A SECRET KIL

Paul Toolan was born in Leeds quite a long time ago and is now a Southern softie enjoying the green landscape of Somerset. After a successful career in Colleges and Universities, he wrote book/lyrics for stage musicals before 'turning to crime'.

His mystery novels feature Inspector 'Zig' Batten, an urban Northerner displaced to the West Country where, to his horror, he discovers they still have crime. Worse, despite a fear of flying, Zig must sometimes forsake cider-land to confront villains in foreign countries such as Spain and Greece.

Like Zig, Paul enjoys walking, fishing, gardens and the occasional whisky. Unlike him, he appreciates sport and the taste of mushrooms, and loves travelling to sunnier climes. His idea of bliss is a slow lunch at a beachside taverna after productively tapping a keyboard to the ebb and flow of the Mediterranean sea.

ALSO BY PAUL TOOLAN

The 'Killing Tree' crime mysteries.

A Killing Tree

A January Killing

An Easter Killing

The Killing of Queen Mab

A Secret Killing

Short Stories.

A View from Memory Hill

A SECRET KILLING

Zig Batten 5

Paul Toolan

Published by Paul Toolan

Copyright © 2023 Paul Toolan

All rights reserved.

This is a work of fiction. Names, characters, places, and incidents are products of the author's imagination or are used fictitiously and should not be construed as real. Any resemblance to actual events, locales, organisations or persons, living or dead, is entirely coincidental.

No part of this book may be used or reproduced in any manner whatsoever without written permission, except in the case of brief quotations embodied in critical articles and reviews. For more information e-mail all enquiries to: paul.toolan1@gmail.com

A SECRET KILLING

PART ONE	1
PART TWO	9
PART THREE	43
PART FOUR	51
PART FIVE	229
PART SIX	257

PART ONE

MALAGA, SPAIN

One

Malaga's quayside, all a-shimmer in the sun's glow, buzzed with weekend trippers, cheery Spanish families – and a sweaty Zig Batten. Though here to work, his eye wandered to a pair of street dancers, teasing the crowd with the slow sensuality of a tango.

The man, tall, in a black suit and hat, eased his elegant partner over the paved promenade, his well-rehearsed face scorning the *bravos* of the Sunday throng. The woman sashayed to a ghetto-blaster's deep bass throb, black fishnet tights chequering her long legs, sleek beneath a bright red dress split to the thigh. Hands barely touching her partner's back, she splayed her fingers like a starfish, sunlight glinting from silver thumb-rings and a twin bracelet of pearls.

Hope my task runs as smoothly, thought Batten, as he watched them coax, spin, tease, and glide, wishing he was the dancer in the suit and hat, Sonia's jeweled fingers softly caressing his back.

But Sonia was in England, a thousand miles away, and he was not here to dance. Digging a euro from his shorts' pocket, he dropped it into an already brimful hat and headed for the shade. From the dark canopy of a line of plane trees, he returned his gaze to a different dancer, thirty yards across the quay.

Unmissable, this figure, a giant Mickey Mouse, tippy-tapping his oversized boots on the promenade, beguiling the Sunday tourists - or the younger ones - with a plastic smile broader than a boomerang. The cool November morning had climbed to a thirty-degree afternoon, and over-dressed for the Spanish sun, Mickey was paying in sweat for his anonymity.

Gaggling groups of children reached up to high-five Mickey's white gloves, and a trickle of Sunday punters pied-pipered after his grinning head to a ticket booth on the quayside. Here, they coughed up hard-earned euros for a catamaran trip around the bay, old olives and flat prosecco thrown in.

When the boat sailed, the Mouse's costumed shoulders wilted in relief. As the ghetto-blaster fell silent and the tango dancers bowed, Mickey turned away from the cheering throng, pulled off his hot head and propped it by the ticket booth. The best part of a bottle of iced water disappeared down his throat and a stained hankie mopped away a neckful of sticky sweat. Then without ceremony, he perched his headless, rehydrated self on a harbourside bench, black Mickey-boots thrust out in front of him like a pair of capstans.

From the shadows, Batten sized up the sub-Disney figure, strolled to the jetty and stood over him, unsmiling, deliberate. The man's voice emerged not as a mouselike squeak, but deep and faintly foreign.

'Don't move,' said Mickey. 'Stay there, stay right there. You make great sunshade. Looking for employment?'

'No,' said Batten, comparing the mugshot in his fist with the face of the half-man, half-mouse. 'No, I'm not looking for employment. I'm looking for *you*.'

Two

To the white-jacketed waiter, the bottom half of a Mickey Mouse squatting at a table in the waterside bar was just another day. He plonked down two cold beers in the welcome shade, and Batten sipped. Mickey glugged his in one long draught and lumped his mouse boots onto a spare chair. 'Well?' he said.

Running a finger down the cool wetness of his beer glass, Batten gave Mickey a long stare, making him wait. Yes, ten years younger than me, but matching my six-foot, he guessed. Faintly Slavic bones, a bit like mine, but a stubbier nose, and no moustache. Mickey stared back, a mouse on the outside only, and dragged the back of his hand across his lips. 'Thanks for the beer,' he said, slamming the empty glass on the table. He dragged his mouse boots from the chair and was about to clump away when he spotted the fifty euro note in Batten's fist.

'Take more than 50 euros,' Mickey said.

'Only if you're here.'

With a flick, Mickey's hand snapped up the note and settled his backside back into the chair. 'Mickey wants to know how many these you got?' he said, holding the fifty to the light.

Batten held up a second note. His client had authorised five hundred euros - "but no more" - should persuasion be required. 'The first fifty's for sitting down. This one's for dropping the Mickey Mouse crap. Pavel.'

Mickey's eyebrows pinched together, his brow a sharp wedge.

'Pavel Ducek, yes?'

Pavel's answer was a tiny shrug, as he slipped the second fifty into his pocket. He wouldn't need to work again today. 'And where is the third?'

Batten silently sipped his beer. In response, Pavel caught the passing waiter's arm. 'Another for me. Large, this time. His bill,' he said, jabbing a thumb at Batten. 'If no third, I drink this beer, go play Mickey.'

'We'll wait for the beer, then,' said Batten. 'And see.'

When the waiter plonked it down, the beer was as cold as Pavel's silence. He glugged a throatful and sat back, open palm upwards, the back of his hand tapping the table, ready to grab the third enticing fifty clamped in Batten's fingers.

'I'm flying back to England tomorrow. Back home, to Somerset,' said Batten, noting Ducek's sudden twitch at *Somerset*. 'In my pocket, there's an extra boarding pass, with Pavel Ducek's name on it.' Batten's raised palm stopped Mickey's anger in its tracks. 'Yes, I have your passport details, and more besides. And more of these.' He rustled the fifty euro note, still planted in his fist.

If the thought of easy money brought a Mickey Mouse smile to Ducek's face, the thought of *flying back* removed it. He glanced over his shoulder at the catamaran, circling the bay. 'Somerset, huh. Boarding pass, huh. But where is your warrant card?'

'I'm not here to arrest you, Pavel. Can't. No warrant card.'

'So, not police? You sm-.' He would have said *you smell like police*, if not for the unclaimed fifty. 'You *talk* like police. Talk painful, like maybe you sit on handcuffs.'

'Ex-police, Pavel.' Batten still felt the tremors when he said so. '*Ex*-cop. Have no fear.'

'Have no fear? Have no fear but you want I get on plane with you, fly back, to *Somerset*?' With a second glance at the catamaran, Pavel picked up his beer, licked his lips but didn't drink. 'Who sent you?' he hissed.

'Not at liberty to say, just yet.'

'Not at liberty? But Pavel *is* at liberty!' Mimicking Batten's flat Yorkshire vowels, he said, 'and Pavel stay at liberty - if it's all t'same to you, *lad*.'

Batten might have said it *was* all the same to him. He'd tracked Pavel down, at his client's request. Offered him a plane ticket. Dangled inducements in his path. Offer refused; assignment failed. Fly back, alone, drop a 'services rendered' bill in the post... *Yet here I am*, he thought, *still poking away at unsolved puzzles*. He flicked the third fifty onto the beer-stained table, anchoring it with his index finger. The banknote waved teasingly on a light sea breeze, carrying with it the confused scents of grilled steak and eucalyptus. 'I can tell you who *didn't* send me. It wasn't your partner.'

'Partner? *Partner?* Hah.'

'And it's in your partner's interests that you return. She's struggling to understand. Either it's you she needs, or closure.'

From the tells twitching his face, Pavel Ducek needed closure too, despite his denials. 'I have no partner,' he blustered, his voice tight with suspicion. 'She's not my partner! Not for…I don't know how long.'

'Three months,' said Batten. 'Three months since you upped sticks, no explanation. In all that time she says you never wrote her a single word.'

'Word? What for? We not married. If she say we are, she have bad memory.'

'She remembers she's still in love.'

'Puh. Who with?'

Batten stared at the gold and green banknote flickering in the breeze. When he slid it into his pocket, Ducek hardly gave it a glance. The note felt damp, from the condensation dripping from Pavel's glass - or from his eyes.

'I don't love her,' hissed Ducek, the desperate lie cracking his voice. The muscles of his face struggled with themselves before clamping into a knot. 'And you won't force me back, Mr-Not-Police.' He thrust his face at Batten. 'What if I knock you down right now, make you see stars, then go play Mickey Mouse? *Huh?*' Batten heard the note of rising panic. 'Or get new disguise, play Donald Duck instead?'

Straightening up in his own chair, Batten said, 'Donald or Mickey, you'll still be Pavel Ducek. And she'll still be in love with you. As for knocking me down, if you fancy trying, be quick.' He pointed over Ducek's shoulder, where clamouring seagulls mobbed a boatload of tourists flicking stale bread into the bay. 'Because your sweaty job is sailing into view.'

As Ducek turned to look, Batten sprang forward and with iron hands clamped Mickey's fingers to the chairback. Pavel fought to free himself, his hands strong too, but his grip slippery with sweat. An elderly couple two tables away smiled at what they mistook for some sub-Disney lark. Batten ignored them, lips whispering into Ducek's ear. 'Push me too far, Pavel, and *Mr-Not-Police* might make *you* see stars.' Ducek tried to pull his hands away, but Batten's grip was steel. 'Or you could just behave yourself? Nod twice for yes.'

Ducek's gaze shifted from his clamped fingers to the catamaran edging towards the quayside. When his eyes fell on the Mickey Mouse head, its frozen grin staring back from the ticket booth, the thought of donning it in this afternoon heat killed off his last dregs of resistance. With a glance at his beer, he nodded twice. When Batten released him, despite his hands shaking from the pressure, he managed to clutch his glass and drain it.

Batten sat back in relief, fisticuffs a last resort for him. Renewed physical strength, honed into shape by renovating his new old house in Somerset, was a brass-neck bluff. Watching Ducek rub the blood back into white hands, he guessed the bluff was working. The half-man/half-mouse slumped forwards, and Batten saw a figure who had lost his love of Spain - or was focused on a greater love elsewhere.

'This plane ticket,' Ducek said. 'One-way? Or return?'

'Your choice,' Batten lied. One-way was his client's request - as was making Pavel cough up his reasons for fleeing to the Costa del Sol, overnight, with not a single word of warning. Either way, the crumpled figure across the table showed no desire to clock in as Mickey Mouse, or even to speak. In the silence, Batten watched the two tango dancers stroll elegantly past, arm-in-arm, the man's free hand clutching an old ghetto-blaster - tired and worn, like Pavel now. 'Well?' asked Batten.

'If I go - *if* - I maybe only talk.'

'And you'll listen, I hope?'

'Listen? Maybe.' He stared at the blue water of the bay, as if the gentle ripples held remembrances of lost love. 'She not make you come here?'

'No.'

'So. Who did?'

'Ah, now,' said Batten, 'that's a longer story.'

'Good,' said Ducek, peeling off his giant boots and dumping the empty plastic shells onto the grass. He looked forlorn in his scuffed Nikes but made a fist of pretending otherwise. 'Good. Because I quit from Mickey Mouse. And long story means more time for beer – on your bill.' With that, Pavel clamped his mouth shut and flopped his old Nikes on a chair, his veneer of bravado failing to hide a face tight with fear. When he spotted the catamaran dock at its quayside berth, he shuffled his chair to the darker shade of a eucalyptus tree and hunkered down, hidden from view.

The passing waiter barely noticed the wary flick of Pavel's empty glass, condensation dripping down its side like tears.

PART TWO

SOMERSET, ENGLAND

EARLIER

Three

The things I do for love, thought Batten, pulling his neck into his coat collar. The reward for climbing to the top of Ham Hill was a vast panorama of Somerset's rural splendour. At the hill's foot, the village of Stoke-sub-Hamdon lay dressed in a coat of blackcurrant bushes and apple trees, fading now into autumn. Burrow Hill, scene of his first case in Somerset, popped up like a one-treed pimple in the valley below. Framed on the far horizon lay the Mendips, the Blackdown Hills and the Quantocks, vague purple outlines against a gunmetal sky. Today, alas, the view was sliced by a raw wind hissing from the Arctic.

He rubbed the frozen tip of his nose, to no avail. 'Don't you get enough death at work?' he whispered to Sonia.

'That's pathology, Zig,' she whispered back. 'This is commemoration. And it's nearly over.' She wrapped her arm round Batten's waist and - he noted - nestled her hand in his coat pocket in search of warmth. The Remembrance Day ceremony had not been overlong, but at the eleventh hour of the eleventh day of this particular November the freezing wind had turned his feet to stone. He glanced across at the Vicar, intoning the names of the more recent dead. Their rank and regiment were also engraved on the hilltop Memorial, a stone pinnacle piercing the sky, surrounded today by fifty or sixty frozen souls, smart and upright in their uniforms or, like Batten and Sonia, huddled together in reverential black, punctured only by the bright lapel pinprick of a red poppy. The silver, blue and green of flags, medals, and regimental banners added colour, but not heat, to the dark gathering.

'*Richard Ellis,*' chanted the Vicar, robes flailing in the chill wind. '*Henry Fallon...Christopher Green...*' Do the clergy wear thermals beneath their God-frocks, Batten wondered, wishing *he* was?

Before the ceremony, Sonia Welcome had pointed to her great-grandfather's details, permanently engraved in the tall stone monument, one chiseled name amongst many. 'I wish they'd stop calling it The Great War,' she said. 'Not great for Billy Welcome, was it? A father at nineteen, dead at twenty, with barely any past to remember.' After the bugler played *The Last Post*, she shed a tear for the great grandad she could never meet, her tears lingering through the minute's silence. When the Reveille sounded, with three mournful notes on the bugle, she said, 'how cruel, to be called Billy Welcome. No welcome back for him. And his only goodbye was a bullet.'

Batten also felt tears on his cheeks, telling himself it was the emotion of the event and the cruel bite of the wind - but knowing the tears were in memory of his own Aunt Daze, his 'mother' from the age of two. Cancer took her, a few short months ago, and today's ceremony doubled as a private remembrance. His tears might have been a nod to his own near departure from the world, at barely forty. Did *The Last Post* sound for his unwanted exit from CID? In the Force one day, invalided out the next, and still unsure how to turn one lost career into another. From habit, he rubbed the permanent lump on the back of his skull.

'*Norman Hadley…Reginald Hix…Andrew Jack…*' The Vicar's drone brought to mind Batten's final day in the CID office in Parminster, the names of his much-missed colleagues engraved on a giant leaving card. DC Eddie Hick had doodled a picture of a bacon sandwich next to his signature. Nina Magnus and Hazel Timms offered glum-faced emojis, Timms adding a sad tear to hers. Sergeant Ball, PC Foreman and 'Prof' Andy Connor from Forensics had merely signed. Batten's premature exit to police-pension-land wouldn't stop their monthly meetings of *The Parminster Cider Club*, in one hostelry or another. At least he hoped not.

He felt Sonia shudder, perhaps from cold, then shuddered himself, from guilt. Remembrance Sunday, and here he was with booze on the brain. Worse, he looked forward to getting out of this icy weather and into *The Prince of Wales* for a warming tot. The entire gathering, clergy and all, were clothed in deep respect – but a bracing drink wouldn't go amiss.

An icy gust of wind whipped the flags and banners into new shapes and colours and when his eye followed them, he spotted the same unreadable face, still there, at the far corner of the gathering. Same closed features, same characteristic underbite, same penetrating eyes. Sonia followed his glance. 'Why is that woman still staring at you, Zig?' she whispered. 'One of your old flames?'

Amid the moving stillness of the ceremony, Batten almost smiled. The woman in question was dumpy in shape, twelve inches shorter than his six-foot, and fifteen years older. That unreadable face, he thought, where have I seen it before…?

As the gathering dispersed down the slope, Sonia rubbed the feeling back into her hands and glanced over her shoulder. 'Zig, that woman's following. What's going on?'

'Not sure. She's been trailing us all morning. She parked three cars away, same car park.'

'How do you know?'

'Because I *used* to be a detective…' When he glanced back, he saw Sonia was right. 'I've seen her before. If I could only remember where.' Batten again rubbed the lump on his skull, the gesture now as permanent as the lump itself. Over a year ago, yet his memory erratic still – except for the crunch of the steel cosh which triggered his exit from the Force. For all he tried to forget, that cold hard shock refused to fade away.

'What if she trails us to *The Prince of Wales*, Zig? Offers to buy the drinks – or, goodness, creates a scene?'

'No, she'll do neither, don't worry.'

'How can you be so sure?'

'Too public,' he said, with a nod of certainty and a glance back at the woman whose name he couldn't remember.

Empty space now. Gone.

*

In *The Prince of Wales*, Batten scrolled down the enticing list of fine whiskies, ordering a Speyside for himself, a warming brandy for Sonia. They sipped and chatted to Remembrance Day attendees by the log fire, near a scrum of well-walked dogs, panting bodies spreadeagled on the flagstone floor.

When they made their way to the car park, the same woman waited in a little red Corsa, three cars away, engine running, presumably for the heat. Easing Sonia into his Ford, Batten closed the door behind her and waved a reassuring hand. The short, fifty-something woman emerged from the Corsa as he moved towards it. And looked squarely at him.

He remembered where he'd seen her before.

But wished he didn't.

Four

Temporary or not, living in three dwellings at the same time grated on Batten's nerves. Worse, of the three, this main dwelling once belonged to a murder victim. Sonia Welcome, no believer in ghosts and curses, had bought the half-derelict hamstone house 'to do up'. She didn't ask Batten -because she knew what he'd say. But with typical directness, she did ask if he was interested in living there too.

'Too?' he said. 'Who with?'

Sonia had waved a mock-fist and said, 'the police tell me it's illegal to punch people.'

His reason for moving in, he claimed, was the grand view across the valley to Ham Hill - but that same night his body, mind and heart knew the deep reason was Sonia. The next day, clearing brambles from around the front gate, he discovered a cracked stone plaque cemented into the wall. Unbeknown to the new owners, and indeed to the postman, the house once had a name. When Batten rubbed away at dirt and moss, faded lettering emerged: *Hillview*. They ordered and fitted a new brass nameplate, and the two of them took a selfie, standing either side of it, proud smiles of ownership on their faces.

Now, though, with renovation under way, he and Sonia were reduced to 'camping' at *Hillview* on a mattress in the chaos of their own creation. When dust and debris made even this impossible, they camped at his cottage in Ashtree. Once the main dwelling was ready and they'd moved in, he would have to choose what to do with his Ashtree home – a painful decision, pushed to the back burner for now.

The *third* dwelling was not strictly a dwelling at all. Batten paid for his new 'garden office' with a bequest from Aunt Daze. When she left him her Premium Bonds, he had no idea she'd squirrelled away fifty grand, which more than covered the building and its installation, and the construction of a private entrance to what he hoped would become his business base. He made sure to site the 'office' in the rear garden with its glorious view of Ham Hill's Iron Age earthworks. Through the frame of the wide window, he could spend all day gazing at it across the valley – if the ingrained need to *work* would let him.

This 'garden office' of the old hamstone house had a modern Scandinavian vibe, cedar-wood cladding, a loo, a kitchenette, a desk – and a chair for *clients*, whoever they turned out to be. The sofa morphed into a bed, but one night's broken sleep on its hardness was enough. So why did he feel better for having a handy bolt hole?

'It's because of your conflicting emotional states, Zig,' Sonia had told him as they lounged in a twilight bed at his Ashtree cottage.

'Thought you were a pathologist, not a psychologist.'

'Both,' she said. 'Luckily for you. The psychology bit means I can pretend to be a satnav, should you lose your way.'

'Didn't lose my way half an hour ago,' he said, caressing her smooth skin beneath the sheets - soft Egyptian cotton at her insistence - till she playfully pinched his hand.

'Because you weren't conflicted, Zig. Neither of us. You were in your *connecting* state.'

'Yes, I seem to remember *connecting,*' he said, snuggling closer.

'You did, happily. But tomorrow, who knows? One of your conflicting states might filter through.'

'What, I've got more than *one*?'

'Several, Zig. You're complex, as am I – we bask together in the glory. But when you're not connecting, you have been known to drift off into *escape*? No?'

Batten sat up in bed, gazing at the familiar prints and paintings on the walls, the bedside tables he'd recycled, the lamps he'd rewired – all carried out in contented solitude. When previous relationships dipped, yes, he had sometimes drifted off, to a place he thought of as *Zigland*, to be pleasantly alone with his thoughts. His Ashtree cottage had become a kind of skin, holding the rest of him together. But Sonia's golden skin held him too, and he didn't want to drift away from her. When he said so, she wrapped him in a gold-leaf smile. 'I know you don't, Zig. I really know. But you do still have a bolt hole in the garden.'

'It's not a bolt hole, Sonia. It's my *office*. I can't become a...*something* without a base, can I? And you won't want me seeing clients in our kitchen - when we get one.'

'Clients? I didn't know you had clients. When did you even decide what to *offer* your clients?'

'I've only decided what *not* to offer. No grubbing under stones to feed the tabloid press. No divorce work, nothing like that.'

'Selective, Zig.'

'I've a premature pension. I can afford to be selective.' He didn't mention the rental income his Ashtree home might provide, because the thought of strangers living there still saddened him. 'Private problem-solving - that's as far as I've got. Haven't even settled on a business name. And it's *one* client. My very first. You saw her. On Ham Hill, on Remembrance Sunday.'

'What, the dumpy older woman with the stare, who followed us? Wants you to make her tall, thin and young?'

'Don't know what she wants. She wasn't overkeen to tell me in public. I only agreed to see her as a test-case. She's coming here tomorrow.'

'Ah, to your *bolt hole*?'

'To my *business premises*. While *you* are at yours.' Batten returned her smile, relieved to have a 'bolt hole' in the garden – and doubly relieved Sonia's working life was separate from his.

Because Dr Sonia Welcome spent most of hers at the mortuary.

Five

Solid oak, the desk. He bought it at auction, re-glued the wonky drawers and polished it, top to toe. But as he ran his hands over the distinctive grained surface, he knew it would take more than a fine old desk to give his new 'career' a kickstart. In the wall mirror, he checked his appearance. A careful shave, a moustache trim, dark hair combed and less unruly – plenty good enough for a first day in the new job. He flopped into the leather office chair - second-hand too, but freshly oiled - and allowed himself a start-the-day spin, as he used to do in his tiny office at Parminster CID. More room here, he thought, when his feet came to rest, and his eyes flicked to the brass wall clock.

Ten-o-clock, they'd agreed, and ten sharp it was when Batten's buzzer buzzed for the very first time. On a long breath, he took in his new 'work environment', its oak floor softened by a sheepskin rug after a gentle nudge from Sonia. Reference tomes stood to attention on the bookshelves he'd built. One tome concealed an unopened bottle of Aberlour and a single glass. A too-shiny metal waste-bin stared back, and a Bluetooth speaker for the music he missed when it wasn't playing. It never played at Parminster CID, and even if it had nobody would hear it amid the raised voices, ringing phones and clang of filing cabinets. Here, it was too quiet, except for the buzzer's second purr.

Feeling more a suspect than a questioner, Batten flicked the wall-switch controlling the private entrance to his undefined 'office'. No plaque or plate graced the door because he'd yet to come up with a business name.

Regardless, in she walked, and took the proffered seat, short fingers gripping the handbag in her lap. Despite the characteristic underbite, the unreadable face he'd seen on Ham Hill seemed a tad more relaxed – or perhaps *he* was, being on home turf. 'Found it, then?' he asked, immediately cursing the lame opening to his first venture. Whatever it turned out to be.

'Oh. Yes. I used to drive past this house on my way to work, when I lived in Parminster. I say 'house', but back then it was mostly covered in undergrowth. I suppose I mean 'overgrowth'. Didn't it belong to that strange woman with the nickname?'

'Yes. Queen Mab. Her real name was Rose Linnet.'

'Was it? I just remember the smell of alcohol, if I had the misfortune to pass her in the street. She was a bit…'

'Dilapidated?' He didn't say *dead*, though he'd spent months searching for her killer.

'I was going to say *disturbed*.' She looked away, into the distance, to some far-off private place. 'Sometimes, people are,' she said, turning back. 'Poor woman.'

The lame opening dwindled into awkward silence as his first 'client' continued to gaze at invisible memories. *Make a start*, Batten told himself. Just because you've got all day… 'You lived here in Parminster, you said?'

'Oh, long time ago. I live in at Wake Hall now.'

Even after five years, the mention of Wake Hall sent a sharp pulse through Batten's veins. His very first case in Somerset had involved the vast private estate with its huge stable blocks, wedding venues, residential wings – and a stately home built not from the local hamstone but from imported white limestone, sullied to a dirty grey by age and weather. Or was, the last time he saw it. He had no desire to see it again, nor its owner, the imperious Lady Wake.

Another sharp pulse sent his thoughts back to Ham Hill on Remembrance Sunday, to the moment he recognised the dumpy figure now sitting opposite, attractive in a mumsy sort of way despite the underbite, hair neatly bobbed, handbag nestling in her lap like a beige sporran. Avril…something? And if she 'lived in' at Wake Hall, more fool her. Reluctant to even open his laptop, he glanced at the few short scribbles on his scratchpad.

'Avril, I never asked your surname. For my notes?'

'Oh, it's Kerrig – I mean Dean. D.E.A.N. Avril Dean.' She stopped, her mind flashing back to a private moment in the past. 'Kerrigan was my married name,' she said, her face momentarily taking on the same unreadable expression he'd seen on Ham Hill. Realising she'd drifted off, she sat upright in her chair.

'And you're still in the same role, at Wake Hall? Still Lady Wake's maid? Batten assumed maid meant 'dogsbody.'

'No, no, more than that. I've been there so long, I'm a fixture. Her

Ladyship's private secretary now. Organise her diary, liaise, keep things ticking over. She's a very busy woman, what with all the new ventures. And I'm one of those 'gets things done' sort of people.'

'Shall *we* get things done, then, Avril? Perhaps tell me what the problem is?'

'The problem. Of course. Yes.' A slow silence drifted across the desk like fog, as Avril's 'yes' faded towards 'no'.

Gut instinct clicking to the 'on' position, Batten dived in. 'I hope I'm not jumping to conclusions, Avril. But if your problem is to do with unfair dismissal then I can tell you now, I'm the wrong person. Industrial tribunals aren't my area of expertise, sorry.' *And certainly not if they involve Wake Hall.*

Without speaking, Avril Dean's face spat out *how dare you!* Her handbag jerked so sharply in her lap he wondered if she planned to hit him with it. And when words did emerge, they carried an acid edge. 'Unfair dismissal? *Never.* I don't know anyone more loyal than I am. And Lady Wake knows the same – because Lady Wake tells me so, and I know she means it!'

Told off in his brand new garden-office, Batten fiddled with his pen to hide his deflation. Why couldn't Avril Dean be a straightforward *man* who'd had a family heirloom stolen, and wanted it back, no questions asked? *That* he could deal with. As if reading his mind, she reached into her bag and drew out her car keys.

Oops, I've pissed her off and she's on her way, he thought – till his eye fell on the keys. On Ham Hill, she'd driven a little red Corsa but Batten's ex-detective eyes spotted a Range Rover fob in her hand. Avril might have been well-dressed, but she was hardly a toff with a string of cars to choose from. She saw him looking.

'It's not what you think,' she said. *It never bloody is*, he thought, but she was on her feet. 'I need to fetch something from the car. To explain. Is that alright?'

Avril's changed her mind, he guessed - about her 'problem', or about *him*. Is 'the car' her polite excuse to leave with dignity? Or does she need a walk round the block, to pluck up courage, to stiffen her reluctant thoughts, whatever they are? He gave a shrug of agreement. 'I'll switch off the gate lock. Just walk back in when you're ready,' he said, meaning *if,* and she shuffled out.

To fill the time, he flipped and caught an imaginary coin. Heads she returns, tails she doesn't. He had no idea which was best, so gazed instead across the half-cleared garden to the half-renovated house. The builders had repaired areas of worn hamstone which after cleaning and pointing would look as good as the already finished front. He could hear the roofers replacing the lead flashing. Every now and then a head popped up above the scaffolding and a hammer disturbed the silence.

Sighing, he re-read his paltry half-page of scribbles, before flicking it into the too-shiny bin. Avril Dean, who used to be Avril Kerrigan and who 'lives in' at Wake Hall. Erstwhile maid to Lady Wake, and now her private secretary. A woman who 'gets things done' - except when asked to explain what her problem is. Who drives both a Vauxhall Corsa and a Range Rover, and whose footsteps, to his ambivalent surprise, he could hear returning. With waning enthusiasm, he bent down to guardedly retrieve his notes from the bin, as Avril slid back into her chair.

When he sat up, it wasn't Avril Dean on the other side of the desk.

It was Lady Wake.

Six

Used to controlling himself in face-offs with toerags or slimeballs, Batten failed to conceal his shock when he stared into Lady Wake's steely eyes. Would he classify her as an old adversary? Old, no. She was about his age, forty-something at most, and expensive skincare was defeating the years. Or was it those facial bones, sculpted for beauty, and her trim curves, wrapped in a black silk jacket so sharply cut it could slice bread? If an adversary, she was a dark-eyed, handsome one, her palpably expensive perfume teasing his nostrils. With one lithe, languid waft of her arm, she ensconced her leather bag on the chairback, without needing to look. Avril had fetched 'something from the car' alright. And having 'got things done', Avril was nowhere to be seen.

Ex-cop and titled beauty stared at each other, in a silence carved from stone, till Batten realised he was enjoying the view. 'It's not my birthday,' he said, 'so you can't be the singing telegram.' Lady Wake pretended to smile before taking in her surroundings with a noncommittal flick of her eyes. 'I'm surprised to see you, I'll admit,' Batten added. 'You used to call me 'that odious Inspector.' When you weren't snidely demoting me to Sergeant.'

'It's possible. I was younger then, somewhat angry. And at a rather painful crossroads.'

Batten had experienced a few painful crossroads of his own but said nothing. He wondered if her dark-blue eyes always sparkled like diamonds - bright but hard.

'And I may have been in a state of shock. From circumstance.'

'Well, when someone poisons your Estate Manager…' It was Batten's first case after moving to Somerset, and the dead rictus of that poisoned face still haunted him. Lady Wake was fortunate - she was never required to view the body. 'And on top of that, wasn't Wake Hall involved in a spot of nasty trafficking? Not to speak of all that laundered money?' She looked away, to hide her embarrassment. Yes, sharp diamonds, those eyes, Batten thought.

'Those crimes were committed by others, not by me, as you and your colleagues established. My mistake was associating with-'

'With Olly Rutter?' Batten's old Northern adversary had slipped south to the West Country long before Batten's transfer – and slipped into Lady Wake's bed at Wake Hall. Rutter managed to poison the vast estate with crime before moving on, to Her Majesty's Prison Bristol where he still stewed, his chance of parole thinner than a hair. Batten guessed Lady Wake declined to visit.

'I associated with the wrong people, at a wrong moment. In a life askew. *Then*, not now.' She allowed the faintest sigh to pass her lips. 'I vainly hoped we might get off to a better start. Mm?'

Batten reined himself in, despite a lifelong wariness of folk who pronounced 'off' as *orfe*. *An orfe is a fish, dammit.* And, in truth, Parminster gossip said Lady Wake *had* moved on from her wrong life with the wrong people. Wake Hall was now a significant local employer – of mostly women, who spoke well of the place. One such was PC Jess Foreman's daughter Susie, a stable girl in the Hall's vast equestrian business. Jess often shared a glass or two with Batten and since gossip cuts both ways, perhaps Lady Wake learned of his post-CID status by cupping a refined ear to the stable girls, or one in particular. He'd already assumed Avril Dean learned of his new situation from the rumour mill, so more likely Avril's ear did the cupping, before 'getting things done.' Whichever, it was Lady Wake in the chair opposite, lips pursed, eyebrows raised, manicured hands in her lap, one exquisite hand tapping on the other.

'A better start might begin with you fessing up why you're here,' said Batten. '*You*. Not Avril.'

'Dear loyal Avril. Was I right in assuming you'd refuse to see me if I made a direct approach?'

Batten's answer was a shrug, and silence. She was on his patch now, free to speak or free to leave. Another tiny, almost petulant sigh crept past her lips before words followed.

'Well. Here I am. With an awkward problem. And in your new private capacity, perhaps you'll consider solving it. With absolute discretion, it goes without saying.'

Mouth shut, hands open, Batten let her carry on.

'Do you remember Vito Valdano? Of *Solo Souls*?'

Vito Valdano once ran posh residential programmes at Wake Hall, for well-heeled single folk, and Wake Hall did nicely from the proceeds. Even Batten's wayward memory recalled the overweight, sweating man that used to be Vito. 'John Lennon glasses and a technicolour suit?' he asked. She managed a refined nod. 'Didn't he wobble off to pastures new?'

'If Vito *wobbled off*, it was to make a fresh start, to a life of philanthropy. He runs an orphanage in Bulgaria, now. Or perhaps Romania? No matter. He somewhat left me in the lurch, since his Residential programmes played a key role in Wake Hall's business plan.'

'I heard they still do.'

'And have grown, considerably. You also recall Vito's assistant, Oksana?'

Batten remembered Oksana too, and her unpronounceable Polish surname. CID were reduced to calling her 'Oksana Thing'. Owing Lady Wake no delicacy, he said so. She almost smiled.

'Thankfully, she has since changed her surname by deed poll. She had hoped to change it by marriage. In fact, that is a small part of our problem.'

Slow down on the 'ours', he thought, but let her continue.

'Regardless, the entirety of Wake Hall breathed a sigh of relief when *Vossialevydipsic* became a more pronounceable *Brok*. Apparently, Brok is a place. In Poland, where Oksana's ancestors were born. Rather challenging, *Vossialevydipsic.*' The name rolled easily from Lady Wake's tongue, but Batten assumed words wouldn't dare do anything else. 'After Vito left, Oksana *Brok* took on his role. Now, she runs my residential programmes with efficiency, aplomb, and huge success.'

'And huge profit?'

'Which I re-invest.' She awarded Batten a diamond hard stare. 'Oksana is an efficient angel, and I cannot do without her.' Lady Wake's antennae sensed the dip in Batten's interest. 'So, we approach the core of the problem. Oksana *Brok* is threatening to leave.'

Inwardly sighing, Batten said, 'Sorry about that, but I don't do employee relations. I seem to remember telling Avril the same. I'm not Human Resources.'

'No. But you *are* both human and resourceful. I came here with a problem, yes. And though it pains me to say so, I came to you because beneath your Northern carapace - if my estimation is correct - you possess a good deal of human sympathy. Indeed, you probably did so long before I learned mine, through painful mistakes and the shame of experience.' He watched her wince as she admitted it. 'You also possess considerable insight and a tenacity I grew to respect, if grudgingly. And you are *ex*-CID.'

A familiar acid pain kicked Batten in the gut when she said so. Now, it was his turn to wince.

'Being ex-CID, you carry advantages, mm? You know about *investigation*. But are under no pressure, shall we say, to share the results in the public glare?'

Batten wanted to ask if she was offering cash or flattery. 'Nice to hear all that, but if Oksana Thing - Oksana *Brok* - wants to leave, what am I supposed to do? Borrow a ball and chain from the Police Museum?'

'It's a complex problem. Are you able to grant me the time to tell it?'

Time was plentiful in Batten's life, but he wouldn't say so to Lady Wake. 'It depends,' he said.

'*Depends?*'

'On how complete the story turns out to be. I mean, so far, you've not mentioned the more obvious problem.'

'I don't-'

'Oksana's brother, Dave? *Dave Vossialevydipsic.*' Batten's tongue struggled with the tongue twister but ground it out. 'Unless he's also changed his name to Brok, wherever he is?' Lady Wake's face was a picture of bemusement. Real or painted? Batten wondered.

'I have no idea who or what you are talking about.'

'That comes as a surprise. CID's been chasing Dave for years – and getting nowhere, with or mostly without the help of Oksana *Brok*. All she ever coughed up was her brother's school nickname - 'Dipstick Dave'. Seems the name stuck, except in his adult presence. Willing and able to defend himself, Dave *Thing.*'

'You have me at a disadvantage. I fail to see how this *brother*, whatever his name, has any relevance.'

'Oksana's made no mention of Dipstick Dave? He's not the reason she's threatening to quit?'

'No. Not at all. Why would he be?'

When Batten eyeballed Lady Wake, classy and beautiful, what did he see in her face? Bemusement? Ignorance? Deceit? Dipstick Dave briefly made the press and media, though five years ago, when Lady Wake's mind might have been on problems of her own. If Oksana Brok was in contact with her missing brother, and knew the full story, perhaps she was keeping the police *and* her employer in the dark? 'You don't know? About Dipstick Dave?'

'Frankly, I don't recall Oksana mentioning this person even once.'

'Well, I can guess why. He's still wanted.'

'Wanted?'

'Yes. For murder.'

Seven

In the side-street outside *Hillview*, Avril Dean sat upright in the leather driver's seat of Lady Wake's Range Rover, watching the honey-coloured walls of Batten's home, and listening to the quiet voice of the car's other occupant.

'Do you think he will?' asked Oksana Brok.

'Take on the task, you mean?'

'Take on *my* task. Agree to find Pavel?'

'Well, ma'am is still there in his office. He hasn't asked her to leave.' Avril almost said, 'hasn't thrown her out', but one didn't throw Lady Wake anywhere.

'She can be persuasive, can't she?' Oksana said, and the two women shared wry nods of agreement. 'Should I have told ma'am about Dave, do you think?' Avril Dean's answer, a silent roll of the shoulders, was not enough for Oksana. 'Does ma'am even know I *have* a brother? Let alone a brother who's a…'

'Who's a *problem*?' Avril knew about problems - and was skilled at solving them. 'She'll know by *now*. You've met the blunt Mr Batten. You've seen how…*direct* he can be.'

Oksana Brok sat back, face as crumpled as the tartan car rug spread over her knees – for comfort, not warmth. 'Perhaps it *is* better if I go myself. To Spain. Better for everyone, I think, if it's me who finds Pavel?'

Avril Dean had heard all this before. She and Lady Wake had discussed how to deal with it. 'Oksana. You have no experience of handling a situation that could be dangerous. You're a highly skilled organiser, yes. But you're not a *finder*, are you? And you don't know the law.' *Nor how to get round it, should the need arise.* She didn't mention the matter of the Hall's reputation and Lady Wake's insistence on privacy – though *ma'am* had, in spades, without sullying her lips with *dirty washing* and *in public*.

'I suppose so,' mumbled Oksana, wrapping the rug more tightly around her knees and pondering *dangerous*. Dangerous for whom? For Pavel? For herself? And what about Dave, her disappeared brother? She gazed through the car window at the thick yew hedge surrounding

Hillview, then at the scaffolding peeking above. The heads of two burly roofers began to move in rhythm with the tap of invisible hammers, the distant sound drilling into Oksana's head like a loud clock's tick. Automatically, she looked at her watch. 'Will ma'am be long, do you think?'

*

After ten minutes of Lady Wake's cut-glass voice, Batten was glad when she remembered Avril still waited in the Range Rover and slipped outside to release her. He sat back in thought, against a soundscape of hammers on the main house roof.

The few words Batten managed to squeeze in had at least updated Her Ladyship about Oksana's brother, Dave - still wanted for murder, five years on. Lady Wake's claim to have no memory of press and media stories about a decaying corpse in a disused orchard was vehement, if her clipped tones could ever be so described. But did Batten believe her?

No reason she should remember the corpse was called Tom Bowditch, Dave's tractor-thieving partner in crime. All the same, he took unfair delight in piling on the more shocking details and watching her wince. Tom Bowditch met his end in an isolated barn, a heavy pair of bolt-cutters embedded in his smashed skull - with Dave's DNA liberally spread on both bolt-cutters and corpse. Her Ladyship slipped out before he could add to the gore.

In the pause, he made coffee from the slick machine Sonia had bought him, the rattle of fresh beans in the grinder bringing him back to earth. As a grudging afterthought, he poured a cup for the returning Lady Wake, enjoying her faint surprise when he placed it on the desk in front of her. With an almost imperceptible shake of her head she declined milk and sugar. *At least we have that in common*, he thought.

'I've sent Avril away – also to have coffee.'

She pronounced it *cawfair*. Batten's Aunt Daze used to say *coffeh*, her flat Yorkshire tones shortening the word. Do money and power make one accent 'better' than another? he wondered, as Lady Wake again looped her designer handbag onto the edge of her chair with a stately curl of her fingers.

'Avril will collect me in an hour or so. Does that suit?'

Did it? Despite the suspicious gaps in Lady Wake's story, Batten couldn't prevent old habits kicking in. Sensing unseen depths in this *iceberg Ladyship*, his toes and curiosity tingled. With an almost imperceptible nod of his own, he sipped black coffee. She ignored hers, hands in her lap, one tapping the other as he went over his notes.

'Pavel *Ducek*?' He spelled it out. 'Is that right?'

She nodded. I'm on nodding terms with a *Lady*, he thought. 'You said Oksana met him at Wake Hall, and they fell in love?'

'Fell? *Plunged*. Rather romantically, as I recall. Pavel worked on the estate-'

'Yes, a blacksmith, you said.'

She corrected him, again. 'A registered *farrier*. Horseshoes, and the feet of horses. No firedogs, no wrought-iron gates. A farrier, and a most reliable one.'

'But not a reliable fiancé. You said Oksana was expecting to marry him?'

'The other way round, in fact. It seems he was the prime mover in the relationship. On the few occasions I saw them together - in an off-duty capacity, that is - he was clearly besotted.' She threw Batten a look in case he doubted her ability to judge true relationships, given the disastrous nature of her own. 'Neither she nor I can fathom why Pavel so abruptly departed. Such a sudden, brutal *fait accompli*. We need *you* to find out why, for our different reasons.'

Different reasons? Why different? Batten asked himself. 'Departed, you say? Or 'went missing'? I mean, did you call the police?'

'I never again wish to see a police car at Wake Hall. Disastrous to one's business reputation.'

'Missing Persons, then? Did you report Pavel's *departure*?'

'Does a missing person bother to pack a bag?' Her glance of disdain had icicles on it. 'Because Pavel *did*. Oksana went to the place he rented, out on The Levels, and his rucksack was gone, along with various items of clothing, razor, toothbrush and suchlike. He didn't hand in his notice, nor say a word of explanation or goodbye. His mobile phone was disconnected. He simply disappeared overnight. And I do mean *literally* overnight. It's been almost three months now, and I had hoped Oksana might recover her spirits. I'm afraid there are two Oksana's, the old and the new. Would that the earlier version could return, because, ever since Pavel disappeared, she has been a distracted woman with a shattered heart.'

'And she wants to leave Wake Hall to track him down? Bit naïve?'

'Alas, not entirely naïve. Not *now*. Her hopeless quest was rather thoughtlessly boosted by…by me, her employer.'

Puzzled, Batten finished his coffee. Lady Wake deigned to sip hers, registering surprise at its quality and sipping again. What next, Batten mused, smoked salmon canapés and *dray waite waine*?

'You may recall I frequently travel overseas? To purchase horses – of the finest quality?'

Batten knew. Olly Rutter, her ex-bad-boy and bed-warmer, made sure to travel with her whenever crimes he'd planned were about to take place in England. CID called him Alibi-Olly. 'But you'd hardly need to travel with a farrier in tow, not even a reliable one, not even a Pavel Ducek?'

She wrinkled the nose at the idea. 'Of course not. But I have eyes. And on my recent equine trip to Spain - Andalusian horses are my favourite, such stately beauty, such flowing manes…' She heard herself personalise and put a stop to it. 'Regardless, I found myself with a little time to spare in Malaga. I wandered by the harbourside, in the Spanish sun, taking in the sights. To my shock, one of the sights turned out to be Pavel Ducek.'

'What, you just bumped into him, arms full of horseshoes, on his afternoon stroll?'

'Nothing of the kind. It was bizarre. Boats were touting for trade at the quayside. Trips round the bay, or some such. One of the boats had a ridiculous man dressed as a Mickey Mouse, enticing tourists aboard. When the boat sailed, off came the giant Mickey Mouse head - it was a warm day - and beneath the costume was a perspiring Pavel Ducek. Making a living, of sorts, I imagine.'

And in disguise? Batten wondered why. 'Did he spot you?'

'I very much doubt it. I was some distance away, in the throng. It was Pavel, without question.'

'But you didn't approach him?'

Lady Wake looked out and up, as the rooftop concerto of hammering resumed. 'I was nonplussed, and quite out of my comfort zone. Wary, truth be told. And what would I have said?'

Batten could think of a dozen useful questions to put to Pavel Ducek, given Her Ladyship's story. He wondered how much she was leaving out. 'So you waited till you got back to Somerset, and told Oksana?'

Lady Wake finished her coffee, more from embarrassment than need. 'Foolishly, I did. I hoped the news might conjure up the old Oksana. And I reward loyalty, you see.' Her piercing look flashed across the desk at Batten, suggesting his loyalty might be rewarded too – if he offered it. 'Alas, the following day, she asked to see me and with the greatest regret gave four weeks' notice. Now, in three weeks' time, she flies to Malaga, in search of her Pavel, unless I - *we* - persuade her otherwise. By finding him and convincing him to return, perhaps?' Her diamond eyes flashed another meaningful glance at Batten. 'If not, I shall be forced to find a replacement for Oksana, heaven knows how, and reorganise my residential business yet *again*.'

Batten scribbled down more notes, despite doubting Lady Wake's motives. The begged question - *whose priorities?* - nagged away at him. Did the opaque priorities of Wake Hall's owner really come second to the welfare of Oksana Brok? Or was he being stubbornly tough on Her Ladyship? Looking up, he saw her watching him. When they locked eyes, hers seemed less diamond hard, softened by need perhaps. For a second time that morning, he gazed at stately beauty that was, yes, intoxicating. He dragged his eyes away.

Such beauty, whether in Lady Wake or her beloved Andalusian horses, could easily kick a man in the head.

Eight

That evening, at the monthly meeting of what the four men called *The Parminster Cider Club*, Batten pressed himself against the radiator in search of warmth. He didn't think November could turn colder but it had, and *The Lamb and Flag*, this month's venue, was only just warmer than the street outside. How cold might his companions turn, if he admitted his involvement with Avril Dean and Oksana Brok, and the inscrutable Lady Wake? He watched the three of them, pints in hand, chuckling at a police in-joke - but he was no longer *in*. If he mentioned Wake Hall, would the jokes screech to a halt, and his old colleagues stare into their cider?

The huge figure of Jess Foreman - who looked like a cop even in his casual clothes – was yet again reminding the gathering that 'Jess' might sound female, but it was still better than his proper name: Jesiah. 'Anyone calls me Jesiah', he said with a smile, 'gets no cider.' Raising his glass in a giant fist, he said, 'And since we *do* have cider, I propose a toast!'

'Since when did you need an excuse to swallow cider, Jess?' said 'Prof' Andy Connor, enjoying a night off from Forensics, and wearing a bright yellow jumper to prove it.

A smiling Foreman ignored him. 'I propose a toast to the *Inspector!*' he said, glass raised and ready. In Jess's Somerset burr, it came out as *Inspeccor.*

Batten groaned at the memory. '*Ex*-Inspector, Jess. Kind of you to remind me. Not.'

'Oh, no, sir' - Batten's old colleagues were still calling him 'Sir' - 'not you, sir. I mean the *replacement* Inspector. I mean Inspector *Ball!*'

When the four men clinked glasses, Batten and Ball avoided each other's eyes. 'It's only temporary,' mumbled Ball. 'Acting Inspector. That's all it is.'

'What, with a national shortage of detectives?' said Andy Connor. 'Nah. Parminster copshop's lumbered with your ugly mug till you get your gold watch. You and Eddie Hick. Did Eddie tell you *his* news, Zig?'

'Er, no, not heard.'

'Well, he passed his Sergeant's. Word is Laura, the new girlfriend, she wrote his portfolio for him. Or at least checked the spelling!'

Batten tried to join in the laughter, to be happy for his ex-colleagues – now Inspector Ball and Sergeant Hick. But the news had passed him by. 'Can't think of two better results,' he said, raising his pint and trying to sound genuine.

'Eddie and I were the cheap options, I expect,' Ball mumbled, toying with his half-empty glass. 'A case of the devil you know. That'll be why.'

The four men swallowed cider in an embarrassed silence till Batten overcame his sense of loss and tackled the elephant in the room. 'It's because you're bloody good detectives, both of you – *that's* why.' This time, he meant it. Despite a hatred of cricket - made worse five years ago when *Batten/Ball* first appeared on the CID roster - he caught and held Ball's eye. 'And tell Eddie I said so.'

Ball held Batten's eye, too. 'I will, sir. I will. And we both appreciate what we've learnt, along the way. From you, I mean.'

'Tell you what you haven't learnt,' said Andy Connor. 'Haven't learnt to buy your round – my glass has been dry for a good ten seconds.'

When Ball went to the bar and Jess to the gents, Connor leaned over to Batten and dropped his voice. 'He was too embarrassed to tell you, Zig. Thinks he's sort of nicked your job.' *Well, he has,* Batten thought. 'You might want to put his mind at ease, in private, just the two of you, should the opportunity arise? Given how well you worked together?' Connor added a raised eyebrow and leaned back in his seat. 'And, you know, for friendship?'

As his erstwhile Sergeant placed fresh pints on the tabletop, Batten wondered how to do as Connor suggested. Might Dipstick Dave, wayward brother of Oksana Brok, be the excuse for a private chat with Acting Inspector Ball? In what capacity? Friend? *Private Investigator*? Or just plain snout? And what if Chris Ball kept calling him 'Sir'?

He slumped against the radiator, in need of warmth. Sipping fresh cider, he hardly tasted it.

Nine

The last time Batten drove through Wake Hall's iron gates was five years ago, on police business of the murderous kind. Today, the huge estate looked little different: farm cottages scattered across the endless green landscape, lakes in the distance, and at the head of a long, gas-guzzling driveway, the Hall itself, an over-ornate block of imported limestone, grey with age. Except it wasn't. Her Ladyship must have had it cleaned. A symbolic rebirth, given how crime-scarred it once was? Whatever the motive, morning sun bounced off the Hall's acid-whiteness, almost dazzling him.

Curious still, Batten swung into the Visitors car park and gazed at rolling fields disappearing over the horizon. A few of those fields once belonged to Sergeant Ball's parents – till old Lord Wake bought their little farm for way below its market value, not long before the bankrupt ex-owners passed away, too young. *Good job Ballie's not here*, Batten mumbled to himself as he trudged beyond the Equestrian Centre's serried lines of stable blocks, one after the other. Does *Her Ladyship* own every bloody horse in the world? he wondered, the clang of buckets and the clop of horses filling his ears, and *horse-horse-horse* invading his nostrils. He liked horses, but not the scent of them, and they were here in such vast quantity there was no escaping the smell. Hurrying to the entrance doors, which seemed to frown down on the untitled, he pulled on a heavy iron chain and somewhere in the grand building's bowels a *Visitor* bell clanged.

Avril Dean's unreadable face let him in, and he was ushered beyond the inner porch to the aircraft hangar of an entrance hall he'd visited before, its high walls lined with old tapestries and fading portraits of what he assumed were the ancestors. Lady Wake, who seemed to wear only silk, graced a leather chesterfield twice the size of his car, and graced it finely. Avril drew out a less opulent chair for Batten, then disappeared through a trompe l'oeil painting of a door that turned out to be real.

Lady Wake pitched right in. 'I have much to do today. Oksana has agreed to, well, to an *interview*. Avril will hover nearby in support. Afterwards, she and I will discuss terms and conditions, and any niceties, including your travel costs to Spain. That will serve?'

Serve? Batten no longer worked for the State and had no intention of being treated as any kind of servant, public or otherwise. He pitched in with his own terms and conditions. 'I think before we go any further, I should make my position clear?'

Lady Wake's eyebrows flicked north in a tiny dance, before she controlled them. 'I assumed we were already *clear*,' she said.

'Not quite. Subject to what Oksana tells me, I'll do what's required – but there are exceptions.'

'And these are?'

'Straightforward enough. As a private citizen, I may need to sidestep an inconvenient law or two, in the interests of natural justice, but I'll only *break* a law as an absolute last resort. Should that happen and I find myself in trouble, I'll expect you to exert, shall we say, a little influence on my behalf. That's my position.'

'Sufficiently flexible, I would have thought?'

'But one exception isn't flexible, and you might not like it.'

With the almost imperceptible sigh he'd heard before, she said, 'Try me.'

'It's this *ma'am* and *Your Ladyship* stuff. I won't be doing any of that, and if you insist, we might as well call it quits right now. Not negotiable.'

A faint rustling of silk on silk disturbed the silence of the room. Batten could feel the lowered chins and frowning stares from every ancestral portrait on the high walls, burning into his *insolence*. For a long moment, Her Ladyship was as speechless as the portraits, till the faintest of smiles softened her face. 'Does this mean you intend to address me as 'luv'?' she asked, mimicking his flat Yorkshire vowels – and doing it well.

Batten brushed aside her question. Every member of his old CID team took the piss out of his accent, and he'd become immune. 'Avril and Oksana are who they are. If I track down Pavel, he'll be Pavel. My name's Zig. Your name's Marianne. If that's not good enough for you, say so and I'll be on my way.'

When Lady Wake rose effortlessly from her enormous sofa, Batten assumed it was to refuse his terms. No matter, he had kitchen walls to paint, shelves to build and half an acre of weeds to attack. He rose too, ready to leave.

'Mm,' she said. 'Then it seems the better half of the bargain will be yours. *Marianne* is, I'm sure you'll agree, a mellifluous name, despite meaning 'rebellious' - or so I am told. But *Zig*?' She flicked her manicured fingers at the air. 'It offers next to nothing in the way of sound, and does it have any meaning at all?' She softened her question with another half-smile. What will it take to make her *laugh*, Batten wondered, as she remounted the Chesterfield in a rustle of silk? 'So. It seems I must grow accustomed to *Zig*,' she said.

'Well, *I* did,' replied Batten, not bothering to tell her it was short for Zbigniev, nor that Zbigniev means 'dispelling anger'. Lady Wake tilted her head an inch to one side and awarded him the slightest dip of her chin.

'And since we're talking names,' Batten said, 'isn't it time I got cracking on Oksana *Brok* and Pavel Ducek?'

She answered with a second dip of her chin, so beautifully-boned he kept his other question to himself: *'Marianne', where Pavel is concerned, are you being economical with the truth?*

As she gracefully rose from the Chesterfield, he wondered how surprised she would be if *Dipstick Dave* cropped up.

*

Eyes. Batten was thinking about eyes. Wake Hall seemed full of them, all different. The portraits full of eyes dangling from the high walls of Wake Hall. The unreadable eyes of Avril Dean. The diamond-sharp eyes of Lady Wake. And now, the dark brown eyes of Oksana Brok, pretty, but flicking nervously up at him, a rabbit-in-the-headlights. Worthless here, his old police habit of looming over a seated suspect, using his height to intimidate, because Oksana Brok was not a suspect, was she? But if she was keeping secrets, he needed to know what they were.

A pair of faux-leather bucket chairs squatted either side of an antique table in Oksana's tidy office in the backwaters of Wake Hall. The chairs match her eyes, he thought. When he sat down in the empty one, she seemed to freeze more solidly into hers, despite the heat pumping from a sizeable cast-iron radiator. Batten pointed across the room at the desk phone and raised a vocal eyebrow.

'Avril will field any calls,' she said, her voice a sigh.

Batten nodded. Avril Dean - or was it Avril Kerrigan - Wake Hall's 'get things done' person? He wondered what else she 'gets done' - but this was not the time to ask. Relaxing his posture, he focused instead on Oksana Brok.

'Before we start, I should thank you for changing your name.' He added a smile. 'Brok is a lot easier to say.'

'Quicker, too,' she replied. 'The whole Estate is relieved. And the residential guests.'

'But *Vossialevydipsic*, it's your family name.' She seemed surprised Batten could wrap his jaw round the syllables. He didn't tell her he'd lost his own Polish-Russian surname - and most of his family - before he was two years old. 'Does it feel like a loss?'

'A loss?' She fell silent. Thinking of a lost Pavel, perhaps. Or lost parents. Or maybe Dave, her 'lost' brother. 'It's not too bad,' she said, looking away. A still-slow Batten guessed she'd changed her name because wanted-for-murder Dave had the same surname – and it stuck out like a bone in an open fracture. Or did Avril Dean give her a nudge?

Oksana found her voice again. 'At least Brok, in Poland, is where my family first made their home. So...' He was expecting at least a *mention* of brother Dave, but she tailed away into silence.

He had the sensitivity to keep Dave out of it and focus on the core reason for his presence. 'Why do *you* think Pavel left? I mean, overnight, without warning?'

Oksana Brok sat up in her chair, not expecting even this level of directness. She flicked her eyes at him, her frozen posture fizzing into sudden passion. 'I do not *know!*' Hearing the loudness of her own voice, she paused, controlling herself. 'I only know he would not choose to hurt me. I will not believe that of Pavel. He is a good man, whose love I have felt. I still feel his love. Here!' She touched her heart, fingers shaking on her chest.

Despite her vehemence, Batten pushed at the moment. 'But Pavel left, all the same. There must be reasons.' When she shook her head, nonplussed, close to tears, he asked, 'had he borrowed money? Was he in trouble?' *Did he find another woman?* Oksana pre-empted him, controlling her passion through tight lips and a clenched jaw.

'Do you think I have not asked myself these questions? I am well-paid, and Pavel is a working man, not rich, but no, no money problems, no debt-collectors. And before you ask, he had no 'mistress' hidden away. I know this, I *feel* it. A hundred other reasons, perhaps, and each one a mystery to me.'

'But Spain? Why did he fly to Spain? Or end up there, at least? Why Malaga?'

Oksana shook her head, her hands shrugging the invisible answer. 'I have never been to Malaga. Pavel has never talked of Spain. We talked of Paris, for…' She sniffed into her handkerchief. 'For our honeymoon.'

Batten gave her a moment. *It was easier in CID*, he realised, *in an interview room, a warrant card in my pocket, tape machine running, uniformed PC standing guard.* Here, in a private office, probing a broken heart, he felt more like an agony aunt.

'How recent was it? This talk of a honeymoon?'

She glanced across the table, holding his eyes. 'Three days,' she hissed. 'Three days before he…flew away. And no, it was not *cold feet*.' This time, she had no need to say, 'I feel it'. Her conviction flamed from her eyes, from her body.

There's strength here, Batten thought. *And confusion.* 'Pavel's friends, then. His social circle. Anyone who might hold a clue to why he left. Is there someone he might visit, in Spain?'

Once more, her hands shrugged away the question. 'He had friends, of course. But they are here, in England, and I know them. They have not seen him. Do you think I do not ask them, again and again?'

Batten took a breath. 'Then what about his past? Did you share reminiscences? Couples do, don't they?' He and Sonia did, he told himself, till he heard her voice in his head: *it's like drawing teeth, Zig, getting you to talk about the past!* Patiently, he'd told Sonia: *I don't have a string of family memories. A few names and places, a handful of old photographs. It doesn't take me long to reminisce.* No parents left alive, no siblings. The death of Aunt Daze, his mother-in-all-but-name, still raw. Was it the same for Oksana?

'I am only 32,' Oksana said. 'Pavel the same. I have little family, just my mother, and she…a Nursing Home.' She threw frustrated hands at nothing. 'Pavel has no family left alive. We talked of the past, yes, and of childhood visits to Poland, of the countryside, there and here. But we talked more of the future, of making a life together. Soon.' She fell silent, as the handkerchief made a second damp appearance.

'Pavel's training then? You don't just *claim* to be a farrier. It's a profession. You have to learn it. Do you know where, when, who with?'

When Oksana stood up, Batten thought she'd had enough of him. But she raised her index finger and opened the door. 'One moment,' she said, and left the office.

In the silence, Batten regrouped. His own past was less rich than some, so why not Pavel's too? But the adult Batten had a career history. He went to university, to Police Training College. He went to conferences, had colleagues... He was still pondering as Oksana returned, gripping what looked like a large, framed photograph.

When she placed it on the table Batten saw it was a certificate from the *Farriers Registration Council*. Pavel Ducek had put the work in, from a young age, completing the required four-year apprenticeship, and becoming a fully registered farrier aged twenty-one. The certificate was studded with official stamps and signed by someone whose title was *Approved Training Farrier*. Batten couldn't make out the name, but Oksana's answer beat his question.

'Frederick Mill,' she said. 'He died. Fred. Pavel took me to the funeral.'

Batten cursed as a potential source disappeared. He scanned the certificate again. Pavel had done required stints of formal training at *The West Country Crafts College*. He'd never heard of it - Somerset was a big county, and Batten still an 'incomer'. 'Do you know this place?' he asked.

'I know where it *is*,' she said. 'But it closed down. We drove past once and Pavel stopped to wave at the caretaker - a watchman now, Pavel said, looking after the place till it's demolished. Developers bought the site. It's a concrete blockhouse, ugly. Knocking it down will be a blessing.'

Not to me, Batten thought. Need to be quick, to beat the bulldozers. He sighed as more 'new career' realities piled up. In CID, civilian staff and Detective Constables stuck their thumbs in the pie on his behalf and pulled out people and addresses. Now, he would have to do it himself. Oksana took pity, stepping over to her desk to scribble down directions.

Batten stared at the caretaker's name - Ronnie Lopen. 'What's he like, this caretaker?' He hoped she'd say 'forthcoming'.

'Like? I've never spoken to him. That's Pavel's world. From a distance he looked old, a little stooped. Apart from that…' Once more, Oksana shrugged away the rest, and Batten got to his feet.

'In that case, I suppose it's back to college for me, for a chat with an old, stooped caretaker. Assuming your boss doesn't object?' Batten's hands opened in a question.

'I'll go and ask Lady Wake,' said Oksana, her brown eyes now almost as unreadable as Avril's. Without another word, she left Batten alone in the office. In a flash he scanned it for clues – but no Wake Hall secrets were on display. All he could do was hope her bloody Ladyship would agree to widen the search. And, once tracked down, that Ronnie Lopen would be more than *forthcoming*.

Ten

'You're not going to make a habit of this, Zig, are you?' Sonia softened her question with the smile he'd sell his soul for.

'A habit? Of what?'

'Disappearing overseas. Without *me*.'

'But I offered. You said you had to work.' Batten's offer had been deliberately vague. For all he knew, the search for Pavel might turn out to be dangerous. He'd brought unintended peril to a previous partner - and imperilled her young daughter - a lesson hard-earned. No way would he imperil Sonia. *Ever*. He thrust a blue, short-sleeved shirt into the badly packed cabin bag which lay open on the bed, in the only finished room in the house. The décor was all Sonia, but he liked it – just as well since he'd got light taupe paint in his eye while painting the ceiling. 'Anyway, I'll be working, too.'

'Yes, working in *Spain*, in the warm, while I'm keeping a cold lonely eye on *Hillview* – and on the builders.' She glared at the radiator, fitted to the bedroom wall, but waiting to be connected to a heat source – whenever they got one. 'And I thought you were going to that college, ten miles away, not a thousand.'

'I was. To see an old, stooped caretaker and track down Pavel's mystery history.' Distracted, Batten shoved a pair of flip-flops into the bag. When Sonia gave an ironic cough and said, 'Work shoes, Zig?' he yanked them out and tossed them into a corner.

'So, this caretaker. Flown to Spain, has he?'

'Course not. It's Her bloody Ladyship.' Batten aped the cut-glass voice. 'Why have yeeoo remained in Somerset when Pavel Ducek is in Speyan? Shouldn't yeeoo be setting orfe? To bring him heyah?'

'Nobody in the world talks like that, Zig.'

'Huh. *She* does - when her dander's up. Didn't quite accuse me of skiving. Just idly wondered if she'd made a mistake and this caretaker was paying my expenses…'

No point telling Sonia of the strange look on Lady Wake's face at their last meeting. Fear, was it? Desperation? *Something*, anyway, something new, making her suddenly shoo him off to Spain as if her life depended on it. And nothing to do with Pavel's old caretaker, he felt sure of that. When he tried probing, Lady Wake's diamond eyes had hardened, her sigh almost a hissy-fit. Wake Hall, a landed estate of secrets.

'So, what choice do I have?'

Sonia did a Mata Hari twirl, freezing into a mock-coquettish tableau, framed by the bedroom door. 'What choice would you *like*, Mr Zig?' she said, in a comic husky voice.

Batten chuckled, then glanced at his watch. 'Sonia, I have to get to Spain. To repatriate Pavel-Mickey-Mouse, daft as it seems.'

'Inane in Spain, insanely on a plane?'

Batten hated flying, and Sonia knew it. He zipped up the bag, put his arms round her and drew her closer. 'You're becoming as sarcastic as me.'

'It's rubbing off, Zig. It's the close proximity.'

'How close?' he said, balancing on one foot and shoving the bag off the bed with the other.

'Closer than this,' she said. With a smile he would sell his soul for.

PART THREE

MALAGA, SPAIN

EARLIER

Eleven

In the harbourside bar, Batten's puny sense of achievement was brief. Not difficult, tracking down a giant Mickey Mouse dancing in full view on Malaga's quayside. But getting him on a plane to England...

Shaded by eucalyptus trees, Pavel Ducek seemed to diminish with every swig of his beer - from man of resolve back to mouse of uncertainty. 'Not changed your mind, Pavel?'

'What?'

Pavel's mind wasn't there to change. Like Mickey Mouse, he was elsewhere, weighing up fresh pros and cons – Spain, Somerset, Spain, Somerset. And maybe weighing the dangers involved.

But when the waiter shuffled by and said, 'Another?' it wasn't Batten who declined with a silent shake of his head. Glancing across the table, Pavel drained his beer and quietly pushed away the empty glass, as if the slightest noise might attract unwanted attention. 'No. Not changed my mind,' he said, voice almost a whisper. He checked the catamaran was still moving out into the bay then pointed to a narrow track beyond the shadowy branches of the trees. 'We will leave that way. Stay in the shadows. And keep up - because I not stop for you.'

With that, Pavel slid a green baseball cap from his pocket, pulled the visor over his face and strode away. Stripped of his giant Mickey Mouse disguise, he looked to Batten like a bloke you might see in the street – tall, gym-toned, his posture squeezed to a faint stoop by debts, or moody teenage offspring, by a hard wife or a hard life. None of these explained Pavel's overburdened stride as the two of them made their fast way along the shaded track, across interlocking roads and into the narrow backstreets of Malaga, dodging between one tall building after another. At least there's shade here, Batten thought, as sweat ran down his back.

Even his long legs struggled to keep up, but whatever Pavel was trying to leave behind, he wasn't telling. 'Where are we?' Batten asked. 'I'm lost.'

'This is Soho. Malaga's Soho, not London's.'

'You live here?'

Pavel shot Batten a dismissive glance. 'On my pay? Keep walking.'

They did. Over a concrete bridge spanning a dry river, then in and out of more backstreets, the buildings older, less well-maintained. 'Wouldn't the main roads be quicker?' said Batten, probing.

'Backstreets safer,' Pavel, said, more a grunt than a voice.

'Safer? Who from?'

This time, not even a grunt - one silent shrug for an answer. The same shrug as when Pavel had waited in the shadows till the catamaran sailed off again, before collecting the remains of Mickey Mouse and adding them to the giant grinning head in the ticket booth. Locking the booth, he'd stood in silence for what seemed an age, deciding. Then with a final glance at the blue waters, dropped the key through a slot in the ticket-booth door…

After twenty brisk minutes, Batten's backstreet journey ended at a nondescript apartment block, its peeling white façade revealing two or three previous paintjobs, none of them recent. Avoiding the front entrance, Pavel skipped down a dustbin-cluttered alley, silently turned his key in a back door and in they went.

Barely gone teatime, but the blinds pulled down. Lamplight revealed a dwelling that would even be small for a real mouse. Expecting chaos, Batten saw the tiny flat was neat and clean. Pavel might be on edge, but he kept his house in order, not that there was much to keep. An old sofa, table and two chairs, small TV, kitchenette tucked into a corner, washed dishes draining on the worktop. No air conditioning, though. Despite a room stuffy with built-up heat, Pavel kept the windows closed. And if he carried memories of Somerset with him, not a single photograph was on display. In a curtained recess lay a bed too big for one but not quite big enough for two.

'Palatial,' said Batten, getting a grunt in reply. Uninvited, he sat down at the table, turning the second chair towards Pavel. After an uncertain moment, Pavel flipped his green cap onto the bed, dragged the chair towards him and perched.

'Brass tacks?' said Batten. Another grunt. 'You refuse to say who or what you're avoiding, but I'm parking that for now, OK? All the same, we have to get to the airport tomorrow. I'd feel safer if you gave me *some* kind of heads-up.'

Fingers tapping slowly on the table's plastic veneer, Pavel quelled his fears and found a voice. 'I came to Spain because I am *made* to come. No choice.' For the umpteenth time, Pavel stopped Batten's question in its tracks with a pained shake of his head. 'You want me to admit I came in fear? Then I admit it. Fear, and the shame of fear. I find a job, of sorts, keep my head down – my head inside a Mickey Mouse head, good disguise. 'But at the quayside I feel the eyes,' he said, 'maybe watching. And I wonder, always, where else.' He swept his hand at the room's closed blinds. 'At least here I am Pavel. No need for Mickey.'

'These eyes, who watch? Why can't you say who they are?'

Considering the question, Pavel dragged two cans of beer from the fridge. 'In Poland, there is a saying: 'a guest in the house, God in the house.' Even if the house is this.' He flicked his fingers at the tiny flat and handed his guest a beer. Flipping the tab on his own, he swallowed a draft. Batten stroked the cool wetness of his, without opening it, and repeated the question.

'Last Friday,' said Pavel, 'a new crewman comes to work on the boat. A big man I have never seen before. His eyes, they watch, all the time. And when his eyes dance at me, he couldn't care less if I notice. In Spain, I thought we would at least be safe. Now I am not so sure.'

'We? You and me?'

Pavel dismissed the question with a curl of his lip. '*You* came here from choice. Your problem.'

'Oksana, then?'

At the sound of her name, Pavel drained the last of his beer and stared hard eyed at Batten. 'Keep Oksana out of this! *OK?*'

Raising his hands in mock-surrender, Batten said, 'This new crewman. Who is he?'

'Who? Someone who works for…a someone. Paid eyes, to make sure.'

'You mean make sure you stay put?' asked Batten, picking at the riddles, with no help from Pavel. 'Why would your presence in Somerset be a problem for this *someone*? Hell's teeth, I don't understand why he wanted you in Spain in the first place!'

The only reply was another silent shrug. *If I can get him home*, Batten thought, *maybe he'll answer a question with enough words to make a sentence.* 'Haven't changed your mind, I hope?'

This time, Pavel almost laughed. 'Do I even have a mind, when others change it for me? Them. You.'

'Well, who's winning? Them - whoever they are - or me?'

Pavel crushed the beer can to nothing in his fist, then crushed it some more. 'Neither. You are only the nudge, the push I maybe need, to make me see I *do* have a mind. Somerset or Spain, both are dangerous now, and we Poles are supposed to be unafraid of danger. A nudge, from fear back to courage, that is you. For months I play Mickey Mouse, take no chances, six days a week. Plenty enough, for anyone. So, Pavel time has come.'

'Six days a week?' said Batten, probing. 'You do get a day off?'

A nod. A tight smile. 'Yes. One day off a week.'

'And what do you do, on your day off?'

'Huh, in the evening, the local bar, learn to speak rough Spanish. In the afternoon I shop, clean, do laundry, pretend to be happy with this.' He swept a frustrated arm at the walls. 'In the morning I wear my cap pulled down over my face, like a fresh disguise, so I can walk freely, breathe different air.'

'It's good rural air in Somerset,' said Batten. 'And less than three hours, the flight.'

In the tiny room, Pavel seemed to open his nostril to draw in the scent of horses, or the memory of whatever perfume his absent partner wore. 'Good air, yes. Good Somerset air.'

'So, how will we get to the airport tomorrow? Despite the eyes.'

'We? *You* will use a taxi.' Pavel pulled an empty rucksack from beneath the bed. 'I will pack this now, and you will take it, through the back door. Nobody saw you enter. Going out, make sure the same. Tomorrow, you take my bag to the airport as if it is yours. Me, I will pull on my green cap and walk freely, empty hands in empty pockets, my day-off stroll. But this time my stroll will end at the airport. Where *I* will find *you*. And then, if I am careful, we are gone.'

And if you're not careful? Batten almost asked. 'Whatever the consequences?' he said. He looked directly at Pavel, who met his eyes, gave an unsmiling grunt of agreement, and began to pack his few belongings.

'I assume your next day off *is* tomorrow?'

A tiny grin of long-awaited relief flashed across Pavel's face, a touch of resolve in it. 'Yes,' he said, 'but so what? From now on, is not every day tomorrow?'

*

Next morning, reaching Malaga airport in good time, Batten entered to the grating sound of tannoy messages, trundled suitcases and the buzz and bustle of the human throng. He found a seat with a view of the busy lines of check-in desks, but didn't check in. The vast, marbled Departures area laced with cafes, shops and information screens, was the perfect place for *someone* to hide in plain sight, but when he scanned the melee of staff and travellers he spotted no eyeballs doing what *he* was doing. Nor did he spot Pavel, whose belongings lay next to Batten's cabin bag, in a rucksack too small to hold a full life. True to form, Batten had been through the contents, which said next to nothing of their owner. Two flight tickets and two pre-printed boarding passes sat in Batten's pocket. But unless Pavel presented himself at the check-in desk...

Sweat began to prickle Batten's skin. *Why didn't you grab Pavel's passport, you idiot, yesterday, while you had chance?* With unfelt nonchalance, he tracked face after face, seeing nobody remotely resembling a tall, slightly stooped man in a green baseball cap.

Time ticked away. When did boarding close? He checked the screen. Fifteen minutes. He tapped his feet, harder, on the marble vinyl floor. He checked again. Twelve minutes now. Green baseball cap, where? Growing pressure, from his own professional pride, from the imagined disapproval of Lady Wake, from the damn ticking clock. He stood up to improve his view - just as a man in a dark blue baseball cap slid into the seat beside him.

Pavel.

Unsmiling, his open hand thrust out, he said, 'My boarding pass?' Batten handed it over but was reluctant to let go of the rucksack. What if Pavel took it and fled? 'In case they ask to weigh it,' Pavel said with a shrug, and they headed for the check-in desk.

In the queue, surrounded by sweating latecomers, Pavel removed his cap and only then did Batten realise it was dark blue and nondescript. 'Clever,' he said, smiling. 'What happened to the green one?'

'Left behind, on my uncomfortable bed. A souvenir, for whoever discovers I am gone.' Pavel smiled a smile of freedom which swiftly disappeared, replaced by the wary, watchful eyes Batten had grown used to. The erstwhile farrier's face relaxed only when the plane taxied down the runway and climbed into the sky, and he blinked away three months of Spanish confusion.

After the knuckle-grinding stress of take-off, Batten saw to his relief that the plane was half-empty and the nearby seats unfilled – a chance to dig away in private at this taciturn ex-farrier. But once the seat-belt sign clicked off, Pavel pulled his clever blue cap over his eyes and either fell asleep or pretended to. Frustration rising, all Batten could do was switch on his Kindle, retrieve his half-read book - *Archaeology for Dummies* - and lose himself in its pages.

PART FOUR

SOMERSET

Twelve

With no hold baggage to reclaim, Batten walked Pavel through Bristol Airport's passport control and out into Arrivals, heading for his parked car - till Pavel nudged his arm and pointed. Avril Dean was standing at the gate, waiting for them. At least she wasn't holding a sign with *Zig* scrawled on it. When she spotted them, a look of relief calmed her face. But when she gave Batten an embarrassed little smile, he guessed what was coming.

'Lady Wake asked me to say how grateful she is. For bringing Pavel home. She can't thank you enough,' she said, drawing Batten aside. 'And I know Oksana will feel the same, when I deposit Pavel at Wake Hall.'

'I thought I was supposed to *deposit* Pavel at Wake Hall?' said Batten. *And sit in, when Pavel spills his guts to Her Ladyship.* 'It's why I left my car here.'

Avril's embarrassed little smile returned but failed to conceal the obvious: Batten's presence at the Wake Hall homecoming was not part of the plan. 'I'm simply doing as I'm told,' Avril said, the implication being that he should do the same. 'We'll gladly recompense any parking fee, of course. You'll add it to your invoice?'

At '*invoice*', Avril's message became doubly clear. *Thanks, there'll be a cheque in the post, now bugger off!* Batten's unsmiling face told Avril everything she needed to know. Even Pavel looked embarrassed as he trailed behind her to the car park, clever blue cap dangling like worry beads from his fingers, pathetic rucksack slung on his back like a snail's burden. Still speechless with anger, Batten stared after them till with an electric *woosh* they departed through the Arrivals door.

Ten yards away, a coffee bar - a double black espresso might drown his frustrations. He phoned Sonia, to say he'd be early, expecting the same soft tones he'd heard on his tender departure.

'*Thank God!*' she said, her voice frazzled. 'The kitchen's been delivered – well, been dumped in the front garden, seven huge boxes of it. I can't lift even one box on my own and sod's law, it's freezing cold and looks like rain. The plumbers left without connecting the boiler and the new builders have been an absolute fright! They didn't turn up today, just when I need them most, and they don't answer their phones - I thought you were them -'

'Sonia. Shh. What are you always telling me? Breathe? *De-stress*? I'm on my way.'

'Thank God,' she said again, her voice closer now to the golden voice he loved so deeply his heart ached all the way down to his shoes. 'I will, Zig. I'll breathe. And you, drive safely.'

In the car park, he took his own advice and tried to breathe away his anger at the hidden secrets of Wake Hall. But turning away from an unsolved puzzle? He didn't know how! The exclusion from Pavel's homecoming irked him doubly – he would neither see the pleasure of Oksana and Pavel's reunion nor hear the answers it would surely provide. Lady Wake's dictat, he decided, could screw itself.

By the time Batten turned off the motorway onto the A358, he began to glow at the thought of his own homecoming. Shifting heavy boxes of flat-packed kitchen would be a struggle, he knew, but it would at least take his mind off Pavel Ducek.

And he and Sonia would be doing it together.

Thirteen

Acting Inspector Ball wanted to be home. Instead, he trudged past the empty nameplate that used to say *Detective Inspector Batten* and plonked himself in the office chair that used to be Zig's. Copying his former boss, he treated himself to a spin. Parminster CID looked briefly better, but when the chair came to rest, the same pale brown walls surrounded him, and the same overburdened desk stared back. Casefiles. Transcripts. Forensic reports. Witness statements. Timesheets. Folders stamped *Crown Prosecution Service*. How could so much paper descend on just one desk, on just one man? Some days, he wished he was still a Sergeant, and today was such a day.

'Sarge? Er, sorry. Boss?'

'Yes, Hickie?'

Unlike Ball, Eddie 'Loft' Hick was happy he'd been promoted. Despite his chaotic exterior, he had a sharp mind - when he put his mind to it. Today was such a day. He leaned on the doorframe of Ball's cubby-hole office, since there was barely room for him inside. 'Boss, got a minute?'

Ball glared at the litter of dead trees on his desk and stared up at Hick. They'd have to find him a new nickname. The old one - 'Loft', because he's full of crap - was *unseemly* in a Sergeant who wasn't. Di was good at nicknames. He'd ask Di tonight. If he ever got home. 'Yes, Eddie. What?'

'I've been thinking about the boss - er, about Zig Batten.'

So had Ball, though he wouldn't admit it. 'And?' *Oh no, thought Ball. I've done it again - shortened a sentence to just one word. I'm having two-word conversations now. There's no time to **talk** to anyone anymore!* 'What about *Mr* Batten, Eddie?'

'I don't know if you know what I know. About, er, *Mr* Batten?'

'That's two of us, Eddie. Tell me, then I'll know if I know what you know.' Ball felt almost relieved to spout a longer sentence.

'That he's working for her?'

'Narrows it down, Eddie – to fifty per cent of the population.'

'Sorry, boss. Her. Lady Wake. At Wake Hall.'

Just hearing 'Wake Hall' gave Ball the shivers – even after all these years. His dead parents' failed smallholding was bought for peanuts by the vast landed estate, and his birthright engulfed. And he'd almost gone to meet his maker at Wake Hall, five years ago. 'Wake Hall,' he said, through gritted teeth. 'Jess Foreman told me about Zig and Wake Hall. So?'

'OK, well, Laura was on a girl's night out-'

'Girlfriend Sergeant Laura?'

'*Fiancé* Sergeant Laura, boss. We got engaged. I told you. Anyway, she overheard a bunch of girls, gossiping about Wake Hall. Seems they worked there, or used to, and there's funny business going on, but Lady Wake's keeping it under wraps, according to them. And I was thinking, if Zig's there, well, does he know - about the funny business? We were all part of the investigation, weren't we - before. When he was, you know, Inspector.'

'Yes, Eddie. The tractor thief murder. I've not forgotten.' How could he? They'd interviewed every Wake Hall human who'd ever driven a tractor – hellfire, who'd *seen* one in the distance. As much use as interviewing the bloody horses. 'But it's five years back. Cold case.'

'That's just it, though. This funny business at Wake Hall might've warmed it up. See, Laura says these girls were talking about Oksana Thing. Well, it was her brother, Dave Thing, who disappeared - that's who we were after, for the murder, right?'

Ball glanced at the paper mountain on his desk. 'Still are, Eddie. Get to the point.'

'*And*, according to Laura, I mean to these girls, the funny business involves Oksana's bloke, boyfriend, whatever. Foreign name, I've got it somewhere. He went missing, months ago, but here's the point - no-one at Wake Hall made any fuss. I checked for a MisPer report – none. So, Dave disappears, and now Dave's sister's bloke disappears - and no-one reports it? Don't *you* think that's fishy? Oksana Thing has to be the link.'

'She *might* be, Eddie. What are you asking?'

'I suppose I'm asking about asking. Can I ask around, at Wake Hall? I mean, if Zig's working there, s*omething*'s going on. Ask why this foreign bloke disappeared? See if it's connected to Dave Thing's disappearance? We're talking murder, after all?'

We're talking Zig Batten, thought Ball, *and his bad influence on Hick. Two peas in a pod now, Zig and Eddie. Dig, dig. Can't let things lie.* He stared in thought at today's paper pile, thicker than yesterday's. But his two-pounds-of-sausage fingers pushed the paper away. *It's this bloody chair. It's been contaminated. It's been Zigged!*

'Acting on information received,' Eddie? Would that be your angle?'

'Could be.'

'Well, you're nearest - to the cold case store.'

An expectant smile creased Hick's face. 'For the Dave Thing file?'

'Eddie, his name's Dave *Vossialevydipsic*.'

Hick's face lit up. 'That's impressive, boss. Five years on, I still can't pronounce it.'

You can't spell it, either, thought Ball. *He* could, from repetition. Because he was another cop who wouldn't let things lie.

Three peas, then, not two. *Three* peas in a pod.

Fourteen

At *Hillview,* his back sore from humping crates of flat-packed kitchen, Batten glared at his phone, still hot in his palm from incessant calls to the builders, but totally cold where Wake Hall was concerned. Sonia had left for her 'office' - he refused to let 'the mortuary' contaminate his skull - and yesterday's missing workmen were still missing today. Heeding Sonia's gentle warning to *de-stress,* he piled their breakfast dishes into the makeshift sink, shoved his mobile in his chinos and slouched over to the garden office. It's electric heater actually worked, so he could at least warm up. But no sooner had he flopped down in his leather chair than the silent desk phone sneered up at him.

'Sod it,' he told the walls. 'Enough is enough.'

Grim-faced, he grabbed the phone and rang Wake Hall. And this time, he would *not* be put off.

Avril was as unreadable on the phone as she was in the flesh. After much muttering, she said she 'would ask.' Fifteen more wasted minutes, him glaring at the phone to make it ring, then her level voice saying, 'Ten-thirty. But a brief meeting only. We have a full diary today,' before ringing off.

A full diary? he thought. When was the last time *he* had one of those? He grabbed his keys and drove to Wake Hall.

*

Even from distance, Batten recognised Allie Chant, silhouetted against the treeline, her gait tightened by muddy jodhpurs, a padded gilet and well-worn riding boots. Five years ago, he'd interviewed her on his first murder case in Somerset. She was Wake Hall's 'head lad' then, till Lady Wake purged the sexism and promoted Allie to a more gender-neutral Yard Manager. Batten was heading from the Visitors car park towards the looming facade of the Hall, Allie doing the same from the staff side.

Drawing closer, she recognised him, and stopped in her tracks. Batten remembered her willingness to gossip so he called out, 'It's OK, Allie. I'm not a cop anymore. All pig-ness gone. Perfectly safe to approach.'

To her credit, she smiled and joined him where the two paths merged into one. Her jodhpurs looked a size larger, five years on. He pointed at her wedding ring. 'Congratulations. Recent?'

'Last year. You met him. *Interviewed* him. Big Neil, the farrier?' Her milkmaid face lit up as warm pride leavened her voice. 'I love him to bits,' she said. 'When he speaks, the room vibrates, even if he's only saying, 'pass the milk.'

Batten smiled, remembering Neil's deep bass voice, the slowest, deepest he'd ever heard. All the same, he was thinking *farrier* - like Pavel? 'I remember big Neil. Made me look a dwarf, and I'm six foot.'

'We had to buy a special bed. You know, longer.' She stopped. Too intimate a subject, even with a 'perfectly safe' ex-cop. Instead she pointed up the pathway at the Hall. 'Looks like we're headed the same way.'

'And looks like you still work here? Despite everything.'

Allie pushed a strand of hair from her eyes, the morning wind stronger now. 'Five years ago, all that.'

'Even so.'

Giving Batten a look of appraisal, she gazed at the vast estate surrounding them. 'It was hard, at first. For everyone. Each time a horse box turned up, especially in darkness. Wondering what else was in it, apart from horses. And wondering if your lot might turn up too, like on that awful night.' She shuddered. 'Things seem worse in the dark.'

Batten had led the police raid that took down Lady Wake's erstwhile bed-warmer, Olly Rutter – his child-trafficking crimes concealed inside the vast horse-sales business he'd spawned. 'You don't miss Rutter's *Wake Hall Horse*, then?'

'*Wake Hall Horse!* Stupid name. Just what you'd expect from that hairy mammoth. Did you know, us folk on the Estate nicknamed it *The Regiment*? It's *Wake Hall Equestrian* now. Bigger, better - and *honest*.' Allie stared at Batten, a challenge in her eyes.

'So, glad to see the back of Olly Rutter?'

'Huh, back, front, top, bottom and sides. But I've not forgotten the pain he brought to this place. And to Her Ladyship.' Allie pointed at the snow-white blockhouse of Wake Hall filling the sky ahead of them. 'She had it cleaned. After, she held a big meeting, all the Estate staff, and told us straight, told us everything, her face as white as the Hall. I used to think the posh nobs who rolled up here were all snoots, you know, looking down their noses at the likes of me. But she just spoke to us, direct, told us her mistakes, everything. Blindness, she called it. A kind of blindness came over me, she said. About Rutter, I mean.'

'You must've believed her, since you still work here?'

Allie folded her arms, switching her gaze from the Hall to narrow her eyes at Batten. 'One of the horse girls, Nell Something, silly cow, *she* doesn't work here no more. After the meeting she says to me, 'that's two of us, then, 'cos I always get *a kind of blindness* at the prospect of a good shag.' Well, I slapped her so hard she went down with a thump, straw, horse muck all over her.' Allie examined her hand, as if remembering. 'Should have seen it, the surprise on her face. I stood over her and said, 'if you're looking for another job, you won't find it down there.' She struggled to her feet, took the hint, and buggered off - without me needing to slap her twice. Horses give you muscle, see.'

Against the backdrop of patchwork fields and mature trees, Allie Chant seemed like a tree herself. Not a tall woman, but strong, Batten noted. Had she made an inadvertent enemy of 'Nell Something', the lippy horse girl?

'So, I did, I believed what Her Ladyship said - because action followed words. Those thuggy men Rutter brought in, you won't find them here now. Five years on, there's no better horse-place in Somerset. She's put her faith in women, at Wake Hall' - again she flung her hand at the vastness of the place before treating Batten to another stare - 'and put her faith in me, so, yes, I'm *glad* to work here.'

Since Allie was as voluble as before, Batten pressed on. 'She's put faith in *some* men,' he said,' because I'm working here too.'

Allie's penchant for gossip had ears as well as lips. 'I heard you got crocked and had to leave. The police, I mean.' She watched Batten's involuntary fingers touch the permanent lump on the back of his neck. 'Heard you were doing something or other for Her Ladyship.'

'Come as a surprise?'

She paused for thought, new responsibilities briefly corking her tongue. 'Surprise? I can see you don't know horses. Surprise you every day, do horses. Painful, sometimes, if your wits are elsewhere. Not ma'am though. Give ma'am her due. A whisperer, she is. Horse *and* human. You ever see her ride?'

Batten never had.

'What's that phrase - *poetry in motion*? That's Her Ladyship. She rides an Andalusian mare, Maya, as classy as she is. And the two together, well, it's class on class. Maya's a mare, but Lady Wake, she could charm the gonads off a *stallion* if she put her mind to it.' She gave Batten a smiley stare, eyebrows raised, a mock-emoji. 'No. No surprise at all.'

'No surprise I'm looking into Pavel Ducek's mystery departure, then?'

'And mystery return, yesterday,' she said, before looking away. 'But I've nothing to tell you about one or the other, because Pavel's only talking to horses. Me and Neil live next door and he's said zilch to us.'

Batten guessed Pavel Ducek was saying *zilch* because Lady Wake had warned him to zip his lip. Did Oksana tell him the same, in private? But what had he already told the pair of them – and the ubiquitous Avril – before his lips were zipped? Glancing ahead, towards Wake Hall, where tight-lipped seemed the order of the day, Batten tried a different tack. 'At least the Hall has its full complement of farriers again?' he said, testing. 'Good news for your Neil?'

But Allie was no fool, and her sideways glance said so. 'When he left the Army, *my* Neil only worked at the Hall on and off. Lady Wake would have employed him, regular, she said, but he likes freelance. Don't get bored that way, he says. Anyway, he gets all the regular he needs at home. With *me*.'

'But home or away, he knew Pavel?'

A nimble-footed Allie Chant kicked at a stone on the path, nudging it to the verge and loitering as if to admire her handiwork. 'We all knew - know - Pavel, if you ever really know the folk you work with. Neil only worked with him a few weeks, before freelance, and farriers don't go much for talk. The noise, you see. Furnaces, hammers, hooves, metal.'

Then Allie herself decided not to go much for talk. Sneaking into the shadow of a large shiny-leaved camellia, she drew her smokes from her pocket and lit up, blowing smoke at the glossy green leaves. 'Trying to stop,' she said, after sucking in more smoke and blowing it out again, for what seemed an age. 'I'm supposed to be an example, to the younger girls. Fags are frowned on here, you see. Hay, straw, and flame, they don't go together - unless you want a fire.' Grinding the stub beneath her boot, she trotted on, but in silence.

Will anyone at this bloody place tell me anything? Either Batten's face must have spoken his thoughts, or the cigarette had done its job because she looked up at the Hall, closer now, and sighed in surrender. 'Since we both work here now, I suppose I don't have to mind my p's and q's. So just bloody ask.'

Directness has its moments, Batten knew, and ploughed on. 'Well, have you or Neil heard anything about Pavel that might help me? Anything about Pavel's past? Why he disappeared?'

'Even if it opens a can of worms?'

'Especially if. But why should it?'

When she stared in thought at the Hall's bright white limestone, her directness faltered for a moment, before recovering. 'Neil's no use to you. Far as I recall, he never knew Pavel that well. Neither of us did, really. Oksana the same, even though we're next-door neighbours.' Again, her hesitation kicked in, before being flicked aside, like the stone on the path. 'It's the other stuff, with the horses. That's where you ought to be looking. *Some* people here think Pavel's behind it, because it began right after he disappeared, though *I'm* not convinced. And if horses aren't why you're heading where I'm heading, it wasn't me who told you. Right?'

Batten, intrigued, was happy to agree, since everyone at Wake Hall knew Allie and gossip were joined at the lip. 'Other stuff? Bit vague?'

'Ah. You didn't know.' Her big mouth uncorked, Allie raised and dropped her shoulders and with a long sigh said, 'the funny stuff, with the horses – I have to report in, to Avril, if more funny stuff happens. And it has, this morning. Or in the early hours, I suppose, because it never bloody happens in daylight.'

This time they both gazed at the Hall's over-heavy portico, close now, looming like an acid-white question, when Batten wanted answers. 'You called it *other stuff*, then *funny stuff*? Any chance of being more specific?'

'I *was* specific! I said, with the *horses*.'

'Horses? *Here?* Hadn't noticed any,' he replied, making her smile.

She turned to stare at the vast fields rolling away on either side of the path and he followed her gaze. The smell of horses had eased as they neared the Hall, yet beyond the flower borders and post and rail fencing field after field swept to the horizon, each field peppered with four-legged beasts, their collective breath a ghostly mist in the morning air. Never had he seen so many in one place. Wake Hall must buy and sell them in their hundreds, the profits way beyond his imagination.

'First it was gates left open. Staff being forgetful, we hoped. Horses are greedy and they'll push at a fence to find the sweeter grass, but they're not so bright they can open a padlocked gate. And you've seen how many horses. When they get out, it takes all day to round them up. Hazard of the job, I suppose, but a costly waste of time. We held an emergency meeting, told the staff to be more careful and thought that was that. But then we found acorns and yew-tree clippings, scattered where the grass was sweetest. Had to be deliberate - they're poisonous to horses, did you know that?'

Batten didn't.

'We thought, it'll be youngsters, from the towns. Having fun, cocking a snook at posh country folk with fields full of money. Like the fields you just walked past.'

'But it wasn't?'

'Can't have been. Too often. And too...planned – that's what I thought, anyway. Avril didn't want to believe me, till the paint started.'

Impatience rose like heartburn in Batten's chest. He heard Sonia say, *de-stress*, and quelled it. '*Paint?*'

'Splashed paint. On the horses. On dozens of them. Bright red paint, and plenty of it. In thick, glossy blobs. Showed up most on the dark bays, but we have to clean them all, dark or light, or shave it off, the paint – and we can't sell the horses till their coat grows back. Would kids or pranksters go that far, then do it again? Lady Wake was floored when Avril told her. Turned white, according to Avril, soon as she heard 'red paint'. And no, I don't know exactly why. My pay grade, we don't ask.'

'So, you're on your way to report more red paint? To Avril, at the Hall?'

This time, Allie stopped and looked long and hard at the equine fields. When she turned back, her top teeth were planted into her bottom lip. 'I wish I was. Wish it *was* just paint. And I wish I wasn't the messenger. It went way beyond funny stuff, last night. More than twenty horses, in different fields, and they've all been cut. Slashed, flanks and necks, poor creatures. We might find more, in the far pasture. Must've been a sharp blade, so say the vets. They're up there, trying to fix the chaos.' She pointed at the horizon, grim-faced, worried. 'Not life-threatening, the wounds, thank God, but that's twenty or more sales out the window. There'll be scars, see.'

'But wouldn't horses kick out?'

'Wouldn't you? Course they would. Cruel bastard, must've managed to keep his distance.'

'Or hers.'

'Male, female or other – if I get my hands on them…'

'Isn't this a police matter?'

'Huh, told you, above my pay grade. But you know Her Ladyship. No publicity *per-lease*. And who can blame her? Took a lot of effort to rebuild Wake Hall's reputation, after your lot had tramped their boots all over the place.'

Batten felt told off. His boots had contributed to the tramping, back then.

'And the media shark fest after, well. Do you know, a convoy of TV vans tried to drive in - as if one channel isn't enough for bad news? Satellite dishes on the roof, the lot. Give Lady Wake her due, snapped her fingers and three giant tractors blocked the road. Two Estate lads in each, nearly as big as my Neil, all six of 'em, against a bunch of titchy reporters. Me and my girls came out to watch, but they chickened out, the wimps, climbed back into their vans and scuttled off. Tried again on the service roads, same result.' She stared into the distance towards the roads in question, a smile on her face, till reminded of her task by the grandiose double doors they had reached without noticing. 'I'd better tramp *my* boots in here,' she said, 'and get it over with.' Gossip done, Allie scraped what Batten hoped was mud from her boots and stared up. 'But you've not come about horses, have you?'

Batten's visit was about humans, but Allie's information changed that. All the same, he shook his head.

'Well, you didn't hear about the horses from me, remember,' said Allie. 'And since *equine* takes priority in this place, I better go first.' With that, she cantered up the stone steps, yanked the heavy iron chain, and an unseen bell tolled somewhere in the building's bowels.

*

Once again, Avril eased back the heavy door. *This woman, the eyes of Wake Hall, is she on wheels?* More likely a camera, covering the entrance, he guessed.

When Avril saw Allie and Batten together on the top step her unreadable eyes twitched, deducing what questioner and gossip had most likely shared. And with a further glance at Allie's worried face, Avril swept her past the ante-room door into the vast entrance hall. 'Lady Wake and I have to deal with this,' she told Batten, pointing at Allie. 'I'll send coffee for you, if that's OK?'

In other words, *wait your turn, here.* Batten pulled a face, impatience not softened by the fact that - technically at least - he was still being paid. The bolt clicked on the other side of the ante room, and he drew out the same once-pink velvet chair he'd squatted on the first time he entered Wake Hall, five years ago. Back then, with a warrant card in his pocket, he was investigating a murder. Now, his pocket held keys, phone, pen and a packet of mints, and he no longer knew *what* he was investigating.

A young woman brought coffee, as promised, in a silver jug on a silver tray. Posh, Batten thought, as he poured and drank. He tapped more questions into the memo pad in his mobile, trying to weave random threads of information into a linear narrative, without success. He drank more coffee, cold now, and tapped his feet, faster and faster.

After half an hour, Avril reappeared and beckoned him to follow. This time, they went through the forbidden trompe l'oeil door that was a real door and across a corridor to a neat office. The walls, a neutral beige, sported a giant pair of year planners. A desktop computer sat on a tidy desk, Avril's coat draped over the back of her office chair. When she drew out a second chair for him, he wanted to ask who it usually belonged to, but she got in first.

'I'm sorry you had to wait. The last few months have been awf…have been *trying*,' she said. Batten's sympathy meter had dropped to nil, and he cut her off.

'Is the boss in?' he said, translating Avril's silent response as, *yes but not, after all, to you.* Detesting wasted journeys, he stood up. 'Well, *when she returns*' – he raised one eyebrow to nudge home the sarcasm – 'tell her if I don't get answers today, she can have her retainer back and I'll find some other stable to muck out. Oh, and as a responsible citizen, I may need to report some nasty criminal activity to the police. Crime is crime, even if the victims happen to be *equine*.' He turned to go but she stood up too and gently caught his arm, her unreadable face softening.

'To understand Her Ladyship,' she said, 'try to appreciate how much horses mean to her.'

'Horses?' he said. 'Hadn't noticed any.' The irony was lost on Avril.

'Mr Batten...Lady Wake may be asset-rich when it comes to land and possessions, but she is an only child, with no living family – and regretfully, is childless.' Avril's hands swept beyond the walls to the Estate's vast acreage. 'With no obvious heir to this...*burden*, what will become of it?' Dropping her hands to her sides, she let the question sink in. 'Her substitutes for beautiful children are beautiful horses. Maya, her favourite, is a thoroughbred Andalusian mare, the most exquisite you will ever see. And when any of your children are threatened, attacked – or scarred...'

Rein yourself in, Zig. He swallowed the unintended pun and said, 'I don't rejoice in any of that, but nor do I rejoice being kept in the dark. I'm not mucking out her stables in blinkers, with my bare hands. When *she* comes clean, I'll do some cleaning for her. Otherwise, it's pastures new for me.' He gave Avril a moment to decide, then edged towards the door.

'Please,' she said. 'Sit down. I'll see.' And she was gone.

At least I'm waiting in a different room, Batten thought, still feeling like an intruder on the other side of the mysterious trompe l'oeil door. Eyeing the Wake Hall year planners on the wall, he resisted the temptation to scan their secrets - but not for long.

The first planner listed residential events, dozens of them, month after month; weddings; banquets; business dinners; literary lunches; an Arts festival. All organised by Oksana Brok, he assumed. The second was equine. Buying trips; horse fairs; overseas trade shows; sales deadlines – and in bright red pen, he noticed, an emergency meeting of all equine staff, three months ago. The meeting Allie had mentioned, warning them to keep the gates locked? Tracing his finger down the planner, he saw a second emergency meeting, in two days' time. The ink was still wet, there, blood-red on his finger. *I bet I'm not invited.*

Avril was standing in the doorway, watching him. Brazen, he turned and said, 'I want to know what's going on. *Everything* that's going on.' He tapped an ink-stained finger on the planner. 'And this meeting, I need to be there. If not, Her Ladyship can muck out the stables on her own.'

Fifteen

After another wait, shorter this time, Batten followed Avril as she ignored the trompe l'oeil door and plodded down a long passage so thickly carpeted it felt like walking on a trampoline. Deeper into Wake Hall they went, past more closed doors and into a stylish sitting room-cum-office, its pastel walls topped by an ornate plasterwork ceiling. An antique desk - solid walnut, he thought, exquisitely done - commanded the bay window. Matching walnut cabinets framed a view Batten had never seen, a formal garden with manicured borders, twin fountains feeding a lilypond, and a central pergola-covered walkway. Lit by a cold sun, it led the eye past a ha-ha to rolling chains of fields abrim with horse after horse. At the room's far wall, ornate fenders flanked a log-fire warming a pale-grey chenille sofa and two Queen Anne chairs. Lady Wake sat in one of them, a cashmere shawl over her shoulders. I'm in her private lair, he realised, cursing himself for thinking he should have worn a suit.

He'd only ever seen her in full make-up, with mascara accentuating her diamond face. She was still a striking beauty without the mascara – removed partly by tears, he guessed, judging by the red rings around her eyes. He could have said, *they're only horses,* but he abhorred the wilful harming of any living creature, man, or beast. And when beloved beasts are slashed and scarred with some kind of blade...

'I'm sorry about the horses,' he said. 'You must be ten times sorrier than I am, but...'

She waved away his condolences, though gently, her hand dipping towards the empty chair. With a nod of thanks to Avril, he sat down.

'M'lady?'

Lady Wake seemed to have forgotten Avril was there. 'Oh. Of course. You'll be in your office?'

Avril dipped her head, closing the door on her way out. The exchange reminded him of his dealings with Sergeant Ball - Acting Inspector now - the shorthand of folk who've worked together smoothly and long.

'She's such an asset,' said Lady Wake, as if reading his mind. 'Not old enough to be my mother, but some days she almost is.'

'Days like today?' he said.

She looked at him, her eyes sad, and dipped her head. 'Zig,' she said, as if needing to practise the name. 'I understand your frustration - or I hope I do. You found Pavel and brought him back to Oksana, to all of us, and I assumed we would have no further need of your services. But after today...'

'Or last night?' he said, echoing Allie Chant.

'Yes. Mischief only seems to happen in the dark. And far more than mischief now. My beautiful horses...' She turned her head away for a moment, before recovering. 'So. Your services are further required. Assuming you are willing to take on the task?'

Trying to find a better phrase than *it depends*, Batten plumped for, 'Frankly, I'm not sure what the task *is*. Every time I ask a question it feels like I'm stepping on secrets.'

Lady Wake emitted the tiny sigh he'd heard before. 'Not *secrets*,' she said. '*Confidentialities*, some of them...awkwardly private. If I say what they are, will you commit?'

Her directness a surprise, he was briefly stumped. Having wondered what lay beyond Wake Hall's closed doors, here he was, uneasy in *Her Ladyship's* private office, feeling like a tradesman who'd used the wrong entrance. Lamely, he said, '*It depends.*'

'On?'

'On these *confidentialities* - and on the task, whatever it turns out to be. For example, is Pavel one of those confidentialities? He's certainly one of the secrets I keep stepping on.'

Drumming her manicure on the arm of her chair, Lady Wake fell into silent thought. Then, with one firm tap, she rose to her stately feet and unlocked a drawer in the antique desk. He watched her remove a white envelope no bigger than his hand, shake out what looked like a pair of photographs and gaze at each for several seconds. Batten could only see the backs. Glancing across the room at him, she seemed to make up her mind and, after relocking the drawer, brought the photos back to the fireplace and handed the first to Batten.

'This,' she said, 'is one of the confidentialities.'

'It's a snap of Pavel,' he said. 'And Oksana. What's confidential about that?'

She leaned closer, expensive perfume teasing his nostrils, and her delicate finger traced a line from Oksana, standing behind a well-loaded buffet and facing the camera, to Pavel who was looking away. 'Can you see what Pavel is reacting to?'

No, I bloody can't! Embarrassed, Batten had to fumble in his pocket for his spectacles, here, in Lady Wake's private lair. She half-smiled as he pulled on his glasses and stared at Pavel, head turned away from Oksana towards a muscular, bearded man, his hand gripping Pavel's shoulder.

'I don't recognise the man. Should I?'

'Probably not. I didn't, at first. I should explain. Oksana gave me the photograph simply because of these.' She pointed at the ornate table dressings, decorating the buffet. 'On behalf of the Hall, Oksana had attended a property company function with Pavel - work and play combined, as they so often are. She saw the decorations, and suggested we buy something similar for our banquets, and in fact we did. Only on second glance did I recognise the man gripping Pavel's shoulder.' She handed Batten the second photo. 'I had it enlarged. This is him, in close-up. I realised where I had seen him - though we never conversed. It was at a rather different function.'

Batten's hand said, 'so what?'

'It was a slightly 'off' business lunch.'

Off, he wanted to say, not *orfe*! Instead, he raised an eyebrow.

'If I tell you it was five years ago…'

Batten's penny dropped. 'You were with Olly Rutter?'

'Alas. I was.'

'So why was this lunch slightly off? No offence, but wasn't every business lunch Olly attended *slightly off?*'

Her sigh, again. 'Admittedly, I should have been more suspicious, and sooner. A sort of…blindness came over me, before I noticed familiar business contacts falling away, and new faces replacing them – harder faces, I now realise. And they spoke to Olly in corners, in whispers, when I was in another part of the room.'

'And this man who knows Pavel - he was one of the new faces?' Batten looked again at the bearded figure in the photograph. Smooth, big, hard. 'Don't tell me, this *associate* of Olly is the real reason I dragged Pavel back from Spain?'

Her response was a firmer stare. '*One* of the reasons,' she said, curtly.

'When I said I wanted him back for Oksana's sake, I was speaking the truth.'

Part of the truth, thought Batten, keeping his mouth shut. 'So, yesterday, when Pavel got back, you flashed the photo and said, *'by the way, who's this?'*'

'Not immediately. He needed time with dear Oksana. But later, yes, I did. And Pavel turned white. Whiter than limestone. Persuading him to say *anything* about the man in the photograph proved a struggle.'

'I hope he said *something*. He's coughed up sod-all to me.'

'*"From the past. Luka is from the past'* - his very words, and precious little else.'

The past. Another country, Batten thought. But at least he had a name to work with. 'First or second?' he asked, momentarily confusing her.

'Oh. First. Luka *Judd*. Pavel said the man's name was Luka Judd.'

'Is that it? That's the *confidentiality*?'

'One of them. Luka knowing Olly is another.'

Frustrated from being kept in the dark, he shamelessly pushed her along. '*And?*'

Lady Wake's nostrils flared, before the self-control returned. 'If Luka Judd's face appears in a photograph a few short months ago, he is or was in the area. And he clearly knows Pavel, as the strong hand on Pavel's shoulder suggests.'

Batten stared again at the photo. Pavel's face was half-turned away from the camera, but the visible half looked surprised - or maybe shocked?

'You have, shall we say, *crossed paths* with Olly, so will have confronted his inner fury, the likes of which I have never before experienced. I had no illusions he would disappear quietly but neither did I suspect, from his prison cell, he could somehow persuade this *Luka* to wreak a belated revenge on me, through my horses – or arrange it, at the very least.'

'Bit of a stretch, isn't it, from Luka being in the vicinity to Luka being the culprit?'

Lady Wake shuffled in her chair. Struggling with another *confidentiality*, Batten concluded. He was right, because this time her sigh was audible.

'For a brief period, Olly and I owned a property portfolio – I sold it, after the removal of Olly's name and, before you ask, after the finances were cleansed.'

'Cleansed of laundered money?'

Her manicure waved in reluctant agreement. 'I'm afraid I allowed Olly to make criminal decisions on my behalf. My blindness,' she said, and fell silent.

'Doesn't explain Luka,' said Batten.

'Alas, it may. The properties were in Bristol, which I now know is Luka's stamping ground. Not far, in fact, from Bristol Prison, where Olly thankfully resides. I had no knowledge of this at the time, but a trusted associate tells me the entire portfolio was in fact bought from a shell company owned by Luka Judd.' Her manicure forestalled Batten's raised eyebrow. 'You are not my only connection to the world beyond Wake Hall.'

'Still tenuous,' said Batten – a phrase he'd borrowed from the Crown Prosecution Service.

'Not so. It seems Luka was desperate to sell. He needed to inject cash into his overseas property schemes. Olly stepped in at the eleventh hour – and when he does favours he expects favours in return. Only fools refuse him, and I doubt Luka is a fool. So. Olly, Bristol, Luka, Pavel – and Wake Hall. A string of too many coincidences.'

Sometimes, that's all they are, Batten could have said, but Lady Wake once more stopped him in his tracks.

'I forgot to mention. Luka's property schemes, for which he desperately needed the money, were in Spain.'

Now, Batten's toes began to tingle. 'Not on the Costa del Sol, by any chance? In striking distance of Malaga, where Pavel was playing Mickey Mouse?'

'Correct.' She took the photograph from his fingers and gazed at it again. 'Until today, until the vicious events of *last night*, I too had doubts – and fears. But I know Olly too well. A manipulator of others, by skill or by threat, whichever works best for him.'

'In CID, we called him Alibi-Olly.'

'How fitting. Yes, safely out of the way while others wreak his revenge – on Wake Hall and on me. By attacking what is close to my heart.'

'Your horses?'

For a brief moment, she closed her eyes. 'My horses. A Chinese torture, aimed at me, through them, I'm certain. Gates left suspiciously open. Acorns and yew-clippings scattered in the grass. Did you know they were poisonous to horses?' Batten pretended he didn't. 'Red paint flung at horse after horse – too often to be childish vandalism. And…'

Suddenly chalk-faced, she rose from her chair, and crossed to the window, staring through it past ponds and pergolas, to the equine horizon. Another *confidentiality*'s brewing, Batten mused, as Lady Wake gazed fondly into the nearest field at a fine-boned, grey-maned Andalusian. From Avril's description, he guessed this was Maya, the classy mare Allie Chant had mentioned, *Her Ladyship's* favourite 'child'.

As he watched, her fond gaze seemed to crack, like ice on a frozen lake, and she uttered just one word, 'Red.' After what seemed an age, she turned to face Batten, the spark dwindling from her diamond eyes. 'Red, bright red…is Olly's colour. He insisted I wear red silk, in…certain situations.' Her cheeks took on the hue, as intimate moments from her private life became embarrassingly public. 'Silk, it suits me. But red, no.' Controlling her discomfort, she added, 'You may have seen the red silk lining in Olly's suits. But not, I trust, his red silk underwear. He would tolerate no other kind, no other colour. It was Olly's…bedroom signature, I suppose.'

Batten shook off his own embarrassment, trying not to picture Rutter and Lady Wake in a red silk bedroom romp. 'And now it's red paint, on the horses?'

Framed in the light from the bay window, he saw her tears, heard the tremor in her voice. 'Olly's message, I'm sure of it. And escalating into red *blood* today, the red blood of my beautiful steeds, their flesh cut, their necks forever scarred. Twenty, last night. How many more if it is not stopped? And what next? *Beheadings?*'

A different bedroom, in a scene from *The Godfather* flashed into Batten's skull. A severed horse's head in the red-stained sheets. He shook it away as tears drifted down Lady Wake's exquisite cheekbones. He felt helpless and hopeless. How is one supposed to comfort a member of the aristocracy? Not, for sure, by warning her that thugs who harm horses might gladly harm humans, too. A supportive silence was the best he could manage, his thoughts a random dance – *What about night security? Who is this Luka Judd? Why won't Lady Wake call the police?* Think straight! he told himself.

'I still don't see how Pavel was supposed to fit in, apart from being vaguely acquainted with this Luka.'

'Who is well acquainted with *Olly*. My surmise - and Avril's - related to knowledge and access. Even in darkness, Luka or his associates knew how to enter, knew which fields to approach, how to unlock, how to leave unseen. Pavel is a Wake Hall farrier, with keys to all the gates. He knows the fields, the roads, the bottlenecks. And the mischief began immediately he disappeared. So, at the time, we suspected he supplied keys and knowledge to Luka before fleeing to Spain - his parting gift a free pass, so my beautiful horses could be scarred in the darkness.'

To Batten, her theories sounded like a desperate search for a scapegoat – one he'd dragged back from Malaga, maybe under false pretences. His ex-CID mind craved harder evidence. 'Not sure I buy Pavel giving Luka a surreptitious guided tour, handing over his keys, then dumping Oksana, overnight, without so much as a by your leave? Not now I've met him. But I assume you double-checked with Pavel?'

'I am afraid I did. Rather gauchely. He was distraught, insulted. Having returned, shall we say he offered to immediately depart again - with Oksana. I apologised, and not just because of her. Now, yes, belatedly, I believe Pavel's protestations. He's become so protective he barely lets Oksana out of his sight. And thankfully, has renewed his farrier contract and returned to normal working life.'

Batten stroked his moustache, pretending it helped him think. *Normal? Nothing's normal at Wake Hall! And if Pavel isn't involved, who is...?* 'Any more *confidentialities*?' he said.

She looked through the window at the threatened fields where her favourite 'child' safely grazed. 'None I consider relevant,' she said.

'And you won't involve the police?'

'Only in extremis. The Estate is still recovering from the last police *invasion*. A business brand is too easily sullied. Currently, I am involving *you*. Zig.'

He wasn't ready to call her Marianne, despite his own insistence. 'CCTV?'

'An outdated system. Unproductive. New cameras are to be fitted, shortly.'

'Security patrols, then?'

'Yes. Avril is doubling them. Two vans now, darkness to dawn, constantly vigilant and in radio contact. Alas, the incidents seem to occur when they are elsewhere.'

'No surprise, on an estate the size of Mars.' *Twenty vans wouldn't be enough.* 'I've never seen so many fields full of horses.'

She dipped her head, assuming a compliment, till the thought of scarred horseflesh disturbed her features. Before she could reply, a discreet hand tapped on the door and Avril entered. Lady Wake glanced at her watch, surprised by the time. 'I shall ask Avril to vet the night security people afresh. And review any outcomes.'

Avril twitched her lips, a shorthand response. Batten had a dozen more questions – about Pavel's past, Luka and Olly, disgruntled employees, security measures, and the imminent emergency staff meeting. He figured Avril was a better bet and rose from his chair. 'Looks like I'm taking on the task, then.'

'And we have every faith it is a task you will complete,' said Lady Wake, as Avril held open the door and Batten took the hint.

Following Avril down the passageway, feet bouncing on the carpet, he tried redefining the task he'd taken on. By the time he bounced into Avril's office, he was no wiser at all.

Sixteen

A mover, not a sitter, Batten inwardly groaned when Avril drew out the same office chair he'd sat in half an hour ago and mumbled, 'You've guessed what I'm going to say. I can see it in your face.'

I wish I could read the secrets in yours. 'You want me to do more waiting?'

'I'm afraid so. Lady Wake's accountant is here. Unavoidable. But I'll slip out once business is underway. Ten minutes?'

He plonked himself in the chair and folded his arms. At the door, a wry-smiling Avril said, 'You could always read the year planners again, while you wait?'

Batten smiled back. Against his will, he was beginning to like Avril, or her readable bits. All the same, when she left he listened at the door - then scanned her desk for *confidential* documents. Nothing. Every desk drawer was locked, and his suspicious mind wondered why. Stumped, he did what he often did where crime was concerned: sat back in his chair, closed his eyes, and put himself in the shoes and mind of the culprits, whoever they were...

I'm Olly Rutter, in Bristol Prison, vengeance on my mind. Luka Judd has a handy gaff in Bristol, just down the road, and owes me a favour - and when I call in a favour... Luka has history with this Pavel bod who works at Wake Hall, so we'll pump him for inside info and hit Lady Muck where it hurts, with a touch of Chinese torture thrown in...

Olly's visitors, in prison? How does an *ex*-CID Inspector get hold of the records? Or dig up what might have been overheard?

I'm Luka Judd, I've got Olly on my back – noxious – while swamped by problems of my own in Spain. Bumped into Pavel, a blast from the past. And he was ecstatic to see me, not. But handy, him working at Wake Hall...

How to track down Luka? If in Bristol, easy. If in Spain...

I'm Pavel Ducek, I have Luka on my back. He's demanded my Wake Hall keys...

And was that how the *funny stuff* began? When Batten opened his eyes, the clear light of day murmured only *maybe*. He would need to question Pavel again - a tougher approach this time, with a photograph of Luka Judd in his hand. Oksana, too; the security guards; Allie Chant; the stable girls. And Lady Wake - how many more *confidentialities* is she withholding?

He was listing more questions when Avril returned. Yes, Batten was 'welcome' at the emergency meeting with the equine staff. She 'would ask' if Pavel might be interviewed, Oksana too. But give Lady Wake more time, a day or two, Avril suggested, leaving Batten in no doubt that where *ma'am* was concerned, he would have to wait. But no more sitting around today. Me and Avril, he decided, whether she likes it or not, we're going to *move*.

*

Climbing into Avril's little red Corsa brought Rutter's red underwear briefly to mind. The car was as clean and neat as Avril, but a tight fit for a tall ex-detective. Her timescale was also tight. 'Thirty minutes,' she said. 'Then I have meetings.' Her reluctant hands steered the car towards the far fields where the latest skulduggery took place, one hand lifting from the wheel to point at various gates previously left open, then at paddock after paddock where poisonous clippings were strewn and red paint splashed over unsuspecting beasts, by unknown hands.

Batten clocked the tangle of roads and tracks weaving to and from the nearest fields and away into the distance. Bewildering enough in daylight, but at night? Five years ago, the police used infra-red binoculars to help catch Rutter's thugs. This time, new thugs - or someone - committed fresh mischief in the dark. If they used night vision scopes to help them see, where did they get their training and experience? Ex-military, he wondered?

He was still wondering when Avril parked behind a green pick-up and a blue van. 'The vets,' she said. 'According to Allie, it's three fields so far, and lord knows how many scarred horses. This is the second field. At this rate, they'll be here for hours. Poor creatures.'

Not sure if she meant horses or vets, he clambered from the Corsa and stretched his long legs. Avril did the introductions, keeping Batten's role deliberately vague. Geoff Markham, the sinewy chief vet, wore a bloodied plastic apron, his handshake like a monkey-wrench. When Markham pulled his surgical gloves back on, they reminded Batten of all the crime scenes he *used* to attend.

Drawing Batten aside, out of Avril's hearing, Markham said, 'I'm over a barrel here. Wake Hall's a massive contract and I can't afford to lose it. But I should be calling the police - except I'm under firm instructions not to.' He flung a hand at the white speck of Wake Hall in the distance, then back towards a distressed horse being tended by a female colleague. 'This is nasty. Malicious maltreatment. It's an offence under the-'

'Animal Welfare Act. Yes.' Five years ago, Sergeant Ball had used the same offence, Rutter's spiteful whipping of a frightened horse, as a pretext for arresting him. Once the money-laundering and tax evasion emerged, the pretext became merely that. *Malicious maltreatment of a horse.* Another link to Olly Rutter? Another vengeful echo of the past? This morning, when Lady Wake passed on her suspicions, Batten wasn't sure. Here, now, the tenuous link to Rutter felt like hard connective tissue, blood-red proof of his vengeance.

'Not squeamish, are you?' asked Markham.

Batten never understood why folk chose to work with wounds and blood. Hell's bells, he lived with a woman who took a scalpel to dead bodies. 'Course not,' he lied, and followed Markham into the field. Allie Chant was already there, strong hands on the head-collar of a fine-looking horse, its flanks a mixture of chestnut-coloured hair and dark blood. She gave Batten a sad glance as a second vet tended the jagged wounds. Batten tasted his breakfast coffee, for a second time.

'Thank God for ketamine,' said Markham. 'Anaesthesia for horses. Might need some myself if we find many more like this.' He pointed at a deeply scored gash in the horse's neck. 'The cuts to the flank are bad enough. But the neck wound, close to life-threatening.'

'Deliberately life-threatening?' asked Batten, glad to turn away from the sight of damaged flesh, shining in the late morning sun.

Markham stroked his chin. 'Not sure. The wound looks random to me. Wounds plural, I should say. And since no horse in the world would stick around to be slashed a second time, my guess is a rope or chain – a flail of some sort, with more than one blade fixed to the end. And a big-shouldered sadist to swing it. I can't see how else these wounds could be made. The horse would bolt – or kick out.'

'A flail, so the perpetrator could keep his distance?'

'Perpetrator?' Markham blew out his breath. 'Bastard, more like. I'm a healer, by profession. But if I get my hands on whoever did this, I'll do more than kick him in the girth.'

'What kind of blade, do you think?' Batten immediately regretted the question, as Markham drew him back to the wound.

'See the clean edges to the cuts? Best guess is agricultural.' At Batten's blank stare, he added, 'Ah, you're not a countryman,' and pointed again at the wound's scores and slices. 'Something with a ring at one end and a bloody sharp edge at the other, like a hedge-cutter blade? Or several of them.' He shook his head, a helpless gesture. 'Who does that, though? *Who?*'

Alibi-Olly might, Batten could have said, through a convenient proxy. In his mind's eye, he saw a vengeful Rutter pulling Luka's strings - or flails - from the safety of Bristol Prison…

Avril's hand on his sleeve broke the thought. Relieved it was time to go, Batten thanked Markham and headed for the car. Before climbing in, he called to the vet, 'The red paint, before, splashed on the horses. Anything special about it?'

'Special? Not to *my* knowledge. But Paula has a theory.' Markham shouted across to his colleague, still tending a scarred horse. 'Paula! The red paint. Tell Mr Batten here what you thought.'

Paula, her apron stained with blood, turned away from the horse and approached, her blonde smile a welcome relief. 'Oh, probably nonsense. I went paint-balling once – three teams, blue, green and red. I was blue, and useless. Got covered in red and green splatters, all over me. And they hurt! The splatters on the horses looked the same. So maybe a paint-ball gun? Could be how they did it?' She shrugged her shoulders and went back to the scarred horse, leaving Batten stroking his chin.

Avril drove them back to Wake Hall in a mutual silence. The paintball gun, if Batten could trace its source, might lead to whoever used it. But the real priority was Bristol Prison.

A vain Olly Rutter would surely agree to a visit, if only to throw more snide insults at the man who helped put him away. Amid the sarky crudeness, maybe a glimmer of useful evidence would snicker from the horse's mouth. Or from the horse's arse.

And where Rutter's concerned, Batten thought, what's the difference?

*

Avril did the decent thing and saved Batten a long walk by dropping him in the Visitors car park, separated from the Official one by a long swathe of fencing and broad swards of greenery, as if manicured lawns and glossy camellias somehow softened the statement of class division. Climbing into his old Ford Focus, he wondered if he would ever graduate to an *Official* permit – or if he wanted to.

The twin car park roads merged at a fountain-dressed roundabout, three hundred yards from the white limestone blockhouse of Wake Hall which swamped Batten's rear-view mirror as he drove away. Mind still on the Pavel-Luka-Rutter conundrum, he failed to spot Sergeant Eddie Hick's Jeep breeze past the roundabout in the opposite direction, heading for the Official car park.

Some days, Hick's disposition teetered towards the literal. I'm on official business, he thought, so it's the Official car park for me. And he pulled into the nearest space, locked his Jeep, bounded up the stone steps and yanked the chain that rang a warning bell somewhere inside Wake Hall.

Seventeen

Arnie Goole, Batten's old Leeds CID pal, was a rotund, apple-cheeked Yorkshireman nicknamed Arnie the Fish. Being a skilled angler he could out-think the fish - and out-drink them, too. When Arnie left the force he moved south, becoming a Senior Prison Officer. At HMP Bristol.

To Batten's surprise, Arnie refused a day-off pub lunch, plumping instead for a skinny flat white and blueberry muffin in Café Nero. In an unpopulated corner, amid piped music, they sat on faux-leather armchairs that reminded Batten of Oksana Brok's office. 'What happened to the pints and whisky chasers, Arnie? You on a health kick?'

Arnie's thick fingers yanked a lump from his muffin and popped it in. 'Shouldn't even be having this,' he said, chewing. 'Supposed to be losing weight. I'm on low sugar, low alcohol, low fat – and low bloody enjoyment! But cheers, all the same.' He slurped unsweetened coffee. 'Nice as it is to see you, Zig, you didn't drive fifty miles to pass the time of day. So out with it.'

Batten returned the Yorkshire directness. 'Olly Rutter,' he said. 'He's agreed to a visit, this afternoon. I'm looking for a heads-up, before the joyful event.'

Arnie put down his muffin. 'Cuh, why didn't I guess? You can pick 'em, Zig. Good job you'll be supervised, safer that way – not that Rutter ever dirties his own hands. Still hiding behind one paid shmuck or another, like he was in Leeds.'

'And in Somerset, Arnie.'

They clinked cups. 'I'd not forgotten, Zig. Just never thought you'd collar him. Nor steer the muscled bastard my way, as if I don't have enough to keep my eye on.'

Batten smiled. Bristol Prison was Category B, for inmates open-minded about escape. 'You keep your eye on Rutter, then?'

'Big sod's hard to miss. Drug-use was bad enough before he arrived. Now, it's worse, get my drift? Mr Drug-Smug, we call him. Always looks like he's up to summat, even when he's not.'

'The *summat* he's up to, Arnie, that's why I'm here,' said Batten, flipping an enlarged photo of Luka Judd onto the table. 'Recognise this fine specimen? Maybe at Rutter's table, at visiting time?'

To Batten's surprise, Arnie stared at the photo but shook his head. 'Zig, I'd remember. And my staff, we share names and faces. Up-to-date info keeps you safe, in there. But Olly Rutter doesn't need visitors. If he wants something doing, there's plenty other routes. God knows how many burner phones he's got up his sleeve. Mind you, they're never in his cell when we search – which tells you summat else.' Arnie dropped his voice. 'Where he gets the phones, who hides 'em, how he knows when a search is planned…' Arnie took refuge in his blueberry muffin. Batten knew what he meant.

'Fingered anyone? A trustee? A member of staff?'

At 'staff', Arnie gave a wink, and brushed muffin crumbs from his chin. In spite of the jazzy muzak, louder now, he dropped his voice. 'Let's just say we have our suspicions - which may shortly be acted upon. But even if you forced a second muffin down my throat, I couldn't tell you more, because I don't know.'

'Any chance you could give me a nudge when you *do* know?'

Pointing to a debris of muffin crumbs and the beige froth in his empty cup, Arnie said, 'After a spread as grand as this, how could I refuse? Next time, mind, if the info's top-draw, you'll be stumping up for a brie and cranberry toastie - to help me lose weight!'

*

A mixture of old and new, Bristol Prison was a hymn to red-brick, and a vast one. Batten drove round the perimeter to get his bearings, surprised how close it was to a primary school and a children's playground. The memory of Rutter's penchant for child-trafficking stiffened Batten's resolve, but once inside the prison walls he felt the same punch-in-the-gut dismay that municipal buildings gave him – hard corridors and raw lighting, faint scents of bleach, the sound of emptiness. Police stations, mortuaries, hospitals. And now this.

For what seemed like an ice-age, he tapped impatient toes on the vinyl, staring across the table at an empty chair. He failed to stop his fingers drumming on a tabletop pitted by scratches and old cigarette burns. *Well-used, like me*, he thought, *now I've turned forty*.

When Olly Rutter was brought in, he looked younger than his 45 years, and darkly handsome still. Prison life had not degraded him, and Batten guessed why. Greased palms, 'favours' - and threats if needed - all ensuring a degree of softer treatment. But the silk suits and designer shoes were gone. Rutter in grey prison garb slid into the chair, his frame barely smaller sitting down. Muscle, not fat, engulfed the space opposite Batten. The prison gym, or maybe press-ups on the cell floor. But today, an interlude, a proxy taste of the outside world, a joust with an old adversary, to help pass the time.

'Well, well, *Ziggy* Batten, you've returned - like acid reflux. I heard you got pensioned off,' he hissed. 'After someone gave you a well-deserved clout on the head.' He leaned across the table and lowered his voice. 'Alas, it wasn't me.'

'Not why I'm here, Rutter.'

'Then if you've come for a loan, I shall have to disappoint. The taxman's been very unkind.' Rutter's eyes became a stiletto stare. 'With help from the likes of *you*.'

Batten's fear of Olly Rutter had long since been replaced by contempt, but he quelled the urge to show it, since Rutter was spewing out enough contempt for the pair of them. Instead, Batten jabbed a stick in the muscled detainee's underbelly. 'Lady Wake sends kisses, but they confiscated the champagne at the gate.'

An eyeball twitch, at her name, then pretending to ignore it. 'Should I require champagne, *Ziggy*, I snap my fingers.'

'Just the kisses, then.'

Rutter flexed his meaty fingers on the table, a silent threat. 'If you're *involved* with that snooty bitch, have some free advice. Where Lady Muck's concerned, keep both hands on your codpiece. She could entice the bollocks off a whole chorus of castrati, yours included.' Olly's fingers twitched, with memories perhaps. 'What do you want, bastard?'

Ignoring the gibe, Batten reached into his pocket, taking his time, and produced a face-shot of Luka Judd. After a casual glance, he flipped it onto the table. There was a flicker of recognition, he was sure.

'What next? Your fucking holiday snaps?'

'He sends his regards, too. But no kisses, this Luka...I've forgotten his surname.'

Rolling his eyes, Rutter glanced again at the photograph. 'How fiendishly clever. Testing poor Mr Rutter's memory like that.' Again the narrowed stare, at Batten, at the photo, at Batten again. 'My memory's sharp. Because I *never* forget. *Ziggy.* This is Luka Judd. There, name confirmed. So fucking what?'

'You'll remember your dealings with Mr Judd, then? The property portfolio he sold you?'

'At an extremely favourable price. I'm good at *business.*'

'So's Lady Wake. She cleaned it up and sold it on – with your name removed from the deeds, of course. Did I say she sends kisses?'

Rutter's hands rose from the table and conjoined, not in prayer but as one giant fist. 'This is becoming tedious,' he said.

'And I bet there's a lot of tedium, in here.' Batten looked round at the piss-yellow walls. 'So, to pass the time, I expect you've been honing your criminal tendencies? With help from Mr Judd?'

'Help? Since when has Olly Rutter needed help? And Luka Judd? Far as I'm concerned, he's history.'

'But he's still getting up to mischief, on your behalf? Been very naughty, unlocking gates, throwing poison into fields, splattering horse after horse with bright red paint?'

'Tuh, that Luka. Always was a touch *carefree.*'

'But *carefree* at Wake Hall, where you still have unfinished *business.* And being pally with Luka, he's helping you finish it. Rutter, Judd, Wake Hall. Too much coincidence. Wouldn't you say?

Leaning back in his chair, Rutter yawned, his muscled arms almost reaching the dreary walls. 'Life,' he said. 'Full of coincidence.'

'No coincidence the other night, though. This time, someone took a sharpened flail to Her Ladyship's horses. Twenty or more of them, flanks and necks, slashed and gashed. Nasty. Unsaleable.'

As Batten watched, a momentary flash of surprise and pleasure ghosted from Rutter's eyes. His yawning arms paused in mid-air and his fingers twitched, till he controlled them. *He didn't know,* Batten realised. *Luka hasn't told him yet. But he knows now - and the look on his face says he's happier than a pig grubbing in muck.*

'The Witch ought to take better care of her *business.* Tut, tut. Whatever *next?*'

Not quite an admission, the faint threat in Rutter's voice, but it tingled

Batten's feet. 'Whatever Luka's planning *next*,' he said, 'he'd better be careful. Tell him that from me, will you? Tell him there'll be extra vigilance, from now on. And when we catch him, he might end up in here, with *you*. What jolly times you'll have, reminiscing, in these palatial surroundings.'

Rutter yawned again, this time as he rose from his bolted-down chair. '*Bored*,' he said.

At the door, Batten called after him, 'What are they like, Rutter?'

Two muscled shoulders turned back. '*What*? What's what like, you plonker?'

'Prison underpants. Do they rub? I don't suppose you wear *red silk* in here?'

The shoulders shrugged and departed, but not before a flash of angry recognition lit Rutter's face. *Red silk, red paint, red blood. All down to you, Olly.* Batten was certain now. *You and your bought minions. But I'll stop you.*

And not because Lady Wake is paying me.

*

Olly Rutter strolled down the glum corridor towards his cell with mixed emotions. Despite the extras, it was still a cell, with a barred 'window' so high and tiny he detested the sight of it. But by the time he entered, bastard Batten's info had lightened his mood, even when he heard the *clunk* as the lock snapped shut behind him. Twenty horses - more than he'd expected. The planned escalation must have gone like clockwork. For the *interventions* at Wake Hall, using a psycho had its merits, especially a psycho with a zip for a mouth.

Grabbing a gold-plated lighter engraved *Olly 1*, he fired up a fat cigar, in flagrant contravention of the no-smoking ban. Prison or not, today would be a better day, improved by plonker Batten chasing his own arse up a tree. With a throaty chuckle, he muttered, '*Luka Judd*. Meddle with that crazy dickhead, *Ziggy*, and you'll get more than a sharp tap on your dodgy skull.' Fixing Batten was not part of the plan of course - but who turns down a bonus?

From his too-firm mattress, he blew twenty slow smoke rings at the ceiling, one for each ruined horse, counting off each smoky ring with smug pleasure. Then he blew a final vengeful ring for *her*. The prison psychologist had tried to sell him anger management, and Cognitive Behavioural Therapy, whatever that was. The only therapy Olly Rutter valued was revenge. He hated what he couldn't have. And he could no longer have Lady Wake…

Extra vigilance? Puh. Batten's warning fell to the floor like ash from the cigar. Olly had plans for *extra vigilance*.

'Lady Muck won't know what's hit her,' he told the walls. 'That bone-china face, it'll turn whiter than Wake Hall. I guarantee. Then turn whiter still.'

Eighteen

Hoping the autumn landscape would clear his head of Olly Rutter, Batten drove home from Bristol Prison via the Mendip Hills. The rolling vistas managed to dispel the thought of hairy-ape Olly, at least for now, but Pavel's untold story still niggled. Though warned to pre-book every 'intervention' at Wake Hall, Batten mouthed *sod it* to himself, pulled off the A37, and turned in the direction of the giant estate. Work should be finished for the day by now, but when he parked outside Oksana Brok's grace-and-favour cottage and rang the bell, the only reply was silence. Peering through the windows, he saw soft embroidered cushions, a thick rug the colour of corn, and walls dotted with pastel prints. Pavel was living here now – in a not very Pavel-like gaff, but comfy compared to the one in Malaga. And not a Mickey Mouse in sight.

The bench in the front garden was comfy too, but Batten had been glumly squatting on it for a good fifteen minutes, the day turning cold, by the time Oksana and Pavel climbed out of a mud-spattered Land Rover. Pavel's, Batten guessed.

From her lack of surprise, Oksana had clearly been told Batten would call at some point, but the look on Pavel's face said the opposite. 'He drives me to the Hall and collects me,' Oksana told Batten, pride and love in her voice. Pavel touched her hand as she stroked his cheek. 'I can walk the five hundred yards, but he insists. He's my joy, my protector.'

Batten only half-smiled at Pavel's romantic side. The begged suspicion lingered: why does Oksana need protecting?

Her eyes wandered between the two men, uncertain. 'Can I get you a drink?' she said.

Batten shook his head. 'Pressed for time, sorry.' *Been tapping my toes for fifteen minutes!*

Seeing Oksana into the house, Pavel called after her, 'I have to clean my kit.' From the Land Rover he lifted a steel toolbox and walked it to a patio at the edge of the garden. When Batten followed, Pavel jabbed a grudging finger at an aluminium table and two chairs.

With feigned interest, Batten watched Pavel remove an array of farrier tools from the box, the clatter punctuating the silence, as hoof trimmers and picks, rasps, hammers, and long-handled pincers landed on the metal table. Working with a scraper and rag, Pavel returned each one to the box neat and clean. Like Pavel's tiny flat in Malaga.

'Well, here we are,' said Batten. More silence. 'When Avril said I could talk to you, I figured by now *speech* would be involved.'

'I never tell Avril to send you *here*. She should ask Pavel first,' he said, dropping his voice and glancing over his shoulder at the cottage.

Batten dropped his voice too, but his words emerged as a hiss. 'Dammit, Pavel, tell me why Luka Judd has you by the short and curlies – or at least give me a clue!'

'Clue, huh. Mr *Detective*. I tell you everything and you make everything *nice*? I don't think so.'

'I brought you back from Spain, Pavel. To Oksana. You owe me for that.'

Pavel glanced towards the cottage as the faint sound of singing floated from the open door. Oksana's voice, but the words foreign - Polish, Batten assumed. 'I not talk here.'

'Does that mean you *will* talk?'

Pavel lifted a pair of pincers from the table and scraped invisible dirt from the jaws. '*The Horse and Groom,* in Hamford? You know it?' Batten did, the nearest village pub to Wake Hall. 'I walk there, Saturdays, just me, before dinner.' He buffed the pincers with a rag. 'Saturday, early, still quiet. One drink. But to sit and breathe, away from horses, from people. You understand?'

It was only Wednesday. *Three more days!* Batten tried to conceal his irritation. 'What time?' he said, on a long sigh.

Flicking what Batten hoped was dirt from a large rasp, Pavel said, 'Six.' He pointed the rasp towards the sound of singing. 'Oksana do dinner, seven-thirty.'

'And if I turn up at *The Horse and Groom*, might you actually *speak*?'

The final knife lay on the table between them. With a small diamond file, Pavel sharpened the edge and tested it by flicking the blade at a lavender bush fringing the patio. A woody stem dropped to the ground like a corpse to a grave.

'If you slice into the wood, lavender won't grow back,' said Batten.

Picking up the stem, Pavel peered at the severed end and threw it over his shoulder. '*I* will grow back,' he said. 'Oksana will grow back – if not scared by the likes of you. Saturday, away from here, I tell my story.' He wiped the knife on an oily cloth, and held it deliberately close to Batten's face. 'But I tell only you. *You* will not tell Oksana. *OK?*'

'Fine,' said Batten, watching the knife slide into a leather sheath, which slid not into the box, but into Pavel's pocket. 'Six-o-clock it is.' If still in CID, he might have reminded this taciturn farrier that carrying a knife, even for protection, is illegal.

And sometimes dangerous.

Nineteen

On the way to *Hillview*, his almost home on the fringe of Parminster, Batten parked in the High Street by the all-day supermarket and bought himself a lazy ready meal. After progress-checking the half-built kitchen, he shoved his curry and rice in the microwave, stirred it liberally and ate it standing up. Sonia was leading an after-work CPD event at Parminster Hospital, light supper included. He wondered what Continuing Professional Development he should do for *his* current role, whatever it was. *Cuh, elocution lessons, so I can talk to Lady Wake!* He rammed his plate into the makeshift sink. The fitters had fixed taps and drains to the new one – maybe by tomorrow they'd get round to plumbing it in.

Tomorrow and *Tomorrow and Tomorrow.* He was not going to watch three days tick by, waiting for Pavel's speech organs to rediscover their function. He stomped over to his garden office, switched on the lamp and dug out the Ronnie Lopen details Oksana had scribbled down. Nearly eight-o-clock - was it fair to phone the old caretaker this late? He did anyway, and to his surprise, the phone was answered at the second ring.

'I'm on lates this week,' Ronnie Lopen explained. 'There's two other old sods like me and we share watchman duties. Ekes out the pension. And if I'm honest, it passes the time.'

Since Ronnie was clearly the forthcoming type, Batten asked if he could have a chat about *my friend Pavel*. Keeping his reasons and status vague, he drew on old skills in this new career: a Northern directness that could unblock a sink; and subtler listening skills. When he mentioned '*ex-CID*' - though it still wrenched his guts to do so - Ronnie seemed to relax, quelling the irrational fear of arrest that people have when a real policeman is in the room. At the mention of Pavel's name, the tone became both forthcoming and friendly. 'Come now if you like. I'm going nowhere till midnight, and you get bored with the sound of your own voice. Bring photo ID and toot your horn at the gate. I'll put a brew on.'

Leaving a note for Sonia, Batten donned a warm coat, climbed into his Ford and ten miles later drew up outside the ugliest 1950s building he'd ever seen. The security lights had a major downside: they illuminated what would look better in the dark - a sizeable run of square, squat workshops and teaching blocks made of crumbling dull-grey concrete, all flat-roofed, with small random-seeming windows punched into the walls. The whole site was surrounded by fencing topped with barbed wire.

Ronnie Lopen unlocked the gate and led Batten into what must once have been a staff room. Three panel heaters pumped out enough heat to cook the old watchman. Cheap leatherette chairs, scuffed and torn, were clustered around low wooden tables, their surfaces stained by spilt tea and cup-rings. Ancient desks and filing cabinets lined the walls and something that might once have been carpet was now a shiny brown mixture of grease and dirt. No wonder they want to knock it down, Batten thought.

He put out his hand to shake Lopen's and heard a growl. 'Friend,' said Ronnie to a large, hairy German Shepherd, and the dog scrunched back into its wicker basket in the corner. 'Unfortunately, his name's Cyril,' the watchman added, 'but intruders don't know. He's getting on in years, like me, but he's big and loud and scares the shit out of any unwanteds. Best if you stroke him, so he knows what's what.'

A reluctant Batten did as advised, and Cyril immediately rolled over so his belly could be scratched. 'He's a tart,' said Ronnie. 'But the hooligans never get close enough to find out. Tea?'

After a cup of brown tar, Batten was surprised when Cyril the dog climbed from the wicker basket, sniffed his shoes and coiled his hairy coat around his feet. 'Seems he wants me to stay,' he said.

'He likes you. Be honoured - the opposite's worse. He'll lie there, my Cyril, listening out for the night security van. The driver always has a biscuit for him, and Cyril's always hungry. When he releases you, feel free to have a look for Pavel in these,' he said, pointing at the filing cabinets. 'He's in there somewhere. The Council are digitising it all, before the bulldozers move in. You're lucky, 'cos they haven't quite reached Pavel's cohort yet. Me and doggie are here to deter thieves, but I don't see why you can't *look*.'

Taking ready advantage of old Ronnie's laissez-faire approach, Batten stepped away from Cyril and riffled through the files. But Pavel's records only confirmed the already known – he came to the college for the theory parts of his apprenticeship, and passed with a grade A.

Ronnie chuckled through brown teeth. 'Cuh, listen to me – did I just say *digitise* and *cohort*? I used to speak Normal. Used to do a lot of things, mind. D'you know, I started the college rock-climbing club, more years ago than I care to remember. Drove the minibus all over, if I had a weekend free. Avon Gorge, Cheddar Gorge, Wales. Your friend Pavel was in it. Not a bad climber, Pavel. I've a photo somewhere.' He dragged open a file drawer and produced a faded scrapbook. 'Let's see…' He flicked beyond pages studded with group photos, male and female, young and not so young, and from the changes in hair and dress, from different decades. 'Here you go, that's me, there. Not worn well, have I? If you'd come five years back, you'd have been re-directed to Musgrove Hospital. Silly sod that I am, I woke up one morning and convinced myself I *wasn't* too old to climb. Turns out I was. Spent nigh on six months either blotto or in physio, serves me right, eh?'

Batten's condolences were only half-felt - his eyes drawn to the other faces in the photograph. A dozen male students, six on each side of a younger Ronnie Lopen, stared at the camera. Some had climbing ropes coiled round their shoulders, others had metal carabiners dangling from their belts. At their feet, more paraphernalia poked out of an assortment of sports bags and backpacks. Pavel stood on the left, smiling. On Ronnie's right, a well-built man had his arms round the shoulders of two others, one young, one older.

The arms belonged to Luka Judd.

'This is an interesting face,' said Batten, hoping he was being subtle, while pointing at Luka's dark beard and receding hair.

Ronnie Lopen nodded. 'Good climber, him, if reckless. Big bugger always had to be first, best, top dog, so he took risks. Strange looking cove. A magnet, though, to women *and* men. Some folk are born persuasive, I suppose, and *he* certainly was. All their names are on the back, but I don't need to see. Luka Judd, the bearded one. Often wondered where he ended up. You know, the staff used to call him Filthy Luka? Not because he was dirty, far from it, always smelled posh, some stuff he rubbed in his beard, I think. But don't leave any cash lying around, they'd say, 'cos Filthy Luka won't - it'll be in his pocket faster than you can say 'thief'!' Again, Ronnie's brown teeth chuckled at the memory.

'I'm surprised the college put up with that,' said Batten, probing.

'Well, they did, and they didn't,' said Ronnie. 'His tutor let slip they 'suggested' he complete his year and then scoot, or else. And he did.' Tapping the photo, he added, 'Two or three of these rock-climbers, Pavel included, they pop by, time to time, and say hello. But not Filthy Luka. Mind you, if he did, I'd let Cyril's teeth deal with him.'

'Filthy Luka wasn't pals with Pavel, then?'

'Now that's a good question because for a while he was. The Poles sticking together, sort of thing. Must've had a falling out because by the year's end you'd think they'd never met. Pavel even stopped rock-climbing, because Luka didn't.'

Another question to put to Pavel on Friday, thought Batten. 'What about these other two? Luka has his arm round their shoulders. Pals?'

'Oh, thick as thieves, all three of 'em.' Ronnie scrunched his face into a memory-ball. 'Let's see if I can remember their names without looking.' He gave up after five seconds and removed the photo from the scrapbook.

Thieves is right, Batten thought, guessing that gaps in the old caretaker's memory stemmed from six months in a hospital-daze five years ago, the press and media coverage of the tractor thief murder passing him by. Before Ronnie even turned over the photo to squint at the names, Batten knew who they were.

'Ah, of course, young Tom Bowditch – keen, but kept falling off. And Dave Whatsit - good climber, but no surprise I forgot *his* name. Never could pronounce it. Time I got to the end, I'd forgotten the beginning!'

Batten pretended to read it. 'Vossialevydipsic,' he said. 'Quite a tongue-twister?'

'If it'd been me,' said Ronnie, 'I'd have changed it to *Smith*!'

Or to Brok, thought Batten as Ronnie's brown-toothed laughter filled the room. In the echoes, Batten's memory flipped back five years, to a twenty-something tractor thief called Tom, his body found in a remote barn, the poor boy's skull split in two – and Dipstick Dave Vossialevydipsic, missing brother of Oksana *Brok,* the chief suspect still.

Batten tried putting his ducks in a row…

Tom Bowditch and Dipstick Dave were 'thick as thieves'.

Luka was pally with Tom and Dave.

Pavel knew all three of them.

Not so long ago, nigh-on a million pounds in quad-bikes, expensive motor homes, and top-of-the-range tractors 'disappeared' on their illegal way to Eastern Europe, and a few unfortunate guard dogs were poisoned along the way.

Batten stroked the soft fur of Cyril the German Shepherd. *Someone with links to points-East managed the false paperwork, the selling on, the laundered money. If Dave and Tom were the arms and legs, who was the brain? Filthy Luka Judd? Pavel Ducek? And what happened to the money…?*

'Can I take a shot of this?' he asked, pointing at the photo and waggling his phone.

'Course,' said Ronnie. 'My generation, we had to send ours off, or take them to a shop. Nowadays…'

'Anything in there about these two?' asked Batten, cutting through the nostalgia with a finger-tap on the faces of Tom and Dave.

'Should be,' said Ronnie. 'Same cohort as Pavel. Luka should be in there too. Help yourself, no skin off my nose. Why d'you want 'em, though, just out of interest?'

Why did Batten want them? He wasn't even sure himself. 'I'm wondering if this Luka Judd's been up to mischief. Maybe his two pals, as well. Or making trouble for Pavel…'

Ronnie considered this. 'Not seen Pavel for months, as it happens. Trouble, you say?'

Batten shook his head. 'Don't worry, he's fine, still happily knocking nails into horseshoes.' No sense telling Ronnie of Pavel's departure to Spain, and semi-reluctant return, when even Batten struggled to understand it. Neither did the filing cabinet help overmuch. Tom Bowditch had completed *Mountain Bikes: Construction and Maintenance*, which tallied with the well-maintained bike found at the crime scene, Tom's prints on the handlebars. The police assumed it was used at night to silently approach the garages and barns targeted for theft. Predictably, Dave's chief skillset was *Tractor Maintenance and Repair*. His extra talents, thieving and how-to-poison-a-guard-dog, were acquired somewhere other than college.

But the magpie-profile of Luka Judd tingled Batten's toes so much he could almost hear them drumming on the stained carpet. Luka's main programme, *Commercial Locksmiths and Property Security*, was suggestive enough, but his strange mix of supplementary courses covered financial management, building skills - and *Spanish for Business*...

With a final stroke of Cyril's warm fur, Batten said his friendly goodbyes to Ronnie Lopen. 'Next time I pass,' he promised, 'I'll bring a thank-you bottle of something strong.' Ronnie beamed at the suggestion. Batten hoped it would improve the taste of the watchman's tarry tea.

As he drove away, Ronnie's *'thick as thieves'* rang in his skull, adding to the conflicts already there. Old CID ethics. His new private role. His Wake Hall employer's insistence on discretion - all struggling for supremacy. Ronnie's information might be useful to Chris Ball.

If Batten told him.

Twenty

Sergeant Chris Ball never used to bring paperwork home. Now, in his *Acting Inspector* role, he pored over files and statements in the spare bedroom, transformed into a 'study' as if by magic. The real magic was his wife, Di, whose wand had moved out the bedframe and mattress, re-painted the walls a neutral grey, and moved in a desk and an office chair on castors. *Great,* he thought, *now I can be at work when I'm at home.* If only Di could magic away the smell of fresh paint and add six hours to the twenty-four.

She'd bought him a new laptop bag, too, posh black leather with compartments for documents. Dinner over, the dishwasher filled, and Di watching re-runs of *Strictly Come Dancing*, he flopped into his office chair, sipped his cider and from his new bag pulled Eddie Hick's report of his Wake Hall visit.

Rumours that girlfriend Laura completed Hick's Sergeant's Competence Portfolio were neither fair nor true. Hick had a good mind, which came with a rag-tag gait and a touch of dyslexia. Ball guessed Laura may have tweaked the odd misspelling in Eddie's Portfolio, but - alas - had no opportunity to correct the text of his latest report.

Arvil Dean, Ball realised, was Avril Dean – because he'd interviewed her five years ago, when investigating the shenanigans at her workplace. A personal maid to Lady Wake then, according to Hick she was now her *Private Secretary*. The rest of the report offered more idiosyncrasies - acting on *edivence recieved* being one of them - but was clear enough.

Hick had not been invited into the private rooms of Wake Hall, and rather than questioning Lady Wake herself, had to settle for *Arvil*. His enquiries about Pavel Ducek, the report said, were met by a puzzled silence. When Hick delved into his disappearance, Avril Dean explained that Lady Wake had many equine contacts in Spain and Pavel, a farrier, had been 'doing something with horses' over there. He was now back, and if Hick didn't believe her he could see the living proof.

Zig Batten's brass neck must have rubbed off on Hick because he said, yes, he would like to see the living proof, thank you very much. He duly did, confirming Ducek's identity via photo ID in the form of a Driving

Licence. Despite the bland prose, Ball could almost hear Avril tutting.

The news that Oksana Unpronounceable had changed her name to Oksana Brok was a comfort to Hick and Ball - but didn't help Eddie get to interview her. Busy in the Conference Suite, according to *Arvil* Dean. Raising the subject of Dave Unpronounceable got him a blank look, but nothing else. Asking if he'd been seen in the vicinity earned him a scowl, a no, and the door.

Clipped to the report was a Post-it, covered in Hick's scrawl. *No sine of Zig,* it said.

Ball finished his cider and slid the report into his bag - Pavel's presence confirmed, Dave's absence ditto. Nothing ventured, worth a shot, another box ticked. Running out of cliches, he breathed a sigh of relief.

No need to cross the hated threshold of Wake Hall, a place of torment for him.

Because his Jeep was on its homeward journey, Hick had not witnessed Avril and an incensed Lady Wake in conflab, their two knotted faces tight with anger. What brought the *police* to Wake Hall *again*? The nerve of it, implying 'Dipstick Dave' is hiding *here!* And how did they find out about Pavel?

Who told them?

Twenty-one

Twelve noon. Lunchtime, in Bristol Prison. Every bloody day.

Olly Rutter heard the clunk as his cell door was unlocked and pulled ajar, then more clunks as the ritual continued down the long corridor. He was peckish, but deliberately stayed where he was, flicking through *Surrounded By Idiots,* a paperback on business behaviour.

A scurry of hungry inmates sped past his door, then a silence, then key-jangling Prison Officer Campbell returned, kicking the door wide open and stepping into the cell. 'Lunch!' he yelled. 'You deaf? *Out!*'

Slowly inserting a bookmark, Rutter closed the book and got to his feet, eyebrows raised in a silent question. Campbell's hooded eyes gave the faintest flick of assent, his broad back obscuring the exchange. Then he snatched the book from Olly's hands in pretended dominance.

'*Surrounded By Idiots?* That's what you think of us, eh?' He riffled a few pages, covertly slipped a folded piece of paper into the book, and snapped it shut. 'Well, this is what we think of *you!*' The book skidded onto the floor. 'Pick it up, messy bastard,' he hissed.

Olly duly did, in silence, and tucked the book - now with its extra page - beneath his pillow for later. *About time too*, he thought. *Lady Muck's Chinese torture is well behind schedule. Mustn't keep the Witch waiting.*

Chuckling to himself, he slouched down the empty corridor, seemingly escorted by the bulk of Prison Officer Campbell, to the grey, neon-lit echo of the dining hall. No need to rush. Sitting in the seat reserved for Olly Rutter was a mistake the newbies made only once.

He patted his stomach. Yes, he was. He was peckish.

*

Because the leaves were poisonous, Nell Warren wore gloves to clip the yew trees and stuff the clippings into plastic sacks, making sure no-one was around to see. Last time, she'd added green acorns, but yew on its own was nasty enough for any horse dumb enough to munch it. This time, she'd chuck yew in every water trough she could locate. Poison soup for thirsty horses. *That'll teach Wake Hall!*

She had nothing much against horses, being an ex-stable girl herself, but plenty against Allie Chant. When the fat-arsed cow punched her onto the stable floor that day, horse-muck and all, the shock and shame of it festered into a writhing tapeworm of revenge. The blue bruise on her face faded after two weeks, but the memory of that punch never did. It swelled, ripened - and burst. *I'll fix Allie's fat arse, just watch me!*

If instead of yelling *stuff your job* she'd let them sack her, she could've claimed false dismissal, taken Wake Hall to an Industrial Tribunal, screwed them for compensation. Her mates were fed up hearing her sound off about it, in the pub. And when she'd had a shot too many, Nell Warren could be *loud*.

She'd been louder than usual that one night and spent next day hungover in her tiny Parminster flat – till a sharp knock on the door made her head throb. She was still hazy when she opened up and saw the blonde woman in the frumpy frock and thick glasses on the doorstep, staring at her. 'How come you know my name?' demanded Nell. 'How'd you find out where I live?'

The woman just shrugged. Alison, she called herself. 'I'm Alison *Smith,*' she said.

Sure you are, thought Nell, with *A.B.* in gold letters on your posh bloody handbag. But when a jaw-dropping wedge of banknotes emerged from it…And since Nell Warren was broke…

'You're not the first,' said Alison *Smith*. 'Wake Hall did the same to me, years ago.'

'Oh yes?' said Nell, staring at *Ms Smith-with-initials-A.B.* But the frumpy-looking woman's eyes stared powerfully back till Nell was forced to look away.

'I swore I'd get even but could never think how,' said the older woman. 'And it's simple, isn't it? They care more for horses than the likes of *us*. So, what if we upset the horses? And make it our little secret?'

Nell Warren, easy to persuade, knew Wake Hall like the back of her hand, even at night. A pushbike, silent, panniers stuffed to the brim with acorns and yew. Handfuls of clippings flung into the fields, when and wherever Alison said. Then handfuls of readies, to spend on nobody but Nell.

She still knew a few stable girls at the Hall and pretended to be shocked when their gossip turned to yew clippings and acorns. When the gossip turned to red paint and *real blood*, Nell's shock was no pretence. Feelings mixed, she guessed Alison *Smith* was throwing in a little mischief of her own. *Still, as long as I get paid…*

And paid she would be, after more mischief in the dark, tonight. More yew clippings, in the horse troughs this time. A poisonous revenge on Wake Hall.

Alison *Smith* loved stupid people. She allowed herself a chuckle at Nell's naivety, while admitting the vengeful stable girl had so far carried out her role rather well. This next incursion, though, would be targeted. She'd borrowed a steel-mesh butcher's glove and, sliding it onto her hand, safely bagged up the pile of vicious-looking nasties bound for Wake Hall. Carbon-black, all of them, the dull, matt colour of a car tyre. Though Nell Warren didn't know it, her pathetic bits of yew were merely a sideshow, a decoy, a sham.

It was Alison *Smith* and associates who would carry out the real mischief, sowing seeds of torment in an altogether different part of Wake Hall. In darkness. Tonight.

Ready for Friday morning…

Twenty-two

'I love to see a man in the kitchen,' said Sonia, coiling her arms round Batten's waist and pressing herself against his back as he stood at the new sink. 'But I'll never understand the male aversion to rubber gloves.'

Enjoying Sonia's closeness, a gloveless Batten rinsed the final breakfast plate and popped it on the drainer in the almost working kitchen. Tomorrow, the fitters promised, the dishwasher would be plumbed in too. He dried his hands. Rubber gloves always reminded him of crime scenes and hospitals – and the gothic horror of Sonia's work at the mortuary.

Nor would he wear gloves this morning when he finished slapping Sage Grey on the walls. Sonia had chosen the colour, 'because I suspect you're colour blind, Zig.' He wasn't, but gladly left the choice to her, his head already full of non-domestic choices. Top of the list was whether to respect the privacy Lady Wake was paying for - or hand everything he'd dug up to *Inspector* Ball.

When Sonia uncoiled her loving arms to answer the phone, Batten wondered if Chris Ball was ringing *him*. But Sonia covered the receiver and whispered, 'It's Wake Hall. Probably want to sell you a horse.'

His smile turned to a frown when, with neither explanation nor pleasantries, Avril 'invited' him to a meeting at the Hall, *forthwith*. No, she said, not the emergency meeting of the equine staff - that has been postponed. Before Batten could ask why, she briskly ended the call. 'Typical,' he told Sonia. 'Spend days kicking at the tall doors to get in, but when I'm about to paint the bloody kitchen they demand my immediate presence.'

He kissed her goodbye and drove off, Radio 4 filling his head with gloomy world news all journey long, to the moment he pulled up in the Visitors car park. A cold November mist still lingered, clothing the white monstrosity of Wake Hall with ghostly breath – which must have found its way inside because when *he* did, his welcome was ice.

Avril Dean's unreadable face now spoke volumes. And when ushered silently into Lady Wake's posh lair the ice continued. *Nope, they're not trying to sell me a horse.* Avril remained standing, arms folded tightly across her chest. Batten was not offered a seat. Lady Wake did the sitting, enthroned behind her walnut desk, dressed in the most exquisite riding gear he'd ever seen. She graced him with her coldest, diamond stare, but managed to stay beautiful, even with daggers in her eyes. And in her voice.

'We have been visited-'

'Not more horse attacks?' he said, cutting in.

She frowned at him. 'We shall come to that. We have been visited by the *police*,' she hissed – and it *was* a hiss, a convincing snake impersonation, behind a pair of anaconda eyes. 'Asking about Pavel's *disappearance*. And about this brother of Oksana, this *Dave*. Avril was questioned by a…' She turned her face an inch towards Avril.

'Sergeant Hick. Of Parminster CID.'

'Where *you* used to work,' added Lady Wake.

Batten caught on. She'd been quick to dump on Pavel, now quick and wrong to dump on him. He would be nobody's scapegoat, and with horses, not goats, in mind, he said, '*Whoa!* I see where this is going.' Had she been less icy he might have admitted being tempted to tell all to the police - while remaining crystal clear he'd told them nothing. He chose the second option. 'If the police turned up, they didn't turn up because of me! That's the unembroidered truth. If it's not good enough for you, say so, and we're done. *Permanently* done.'

Again, Lady Wake's chin shifted an inch towards Avril. In the silence, Batten saw tiny facial twitches pass between them, a sort of Wake Hall Morse code, before *Her Ladyship* rose from her desk and enthroned herself in the Queen Anne chair she'd occupied the first time he was allowed in her lair. She waved Avril towards the sofa and, after an icy pause, threw her disdainful fingers at the second chair.

'Nice to get the weight of my feet,' Batten said. The glacial pause froze into an interval, but when Lady Wake did speak, her voice held more exasperation than ice. 'If not you, then tell me *who would*? And please omit Allie Chant from your answer. She has already been questioned.' Again a silent exchange of Morse code. 'Avril is satisfied she is not the culprit.'

What could Batten say? Where Pavel was concerned, his fellow farriers, or the stable girls? Hell's bells, any drinker in the nearest local, *The Horse and Groom,* with or without a hearing aid. He opted for the 'police professional' line. 'Pavel? Local gossip is my guess. Dipstick Dave? He's a suspect in an ongoing investigation. Maybe a routine reassessment of a cold case. Maybe a police informant dropped a hint, which was followed up. And several other explanations – none of them *me*.'

Lady Wake closed her eyes and her exquisite head dropped back against the chair. The faint sigh he'd heard before crept from her lips. 'We are at a loss,' she said. Her eyes opened and a pair of diamonds flashed at Batten. 'On top of the *police* visit, we suffered further equine interference last night – yes, again covert, again in darkness.' She twitched a muscle at Avril, as if pulling the string that worked the ventriloquist's doll.

'More yew clippings,' said an exasperated Avril. 'We had almost grown immune, but this time our nocturnal *visitors* targeted the water supply - poisonous yew, in dozens of horse troughs, spread across the far pastures - the vets and half the stable girls are up there trying to quell the chaos.' When she ran out of breath, Lady Wake took up the thread.

'Advise us. Please. What action can we take?'

'You won't *take* my advice,' said Batten. 'Tell CID about these attacks. You're risking charges of concealing a crime and obstructing the police.'

Marianne Wake lifted her chin a millimetre or two and he thought the aristocracy must be trained in the frugal movement of their body parts. 'The presence of police - imposed or requested - is anathema to me. Memories of their previous interventions are too…disturbing. And I thought I'd made it clear: Estate problems require Estate solutions.'

Batten shrugged. 'OK, security patrols, then? Cameras? Any progress?'

This time, Lady Wake's hand came into play, twitching marginally towards Avril, her permission to speak.

'An extra van, from tomorrow, both now fitted with searchlights. A guard in each van, on constant patrol, and in constant radio contact,' said Avril. 'New cameras will arrive soon, to be installed as a matter of urgency.'

'Infra-red?' he asked.

'Of *course*,' said Avril, with a do-you-think-I'm-stupid look. 'And what of *you*? Any *progress*?'

Wondering if the mention of Olly Rutter would be too disturbing, he plunged in. Both women winced at 'Rutter' but perked up when Batten described the visit to Bristol Prison and his suspicions about Rutter's links with Luka Judd. When he mentioned Ronnie Lopen and Luka's history with Dipstick Dave, they perked rapidly down again.

'I can only repeat what I told Sergeant Hick,' said Avril, her voice sharp. 'Dave has *not* been seen here. Oksana was far too busy to be confronted by more *police* questioning, but frankly, had Dave appeared, I doubt she could conceal the fact.' She dipped her deferential head towards Lady Wake. 'I - we - are not sure where that leaves us.'

Batten had his doubts too. 'Look, the police are *supposed* to search for Dave. He's wanted for murder, not parking on a double-yellow line. If I can pick up Dave's trail first, and it leads to Judd and Rutter, I'll have a better chance of stopping their dirty work. And the safer your horses will be.'

When he fell silent, a strangely testy Avril said, '*And?*'

Drawing on his own frustrations, he said, '*And* it would be easier for me if I had a bit more freedom of movement around here.' Lady Wake looked over her nose at him, as if he planned to plonk his feet on her solid walnut desk. 'I want to turn up, park my car, poke around and ask questions. Instead of ringing the Wake Hall doorbell for permission to blow my nose. Every Tom Dick and Jane on the Estate knows I'm working here, wouldn't you say?'

After a Morse Code session with Avril, Lady Wake found her voice. 'Ask questions of *whom*?'

Ignoring her implied, *you'll damn well make an appointment with* **me**, Batten listed names on his fingers. 'Pavel, Oksana, the farriers and stable girls, the vets, the night security guards, for starters.' Ever the opportunist, he added, 'And since you've dragged me here, I'd like to begin right now.'

Lady Wake glanced at her watch and rose abruptly from her chair, Avril too. Batten stood up in automatic deference, immediately hating himself for doing so. Passing the baton to Avril with a twitch of her fingers, she said, '*I* must get on,' pronouncing it *orn*. On a horse, Batten assumed, given her posh riding gear, but without another word she was *gorn*, leaving Avril to deal with Batten.

He took a moment to prioritise. On Saturday, gutting Pavel in The Horse and Groom might throw light on Dave and Luka. Today, at Wake Hall, he homed in on Pavel's partner.

'Oksana,' he said. 'A bit of a closed book to me.'

Avril's testy voice snapped back. 'Is Oksana not entitled to a degree of privacy? And what of the rest of us?' Batten watched her gaze through the window at the private gardens. 'How would you feel if there were suspicions about *your* relatives?' Her eyes swept beyond the ha-ha to the vast horse-filled carpet of pasture and hedgerows.

'Relatives?' he said. 'Whose relatives?'

Avri's underbite twitched as she back-pedalled, glancing at him then quickly looking away. 'I mean... *Oksana's* relatives. Imagine *your* brother being a murder suspect and 'on the run'?'

It was his turn to stare at space. *I don't have a brother. Nor any relatives worth a mention.* He guessed it was the same for Avril. 'I'm not going to *grill* Oksana,' he said. 'But she was at the same event as Pavel and Luka - you saw the photograph. She may have information and not realise - or be keeping *secrets*. In my experience, people *do*.' He held Avril's cool stare till she looked away. 'And isn't experience what you're paying me for?'

In a pensive silence she wandered closer to the window, as if it held answers. Her face, reflected in the glass, looked wary and worn.

'She *is* around?' he said.

At Avril's nod, Batten sat back down in Lady Wake's super-comfortable Queen Anne chair. 'I'll wait, then,' he said.

Avril strode to the door and held it open. 'Not in here you won't,' she said.

Twenty-three

Stall 20 in stable block D was an almost palatial horse-house, befitting the regal mare of its owner. Maya was saddled and ready when Marianne Wake emerged in her pristine riding gear, a white silk scarf exquisitely ruched around her neck. Amid the turmoil of the last few months her one comfort had been Maya - and would be again today. She rode her without fail every Friday morning, Avril ensuring the diary never encroached. At the mounting block she stroked Maya's flowing grey mane and smiled when the fine-boned horse gave a whicker of welcome and nuzzled against her cheek and neck. 'I see Pavel has given you brand-new shoes,' she said. 'Shall we try them?'

Gently taking the reins, she mounted with aristocratic ease, enjoying the clip of new metal on the stable yard floor. For all her doubts about Pavel, when it came to horseshoes he was skilled and consistent. Would that the other men in her life had been as reliable. Or had she been an unreliable judge? In thought, she turned Maya towards the exercise arena. The shredded rubber floor, though dull in colour, had a safe, comforting bounce to it, which drew from horse and rider a corresponding bounce. She would put Maya smoothly through her paces, and for one blissful hour forget unreliable men and the heavy burden of Wake Hall.

Barely touching the reins, she steered Maya across the yard and headed for the empty arena. The stable staff knew to steer clear on Friday mornings - *Keep out, it's reserved for ma'am,* the newbies were swiftly told. At a leisurely walk, she and Maya headed for its unsullied floor, horse and rider gliding as one.

The grassy drove between stables and arena felt soft and safe - till Marianne Wake sensed sudden movement, then heard a loud scream, a yell, and was shocked to see Pavel sprinting straight at her, his face screwed into a tight knot, laced with tension. She gasped when his right hand shook at her, and she saw the glint of morning sunlight flashing from his knife. She gasped again when he raised his left hand which dripped red with blood.

Blood! she thought. *Pavel! He's attacked my horses! And wants to scar my beautiful Maya! Or am I the target?* In fear, she kicked Maya forward and picked up speed, all the while mesmerised by the knife, the blood, and Pavel's twisted face. If she made it to the arena, the automatic gate would snap shut behind her, and she could gallop to the far side and be free.

But Pavel was long-legged, swift and suddenly *there*, his bloodied hand clawing for the reins, his raised voice screaming at her.

*How **dare** he? What does he think I am, a fishwife?*

But the strong-armed farrier was pulling back on the reins, and Maya's eyes staring wide in the same confusion and fear as her owner. Pavel dragged the bridle down, screaming, cutting off her escape, neither horse nor rider able to reach the gate nor enter the soft, comforting arena floor.

'STOP! screamed Pavel. *DON'T GO IN THERE! LOOK!'*

As he opened his bloodied hand, she saw the point of a metal spike embedded deep in his flesh. With a gasp she peered closer. The single spike was one of a cluster, welded together in the shape of a vicious star, the spikes pointing this way and that, each point sharpened and barbed. Carbon-black, the spikes - the same dull matt colour as the arena floor...

'CALTROPS!' yelled Pavel. 'CALTROPS!' In the ring! It's full of them! This one caught me!'

In shock, Lady Wake slid from the saddle to the ground, her face a mixture of relief and guilt. Words of thanks tried to form in her throat, but her legs buckled, and she staggered against the post and rail fence, unable to speak. Time froze, then Allie Chant was beside her, taking Maya's reins. Someone had called Avril, because she rushed there too, Batten following, and a trail of stable staff racing towards the scene.

As Batten neared the arena fence, Pavel called to him – *'DON'T GO IN THERE! They'll skewer your feet! They're everywhere!'*

Batten did as he was told. Instead, he got down on hands and knees and peered along the arena floor to spot what Pavel called *caltrops* – a word he'd never heard before. Camouflaged against the shredded rubber, a barbed metal cluster spiked at him, then further away another, then many more, their pernicious tines awaiting innocent victims, rider or horse. Small enough to go unseen, they could drill equally into foot or hoof.

The yew-tree clippings scattered in the water troughs must have been a decoy, he guessed, to draw attention from this far more deadly scattering. But who scattered them? Who spread yet another clutch of hidden secrets at this godforsaken Estate? For sure, not Olly Rutter and Luka Judd in person. Just how many nasty-minded minions did these two have at their disposal?

Climbing back to his feet, he flinched as Pavel gritted his teeth and dug the barbed point from his bloodied hand by cutting into his own flesh with a hoof-knife. Then Oksana was there, wrapping Pavel's hand in a handkerchief and kissing him tenderly on the cheek. Lady Wake gazed like a gargoyle at the pair of them.

Typical, thought Batten. *Ma'am didn't offer her white silk scarf for a bandage.* But when he moved closer and saw her face, the same white colour as the scarf, and watched her whole frame shake like a willow in the wind…He caught her before she fell, slipped off his coat and wrapped it round her. Taking both her hands in his, he rubbed the blood back into them as she stared at empty space, and he could have been the man from Mars.

Disparate voices blurred together, a chaotic babble: Oksana to Pavel - *You'll need antiseptic!* Allie Chant to no-one - *My Neil's got a metal detector, I'll fetch it!* Avril Dean to the throng - *Someone tell me what a caltrop is!*

All were shocked to silence as Lady Wake slowly found her voice.

'The French call it a *chausse-trappe,*' she whispered. 'Medieval. Older. A weapon. For use against cavalry… But I never thought to see one here, at Wake Hall.'

One? thought Batten. *There's dozens of the bloody things!*

'The barbed points would have pierced Maya's feet…Or mine.' Her controls fell away, and tears flooded her cheeks. When Avril eased a tissue into her hand she wiped away the tears and threw her arms around Maya's neck and mane. Batten's coat slipped from her shoulders and dropped unnoticed to the muddy ground. Maya, her hooves undamaged through Pavel's vigilance, rested her neck tenderly on the shoulder of her mistress and both horse and owner closed their eyes in soulful relief.

Looking on, Batten understood the mysterious bond between human and beast, and again wondered if he should get a dog.

Then Lady Wake was thanking Pavel and wincing at his punctured hand. 'It needs stitches,' she said, waving away his protestations. 'Avril will send for my doctor.' Reaching down for Batten's coat she held it out to him, her eyes nothing like the hard diamonds he'd grown used to. 'I am grateful,' she whispered, reliving the power of his arms around her and his warm hands teasing the blood back into hers. Deep pools of beauty now, her diamond eyes, enticing him. But when her tender fingers brushed his wrist, he remembered Allie Chant's words - *Her Ladyship? She could charm the gonads off a stallion, if she put her mind to it.* Between temptation and disquiet, he stepped away, and Marianne Wake became his employer once again.

'It would seem, Zig, we have more to discuss?'

Supported by Avril, she headed for the Hall, her question a familiar veiled command. Oksana followed, holding Pavel's bandage in place. Warm sweat prickling his skin, Batten trailed behind in their 'wake'.

*

'They knew, didn't they?' Lady Wake said. 'Knew the arena is reserved for me on Friday mornings?' She slid wearily onto the reception room's vast Chesterfield sofa and motioned the others to sit.

'Ma'am, everyone on the Estate knows.'

Batten was glad Avril beat him to the answer. Interviewing the vast squad of Estate workers would take weeks.

'I thought it was a stone,' said Pavel. 'Stones are not kind to hooves. So I reached in to pick it up.' He clutched his pierced hand, too proud to show pain. 'Then I saw the other caltrops scattered there...'

Lady Wake flinched at the reminder. In response, Avril ushered Oksana and Pavel through the trompe l'oeil door, to wait for the doctor. Returning, she poured a restorative brandy for Lady Wake - but not for Batten - and the three of them sat in silence.

'This has to stop,' said Marianne Wake.

'The police might stop it,' said Batten.

'*No.* I refuse to endure the police *again. You* are my police, Zig.'

'I'm one man. I don't pack a Superman suit.'

After a brandy-sipping impasse, Lady Wake agreed Batten could recruit extra help. He wasn't sure who just yet, and Her Ladyship didn't ask. Her mental adding machine had counted the cost of twenty lost horse sales and an unknown number of poisoned horses. After today's incident with Maya, he guessed her head and *heart* knew the greater cost of any repeats.

'Avril will require details,' she said.

He promised to send them, and the meeting was over. Waiting in the ante room for Oksana, his thoughts toggled between ways of stopping Luka Judd, and the soft invitation of *ma'am*'s diamond eyes.

A Superman suit would be useful, he thought, for both.

Twenty-four

Morning became lunchtime by the time Batten got to see Oksana. In her office, the tea too weak and the ham sandwiches too thin, he asked his questions. Her replies told him little of value - and nothing at all about Luka Judd, the figure standing behind Oksana in the photograph. She swore she'd neither seen Luka before nor since, then glanced at her watch. Hearing Batten's sigh of frustration, she said, 'It's not what you think.'

It never bloody is! he wanted to shout.

'Today's my afternoon off, and I need to…be somewhere.' She hesitated. 'It's my mother. She's in a home, and I visit.' Again the hesitation. 'Sometimes she knows me, sometimes not.' A laugh of disappointment. 'Sometimes both together. The home she's in, *The Greenfields*, you wouldn't believe their motto. *Felix Memorias* - happy memories. Hmph. Of course, she chose the home herself, before her decline.'

Silence took over. From experience, Batten let it ride, till Oksana found her voice again. 'She never asks how *I* am, just Dave – David, to her. Always *correct*, my mother. And of course I tell her the same lies - that he's working overseas…successful but busy. After a few seconds she forgets she's asked, then two minutes later asks again, forgets again. And so, we stumble along, she and I.'

'Does she ever *tell* you about Dave - *David*?'

'Rarely. Even then, it's part fantasy…' Her hands threw the thought at the ceiling. 'She would probably talk to you, of course, because…' A little embarrassed, she smiled up at Batten. 'Because she likes handsome men. My father was a rogue, but a handsome one – it's why mother married him. From my birth to his death I was mostly ignored in favour of Dave. A man's man, my father. But now there's only her. And of course, me. The *women*.'

Half supportive, half opportune, Batten said, 'If you think she would - talk, I mean - I can make time?'

Oksana' wan face considered the prospect of another lonely journey to an empty conversation, and the silent journey back. 'It can be a…difficult experience,' she said. 'In a blink, from sense to nonsense. But I can't deny a male voice would be helpful. Nor deny that even before he…' She let the thought of Dave's predicament slide by. 'Even before, Dave rarely visited.'

Batten allowed her a quiet moment. When the silence grew loud, he said, 'Your car or mine?'

*

'*Ahah*,' said Oksana's mother, giving Batten a stare. 'Got yourself a *man* at last! And good-looking too. Hold on to this one, Oksana. Tie him down.' All this as if Batten was deaf, not present in the tidy, beige-walled room smelling of over-sprayed cologne, nor sitting on a hard chair a foot from Danuta *Vossialevydipsic*'s bed. He'd drawn up the easy chair for Oksana, and she sat opposite, face beetroot with embarrassment. The basket of fruit she'd brought as a gift lay shipwrecked beside the unlit lamp on the bedside table.

'No, mother, this is Zig. He's a friend, from work. He gave me a lift here, that's all.'

'Ah, a *chauffeur*, better still. And *Zig*, you say. A Polish name?' She peered at him through horn-rimmed specs. 'Not *Russian*, are you?'

English-Polish-Russian, he might have said. 'A bit of everything,' he mumbled, handsome smile in lieu of credentials. 'Good to meet you.'

Danuta brushed a wayward strand from her brow and peered at him again. 'Remains to be seen,' she said, her face creasing into such a wicked grin he guessed she was a character in her day. She jabbed a finger at Oksana. 'And who's this you've brought with you?'

Oksana's beetroot face faded to the colour of chalk, whiter than her mother's hair.

'This is your daughter, Oksana,' said Batten. 'She's come to see you.'

The horn-rims peered again. 'Oh,' she said. 'Joanna, yes. But is David not here?'

'He's overseas, mother. I told you. He's working abroad.'

'Don't be silly. I saw him only the other day…or was it a week? Well. I saw him.'

Catching Batten's eye, Oksana shared a tiny look, somewhere between acceptance and dismay. Batten took over.

'Was he well? Haven't seen him for ages. Must have been a nice surprise, him visiting?'

'Visiting? Hardly call it a visit, pitch black outside, almost bedtime. Why did you make him do it, Susanna?'

Confusion clouded Oksana's face. 'Make him do what, mother?'

'Tuh, grow that *beard!* Practically covered his face. Only just recognised my own son. A moustache would be acceptable, I suppose, like yours…er, Zack. But a beard? I said to David, I see you've just returned from, you know, from *foreign.* Suntanned, what little of his face I *could* see. And of course the dark glasses, never took the damn things off. But all the film stars wear them, don't they, even at night? Was David in a film, overseas? Find out when it's on the television, er…Joanna. I'd like to watch it.'

Batten flashed a silent query at Oksana. Her shrug of abdication invited him to continue. 'That's exciting, him being in a film. Did David have much to say for himself?'

'*David?* What are you talking about? N*o, no,* not *David.* It was his friend. I'm excellent with names, and his name was…was like one of those board-games we played, when you were a child, Susanna…' With a single eyelid flicker, she spasmed - dead, but breathing - into an invisible world. Oksana hid her face behind her hands. To avoid staring, Batten retreated into memories of childhood games from his own invisible world, in the backstreets of old Leeds - *Kiss Chase,* the one he remembered most. Danuta's loud shout from nowhere shook the pair of them.

'*Ludo!* That's the game. Yes, David's friend, Ludo. Did you meet him, Susanna?'

Speechless, Oksana looked at Batten for help, but drew only a look of surprise. 'I don't think I did, no. What was he like?'

'Like? *Who?*'

'This Ludo, mother. The friend of David's?'

'Well in future, say so! I suppose his beard, which covered most of him, was to make up for the hair!' A cackle of a laugh filled the room. 'Bald as a coot when he took his hat off! *Quite* handsome, behind the dark glasses.' She dropped her voice to a conspiratorial whisper and patted Oksana's hand. 'But not as handsome as your Zack, eh? Make sure you hold on to him, Joanna, mm? Like hen's teeth, a good *chauffeur.*' She noticed her hand still tapping up and down on Oksana's and removed it. 'Oh, yes, Ludo. *Big*. I like a man with plenty of muscle on him,' she said, giving *Zack* a knowing glance.

'Nice of him to visit? This Ludo?' Batten stopped himself saying *Luka*, not that Danuta would have noticed.

'*Visit?* Hah, two minutes waffle, pulls his hat back on, and off he goes. Without bothering to close the door!'

'But he asked after Dave, I hope?'

'Dave? Ah, *David*. Well of course he did. Very successful, overseas, David. In the film industry. Though it must be hush-hush because Ludo said *nothing* about the film David is making. Has made? When Oksana turns up, I shall ask her.' Danuta began to retreat into a forgotten world. 'They never visit, those two, never. It's *shameful*.'

Even Batten was shocked to see Danuta crumble, in a millisecond, as if she'd been punched from within. Her energy drained away, her face a cake of distress, topped by the cherry of a tear. When he saw a second cherry sneak from Oksana's eye and roll sadly down her cheek, his zeal for digging faltered. He should wait in the car and leave these two in a private peace - if peace it could be called. Then Danuta was staring at him, confused, her eyes large pearls behind her glasses, a different energy in her voice.

'David? *David!*' she said, addressing Batten. 'Whatever's keeping Oksana? You said she was coming to see me. When is her film on television? Your friend, *he* had no idea. And in future, don't tell your friends you've left things here when you haven't. It's *unseemly* to be asked. And a backpack? What would I do with your backpack - go hiking? Heaven's sake, where would I keep it?'

Her shaking fingers flicked at the bedroom walls. Apart from the bed, chairs and TV, there was space only for a small wardrobe, a chest of drawers and an even smaller dressing table, scattered with a muddle of brushes, and bottles of pointless perfume.

Unseen, Batten toed the gap between bed-frame and carpet, too low to conceal even a bed-pan. 'Oops,' he said, pretending to shift his chair while bumping the frame itself. Solid, no cavity within. When Danuta closed her eyes, Batten searched out Oksana's. The tears were gone, replaced by a look of bafflement. Then Danuta was babbling again.

'That Ludo fellow, he had the audacity to rummage in my drawers! And my wardrobe too! I was outraged! I shan't need my *negligee* for the likes of *you!* I said, as he left. Shouted after him, you're not *handsome* enough!' With a twitch of her head, she glanced at Oksana. 'Ah, you're the new girl, aren't you? Have you brought my tea?'

Frozen now with his own embarrassment, Batten was relieved when Oksana struggled to her feet, her lips clamped together to contain her sobs. With an effort he could hardly bear to watch, she opened her mouth an inch and whispered, 'I'll fetch it for you.'

Her mother stared at a speck of nothing, trapped in the ceiling's cold white paint, and said not a word of goodbye. At the door, Batten and Oksana looked back, but what little remained of Danuta Vossialevydipsic neither noticed their departure - nor remembered they had ever arrived.

Downstairs in *The Greenfields'* Visitors snack bar, it was Batten who fetched the tea, made sure it was hot and made sure Oksana drank it. She slumped in a plastic chair, elbows on the table, her face a frozen wasteland. Batten dragged his eyes from *The Greenfields'* coat of arms, proudly dangling from the pastel wall. Its motto, *Felix Memorias,* continued staring down at Oksana, an almost-orphan with an almost mother. She sipped her tea and stared past empty space to memories he could only imagine. His own memories of mothers and waiting rooms jerked him back to St James Hospital in Leeds, and the cancerous decline of Aunt Daze, his lifelong 'mother' since he was two years old. The image clicked off when Oksana spoke.

'Mum meant Luka, didn't she? Not Ludo.'

Batten nodded. 'If...'

'If she didn't imagine it, yes. But I can usually tell.' In answer to his look, she said, 'True. I'm almost certain.'

'And recent?'

She shrugged away the question. 'Yesterday? Last week? A year ago? That's the way poor mother is now.'

Her tea became an excuse not to say more, and he gave her a moment before duty broke in. 'So Dave did have a backpack? I mean, you've seen him with one?'

Though upset, Oksana's intelligent eyes decoded the layers in his question. *Had she seen Dave recently, after all? Was he carrying a backpack? What was in it? Where is it now?* 'No to everything,' she said, unsmiling, till hot tea revived her. 'Dave *was* sporty, years ago. Hiking, climbing, the gym – and he would have had a backpack. But when I told you I hadn't seen Dave since…since he disappeared, I was speaking the truth. The only place I see my poor brother is in my dreams. I told the last detective the same. At least he had the sensitivity to come to my cottage, and not *interrogate* me at the Hall, with people staring.'

'This would have been Sergeant Hick?' Avril said Oksana was busy when Hick called, so Batten guessed Eddie fulfilled his new Sergeant responsibilities by returning later, to tackle Oksana after work.

'Hick? No, no, not him. I remember him from before. The one who twitches?'

Hiding a smile, Batten nodded, and pondered. 'When *was* 'last time'?'

Finishing her tea, Oksana scanned the snack bar, pleasant enough despite the wipe-clean furniture. A Formica table in insipid blue held newspapers and magazines for visitors to browse. With no other visitors, the room was as empty as her, right now.

'The last time?' she said. 'The last time, of many. A few months ago, I suppose, just after Pavel disappeared. I hoped this detective - somehow - was searching for my Pavel. I was upset, almost didn't invite him in. But as usual, it was about Dave. Have I heard from my brother, do I have any of his belongings, have any contact details turned up since I made my statement? Did I realise that withholding information is an offence? I was going to offer him tea, but when the questions began I decided he could die of thirst. I told him the only thing Dave left behind was sorrow.'

'Presumably he showed you a warrant card?'

Again, a shrug. 'I've seen so many I hardly looked. Detective Constable Something. Not Hick, no, but short. Ridge? Bridge? Maybe one of those.' She read Batten's eyes, as earlier he had read hers - and realisation broke through. 'Ah. Asking about Dave's belongings. This *backpack*?'

'Maybe. Could you describe your 'policeman''?'

Oksana shrugged away the question. 'Not sure I'd recognise him if he walked in here right now and sat in your chair. Clean shaven? Neither big nor small?'

'His clothes, his car?'

'Phh. Greyish jacket? Just a car. Blue?'

How many times in CID had Batten heard similar descriptions? The 'uniform' of the forgettable impostor - bland looks, clothes, everything. But it wasn't Luka Judd. Oksana might have recognised him. Another faceless Luka minion, then? And what did he want with Dave's *belongings*?

'You're not suggesting…?'

'That he wasn't a real detective? My hunch is a fake cop, looking for whatever Dave had hidden away. Can you remember exactly what he asked?'

She shook her head. 'Nothing more than I've said. He didn't stay long. I just recall him telling me it was all 'routine'. As if any of it feels routine to me.' Face clouding over, as Danuta's had done, she glanced at her empty cup and got to her feet. 'I need to get back.'

In the car park, Batten's keys jangled in his hand, as if bewitched by Oksana. But he knew she wasn't the cause.

It was Dave, her brother.

And Luka Judd.

Twenty-five

On Saturday morning, without telling Oksana Brok, Batten returned to the silence of *The Greenfields*, not with *happy memories* in mind, but the memory of *Ludo*, covertly searching Danuta's room. Yesterday, he and Oksana signed in and signed out before doors were unlocked. Did 'Ludo' do the same? What about CCTV?

He was lucky. The over-smiling receptionist - Faye, her name badge said - had much sympathy for the long-suffering Oksana, and a brazen memory of the tall, rugged Batten.

'She's been faffing about with entry systems for months, has the owner,' Faye explained, betraying confidences in a low, confidential voice. 'And it's all down to money. Posh entry systems aren't cheap, so we've never had a proper one before.'

'But now?' he said, hurrying her along.

'Not *quite* now. We're getting a Visitor Management System. You know, QR codes and CCTV and magnetic doors. Pre-booked entry only. Even for *you*,' she said, flicking at her hair with a ringless finger, and over-smiling at Batten.

He smiled back, shamelessly milking the moment. *For the greater good*, he told himself. 'Gosh,' he said. 'A resident has a visitor, even *me*, and just signs in? No CCTV, no ID?'

With a coy laugh, she said, 'the new system has both, and more besides. We'll be a *fortress*.' Then Faye's husky whisper added, '*but not quite yet,*' the four words loaded with suggestive meaning.

Batten thought he'd better hurry up, before Faye unbuttoned his shirt. 'Oksana's mum had a visitor a while back, a man, and you know how it is with Danuta – she couldn't remember his name. Oksana wants to get in touch, to see if he'd share some of the visits. But…'

At the mention of Oksana, Faye gave a little sigh. 'Poor woman, I don't know how she copes.' Fingers hovering in a tease above her keyboard, she said, 'as it happens, we *do* keep a log of visitors, for each resident.' Her fingers caressed the keys, but Batten couldn't see the screen when she ran her eyes across it. 'Mostly Oksana,' she said. 'And *you*, of *course*.' Her screen eyes were about to dilate into a bedroom version when, from the staff corridor, the sound of approaching footsteps broke in. 'Only one other visitor,' she whispered. 'But no address. A man, Luke Jones.'

As the footsteps drew closer, Faye's whisper became a loud professional voice. 'And I would happily arrange a tour of our excellent facilities, Mr Batten. Please, take my card. You can ring me anytime - day, or *night*.'

'Very helpful, thank you,' he said, leaving Faye *coitus interruptus* behind her desk. As he escaped to his car, two false names and a real one echoed in his skull - *Luke Jones, Ludo*, and Luka Judd. And a police impostor, sent by Luka perhaps, to question Oksana about Dave's missing belongings. While Pavel, her protector, was safely away in Spain?

In the car park, he asked himself what was more important to Luka - the mysterious contents of Dipstick Dave's backpack, or attacking Lady Wake's horses? Unsure of the answer, he wondered if opportunist Olly was pulling Luka's strings – or Luka pulling his own?

Whichever, both men were *parasites*. Batten spat the words as he started the car. He almost flipped Faye's business card into the bin by the gates, but his new freelance voice hissed, *No! Information is all. Even when the source wants to kiss you to death.*

*

Back home, he made himself a lunchtime omelette on the new range cooker and plonked the dishes in the now-working dishwasher. His mood dipped when he set about the latest DIY task – a wall-mounted plate rack, bought online. He read the self-assembly instructions, the English translation a marginal improvement on the original Chinese. The confused jumble of struts, screws and washers reminded him of the jigsaw puzzle Wake Hall had become.

Roll on this evening, he thought, and a crack at Pavel in *The Horse and Groom*.

*

In his Bristol Prison cell, Olly Rutter tried to forget what goodies the weekend would offer were he fancy-free in the world outside. To resist the teasing thought, he drew *Surrounded by Dummies* from beneath his pillow. Lying back on his bed, he pretended to flick through it, while again studying the single sheet of paper covertly slipped into the pages by Prison Officer Campbell.

On one side, a terse message: *Thursday night, as planned.* Olly's face became a gargoyle-grin as he read it. But Thursday night was gone, and he itched to hear what happened on Friday morning. And even that part of the plan was a smoked salmon starter. The main course yet to be served up, the hefty chunk of roast beef, would turn Olly's grin into a snort of ecstasy.

On the reverse, two hyphenated lines of numbers stared up at him. Below, more numbers were arranged in a grid-like pattern. Olly knew exactly what they signified. A single typed word graced the bottom of the page: *Soon.*

The news warranted a fat cigar - but first, he checked his monstrous watch. Yes, time for the important call. Under the mattress, on the side away from the door, his fingers found the burner phone stashed there by his palm-greased prison officer.

'Well, well, who put that here?' he sniggered to himself as he turned up the volume on Kiss FM. Tapping in the memorised phone number, he made the only call the phone would ever make, reading out the long lines of numbers, then the second set, in its patterned sequence. When the invisible voice read them back, another smug grin cracked Rutter's face. 'Correct,' he said, with a laugh like a drain being cleared. The laugh became a hiss. 'But *soon* isn't good enough. I prefer *when*. So, the big event? *When* is it?'

His smug grin widened as he listened to the answer. Closing the phone, he replaced it under the mattress for Prison Officer Campbell to covertly dispose of. With a click of his gold-plated lighter, he burnt the piece of paper over the aluminium loo, flushed away the ash and flopped back onto his bed.

Then Olly Rutter lit a fat Cuban cigar and watched a giant, vengeful smoke-ring waft towards the ceiling.

Twenty-six

At six-o-clock, *The Horse and Groom* was quiet. A hatless Pavel, his hair wind-blown, chose a table away from the bar at the far end of the flagstone-floored pub, its ceiling beams genuinely old, its walls cluttered with framed prints and photographs of horses, ancient and modern. From an oil painting above the fireplace, three magnificent thick-maned horse-heads stared down at Batten. Weary of horses, he dragged his eyes away and glared at the fire itself – mostly smoke and smelling like it, yet the pub a fridge.

'How's the hand?'

Pavel waggled his fingers. 'Stiff. But it can hold a glass. And it earned me a pay-rise. Cash for a Hero, eh?' He'd insisted on buying the drinks and slid Batten's across the scrubbed table. 'My turn, after Malaga.'

Batten seized the moment. 'Why Malaga? You've been coy about Spain.'

Pavel pointed to his beer. 'In England, one drink. In Spain, three, four, five.'

'But you didn't fly to Spain for liver damage. So? Why?'

A third of Pavel's beer slugged down his throat before he replied, in a low, careful voice as if someone was listening. Nobody was. Batten had checked, too.

'She told you, about Luka? Luka Judd?'

'She? Oksana? Avril? Lady Wake?'

'The third. The big one,' he said.

Batten nodded, pleased he wasn't alone in lacking deference for the titled classes.

'Luka, he scares her. She tell you that too?'

'More or less. She thinks he's behind the attacks on her horses.' Batten drew from his coat the photograph of Luka, hand gripping Pavel's shoulder in a less than friendly way. 'And *Her Ladyship* is worried about this.' He dropped the photo onto the table. 'Despite your heroics, she's still concerned about your connection to Luka.' *And so am I.*

'Connection? Hah. I turn up at some dinner - and Luka turns up too. What *connection*? Do I suddenly give Luka my keys, she asks me, so he can come and go at night and harm her horses?'

'She doesn't think that now, Pavel. Not since you saved her and Maya from the caltrops.'

'Vicious things,' said Pavel. 'All my life I work with horses – I respect horses. Intelligent, loyal. They talk to me, in their way. *Thank you, Pavel, for my new shoes, very shiny.* And I would help Luka harm them?' Pavel sank another third of his pint and wiped his lips, as if to wipe away the very thought of red paint, poison, sharp blades and caltrops.

'But Luka was from your past – that's what you told her. So you do know him.'

Fire in his eyes, Pavel pushed his face at Batten, who wondered if the farrier's knife was still in his pocket. '*He* knows *me!* That is the connection.'

'Come on, Pavel,' said Batten, pointing at Luka's hand gripping Pavel's shoulder in the photograph. 'You might not look pleased to see him, but soon as he shows up you bugger off to Spain without so much as a by-your-leave. And the day after, the *funny stuff* with horses begins. What were folk supposed to think?'

Pavel finished his beer and waggled the empty glass at Batten. 'Your round now.'

'You said *one drink*, before dinner?'

'Oksana knows I am late, tonight.' As Batten stood up, Pavel caught his arm. 'You like Sherlock Holmes?'

'*What?*' On the shelf in his garden office sat *The Complete Stories*. 'I've read the books. What the hell's Sherlock Holmes got to do with it?'

'I see Sherlock Holmes on TV. He has very tough case. Says, "Watson, this is a two-pipe problem." The mock-posh accent came out faintly foreign, almost comic. 'Well, Pavel has a two-*pint* problem. Maybe more.' He slid the glass across the table. 'So.'

At the bar, Batten's feet tingled with possibilities. His fingers too - he almost spilt the drinks. They sipped in silence before Pavel pulled his chair closer and slowly rubbed his chin with the back of an awkward hand. Batten had seen similar gestures in dozens of interview rooms, when a suspect knows in his gut that the time has come – and spills the guts that know it.

'Before, I do not live all the time at Oksana's. I rent a little place, out on the Levels. A shack, all I need. Outside, just trees, water, sky. I like the silence, the peace. Flat wetland stretching away, far as the eye can see. Nobody comes there, not even Oksana, not after she saw it. Me, sleep anywhere. Oksana, feather bed, central heating.' He smiled at the thought of her. 'But one night I come home, and a car is there. Big Mercedes. Nobody in the car. I look all around, nothing. I get my keys, to go in, but the door is unlocked. And when I switch on the light, Luka Judd is in my chair, a king on his throne, drinking my beer. With that crooked smile of his.'

'Luka didn't need a key,' said Batten. 'He trained as a locksmith, at the *West Country Crafts College*, where you did the theory part of your apprenticeship. It's where you met Luka - and Oksana's brother, Dave.' When Pavel raised his eyebrows, Batten shrugged and said, 'You're a farrier, I'm a detective. I haven't forgotten *my* training, either.'

'Huh, since you know my story, maybe we just have a quiet drink.'

Not bloody likely. 'I've told you all I know,' lied Batten. 'Now tell me what I don't.'

Pavel's awkward hand again stroked his chin. 'At college, true, there was me, and Luka, and Dave. Polish descent, all three of us, so we are friends. At first, we go climbing together, talk of what we will do, in life. Dreams, mostly. Luka and Dave, though, they whisper together, those two, serious, often, and one day I interrupt and say, *planning to rob a bank?* But when I laugh, they don't join in. Not a *bank*, whispers Luka. Who robs banks, these days? And he looks at Dave, and Dave looks at him and nods, and we get in Luka's old car, me in the back seat, and drive down narrow roads to the middle of nowhere, and stop - a layby, but no cars, just trees. Then Luka turns round from the driver's seat and offers me 'big chance' to join what he calls 'an enterprise.' Dave he nods his head, to encourage. But I know Luka by now. *Filthy Luka*, they used to call him. I guess what kind of 'enterprise' he has in mind.'

Batten was beyond guessing, certain now that Luka's criminal talents matched the role of crime-fest planner, the unseen third man of the 'enterprise'. Maybe Pavel thought so too, because in the cool, near-empty pub, bubbles of sweat began to stipple his brow.

'I shake my head, and Dave, he just shrugs. Dave is black or white, yes or no, decide, move on, no problem. But Luka, he is only *yes*. When I say *no*, his face turns hard, turns mean.' Pavel swallowed a throatful of beer, perhaps to sanitise the memory. 'Luka asks me again, his voice flat now. I glance at the car door, has Luka locked it? He sees me looking and a grin spreads across his face – a grin from hell, his face like those carved faces on a church…'

'Gargoyles?'

'Gargoyles! *Demons*. Because that's what Luka is. And strong, too. I know in my bones, if Dave is not there, his fingers on Luka's arm, stopping him, maybe I not leave that car with all my teeth. Or much worse.'

Batten saw the sweat of memory creep down Pavel's brow to his cheek before he brushed it away. 'But you did leave. You're here, in *The Horse and Groom*.'

'Because Dave is Dave, and he stops Luka. I know the police still look for Dave. Everyone knows. Oksana is torn, changes her name, pretends she *doesn't* know. Pretends he's emigrated, Mongolia, the Moon. But Dave is not an evil man. Greedy maybe, easy to persuade – and Luka, top of the tree at persuading.'

'He didn't persuade *you*?' Batten left a faint hint of doubt in his voice, which Pavel detected in a flash, his eyes burning across the table.

'Pavel stays *honest*! But Luka, he was born a thief!' More sweat rolled down Pavel's cheek, unhindered. 'He unlocks the car door, tells me I can leave, no harm done. *Hah! No harm done?* Eight, nine miles we drove, the car in woodland, a place I have never seen before. I say, am I supposed to walk? Luka shrugs, but Dave, thank God, he shakes his head and makes Luka start the car. But before we drive away, the demon says to me, Pavel, you turned down big money, said *no* to an offer we didn't need to make. How can we be sure you keep the secret, keep your mouth shut?'

An image of gossipy Allie Chant flashed into Batten's head. Compared to her, Pavel's tongue wore a padlock. For an absurd moment, he thought Luka had nothing to worry about.

'Before I can speak, Dave says, Luka, this is Pavel, our countryman. You think he would betray us? And Luka stares at us both with those lizard eyes, then drives us back, silent all the way. I tell you, nine miles, but the longest journey of my life.'

From toughened-up experience, Batten poured fuel onto the flames. 'Longer than your flight to Spain?'

At 'Spain', Pavel took a hankie from his pocket and wiped his face and brow. 'For Spain,' he said, 'I think my two-pint problem is maybe three.' And without another word he clomped across the flagstone floor to the wood-panelled bar.

'I'll pass,' Batten called after him. In the circumstances, he needed neither the breathalyser nor a cider-fuzzy head.

When Pavel slid back into his chair, his third pint was half gone. 'At the college, I keep my mouth shut – yes, I admit, from fear. But one day Dave draws me aside and whispers, Pavel, if I were you, I wouldn't go climbing anymore. Carabiners, harnesses, ropes? They can snap, can make you fall. Better to be safe, yes? And he goes silent, just nods his head till I see what he is trying to tell me. Then I nod back at Dave. But when we walk away, it is in opposite directions. You ever climb?'

'Climb? Not bloody likely.' Batten thought of the nerve-jangling flights to and from Spain, Pavel the cause. 'Hardly the best of friends, me and heights.'

'Heights?' said Pavel. 'You know how far you need to fall, to never get up again? Thirty feet, no more. Thirty feet onto rocks and you are dead. So I take Dave's hint. I stay away from climbing and from Luka. I stay away from Luka's car, too, but I notice a new face who doesn't – Tom, the tall gumby from the climbing club. You know who Tom is, of course?'

A nod. Tom Bowditch, the tractor thief, and Dave wanted for his murder.

'Tom is young, easy. I watch the three of them whispering, up to no good. Then Tom and Dave drive off together, many times. Luka, though, he drives away, alone.'

Batten was reminded of Olly Rutter, sharpening the knives of crime but making sure others did the stabbing. Was Luka cut from the same cloth? 'It's a long way from a theory class in college,' he said, 'to Mickey Mouse in Spain.'

Pavel stared at his half-empty pint. 'It was Spain made me drink,' he said, pushing away his glass. 'I told you Luka turned up at my shack, a Mercedes now, not an old car? And sitting in my chair when I come home from work?'

'You did. But not what happened next.'

'Next. I wish I could forget what happened next. He gives me no chance to speak, not that I *could* speak, but his voice is new, smooth, a bank manager voice – if bank managers carry guns, because Luka slides one from his pocket. Never had I seen a gun before. Silver, like the Mercedes. He shows me, but close, the gun pointing at my face. Ever happen to you?'

Batten shook his head. Not a gun. But a gunmetal cosh, crashing into his skull…

'And Luka says, do you know, Pavel, even the bullets are silver - isn't that nice? *Nice? Hah!* And his arm curls round my shoulder, tight, not friendly. He steers me outdoors, in the half-dark, waves the gun at me and at the empty landscape. Look at those deep, fast drains, he says. Those ditches and stagnant pools. Nobody comes here, Pavel. Maybe they would never find you? And his eyes are like drills. I want to say, Oksana will find me, but I dare not even mention her name.'

'You and Oksana were an item, by then?'

A sad nod. 'Dave introduced us, years back, of course. But we only met again when I began to work at Wake Hall. A happy time. Till Luka turns up.' Pavel fell into a blue silence, and Batten could almost touch the fear in his face. 'That *demon*, he already knows about Oksana. He steers me into the shack and takes her photograph from the mantlepiece. In a frame, silver, like his gun. Her eyes are smiling - not like his lizard eyes, flicking from me to the photo. Pretty girl, he says, nice skin, not even a…*scar*. His bank manager voice draws out the word and I want to take him by the throat and squeeze the life from his body. He waves the silver gun, pretends to replace the photo but makes it fall to the stone floor. Oh dear, he says, when the glass shatters.'

Pavel's looking shattered too, thought Batten. Stress-lines were slicing through his face like shards, lengthening and shortening as his jaw moved in speech. 'The photo of my beautiful Oksana, criss-crossed with jagged scars, and Luka is sneering down at her. Never, *never* again will I keep her photo in a frame, for the Luka's of this world to see!'

As Batten recalled the tiny flat in Malaga, with not a single photograph of Oksana on display, Pavel reached for the glass he'd pushed away and sank the contents. Again, his hand wiped his lips before rubbing his chin.

'The demon thrusts a plane ticket in my hand, says Spain is warmer, this time of year. I look at the ticket, my name on it - a single ticket, no return - and say, *it's for tonight!* Luka, lizard eyes, steel eyes, he says, hurry up and pack then, wouldn't want you to miss your plane. And those lizard eyes flick between me, the gun and Oksana's broken photograph.'

'So you packed-'

'Huh, after a fashion. And he says, remove the Sim card from your phone, Pavel, if you please? Polite, yes, with the gun in his hand, and he takes the sim card, with all my contacts on it, and drops it into his pocket. I'll keep this safe for you, he says. We go towards his car, and he throws my phone into the nearest drain. Don't make any calls, he says. *None*, you understand? And what can I do?'

Batten wondered what he would do, in similar circumstances. Against a loaded gun, and threats to Sonia, might he have packed? He didn't know the answer. 'And you ended up in Malaga, that same night?'

'Luka makes sure I catch the plane-'

'But he couldn't take a gun into the airport. How did'-

Pavel's voice hissed out like steam. '*He needs no gun! He has my sim card. He has Oksana's photograph!*' Glancing at his glass, craving drink, Pavel saw it was empty. 'Stay in Spain, tell no-one, he says, and Oksana will be safe - no *scars*. If not... It's why I must go! It's why I keep quiet! He gives me euros, says forget Somerset, zip your mouth, find a job, eyes are watching, make no mistake. I climb down from the plane at Malaga airport and begin to feel them, the eyes I never see. And what choice do I have?'

When Batten said nothing, Pavel's face twitched with frustration, with anger.

'*You*, I suppose you would have stayed? Told Luka, go to hell? Phoned the police? Oh yes, the police protect me. Hah! From Luka? And at Wake Hall, with Oksana? Every night, wondering if he comes for me and deals with her instead. *Scars!* I love her too much. I cannot make danger for her. Instead, I get shit job as Mickey Mouse, a job nobody wants, you saw why. At least it hides my face. Big plastic grin for Pavel, but inside, he is not smiling.'

'Maybe you can smile now?' said Batten, mixed loyalties nudging him along. 'What if the police got on Luka's trail? He'd be a fool to stick his head above the parapet.'

'Fool? Luka Judd? Nobody's fool, that man. Not a man, a crazed beast.' Pavel looked round the pub, still almost empty, before producing the sharpened farrier's knife he slipped into his pocket three days ago. 'After work, I lock my tools away, but not this.'

'Against the law, Pavel, carrying a knife. And dangerous.'

Pavel stared at Batten. 'Puh. OK for you to say. You'll protect Oksana? I don't think so.'

'No-one's protecting her now,' said Batten, with a glance at the pub clock, the minute hand in the shape of a horse's leg.

Something close to a smile broke into Pavel's face, then disappeared. 'You know Allie? Allie Chant?'

'Allie the Yard Manager. I know her, yes.'

'She lives next door to Oksana. Her husband, you know him?'

'Neil? Hard to miss.' Allie's husband was a giant with potato fists, and muscles on his muscles.

'A farrier, like me. I tell him some things, not all. And when I am out, like now, Neil watches for me. Some guard dog, eh?'

The soft fur of Cyril, Ronnie Lopen's German Shepherd, came to mind. He shook away the distraction. 'Pavel. I'm convinced you didn't - wouldn't - give Luka your Wake Hall keys.' Pavel gave a wry nod of thanks, since Luka's locksmith skills would take him past any gate he chose, without Pavel's help, and both men knew it now. 'But why did Luka want you out of the way? Nothing you've said explains that.'

'You think Luka bothers to explain? With a gun and an airline ticket in his hand?' Pavel's farrier-fingers squeezed his empty glass, as if it was Luka's neck.' And, huh, you think Oksana doesn't ask me?'

'Oksana's ecstatic to have you back, I saw, and I'm pleased for you both. But she's an intelligent woman. You must've told her *something*.' Batten almost said, '*even* you.'

Pavel nodded, his fingers a metronome, slowly rocking the empty glass against the table. 'Yes. And no. I tell her about Luka, that he threatened me because of something in the past, something innocent. I say I went to Spain to fix it, no choice, very difficult. It troubles her still, and troubles me - because I want no secrets between us. But what would good would it do to tell her *she* is threatened. Why would I frighten who I love?'

'And she believed you?'

Once more, Pavel leaned into Batten, his voice a hiss. 'Everything I told her was *true*!' The pub had begun to fill up, and a middle-aged couple two tables away raised their eyebrows at Pavel's body language. He shot them such a fierce glare they ushered themselves and their Yorkshire Terrier off to the dining area. 'What I don't tell is what is also likely to be true – though I cannot prove it.'

Batten waited for Pavel to speak, but the silence lingered. Pavel looked at the clock on the wall. 'Oksana. I must get back to her.'

No you bloody don't, thought Batten, and he planted his hand, friendly but firm, on the farrier's forearm, instantly feeling the new strength of Pavel's back-to-work muscles. It was Batten's turn to hiss, 'I've been a model of patience up to now. But if you don't tell me 'what is likely to be true,' I swear I'll take your empty glass and insert it where the sun don't shine. Are we clear?'

Pavel almost laughed. 'What do you know of patience? Try being Mickey Mouse for months, in Spanish heat – *that* is patience.'

'But you're not in Spain, Pavel. You risked returning. And I'm trying to help, so for God's sake risk telling me the truth!'

Rocking his head from side to side, as if weighing up pros and cons, Pavel dropped his voice to a low whisper. 'Why Luka Judd exiles me to Spain, is because I know of him, and of Dave and Tom. When Luka offered me a way into crime, I refused. But how can I *un-know*? Luka wants my silence. And the clever demon knows if I am in Spain, I cannot protect Oksana. So, in Spain, I keep his secrets. And since you know his secrets now, maybe a knife in *your* pocket is a good idea, *Mr Zig*.'

Batten was about to say, 'what secrets?' when Pavel removed Batten's hand from his arm, without effort, his grip an iron pincer, and headed for the door.

Outside in the shadowy car park, a line of tall conifers peered down like jurors in a badly-lit room. Hoping for more, Batten said, 'I'll run you back.'

'*No*. I'll walk. Good evening air. Thinking time.'

'Thinking about Luka?'

Pavel shook his head. 'About Dave. Because there is another thing 'likely to be true'. Luka, he sees me off because he fears a policeman's hand on his collar. But *Dave* and Luka? Criminals together, yes, and Dave has more than knowledge of Luka's secrets. Somewhere, he has the-'

'Evidence?' *I'd like some too,* Batten could have said.

'*Evidence.*' Pavel spat the word like a pip from an apple. 'A policeman word, *evidence*. But dangerous for Dave to know. And money will be a further reason for Filthy Luka, be sure of it. So does he look for Dave, here, in England - if Dave is here? Much sorrow for Oksana if the police find Dave. But if Luka finds him first…'

'Two thieves falling out,' said Batten, more directly than he'd intended.

Pavel's shoulders dropped, a sad shrug. 'Two, yes. But not three. Where would I be now, had I joined Luka's 'enterprise', instead of Tom?'

Dead, like Tom? thought Batten.

'I never would say yes, but I wish, every day, that Dave had also said no.' Pavel aimed a long sigh at the thickening clouds. 'Oksana, she is a swan. Calm beauty, on the outside. But, every day, I watch her shiver inside with pain for her troubled brother.'

Batten might have said *for her troubled mother too*. Instead, he turned to go, as Pavel's powerful hand shot out and clamped onto his arm, stopping him in his tracks.

'You are not police anymore. But you *know* police. One came to see me, at Wake Hall. Maybe it was you, who told him? Maybe I would do the same, were I you, and not a farrier.' His grip tightened like a vice, and Batten felt the man's passion and power. 'But if Oksana is hurt…You understand?'

Without another word, Pavel flicked Batten's arm aside and strode away, one hand in his pocket, the pocket with the knife. Batten stared after him, rubbing the blood back into his arm and wondering what else Pavel knew.

*And do I tell CID what **I** know?* Old loyalties and new commitments played tug-of-war, there in the car park of *The Horse and Groom*. Despite the car keys jangling in Batten's hand, he almost went back inside to drown his sorrows. Instead, he plonked himself in the driver's seat, tapped his fingers on the steering wheel and re-ran Pavel's story.

Luka wanted him out of England, Pavel claimed, because he knew of Luka's crimes. And Oksana was Luka's bargaining chip. But Batten's feet still tingled at stronger possibilities: with Pavel out of the way, Oksana could be watched and questioned, about Dave, his whereabouts, and the contents of his backpack. What did Pavel say? *Money will be a further reason for Filthy Luka, be sure of it.*

Batten tapped thoughts into his phone's notepad - then stopped. 'Am I leaping to the wrong conclusion?' he asked the empty car. 'What if Luka didn't want Pavel out of England – what if he wanted him in *Spain*? And not to sweat in a Mickey Mouse costume. *Why then?*'

The night air, and Luka, had chilled the car. Batten switched on the engine to run the heater, still staring at the growing puzzle of notes on his phone, relieved Lady Wake had agreed he could bring in help. 'Too much for one man,' he said aloud, and as the car warmed he came to a decision.

Composing a pair of texts, he pressed *Send*.

Twenty-seven

Only when *Inspector* Chris Ball squeezed his squat body onto a bar stool in *The Jug and Bottle*, did he realise how deeply tired he was. Of late, his once-familiar home in the village of Stockton Marsh had become a second office. So much paperwork swamped his head it was almost an effort to pour cider down his mineshaft of a throat. Only when a long glug revived him did he feel the different vibe in his 'local'. From the roof beams, swathes of tinsel and fairy lights flashed and glowed, and on the bar-top a giant plastic Santa Claus grinned at him. Electric candles behind Santa's eyes threw an eerie-weary light at Ball's face, reflecting his mood.

'*Christmas?* Too busy to notice,' he told Rita, the landlady.

'Wa-aal, it's getting arn for Christmas,' she said in her Somerset burr, jabbing a finger at the garish Santa. 'Haave to get you customers in the mood, don' I? Christmas is *business*, my motto.'

Savouring his drink, Ball considered his own motto: *There's Always Time For Cider*. Now, he had no time for anything, not even *The Jug and Bottle*. First Saturday evening he'd sat at the bar in three weeks - and Rita knew it.

'Where you been hidin', Christopher Ball? Hope you're naat tiring of cider?'

'Rita, I'd rather bleed.' To prove it, he slid his empty glass across the bar. 'Pull me another, eh,' he said, 'since you're so good at it.'

'Thaat's because I pull every night,' she said, with a wicked grin. 'Turn up more offen, you'd notice.'

'Just busy, Rita. New job. It'll settle down.' As if to disagree, his bleeping phone announced yet another message. Dragging it from his pocket, he swiped the screen. A text, and from a rare source these last few months.

Zig Batten.

*

That same evening, in darkness, and a safe distance from Wake Hall, two nondescript cars, the first a faded green, the second dark grey, trundled along the A358 from opposite directions. Separately, at a pre-arranged point, the drivers turned into a side road, came to a halt in a remote lay-by and doused their lights. Remaining behind the wheel till a lone JCB tractor chugged past, a small, wiry man, cap pulled down over his face, emerged from the first car, crossed to the second and climbed in the back.

The driver was a giant. Next to him in the passenger seat, a woman in a blonde wig and thick glasses nodded to the wiry man, in silence. Indeed, few words and no handshakes were exchanged. This was business, and the less time they spent together the better.

The small man passed a harmless looking holdall to the driver, his shoulders the size of wardrobes. Potato hands checked the contents: ski-mask; two-way radio; latex gloves, false numberplates. From an expensive handbag sporting the initials *A.B.*, the woman drew two envelopes heavy with used banknotes, handing the men one each. Two single sheets of paper followed, the first a line of numbers, the second more numbers arranged in a pattern. The wardrobe-shouldered man assessed their import, then proposed a time, a place, a route. Gruff, the exchange, no nonsense, no wasted words. The wiry man nodded. The woman sealed the agreement. Transaction done, time to go.

Ninety seconds later, the two cars drove away in darkness - separately, unobserved and in opposite directions, just as they had arrived. Soon enough, when the crusher did its work, the old green and grey cars would disappear. Well paid, the drivers, for the extra security.

But all three knew the man pulling their strings - more demon than man - was the real reason. A reason only fools would ignore.

*

It was dark by the time Detective Constable Hazel Timms slotted two carrier bags into the boot. Nothing much in them, but plenty for one. *Here you are, Hazel,* she thought, *supermarket shopping, on a Saturday night, how modern.* Though her new status - 0.6 of full-time - was at her request, she had yet to balance its upsides and downsides. The upsides were a four-day weekend, from Friday morning through to Monday night. The downsides were exactly the same.

Timms paddled her fingers against her lips. Life had changed, for worse and for better, after her parents died. She doubted the sting of two funerals in a few short weeks would ever fully depart, but her life changed again when the will was read. Parents and offspring, do they ever truly talk? She had no real sense of mum and dad's investments till, as sole heir, and to her jaw-dropped surprise, she inherited the mortgage-free house she'd nursed them in, and life insurance and savings worth a smidgeon over four hundred grand. *Hooray, I'm a well-off, unmarried orphan*, she mumbled to herself, starting the engine, *with four days out of seven to kill.*

Her new car, an electric Nissan, slid past shop windows stuffed with garish Christmas adverts, Santas in sleighs, and plastic Rudolphs hung with a white mesh of fake snow. *Christmas,* yet the two gut-wrenching summer funerals still felt like yesterday. In what seemed one minute instead of ten, she reached the outer suburbs of Parminster and pulled into a bay-windowed house no longer feeling like home. Poking up from the front garden, the tall weed of a *For Sale* board greeted her. Maybe the footfall of strangers viewing the house will yank me from my limbo, she thought, and force me to make a new home in fresh surroundings.

She slid the car into the garage, plugged in the recharging cable, and realised why the journey from shops to 'home' had felt so short. She'd spent most of it planning what to do with herself tomorrow. And come up with nothing.

She checked her phone for messages. One, and one only. '*Cuh, how to cope with all these demands?*' she said aloud, since there was no-one to hear.

One text.

From *Zig Batten.*

Twenty-eight

Sonia Welcome was a great kisser. Alas, she was fully-clothed, and her Monday morning kiss was the goodbye version. With her wickedest smile, she said, '*One* of us has to face the rush hour traffic, Zig - and the mortuary awaits.'

Batten hated the word *mortuary*. 'Can't you just say you're going to *the office?*' he told the back of her departing head, but the only reply came from the engine of her old Vauxhall as it drove away. Despite welcome heat from the now-working radiators, he lay disappointed in the warm bed. Sonia had many wonderful characteristics, but on this lazy morning he wished punctuality wasn't one of them – till he remembered Chris Ball had reluctantly agreed to drop in on *his* way to work.

'At least it's only a ten-yard walk,' Batten reminded himself, 'to *my* office.'

Scents of furniture polish and coffee confronted Chris Ball as he sat down and scanned Batten's new space, relieved that no premature Christmas tinsel graced the door and windows. The desk and swivel chair reminded him of his new study, magicked up by Di from their spare bedroom. Even the paint on the wall was similar. 'Enjoying it?' he asked Batten, waving an arm at the garden office but curbing the '*Sir*' he'd grown used to. In time, *Zig* would filter into their exchanges, but felt awkward today.

'This place? Definitely.' Batten refused to call his new base a *bolt-hole* – that was Sonia's term. 'I've even got a filing cabinet.' He pointed at a steel box standing to attention against the wall. 'Like the one Eddie Hick used to collide with, at Parminster CID.'

'Anything in it?' asked Ball, after a sip of coffee. Too early for cider, and he had wall-to-wall meetings at HQ.

Batten glanced over his cup at his old Sergeant. *Best get it over with*, he thought. 'Yes. My first case. Wake Hall.'

Chris Ball duly winced, glugging too-hot coffee to wash down the sharp taste of those painful words. *Wake Hall*, scar tissue to him – old, but tender. 'I had heard,' he mumbled.

'And complicated, Chris. I began as an expensive courier, but there's more going on than I thought. Wouldn't be surprised if bits of it wandered your way, soon enough.'

'Then I'll need a bigger desk. Your old one...' Ball faltered, still feeling an intruder whenever he sat in his ex-boss's cubby-hole office, at his desk, in his chair. 'As it happens, Hick paid a visit to the Hall, the other day. Came back with nothing *new*.' He let the thought linger, hoping Batten might fill in any gaps. *The reason he invited me,* he assumed.

Torn by his own mixed loyalties, Batten slid his cup onto the table. 'They should call that place *The Hall of Secrets*. You go through those giant doors to pull teeth, but when you come out, your own molars are missing. So far, my gums are sucking on scraps.'

'CID-worthy, these scraps?'

It was Batten's turn to pause. 'I doubt the Crown Prosecution Service would think so. Not yet. It's why I sort of need your permission.'

If Ball was expected to conjure up *permission*, he'd prefer cider as a lubricant. And he was already crystal-Ball-clear about the boundaries of his new role. 'I might have to disappoint you, then. No permission to 'borrow' a casefile, no proxy use of the police computer, no loitering with intent in the CID foyer. No permission for any of that, sorry. And not just because Area Superintendent Wallingford would have my guts.'

A nod of admiration was Batten's reply. 'I'd expect nothing less, Chris.' *Despite your previous departures from the rules.* 'I was only seeking permission to approach Hazel Timms.'

'Permission to approach? You under a restraining order or something?' said Ball with a grin - before suspicion began to niggle. 'Approach her? About what?'

Even Batten wasn't sure. 'She dropped down to 0.6, is that right, after she inherited?'

'Inherited?' said a wary Ball. 'Heir to a bad brew of money and sorrow, more like. Now, we only get her three days a week, God knows why. Rumour is, the other four days, she twiddles her thumbs.'

'I was wondering if she'd twiddle them for me – so to speak.'

Cottoning on, Ball pushed away his coffee cup. 'You want Hazel - *CID* Hazel - to join your new enterprise? That's the *permission*?'

'Plenty of cops have second jobs, Chris, to pay the bills. In Hazel's case, to give her purpose, maybe?'

Ball folded his arms, tight. 'There's no lack of purpose at Parminster. You should see her desk. And *mine!*'

Batten had seen those Parminster desks every day for five years. 'As I said, Chris, plenty of cops have second jobs. I'm only asking permission to make an offer.'

When caught between two stools, Ball either stretched his legs or cracked his knuckles. Neither improved his height or dexterity but when he stood up and duly stretched, his cogs turned over. 'You *do* know she's not allowed to do anything related to private security? Er, or contravene the Force's ethical rules…' He faltered, struggling to remember the new *Inspector* bumph he was still ploughing through.

Drawing on long experience, Batten helped him out. 'Correct. Nor use police time, equipment, or resources. She won't, Chris. She'd use mine, here.' He waved at his new office. 'And any arrangement, yes, would be annually reviewed - assuming the Chief Constable OK'd her *Notification of Secondary Business Interests* form, of course.'

'Which would depend on what she put in it, *of course.*' Ball wondered if his old boss was after a backdoor route into CID - via the Trojan Horse of DC Hazel Timms.

'Well, research work? Background digging? Record-keeping? She'd be mostly clerical, not field. Too much for me to do on my own.' He pointed at his new desk. 'And she'd do it right here - and answer the phone, while I'm away sniffing out naughtiness.'

'Within the law, I trust? And passing all significant discoveries to the *police?*'

Batten raised his arms in mock-surrender. 'Naturally, Chris. I'm Citizen Zig now. So? What do you think?'

By nature a people-pleaser, Ball wasn't sure what to think. He cracked his knuckles.

It didn't help.

*

When DC Timms' *Notification of Secondary Business Interests* form finally landed on Area Superintendent Wallingford's Central HQ desk, he barely glanced at it. Drawing on his favourite word - *efficiency* - he clobbered it with his rubber stamp. Keeping Timms on a reduced CID contract may not suit crime detection but it suited Wallingford's covert plans for Parminster – and his balance sheet. And if the silly cow chose to fill her time outside the Force with 'agency work: clerical and research', more fool her.

Sliding the form across the desk's shiny surface he slotted it into his *Out* tray, then moved on to more important number-crunching. On his say-so, the Chief Constable would ratify Timms' request, then move on to balance sheets of her own.

*

Oksana *Brok* sat down at her Wake Hall desk, dropped her house keys into her tidy handbag, took out her reading glasses and, despite the recent upheavals, got cracking.

Signing off the accounts for *Booker Prize Novels, the 1980s,* she allowed herself a smile of satisfaction at the balance sheet. A keen reader, she'd designed the ten-week programme herself, and many others like it, the enrolments far exceeding break-even. Some of the attendees were even new faces, from further afield, a positive sign. With Oksana's help, Wake Hall was rebuilding its reputation – and its profits.

The programme tutor being an old hand, Oksana's involvement on the day had been a breeze. She did the introductions, organised break-out rooms, double-checked the expensive lunch - then discreetly enjoyed the discussions and general ambience. Some days, work was a pleasure.

With the smile of satisfaction still gracing her attractive face, she scanned the new names on her attendance list for today's follow-up course - *Booker Prize Novels, the 1990s.* Ten more novels over ten more weeks, same tutor, same set-up - so work was sure to be a pleasure this time too.

Well, she hoped so...

Twenty-nine

After the Chief Constable's permission came through, Hazel Timms sat in Batten's garden-office, staring through the window at the long dark hedge of English yew, *Taxus baccata*. Her father used to know the Latin name of every garden plant, till his own name became a mystery - and his wife's, and his daughter's. *Cory*, he called her, in his final months. Or *Evelyn*. Sometimes both together. *Corylus Avellana*, the Hazel tree – at least he'd half-remembered that.

To break the sad memory, she ran her fingers through her newly-styled hair. Batten had surprised her, first by noticing she'd had a hairdo, then by saying he liked it. Nevertheless, she still wondered if being here was such a good idea.

Working together on the Queen Mab murder, the pair of them had developed a rapport, but this was different. When he described his freelance Wake Hall role, equine metaphors had trotted into her thoughts. Would he be out riding the horse, while she was stuck at a desk tracking down pedigrees and ordering fresh hay? And not one horse, but two, because she'd have to switch horses on a weekly basis. CID, private, CID, private. And, as Inspector Ball had more than firmly reminded her, keep the two roles professionally apart. She glanced up at Batten, in T-shirt and chinos, his work-suit gone, but a familiar eyebrow raised in expectation.

'I'm still not sure about the overlap,' she said. 'I'm still CID, three days a week. And if you and I dig into crime on the other two days, won't I be compromised?'

Batten had considered this. 'Similar process, of course, but we'll be working directly for the victims, for the concerned. And if we do home in on criminals, it'll be CID - on behalf of the State - who make the arrests. In a way, we'll be relieving some of their pressure.'

Given the national shortage of detectives, Timms found it hard to disagree with Batten's logic. So why had she added to the shortage by reducing her hours as a Detective Constable? For a second time, she stared through the window at the yew hedge, nodding not at Batten but at her own silent reasons. Because after two funerals and an overflowing in-tray of wife-beating, theft and thuggery, she was burning out - and knew it. Change. She needed change, pastures new, maybe a permanent farewell to police work. But not, she hoped, via an invalidity pension, triggered by a cosh to the skull. Falling back on horse metaphors, she wondered if to stay safe around Batten, she'd need a body protector and a riding hat.

'What if we try it for a month or so?' she said.

'Suits me,' said Batten, pleased with the *or so*. He had total respect for Hazel's professional skills, but just as important, he liked her as a person. 'Right,' he said. 'When would you like to begin?'

Begin? Yesterday! 'Well. I'm here, so…'

*

Trouble with you is you're too bloody innocent! That's what Phil Kerrigan, Avril Dean's ex-husband used to tell her, jabbing his big finger in her face. *For this bloody world, screw innocence – grow a suspicious mind!* Well, she thought, the world *and* Phil Kerrigan screwed my innocence, and that's a fact. At her neat office desk in the bowels of Wake Hall, she stared at the phone. Yes, she'd promised to ring Zig Batten, day or night, if anything *suspicious* happened on the Estate. But a lost handbag? Was that *suspicious*? She once left hers on a train…

No. She picked up the phone. This was Oksana's handbag, and Oksana was rarely forgetful. Nor did she leave hers on a train, a plane, a bus. It 'disappeared' from the Conference Suite. In the Residential Wing. At Wake Hall. And if punters can afford *Booker Prize Novels, the 1990s,* they can afford a handbag of their own…

Batten Formula One'd his Focus to Wake Hall – a bit too fast for Hazel Timms, who gripped the edge of the passenger seat throughout the journey. 'Your desk work includes follow-up digging,' he explained. 'And since Avril says it's urgent, why not follow it up today?'

When Hazel flashed an *oh yes?* he said, 'Simple!' in a mock-Meerkat voice, to soften the half-truth.

Introductions done, they set to it, Timms following Avril to the scene, while Batten met Oksana in her office. Déjà vu, the pair of them sat in the same faux-leather bucket chairs as last time.

'My purse, fifty pounds in notes, my credit cards,' she said in answer to his question. 'I cancelled the cards as soon as I realised. But at least my phone was in my pocket, and thank God, so were my Wake Hall keys – they open all the main gates and doors. Can you imagine Her Ladyship's face if I'd lost those too?'

Lost - or stolen? Batten's feet tingled. With keys to the Hall, whoever was behind the horse attacks would have an open door to the humans who lived there. 'What about your house keys?' he said.

Oksana turned pale. 'Yes,' she mumbled. 'Gone. But because of the Detective who came to the cottage, the one you thought was fake, I sent Ben Roche, our Health and Safety officer over there, to sort of stand guard. He has a Security brief too, you see.'

'How soon? I mean, how soon after your bag went missing?'

Even paler now, Oksana said, 'At least an hour, I suppose. Probably longer. The tutor was running discussion groups in separate rooms, and I was nipping between, then organising lunch. I only noticed when clearing up later, in the Conference Hall. I *think* that's where I left my handbag. These last few months, it's been…difficult.'

These last five years was the silent elephant in the room. Batten feared the worst but tried to lighten the load. 'I'll ask Avril to send for a locksmith. To change your locks. Just in case. We'll sort it, don't worry.'

Empty words, nor did they curb the equine metaphors. A locksmith might newly bolt the door. But had the horse already gone?

Professional skills to the fore, Hazel Timms rapidly surveyed the scene, clocked entry and exit points and where they led, and acquired an attendance list for the course in the Conference Suite. 'I interviewed Ben Roche, the Health, Safety and Security Officer,' she told Batten. 'He couldn't get into the cottage, front and side doors both locked, but he looked in through the windows and the place has been ransacked, in spades. The cottage next door-'

'Allie Chant's, yes. She and her husband, Neil. They'd be out at work?'

'They were. Ben said he knocked and got no reply. He glanced through their windows too, and everything was normal.'

'So Oksana's place was targeted?'

'Looks it. Nobody around by the time Ben arrived, of course.'

Batten drew Avril Dean to one side. 'Pavel has keys to the cottage. Have you...?'

'Good heavens, no. The last thing I want is a frantic Pavel. The Estate Office is sending master keys.'

Master keys set off a fresh tingle in Batten's feet, but almost immediately the keys arrived and, treading carefully, he went in. Timms shuffled Oksana back to Avril's car, 'just in case,' then joined him. No intruders, but an invisible presence had left behind a chaos of ransacked cupboards. Discarded belongings were scattered over every floor. Upstairs, even the loft hatch was open, the loft-ladder dangling down, no cavity left untouched. *Experts*, Batten mumbled.

Oksana doesn't need to see this, he decided. 'Best you take Oksana back to the Hall for now,' he told Avril, 'and check for any strangers or strange vehicles in the vicinity. Hazel and I will do a thorough search here.' Avril met his covert glance at Oksana with a nod of understanding.

Alone, Batten and Timms scoured the cottage for obvious evidence – she'd already insisted they both don latex gloves. 'It feels strange,' said Timms, 'not waiting for Forensics. Not fingerprinting.' *And not calling the police...*

'It'll feel even stranger in a sec,' said Batten. 'Oksana and Pavel don't deserve this mess. For their wellbeing, we'll put everything back where it belongs.' He neutralised her look of surprise with a shrug. 'Anything obvious missing, tell me. And for propriety's sake, you can deal with the knickers and bras.'

He left Hazel to it and checked outside for tyre marks, scanned the front and side gardens for footprints, and delved into the shrub-lined ditches at both ends of the lane, in search of discards. No sign anywhere of a gutted backpack, if that was the intruder's objective.

When he returned, the cottage was almost pristine. 'Blimey,' he said. 'Wish my house was as clean. I'm still wiping up builder's dust. Anything?'

Timms shook her head. 'But I'm thinking two people.'

Batten was on Timms' wavelength. In his mind's eyes, he saw an 'innocent' vehicle parked outside, keeping watch, while a second thief took the cottage apart.

'Do you think Oksana *was* hiding a backpack – or hiding *something*?'

'*Think?* At Wake Hall?' He let out a sigh of frustration. 'What about the attendance list? Anyone on it called *Will Burgle?*'

Timms pulled a face. 'No, but two of the punter's didn't turn up for their pricey lunch, and they'd paid in advance. Oksana's checking they're pukka.'

'Male or female?'

Timms nodded at the question's import. A man with a woman's handbag might look a tad out of place - even at Wake Hall where everything seemed out of place today. 'Female, both.'

Batten blew out his breath. Even with Timms' help, how was he supposed to prevent more *invasions*? Olly Rutter and Luka Judd had helpers galore. Invisible nightbirds, poisoning *Wake Hall Equestrian*, scarring the flesh of its horses, scattering hoof-piercing caltrops. At least one ordinary-looking male, with a bogus warrant card. Today, a female thief and a driver. And how many others? Wake Hall was becoming a mountainside.

Sensing his dejection, Timms tried cheering him along. 'The tutor told me the name of the course - *Booker Prize Novels*. A posh book club, really. Different novel each week, with a pricey lunch thrown in. Guess the title of today's book.'

Not in the mood, Batten shook his head.

'A.S. Byatt's winner, from 1990,' Timms said with a smile. '*Possession.*'

With a half-hearted smile, Batten watched Timms tuck Oksana's remaining possessions into place. On the way back to the Conference Suite, he wondered what possessed him to say 'yes,' that fateful morning when Lady Wake silked herself and her 'confidential' bloody problems into his office.

*

'Paula Meadows, Mrs. She had to leave early because her husband was taken ill. But she's a regular,' said Oksana. 'I mean, we know her. She lives in Parminster.'

'But the other early departure was also a woman, yes?' asked Batten. *A woman who purloined your keys and burgled your house.*

Oksana scrolled down her laptop screen, which sat on a desk far steadier than its owner's nervy fingers. 'Yes. Her name's...Alice Brown. New to us. This was her first programme.' With a sigh she added, 'Her only one, I suppose?'

Flopping into a bucket chair, Batten nodded, silently wagering *Alice Brown* arrived with a bigger prize on her mind than a Booker Prize Novel, and maybe left with one. 'Could you describe her?'

'I didn't think I'd ever need to. Blonde hair? Thickish glasses? Bit of a thirty-something frump, I suppose. Bit colourless?'

Blonde on bland, Batten thought. 'How did she pay?' He already guessed the answer.

'...Ah. Cash. Unusual, but it does happen. We do have an *address.*'

Batten remembered Pavel's comment about Dipstick Dave's 'address' - Mongolia, or the Moon. And Olly and Luka's Bristol connection. 'Don't tell me. Bristol?'

Oksana returned to the screen. 'Yes. How did you...?'

'Long story,' said Batten, assuming the address was false. 'This Alice Brown, did she drive here? A car registration?'

Eyes scanned the screen. 'She arrived via our minibus service, from Crewkerne Railway Station, but-'

'But the minibus is yet to depart, yes. All the same, *Alice Brown* is gone. And I doubt she left on foot...'

Thirty

A tetchy Avril Dean showed Batten and Timms into the CCTV area, at the rear of Wake Hall's maintenance workshop, then hurried off *to get things done*. Tools for all eventualities dangled from racks above a well-used workbench smelling of oil. Its clutter of unwashed cups and discarded food wrappers suggested the room also doubled as an escape zone for the 'servants.' Batten sympathised, as the fast fingers of Ben Roche, the HS&S Officer, ran the old-fashioned video tape back and forth.

'The cameras only cover main exits and entrances,' Ben said, an embarrassed note in his voice. 'Old system, I'm afraid.' Old or new, he went too fast for Batten's sensitive eyeballs, but not for those of Hazel Timms.

'Stop, there,' she said. 'Back a bit. Bit more. There! What's that?'

The room of eyes looked closer. 'Just the plumber's van driving in,' said Ben, switching the screen to close-up. 'Used the same firm for years. See? *Elliot's Plumbing Services*, on the van, and an official parking sticker on the windscreen.'

The passenger seat was empty. 'Can you home in on the driver,' said Batten. When Ben did, they saw little more than a peaked cap, its brim pulled down over the face wearing it. But probably male.

'Can you fast forward to the van leaving, if it has?'

The tapped keys and jiggled controls echoed Batten's tapping foot, slow at first, faster, then staccato. But not for long, because the van arrived and left within an hour and half. 'Same van,' said Ben, 'same registration, driving out through the gates, as normal.'

Same recently *stolen* van, Batten guessed, peering closer at the screen. Timms beat him to it. 'If it's as normal,' she said, 'how come your plumber arrived alone, but left with a passenger?'

Surprised, Ben zoomed in. Next to the driver, a frumpy skirt was visible, and a headscarf shadowing a woman's face. Not that it mattered what *Alice Brown* looked like.

Since she didn't exist…

At Batten's suggestion, Hazel Timms handled the questions when they returned to Oksana's office. This time, they took the faux leather chairs and Oksana sat at her desk, face impossibly paler than before.

'You haven't seen your brother Dave for five years,' said Hazel. 'Is that right?'

In a slow whisper, Oksana said, 'Dave was always somewhere else. And before you ask, up to no good. But a brother is a brother and, apart from mum, he's my only living family. Yes, five years ago. He came with me to see our mother on Christmas morning and stayed to eat Christmas lunch here in the afternoon. By evening he was gone, and that was that. The police think I know where he is, and I wish I *did*.'

At least she's stopped pretending Dave's in Mongolia or on the Moon, Batten thought, as Timms worked towards the bigger questions. 'I guess Dave drove here, on Christmas Day? No trains, no buses, so he had a car?'

'A motor bike, an old one. But safe. He's a mechanic.'

Batten and Timms shared a look. Harder to carry a backpack on a motor bike, but perfectly possible. 'I guess he brought Christmas presents?'

'Of course he did. A shawl, a pashmina, expensive, for mother. I gave him a cashmere scarf. Dark brown, like his eyes.' She fingered the silver locket she always wore. 'He gave me this. It has a photo of the two of us, as children. The only photo I have of Dave. Camera-shy, my brother.'

All the police ever had, Batten recalled, was an unsmiling passport photo of Dipstick Dave, less good-looking than his sister and only a hint of family likeness.

'May we see?' said Timms. Oksana unhooked the chain, opened the heart-shaped locket, and passed it across. Two smiling children, arms linked, in front of a distinctly non-English building, against a background of tall fir trees and snow.

'It was taken in Poland,' said Oksana. 'We went with my father when we were young. It's at a place called Brok, where my great-grandfather was born. *Brok*. My new surname, since Dave…'

'It's double-sided,' said Timms. 'May I open the back?' Not attuned to jewellery, Batten hadn't noticed.

'Dave sealed it up. He said, when I have a child, I'm to open it and put a photo in the blank space. He wants me to call him *David*. Typical, he assumes I'll have a boy.'

'You've never been tempted to unseal it?' asked Timms. 'Me, I'd want to know if it held a surprise.'

Oksana decoded Timms' question and shot her a glance. 'A surprise? You mean a secret? *No*, I've never been tempted. It was a Christmas gift, a moment of Dave. I've precious little else!'

In the tight silence, Batten quietly took back the lead. 'Oksana, if there's the slightest chance Dave hid something in the locket, we need to see. We've so little to go on.' When she hesitated, he said, 'I saw a soldering iron in the maintenance workshop and I'm quite handy. I could unseal it and seal it up again and you'd never be able to tell.'

Oksana was a picture of uncertainty. From experience, Batten slowly climbed to his feet to hurry her along.

'If you must,' she said, and the three of them trooped back to the CCTV room…

'It shouldn't take long,' Batten told Oksana, as the soldering iron heated up. When he fumbled for his specs, Timms gently eased him aside, moved to the workbench and had the locket open in no time. Spectacles now on his nose, Batten peered at the contents, unsure what to expect. Another photograph?

From inside the silver heart, Timms shook a small coil of white paper. 'It might be a personal message,' Batten told Oksana. 'Best if you open it.' He itched to open it himself, but Oksana was at his shoulder. Breath held, he watched her nervous fingers uncoil the paper and flatten it out. The handwriting was tiny, a black ink scrawl. Oksana's hushed voice whispered the words.

'*I may be here*,' she read. 'Then there's an address. Dave's address?' Her fingers covered up the thin piece of paper, only her eyes speaking: *I want to know where Dave is. But must others know?*

With a reassuring smile, Batten gently eased the paper from beneath her hand. '338 *Calle del Barrio Alto, Casares*,' he read.

'I don't know where that is,' said Oksana.

'I do,' said Batten. 'Casares, in Spain, one of the famous 'white villages.' It's up in the hills near Estepona. Costa del Sol.' Nor was it far from Malaga, where Pavel had played a reluctant Micky Mouse. Oksana could do without the reminder.

'I must go there,' she said, her voice a mixture of resolve and fear.

Lady Wake will have something to say about that, thought Batten. But *someone* will have to go – him probably, another nervous flight at 30,000 feet. And didn't *Barrio Alto* mean 'high neighbourhood?' As far as Zig Batten was concerned, Casares was a mountain-top, and his default position was flat ground at sea level.

Oksana reclaimed the flimsy slip of paper with nervous fingers, her eyes flicking between the address, Timms, and Batten. One moment it was a winning lottery ticket, next moment the gate to Hell. 'I don't know what to do,' she whispered.

Timms and Batten looked at each other. Neither did they.

Thirty-one

In Wake Hall's cavernous reception room, Avril Dean looked flustered. Her surprising vexation soared as Batten narrated the day's events – especially the news of Dave's address in Spain. She drew Batten away from Hazel and Oksana, voice a tight whisper, as if the portraits on the walls might overhear.

'Do I need to remind you of Lady Wake's wishes?' she hissed. 'You are supposed to focus *not* on Dave Vossialevydipsic but on Judd and Rutter.' With a peremptory finger-jab at Timms, she added, 'The *two* of you are here to prevent more damage to Her Ladyship's equine business - and being paid for it!'

To avoid glaring back at Avril, Batten glared instead at the nearest painting, of a rotund mid-Century male in a pristine business suit, a watch chain dangling from his waistcoat and a pair of gold spectacles in his hand, as if the portrait artist had rudely interrupted his perusal of a bank statement. From previous visits, Batten recognised old Lord Wake, feckless dead father of the current incumbent.

When she followed Batten's gaze to Lord Wake's portrait, Avril's face turned scarlet, and her hiss became snake-like. 'Kindly drag your attention from...portraiture, to the matter in hand. Which is *here*, at Wake Hall, not in Spain! Dave may be important to Oksana, but he is *not* priority one!'

Puzzled by the dip in Avril's empathy, Batten gave her a cool stare. 'I'm not sure about that,' he said. 'I think there's crossover.'

'*Crossover?*'

'Yes. Find Dave and he leads us to Luka, then to Olly. Two criminals for the price of one.'

'*Two?*' she hissed.

This time, Avril's face was readable. Not two birds, but *three*. For Avril, Dave belonged squarely in the criminal category – a murderer, guilty till proven innocent, and if Oksana believed otherwise, tough luck. Batten retaliated, shooting Avril a frown. Even the eyebrows on the portrait of old Lord Wake seemed to squeeze together. 'Leaving Spain aside - for now - what took place *here*, today, was a well-planned theft. So perhaps you should do the obvious? Report it to the *police* who have more resources than the *two* of *us*?'

Avril's lips tightened to a thread and in response she flumped across the room to Timms and Oksana. '*Lady Wake* will decide how to proceed,' she said, shooting a backward glance at Batten. 'She is away till Sunday on business, and I am not to disturb her. We will re-convene in my office. Monday morning, 8.30?'

With the palest of nods, Oksana dragged herself away. Timms, with nothing better to do, was available every Monday now. Batten would just have to wait. Avril added the meeting to a pocket notebook, her writing neat, small, contained – like the understated *ting* of her phone as a text arrived.

'The locksmith is here,' she said. 'For Oksana's cottage. To change the locks. And then I suppose Pavel will need to be *mollycoddled*. You'll excuse me?'

Batten half-smiled at Avril's only-just-polite British euphemism for *piss off*. Driving Timms back to Parminster, the smile faded: no new lock would impede Luka Judd, if he turned up in person to pick his way past Oksana's door.

*

In the absence of Lady Wake, Avril Dean was practically running Wake Hall. Despite being a 'get things done' person, the strain was beginning to show, on her face and in her voice. Nevertheless, when Batten and Timms departed she sent Pavel a text then flopped down at her office desk to triple-check the vetting sheets of the new patrol drivers from *Nightwatch Security*. Harry Greene and Mike Bromley had sound credentials, on paper at least. Both ex-military, and plenty of muscle on them. Both had honourable discharges and strong recommendations. *Reliable* cropped up more than once. All the same, she'd had them in her office for a grilling, despite the multitude of other tasks on her plate.

'Just grin and bear it,' warned Walter Moon, the *Nightwatch Security* boss. 'You'll forget she's a dragon once Wake Hall's Christmas bonus fills your pocket.'

'Christmas?' said Harry. 'Can't wait that long. Any chance they'd pay it early?'

'Cock things up and they won't pay it at all,' was Moon's terse reply. 'Now piss off out my office and check your vans and equipment!'

Since weekend work paid extra, Harry and Mike did as they were told, but not before drawing on their playful sides by dressing their dashboards with battery-operated plastic Santas, their eyes bright beams of yellow light. Setting the frequency on his shiny radio, Harry said, 'Testing, one two, three, four?'

Mike's radio crackled into life. 'Received,' he replied, glancing at the crib sheet clipped to his instrument panel. Walter Moon had divided Wake Hall into zones, to be patrolled in a pre-arranged sequence. 'Looks like I'll be starting with Zone 3,' Mike told his radio. 'Then scooting over to 5.'

'I'm Zone 8 first, then 11, right over the other side. Miles away from your smelliness.'

'Huh. Just make sure you don't nod off. And I'll meet you halfway for a break. You still on the cheese and pickle?'

'Yup,' said Harry. 'Same as ever. Yours?'

'Dunno. Always smells like fish paste.'

'Well,' said Harry, 'so do you!'

Tests and checks complete, the two men locked up, and with double-time and Christmas bonuses in mind, went home to sleep, When their night shift began, four Santa Claus eyes would pierce the darkness, not with seasonal joy, but with the ghostly yellow light of expectation.

Thirty-two

At breakfast in *Hillview*, Batten's head was still full of Wake Hall puzzles. Without realising, he was beginning to fill Sonia's head with it too. 'Can't have been Luka Judd in person, at the burglary, can it? Someone might have recognised him.'

'Then it was someone *else*,' said Sonia, loudly scraping butter onto her toast.

'But who? If there's a middle-man, the middle-man must have middle-men. Unless he's a she?'

Swinging her recently unpacked silver spoon like a hammer, Sonia demolished the top of her boiled egg. When Batten heard the crunch and saw the pulverised shell, he decided not to mention his likely return to Spain - without her.

Sonia decided it was time to take Zig's mind off *all* of it. Instead of criminals and horses, their Saturday morning would involve Christmas trees – a six-foot version from the local garden centre, for the recently-painted kitchen/diner.

She got her way, but the afternoon rang with curses as Batten failed to untangle the twisted maze of last year's fairy lights – each snag and knot reminding him of the Wake Hall conundrum his first-ever case had become. He mentioned it to Sonia. Several times…

On Sunday morning, Sonia Welcome tapped him on the shoulder with an ultimatum – though she referred to it as a *surprise*. 'I bought the last two tickets, Zig, as an antidote to Wake Hall. It's time we *both* had a break.' Sonia's way, act first, seek agreement later.

'I seem to recall your antidote to my last case was buying the victim's *house*,' Batten retorted. 'And persuading me to live in it, *here*.'

'Yes, but with *me*,' she said, eyes a-twinkle. 'Get dressed. I'll drive…'

Later that day, he groaned when she parked at the top of Ham Hill, in much the same spot as on Remembrance Sunday. Thankfully, Avril Dean's unreadable face was nowhere to be seen this time. Batten followed Sonia into the temporary Archaeology Centre, where they took seats at the front, near a lurking projector screen. 'It's just a glorified tent,' he whispered.

'Stop pretending you're not interested,' she said. 'You who endlessly waffles on about the Ancient Britons. You're an archaeologist manqué, Zig.'

Folding his arms in defence, Batten watched a tall, professorial man step onto a raised dais, draw the microphone closer and introduce himself as Dr Quinn, from The Council for British Archaeology. Batten controlled a secret envy. His jacket pocket held a shiny Roman pottery shard - Samian ware, 2000 years old, dug up from his Ashtree garden. He sometimes ran his fingers over it, to remind himself what a miniscule speck in history he really was. *We dig for evidence,* he'd often told the long-suffering Chris Ball, *so we're archaeologists for justice.* Lord knows, trying to unearth Luka Judd felt like archaeology.

The audience of forty or fifty listened avidly as Dr Quinn unpicked the findings of recent excavations on Ham Hill, illustrating his talk with dusty images of pits and sieves and measuring sticks. Cambridge and Cardiff University teams did the hard yards, Quinn was saying, on the most recent digs. Not recent in an archaeological sense, he joked, drawing dutiful chuckles from the audience.

With deft finger-clicks, he power-pointed photos across the screen, Batten paying less and less attention - until photographs of human bones began to appear in surprising, shocking quantity.

When the next slide flashed up, the audience took a collective breath. 'A thigh bone,' Finn explained. 'One of very many. And yes, these are knife-scoring marks, where this body - like the others - was almost certainly de-fleshed.'

De-fleshed triggered polite but concerned whispers in the audience. For an uncomfortable moment, Batten saw the slashed, gaping flesh of Lady Wake's fine horses. As more and more knife-scored bones filled the screen, Batten and Sonia looked at each other in puzzlement. Is this benign academic suggesting cannibals once roamed the trackways of ancient Somerset?

Quinn squashed the invisible thought. 'Instances of de-fleshing, one or two, *have* been unearthed on these shores, but the Ham Hill case is rare, and characterised by sheer quantity. Quantity of de-fleshed bones, that is.'

From the rear of the room a voice asked, 'If not cannibalism, what then? Even 2000 years ago, why would anyone choose to strip bodies of their flesh? Can we assume the bodies were already dead?'

'Best if we do,' said Quinn with a smile. 'Theories are problematic, because of course we have no documentation, no affidavits, no witness statements.'

Huh, Batten thought. *Sounds familiar.*

'We have bones and mass burials, yes, but little in the way of context. We know the invading Romans trounced our British ancestors and conquered Ham Hill, but evidence of the Romans de-fleshing their British foes is almost non-existent. If, as is likely, the Britons themselves were the culprits, then possible theories include revenge, yes, of the brutal kind. Revenge on a rival tribe, for example? Or a display of dominance over others? Or a warning to potential opponents?'

'Well, it's made me think twice,' said the voice from the rear, and the tent walls rippled with the nervous laughter of relief. Batten was thinking of Olly Rutter, an expert when it came to warnings, dominance – and revenge.

With a flourish, Quinn switched off the power-point display and in the new silence brought his lecture to a close. 'Archaeology is driven by our need to know,' he said. 'By our desire to unveil past secrets. In the case of Ham Hill, we know a large cache of bodies was buried there, and that their flesh had been removed, for whatever motive - the approval of friends perhaps, the dominance of foes, or to intimidate rivals? These killings were no secret 2000 years ago. But for us, until we unearth more evidence, a secret they remain.'

Batten stared at his idle hands as they added to the applause filling the tent. Quinn's words resonated only too well with his own investigation. Evidence. The past. Secret killings and secret motives. *Get digging,* he told himself, *even if the answers stick in your throat like a de-fleshed bone.*

Sonia nudged him with a gentle elbow - they were blocking the exit. 'Wake up, Zig,' she said. 'I didn't bring you here to fall asleep. And the Christmas lights won't untangle themselves.'

Moving along, he smiled back at her. *No, they won't,* he thought. *And neither will secrets.*

Thirty-three

Early starts didn't bother Susie Foreman, even on Monday mornings in winter darkness. Her old Mini's headlights threw weird shapes onto the bare trees as she drove from her house to the stables at Wake Hall. Though the back roads were deserted, she made sure to stay within the speed limit all journey long. *When your dad's a policeman…*

He's more than that, she thought. He's like a best friend, is Dad. And were he not tucked up in bed after a late shift, PC Jess Foreman might have agreed. He was proud as punch of his daughter, a fine young woman with a secure job she was happy to get up for in the mornings. Asleep or awake, he was pleased to have passed on his values. Patience. Application. Integrity. Concern for others – man, or beast.

To Susie's relief, she had not inherited her policeman father's physical robustness. Six-foot two in all directions was how his colleagues described him – with some truth. At nineteen, Susie was slim and lithe, though strong enough to quell a feisty horse if need be. She would have loved to ride to work on a four-legged friend, but her ancient red Mini did the job well enough. To get in the mood for Christmas, she'd dressed the seats and rear window with gold and silver tinsel which glittered against the gatepost lights as she drove through.

Sometimes she arrived even before the Yard Manager, Allie Chant, had finished her early morning rounds. She liked Allie, without envying the huge responsibility for enough stables to house a cavalry regiment. Susie was in charge of just one block, plenty for now.

Just before 7.30, still dark, she parked behind the stables in the staff area, grabbed her packed lunch from the passenger seat and her mucker-boots from the boot, and locked the car - not that she needed to. Wake Hall was a safe haven, for horse and human alike - Lady Wake's promise to all the staff, these days. And Lady Wake made sure you were trained for the job. The day after Susie passed her British Horse Society exams, she received a letter of congratulations from Her Ladyship - and a week later, a promotion from stable-girl to stable-block leader.

Slipping on her muckers, she walked herself and her lunch past a criss-cross of frosty tyre-tracks towards a strangely silent Block D, proud to be 'in charge' of its twenty fine horses - and especially proud to be trusted with Lady Wake's favourite horse, Maya, a beautiful, grey-maned Andalusian mare, whose every step, trot or gallop smacked of thoroughbred. Susie always mucked out Maya first, in case Her Ladyship wished to ride. Though only nineteen, she knew all about preferential treatment.

The trainee stable girls were due at eight, but Susie would make a start by herself. Maybe when she got home, dad - for once - wouldn't ask her if work was piling up, or at least remove the silly grin from his face when he said it. She guessed the automatic lighting must have failed because Block D remained in darkness as she approached. Fumbling in her pocket for her pen-torch and the stable key, she strode through unimpeded, surprised Allie Chant hadn't clicked the lock and checked the lights on her early morning rounds. But even Allie was allowed to be bleary-eyed before sunrise, or as Dad called it, 'sparrow-fart.'

When she threaded her way down the shadowed walkway dividing the stables into two banks of ten, Susie Foreman was still nineteen. And still nineteen when the sound of her boots on the wooden floor echoed past nineteen whickering horses to the stall at the far end, where the twentieth, Lady Wake's favourite - sleek-boned, grey-maned Maya, as stately as her owner - would be waiting. When she heard the eerie whine of the far gate, swinging on its hinges, and saw the wide-open stable door, Susie was nineteen still. Even when she heard not Maya's whinny of welcome, but a disturbing silence, nineteen she remained.

With the dullest, coldest thud, her packed lunch hit the ground and her tender years hit the sky when her eyes fell on the floor of the open stall. The stable's rubber matting stared back at her, its straw and shavings besmirched into crude, coarse shapes. Another crude, coarse shape lay atop the straw, a shape doomed to stay imprinted in Susie's skull, no matter how desperately she strove to erase it. There, in the half-dark, she gaped at the lumpen, twisted form, spattered with dark red stains that could only be blood. Taking in the red spatters on the stable walls she tasted her breakfast for the second time that day as a lead-heavy coldness froze her bones. Without asking permission, the foul and monstrous image invaded her.

Susie Foreman backed out of the stable, backed across the walkway and would have backed another hundred yards but for the opposite wall, which did at least support her as, in the gloom of early morning, she slid in horror to the cold wooden floor - and became much, much older than nineteen.

Thirty-four

In CID, Batten's habit was to arrive early at a suspect's home, when they were under-prepared for his questions. By the same logic, he collected an eager-looking Hazel Timms in good time for their Monday meeting and drove the pair of them to what he now called *The Hall of Secrets*. 'Maybe today you'll find a magic key,' Timms said, with early-morning optimism.

Batten doubted it. 'Find a key in that place, bet your life they've hidden the bloody door.'

Timms smiled at the Yorkshire cynicism she'd grown used to at Parminster HQ – and had begun to miss. They drove along back lanes, the bare branches of roadside trees speckled white with frost, and Batten hands cold on the steering wheel. 'New boots?' he said, flicking a finger at Timms' feet, clad in knee-high brown leather.

Still surprised her old boss even noticed, Timms assumed Sonia Welcome was successfully nurturing Batten's feminine side. She'd only met Sonia in her pathologist role - but liked her intelligence and, Lord knows, her welcome care for the dead. 'Yes,' said Timms. 'Last time, I had to watch where I put my feet. Can't be sure what you're stepping in at Wake Hall.'

'No,' said Batten. 'And it's never rose petals.'

His Yorkshire cynicism deepened when on the approach road they saw a police car turning into the *Official* car park. He and Timms shared looks of surprise. As they drew up on the *Visitors* side and peered across, Batten spotted Geoff Markham's green Vet's pick-up parked there. Nothing unusual about that, he thought, till beyond it he saw more police cars - and the familiar white shape of 'Prof' Andy Connor's Forensics van.

Timms' surprise turned to alarm when she sized up the implications. 'Zi-ig,' she said, first name terms still awkward, 'I don't see how I can be CID and private on the same day.' Struggling with his own ex-CID status, Batten sympathised - doubly so when Timms shrank down in the passenger seat in case a police colleague said *nice of you to drop in*.

With a silent curse, Batten removed his house keys from the car key fob. 'Ouch!' he muttered, as the split ring nipped his finger and a blood blister formed. He hoped it wasn't a bad omen. 'Let's keep you out of trouble,' he said. 'Here, drive my car back and shove the keys through my letterbox, I'll find my own way home. And, yes, keep your head down.'

When Timms drove off with relief, a bemused Batten was left standing in the car park, struggling to think of ways their business partnership could work. For now, he did the only thing possible - kept calm, carried on, and headed to the Hall's double doors and the so-far-uncancelled meeting with Avril, Oksana and *Her Ladyship*.

The door opened as he approached and Avril surprised him by stepping out, a padded coat adding to her dumpiness. Yes, a camera covering the entrance, he decided. She turned towards the stables, face grim, shiny black coat swishing, and beckoned him to follow. He looked back at the double doors. Either Lady Wake had stayed inside or was invisible.

Needing a heads-up he opened his mouth to ask, but Avril closed him down with a silent shake of her sheepskin glove, a reminder of how sharp and cold the day was. In curious silence they plodded beyond the white limestone façade to the vast landscape of stable blocks, yard after interlocking yard whickering with horse after horse. To Batten's surprise, no humans were to be seen or heard amid the grey-brown walls of blocks A, B or C, and when they turned towards block D they saw the reason why. Twin lines of police tape barred their way. Roughly tied to stanchions and gateposts, the blue and white tape twisted and flapped in the icy wind, as if trying to escape.

To the left of the block, uniformed officers had corralled a large crowd of disgruntled stable girls, sporting a multi-coloured mix of jodhpurs and mucker boots, rubbing their hands against the cold in lieu of throttling the uniforms. A collective white mist of breath wreathed up from the throng. To the right, stood a smaller group of mostly males - farriers, Batten guessed, though why was Pavel not amongst them? All glared at their police herders and wished to be anywhere but here. Wishing is a waste of time, Batten could have told them. Interviews and statements were now the order of the day - and whatever else Inspector Ball decided. Because Ball was trudging across the yard towards Avril and Batten, ginger hair tousled by the wind, with not a glimmer of a welcome smile on his face.

Batten had never seen his erstwhile Sergeant pursue his new role at what was clearly a crime scene - and at his most hated place in the world. The familiar loose jacket and trousers were gone, and Ball shuffled closer in a dark blue suit that needed breaking in.

'Madam. Sir,' he said. Not the habitual 'Sir' of Batten's old CID workplace, nor the tentative 'Sir' of their last *Parminster Cider Club* meeting, but the brisk, formal *Sir* of a policeman addressing the public. Well, Batten thought, that's put me in my place.

'We'll be interviewing all and sundry, by and by. No exceptions. I must ask you both to wait here, if you wouldn't mind?' A loitering uniformed PC made the request a formality. Ball turned to Avril. 'I was told Lady Wake was available?'

'Soon,' said a curt Avril. 'Her Ladyship arrived back very late last night.'

From where? thought Batten.

Ball's response was no more than a flick of his head. 'For now, you may like to get out of this wind,' he said, pointing at the lee of an adjacent barn.

Avril needed no second invitation, but Batten lingered, in hope.

Ball edged away, awkward, then returned and dropped his voice. 'You've seen the situation. It'll come as no surprise to hear there's been…shenanigans. In the stables. Well, in this one.' He pointed to the cordoned-off Block D, a tiny brick in the Estate's vast equestrian wall.

Having clocked Andy Connor's Forensics van and a clutch of police cars, Batten knew there'd been *shenanigans*. The parked Vet's van, more ominous now, made him shiver. He imagined Lady Wake's mascara bleeding down her cheeks when she learned more equine children had been attacked. 'How many?' he said, dropping into the shorthand he and Ball once used.

'Thankfully, just one,' said Ball.

Batten felt a false sense of relief – till horror boomed in his skull. Block D was where grey-maned Maya, Lady Wake's favourite Andalusian mare, was stabled. For a second, he was back in Bristol Prison, confronting the nasty look of pleasure on Olly Rutter's face, hearing the concealed threat in his iron-hard voice: 'The Witch ought to take better care of her *business.* Tut, tut. Whatever *next?*' Dropping his voice to a whisper, Batten said, 'Cut? Or dead?'

Ball peered back in surprise. 'Stone-dead,' he murmured, turning away.

Heart thudding, Batten touched his fingers to Ball's arm. 'Chris, for old time's sake, please tell me it's not the Spanish horse with the long grey mane?'

Eyebrows aloft, Ball said, 'Horse? It's not a bloody *horse*.' He swung an arm at the surrounding chaos. 'What planet are you on? Do you think we'd turn up mob-handed for a *horse*? It's a human. Or it used to be.' Grim, he strode away towards Block D, but when Batten tried to follow, the two pounds of sausage that Ball used as a hand stopped him in his tracks. 'This stable block's a crime scene now. Leave the *inspecting* to the police. *Sir*.'

Thirty-five

A told off schoolboy, Batten watched Ball's back disappear, then joined Avril in the lee of the barn, barely warmer than the open yard. His face was as pale as hers now, the icy wind only part of the reason. 'Want to fill me in?' he said, in hope.

Though not a hands-in-pockets sort of person, she thrust her gloved hands - tight fists now - into her coat. Her breath emerged as a white mist in the morning cold. 'Fill you in? I'm waiting for someone to fill *me* in. The police have everyone incommunicado. Allie Chant rang me, early. She was out in the pastures, in case of more horse-trouble, when young Susie Foreman rang *her*. In a state, she said, mostly garbled. Seems Susie had phoned her dad, asked him to come, pronto, and he's one of yours, isn't he? I'm saying to Allie, 'Phoned him about *what*?' when the line goes dead. Hopeless signal up there. And no signal at all when I tried ringing back. And yes, *of course* I tried more than once!'

'Susie phoned her dad? Phoned Jess?'

'Jess? Isn't that a woman's name? I always call him Mr Foreman - he picks her up sometimes.' Her mind a trampoline, Avril stared in a daze at Block D. 'When I tapped on Lady Wake's door there was no answer, so I got dressed and came here. But Allie was gone and there was only Mr Foreman. I could see Susie in his car, whiter than the frost, a rug or something wrapped round her. Yes, she'd phoned him, in a panic, he said. 'Panic about what?' I asked, fearing the worst, because of what happened before, to the horses - the paint, the poison and their poor flesh cut. My legs were jelly. You see, Susie looks after Lady Wake's favourite horse, Maya. Beautiful Maya.' She pointed across the yard. 'There, in Block D.'

Batten needed no reminder. Avril continued staring, bug-eyed, at the stable-block, the police tape flapping harder in the rising wind, a piercing whine zinging from its stretched surface. He followed her finger, frozen in time, still pointing beyond the tape to the tunnel of shadowy stalls. 'And Jess - PC Foreman - what did he say?'

She noticed her finger still in the air and thrust her hand back in her pocket. 'Say? *Nothing.* I tried to go to the stable, to see for myself. He blocked my way. Plenty of him to do the blocking, isn't there? Wouldn't let me go past so I shouted at him, *'Tell me!'* He just puts a giant hand on my arm and steers me back towards the Hall. 'Best you inform Lady Wake,' he says, big deep voice. She's not up yet, I told him, didn't get back till after midnight. 'Well,' he says, 'best you wake her.' Me, I laughed, couldn't help it, shock I suppose. Laughed in Mr Foreman's face at the thought of Lady Wake being *awake*. He looked at me as if I was demented. *Half*-awake, I told him. Hardly going to appear in her nightwear, is she?'

Putting out of his mind the image of Olly Rutter and Lady Wake in red silk 'nightwear', Batten pressed on. 'Jess Foreman must've told you *something*?' he said.

'*He* didn't. I staggered back past this very barn and spotted Allie Chant. She's the Yard Manager...' Avril was drifting again.

'No sign of Allie now,' Batten said.

'That po-faced Mr Foreman cordoned her off somewhere.'

Standard police procedure, Batten knew. Jess would have snaffled Allie Chant's phone, in case of collusion. And secured the scene and any witnesses - or suspects - as best a solitary off-duty constable could. But what scene was he securing? Batten looked for answers in the long lines of stable blocks, then again at Block D.

'In a blink more police arrived, and then more still. They took Allie away.'

'What? *Arrested* her?'

'*No*! To *grill* her. Like you're grilling me!' Hearing her own raised voice, Avril drew in her breath to calm herself. 'They commandeered the Feed Store.' The same glove emerged from her pocket and jabbed at the distance. 'Probably boiled the kettle and emptied the coffee jar by now. They took Allie and Susie in there. To explain what's gone on, I suppose. And you've seen the other staff, freezing their feet off, waiting their turn, when there's horses to be mucked out and fed and shod, and a mountain of work to do. Lady Wake will have a fit.'

'But did Allie tell you anything, before all that?'

With a grimace, Avril said, 'She couldn't. Poor woman was throwing up. That's why they let her out, I suppose. I had to wait, for decency's sake. Chalk-white, she was, and giving me the weirdest, piercing stare, as if she was demented – or looking at me as if she thought *I* was. Seems she got back from the pastures just before Mr Foreman arrived. Susie couldn't speak, she said, just pointed a shaking finger at Maya's stable. So Allie goes to look, doesn't she? And what she sees turns her stomach. When *he* rolled up and saw it he blocked the way and scooped up Allie. Then he's on his phone, and before you can say *horseshoe* there's one police car after another and big-booted uniforms milling around and it's five years ago all over again, a ghastly mess all over again, and of course it's me that will have to tell Lady Wake!'

Déjà vu, thought Batten - he was one of the big-booted police five years ago. And was Alibi-Olly pulling the strings this time too, with Luka's help, while both men were comfortably elsewhere? Batten wanted to throttle the pair of them.

'Why must it happen so near Christmas?' said Avril, banging a fist against the side of the barn and turning to go. 'I'd better chivvy along Her Ladyship. If your Inspector Ball asks why I've - what's it called, *fled the scene* - feel free to explain my absence. Or not. I'm past caring.'

'What will you tell her?'

Avril shrugged away the question. 'What *can* I tell her? Ma'am, the police are here, *again*, it must be Christmas! They request your urgent presence in the vicinity of Block D, where your favourite horse happens to be stabled?' Eyes flicking between the stable in question and the white limestone bulk of Wake Hall, garishly whiter in the morning frost, Avril faltered. Her black padded coat seemed to wilt around her, till she sucked in a long deep breath and re-formed herself into Avril-who-gets-things-done. 'Her Ladyship, alas, is highly intelligent. She won't need me to say much at all.'

But should Batten? *Don't worry, Avril, it's not a dead horse in Block D. It's just a dead human.* Given the events of five years ago, that would surely make things better. *Not.* Torn, he kept his mouth shut.

Maybe Ball was right. Leave the inspecting to the police. *Sir.*

*

Watching Avril's black coat trudge towards the Hall, Batten pulled his own waterproof tighter as Allie Chant emerged from the Feed Store. Her muddy jodhpurs tottered a safe distance away from anything flammable and, hands shaking, she slumped against the post-and-rail fencing to light a desperate cigarette. The smoke seemed to form words in the air: *So, arrest me!* When Allie flashed Batten a rueful shrug he thought she looked older. Despite hating the smell of cigarettes, he loped across.

'Been grilled, then?'

'Hmph. Grilled, kippered, *and* fried. Might as well get smoked too,' she said, between puffs. 'It's a bad dream. I've gone back five years, to the last time your lot rolled up. At least my jods were a size smaller then.'

Despite her pallor, Batten delved. 'Not a great morning, eh?'

But Allie Chant, nobody's fool, spotted his angle. 'The squat one in the new suit, he says I'm not to discuss the *events* with anyone. Colleagues. The press. *You*.'

'Are you sure our mutual employer would agree?'

'Thought she'd have turned up by now,' said Allie, between puffs on her cigarette. 'Be better if she didn't.'

Batten pointed at Block D. 'Because of that, you mean?'

Crushing her cigarette stub into the cold ground with a riding boot, Allie gave Batten another stare. 'You should take up smoking,' she said. 'That way, there'd be a gap between your questions.'

'Sorry. Paid to ask. By *her*.' He pointed at the distance. The dumpy shape of Avril Dean trotted a little behind the lithe figure of Lady Wake, decked out in a top-grade olive-green waxed jacket and hat, and pristine leather boots. Allie's muddy toe aimed a kick at the cigarette butt which skittered across the yard.

'I can't face another grilling,' she said. 'I'm making myself scarce.'

Before she could scoot away, Batten gently placed his hand on her arm. 'Believe me, I know what it's like when you walk in on a corpse.' Allie winced at the word and turned whiter still. 'And I wish I could tell you the image will disappear overnight, but it won't. All the same, that corpse is someone's daughter or son. So *please*, give me something to work with.'

Caught between Batten and the approaching Lady Wake, Allie mumbled, 'Son. It's someone's son. I'm allowed to tell you that much, I suppose.'

'Old, young, large, small? A stranger? Someone you recognised?'

At 'recognised', Allie froze, then flicked away Batten's hand. 'I'm saying nothing more,' she said, with a nod at the two approaching figures. 'Ask her, not me.'

Exasperated, Batten struggled to keep his voice calm. '*Her*? Lady Wake?'

'*No! Avril!* Nothing round here gets past Avril. If *she* can't say, then horses shit rainbows!'

With that, Allie Chant scuttled across the yard on a blast of icy wind. When Batten switched his gaze to the approaching Avril Dean, her face took on the unreadable expression he'd first encountered on Ham Hill mere weeks ago – though now it felt like a hundred years.

Thirty-six

At last, Batten's chance to tackle Avril with some serious questions - or must he to defer to Lady Wake, tug his forlock and apply for permission? About to decide, he turned towards the pair of them just as a parade of twitches - unmistakeably Sergeant Eddie Hick - flashed across his vision and intervened.

'Er, Madam, sorry, ma'am, er, Your Ladyship?' Lady Wake's diamond hard eyes sliced Hick in two. 'Inspector Ball, er, he requests your presence. Over in the Feed Store. Temporary HQ. For today, I mean.'

Despite wilting beneath Lady Wake's stare, Hick drew on his new authority and stood his ground, arm twitching in the requested direction. With a Morse Code glance at Avril Dean, Marianne Wake reluctantly complied, leaving Avril alone. *At last,* thought Batten, taking a pace towards her.

'You too, madam,' said Hick, his outstretched arm twitching faster still. With what Batten could have sworn was a look of relief, Avril trotted after her mistress to the Feed Store. Hick, winter coat half-undone, turned to Batten and dropped his voice. 'Sorry, er, sir, but the Inspector would like you to wait here a few minutes more. If you'd be so kind.' Hick's discomfort at giving instructions to his erstwhile boss blew away on the breeze. Voice almost a whisper, he said, 'We're short-staffed. Today, sod's law, Hazel's off and Nina's on - on maternity leave, I mean. Area's sending more troops, but…' Tired by the longer sentences, Hick jerked his shoulders into a shrug and careened his frame towards the marginally safer ground of his new Inspector.

Watching the bundle of twitches jolt out of sight, Batten remembered it was DC Nina Magnus who'd suggested Hick was part windmill, part wrecking ball. Now Nina Magnus was on maternity leave? Out of the loop, Batten had forgotten. Leaning against the old barn, a strong scent of manure in his nostrils, he tapped his frosty toes. Wait his turn to be on the wrong side of an interview table, *if you'd be so kind*? 'Sod that!' he muttered and slipped away towards the Official car park. His old Ford Focus wasn't allowed there, but no-one had banned his size nines.

Picking up pace, he ducked past clumps of camellia and viburnum and made a beeline for 'Prof' Andy Connor's Forensics van, crossing his fingers Andy was sitting in it, checking and recording juicy details - 'my data', as he mock-pompously insisted on calling them.

Alas, no Connor - presumably still at the scene. The on-duty pathologist, however, must have finished whatever grisly work today's body required, because the pathologist in question, leaning into the boot of a familiar Audi, was instantly recognisable. Dr Benjamin Danvers had ditched his crime scene suit and his brown hair was sticking up like a lightning rod where he'd shaken off the hood. Much relieved to confront Sonia Welcome's boss, rather than Sonia herself, Batten said, 'Allow me,' and smoothed Danvers' locks back into place.

'Why, thank you, Inspector. Most kind,' said Danvers, before correcting himself. 'Ah. Force of habit. Not Inspector. And if I'm allowed to say, *sadly* not?'

'You are, Doc. But I'm more interested in what else you're allowed to say.'

Danvers closed the boot with a loud click which Batten hoped wasn't metaphorical. 'Ah now, allowed to say? Mm. Not allowed to say much at all, to a member of the public. I should really have said, 'Good Morning' and driven away, yes?'

'Come on, Doc. You're here because there's a body. Male. Deceased.'

Over his spectacles, Danvers graced Batten with his wryest look. His distinctive tie, little stethoscope motifs etched into the cloth, rose and fell as he gave a mock-sigh. 'Only here five minutes and you already know. Not changed a bit, mm? Oh - apologies - apart from the…' Danvers wobbled a finger at the small but permanent lump on the back of Batten's skull. 'Trouble you still, at all?'

'I'm not here for a check-up, Doc, but thanks all the same.'

Danvers jangled his car keys. 'Oh, we both know why you're here. As I say, not changed a bit.'

'Then what about it, Doc? Old time's sake?'

Hand on the driver's door, Danvers paused in thought. 'What if I confirm the facts you already have? Will that serve?'

No! I don't have any! Batten improvised. 'Well, it's not Lord Lucan or Elvis Presley.'

'So I understand,' said Danvers, enjoying himself. 'But, assuming I had a name, you surely wouldn't expect me to provide it? Unless you happen to be next of kin, which I suspect you're not?'

'Relieved to hear it, Doc. So it's…someone in jodhpurs. Er, five foot nothing, and anorexic.'

Again the Danvers chuckle. 'Kitted out for rural pastimes, perhaps. But better-fed than your over-imaginative guess.'

'And not dead from natural causes?'

Danvers wavered, but only for a moment. 'Since the great British public will know before the day is out, I am able to more or less confirm that, yes.'

'OK. Cause of death. Not a shotgun?' Someone would have heard the noise - and reported it.

'*Correct!*' Danvers was in the driver's seat now, the door still open. Face beaming with wry pleasure, he slid the key into the ignition.

'For old time's sake?' Batten repeated.

'You know my ways, *Mr* Batten. Exact cause of death still to be decided. My slab awaits the doughty work of our underpaid body snatchers. Until Mr Body is placed reverently upon it, my trusty slab can offer few conclusions.' Before Batten could speak, he added, 'But no guns, no knives, no *exotica*.'

'Ah, blunt force trauma. Yes?'

'Ye-es.' Danvers started the car, his smile still wicked. 'And also *no*. Because blunt force trauma may simply be a trigger for other causes of death?' Danvers' eyes twinkled as the car door closed. Before driving off, he rolled down the window to enjoy - as ever - the final word. 'And speaking of blunt force trauma: do please look after that skull of yours. We are graced with but *one*, and further damage to yours is…inadvisable.'

The window rolled up and the Audi rolled away, the Doc gracing Batten with a final one-handed wave – like his flowery language, a deflective response to the stomach-churning impact of violence and death.

Thirty-seven

By the time Batten made it back to the barn where he was supposed to wait, Danvers' *underpaid body snatchers* had turned up – two stocky males, professional neutrality plastered onto their faces. But there was no way to hide the long trolley with its body bag, nor prevent the noisy trundle of its wheels on the pockmarked surface of the yard, a mixture of white rime and frost-hardened ridges of mud. The stable girls yet to be interviewed tracked every squeak and bump of its wheels, the youngest girl turning away, her face as blank as the *body snatchers*, and not from the cold.

Beyond the flapping lines of police tape, Batten spotted 'Prof' Andy Connor emerging from the white police tent now clothing the stable like frost. Slightly hunched frame unmistakeable even in a Forensics suit, he beckoned at the near distance and two tired-looking figures emerged from the direction of the Feed Store. Hick's twitches had frozen to a tight stillness, as they did in the vicinity of a corpse. Inspector Ball's new blue suit looked like he'd worn it to muck out a horse. Donning crime scene bootees, they disappeared into the police tent and Batten almost followed them, from habit. Instead, he did what he hated most: he waited.

The white police tent walls billowed in and out, as if breathing – unlike the large male corpse recently removed. 'Confirmed now, Prof?' asked Ball.

'His ID, you mean, or his relationship to the world of the living?'

'*Prof*,' said Ball, reverting to one-word sentences. Frazzled and short-handed, he was in no mood for deflection, not even from cider-drinking chum Andy Connor.

'Sorry, Chris. I can only repeat what three living souls have told you. The Yard Manager whose name I've forgotten, and Avril Dean, they both concurred, separately. Then Her La-de-da-Ladyship said the same - and who's going to argue the toss with *her*? All three either genuinely gobsmacked or Oscar-winning actors. Tears a-plenty. Be no surprise if they're still flowing?'

Ball nodded. 'We've had to give them a break. More to tell maybe, but none of them seem to know why the deceased turned up unannounced in the middle of the night and ended up dead on a stable floor. Interesting, though?'

'*If* it's who they say it is. No wallet, no driving licence - and, gosh, clever me, I even remembered to check the lining of his coat. Maybe Fingerprints will reveal if our three Equine Graces are spinning a line. I get the impression if Lady Wake says Monday's Thursday, then Thursday it is.'

'That I *can* confirm' said Ball, assuming the deceased arrived without ID to confuse any Security staff he might bump into. Or maybe some sidekick emptied his pockets post-mortem - for much the same reason. But ending up dead on a stable floor? 'Is the Doc any more certain about time of death?'

'Danvers? Certain? What world are you liv-'

'*Prof. No.*'

Connors raised his hands in apology. *I keep thinking I'm talking to sarky Zig Batten.* 'It's still what he told you. Sometime between 2 and 4am, give or take. You know, cold night.'

'Cold or not, night deliveries don't stop for winter – unless the Yard Manager's also spinning us a line.'

Sergeant Hick thought if he didn't speak, they'd demote him. 'Er, boss, I checked her transport diary – plenty of night deliveries. But none for *last* night…'

'So one turned up unexpected - and left a pile of manure for *us*. Trace evidence, Prof?'

'There's always trace, Chris.'

'Useful?'

Connor shook his head. 'Nothing yet, apart from the obvious.' He pointed at the red splatters on the stable walls. 'Might look like blood but it's not. Even you two noticed, eh? Red paint, which I shall analyse forthwith. In splodges, but no clue how it got there. A fair bit on the dead man's torso and face but from the angles, he was likely prone when it splashed him. Poor Susie Foreman, she walked in unsuspecting, thought she saw a blood-covered corpse. And by the way, short-staffed though you are, if you're done with Susie it'd be a kindness to let her dad take her home?'

'Already offered, but typical Jess, he said no, too much to do. Mrs Foreman's on her way.' Ball tried to stem a yawn but failed. 'Sorry, Prof. Anything else?'

Chris Ball's struggling, thought Connor. Yes, too much to do. 'Well, not a single label on the body's togs, including the black ski-mask. His latex gloves are bog-standard but speaking volumes. And when we managed to turn him over - God knows what it must've cost to feed the poor sod - these were in his back pocket.' Connor drew two labelled evidence bags from his case, a single piece of white paper in each, and held them up. 'I'll send digital copies. This one looks like numbers in some sort of pattern. The other's just strings of digits – not phone numbers, according to my SOCOs, so don't bother ringing.'

Ball and Hick peered at them. 'Combination to a safe?' said Hick. 'Or next week's National Lottery results?' When Ball flashed daggers, Hick reverted to Sergeant Serious. 'I asked Danvers about cause of death. He gives me a funny look, mumbles something about maybe a horse did it. What bloody horse, Prof? Body was in this empty stable.'

Connor was half-listening, his focus on Chris Ball's pallor. Was Ball cut out for the stress of senior leadership? Another fine Sergeant succumbing to the Peter Principle? As if sensing the thought, Ball said, 'He told me the same. Not much help, as usual, the Doc.'

'He was waiting to compare data with jolly old *me*. Those contusions on the body's chest - you saw them - well, me and the Doc have seen similar elsewhere. Early reddish bruises displaying as two overlapping shapes? And looking for all the world like the imprint of a pair of horseshoes? We're moderately certain that's what they are.'

'Horseshoes?' said an incredulous Hick. 'What, a *horse* gave this bloke a kicking?' A *horse*?'

'Ever been kicked by a horse?' said Connor. Hick twitched a *no*. 'Then don't be. Metal shoes and 600 pounds of muscle. Remember Newton's Third Law of Motion – action and reaction are equal and opposite?' Hick, bemused, looked to his Inspector for help, and got a tired shrug. 'Sergeant, if a 600-pound horse kicked the deceased, he'd have recoiled across that stable like he was shot from a gun. And a powerful two-hooved kick in the chest? It's where he kept his heart, and the Doc seems to think he did have one - before it permanently stopped. Cardiac arrest, most likely. And before I have one too, I'll take my leave and go dibble-dabble my *data*.'

As Connor left, Sergeant Hick dragged a weary hand through his hair. 'Is someone taking the piss, boss? The stiff turns up unannounced in the middle of the night, in latex gloves and a mask, yeh? No ID but a jumble of numbers in his back pocket? Then he's kicked to death by a horse, before getting splodged with red paint? And the invisible bloody horse, I suppose he made a break for it?'

'*She*,' said Ball. 'This stable belongs to a mare called Maya, so I'm told.' He had interviewed Lady Wake and was still recovering. 'Maya, the nag in question, happens to be the priciest horse on the Estate - Her Ladyship's personal ride. Not that she knows where it is right now.' Ball remembered the sudden ghostly tightness shackling Lady Wake's face when told Maya was missing. And the sharp silence as she closed her eyes and turned away. 'Her parting comment, through gritted teeth, implied I'd be more use if I galloped off to look.'

'Huh. Killer horse on the run,' mumbled Hick. 'What a bloody start to the week.'

'Maybe on the run, Eddie,' said Ball. 'Maybe abducted. We could be looking at suspicious death *and* theft.'

Hick wished he knew what they were looking at. 'So if the stiff arrives with theft in mind, boss, and ends up a corpse, is it accident, manslaughter, murder, or what?'

Ball blew out his breath. 'Till we get the Doc's report, or our missing mare canters back for an interview, I suppose it's 'or what'. Anything on CCTV?'

'Up next,' said Hick, 'Ben Somebody, the Wake Hall Security man, he's taken his time getting here – *and* he doubles as Health and Safety, so I've low expectations.'

'Low expectations but plenty of work,' said Ball, staring in thought at the red paint splattered on the empty stable walls. The tent becoming claustrophobic, he stepped out into the cold light of morning, still wondering why *Nightwatch Security* had failed to live up to its name.

*

Batten watched Andy Connor's back grow smaller as it headed for the car park. About to follow, hoping to pick *data* from Andy's brain, he saw Ball emerge from the police tent, remove his crime-scene bootees and glare in his direction. Not the best time to ask an overworked cop who the body was.

Blue suit merging with the cold blue sky, Ball mumbled something to Hick and disappeared in the direction of the Feed Store. Hick twitched towards his old boss, a sheepish look on his face.

'Sorry for keeping you, er, Zig. The Inspector says under the circs, best if you, er, if you disappeared. Uniform, er, a uniformed officer, will make contact, routine, take your statement. And the like.'

'Oh, Eddie, thank God I'm not a suspect,' said Batten, trying to lift Hick's mood.

'No, no, of course. Just…a lot to do, here, right now. And not enough bodies.'

'Unfortunate choice of words?'

'What? *Oh, sugar! Bodies!* Rotten day. Bloody rotten, all round.'

'I'll be my charming self with uniform, Eddie, worry not.' Still worrying, Hick twitched away. '*Eddie!*' Batten called after him. '*Get some sleep!*'

Whether Hick heard or not, made no difference. Sleep was the last thing the Sergeant and his Inspector would get tonight.

*

With no sign of Avril Dean or Lady Wake anywhere near the stables, Batten turned for the Hall - just as his phone rang. It was Sonia.

'Zig? I've just had a strange call from Andy Connor, on the land line. He wanted to leave a message for you, and when I suggested he ring your mobile he said, '*definitely not*' – his very words. Haven't fallen out, you two?'

'You're still at home, Sonia?' Batten wished *he* was.

'Yes, Zig. Paperwork. About to leave.'

'Andy's message?'

'Bizarre, really bizarre. You're to pick him up from his house, tonight, but not till it's dark, and only from the back door. That's it. Why the cloak and dagger, Zig?'

Batten had a vague idea, but explanations could wait. 'Tell you later, love,' he said. 'A funny day, that's all.'

A funny day? He pocketed his phone. Nothing *funny* about today at all.

Thirty-eight

Manny McRory banged his head against the steering wheel of the 4x4. By no stretch of the imagination could his night be described as *funny*. A short, wiry man of limited vocabulary, he nevertheless had a piercing Scouse voice. '*FUCK!*' he cursed, aloud, with no-one to hear him in the blackness of the abandoned field. '*FUCK AND FUCKUN' FUCK!*'

That crazy nutcase should be hearing him, that giant crazy nutcase whose bulging frame *should* have been spilling over the edges of the passenger seat - and who *should* have carried out Olly Rutter's grisly instructions. *Nab Lady Muck's posh horse, carve her up, and plant the shaved head on a pole where the Witch can't miss it!*

A horse-guy from his flat cap to his jodhpurs, Manny had no stomach for carving up a nag. His oppo though, cuh. Manny called him *FUG – Fucking Unfriendly Giant*, though never to his face. The giant's butchery kit sat unused on the back seat – stun-gun, meat-saw, hatchet, knife a foot long. '*FUCK!*' Manny repeated, despite escaping from Wake Hall without *his* head on a pole. He *told* Olly not to use Fug because the bloke really *is* a certified nutcase. Or used to be. Prepared and careful, that was Manny. But Fug? Fugged up the plan! *I knew he would!* That's why I reminded him, twice…

'Norra sound, OK? I reverse the trailer, air-gun the security lights, while you do the locks, ar-right?'

'Yeh, yeh. I'm not a goldfish. I've got a memory.'

Manny had nodded, even smiled at Fug. Always that, slow, deep voice, unchanging, so you could never tell what mood he was in. 'I drop the tailgate and you gerra head-collar on the nag. Then I squirt the red paint while you get horsie up the ramp. Don't forget, you gorra lock the tailgate behind her. Once I start the engine, we scarper. Gorrit?'

'*Gorrit* before, Manny. Not suggesting I'm a dope, are you?'

Confronted by the *Fucking Unfriendly Giant's* potato face, and two giant fists planted on his hips, Manny muttered, 'Course not.'

But he *was* a dope, was Fug. A man who knows horses, but stands behind one? Serves the bastard right - got kicked for being *dopy*. Manny came out in a sweat when he remembered the rest of it…

...All going to plan, slide into the stable yard - used to run *Wake Hall Horse* in the good old days, when Olly was in charge, could find that stable in a blindfold. Kill the security lights, do the locks, head-collar on, tailgate down, and I'm in the cab for the paintball gun when WHACK! – and when you're around horses, you know the meaning of a noise like WHACK. I rush to see, and bloody Fug's clutching his chest and staggering back into the stable while poncy Maya's sniffing the hay net stuffed with apples and carrots and dancing up the ramp to tuck in.

Quiet as I can, I sneak up, close the tailgate and lock it behind her. Then it's grab the paintball gun from the cab and go sort *Fug* in case someone heard the crunch of hooves on idiot. He's flat out on the stable floor by the time I get there, straw and muck all over the place and behind the ski-mask the crazy bastard's eyes are blank and his lips are turning blue. When I feel for a pulse there's nothing, not a whisper, and I'm not giving the big sod the benefit of *my* lips on his kisser and anyway it's panic time by then and I've still got the red paint to squirt - Olly's orders, and that means *do it*. I'm so lathered up there's red paint everywhere and some hits Fug, but he doesn't notice, does he? Checked his pockets just in case and, nice surprise, find his brown envelope stuffed with readies, so I grab that too, stash it with mine. Earned a double bonus, didn't I, fuck's sake?

Tried turning the big bastard, nearly give myself a hernia. He could've picked me up under one arm and slung me in the cab, but I can't budge him and anyway the clock's ticking and it won't stay dark forever.

I get going, fast, and at least the posh horse is quiet in the trailer, munching on treats. I make good time out of Wake Hall, and five miles on I pull in, to the abandoned field with the high hedges where Fug's supposed to butcher the horse.

And I'm still bloody here!

Manny McRory banged his head on the steering wheel again. This would be the third time he'd fucked up one of Olly Rutter's schemes. The last two, he'd ended up inside, saying *no comment* and sod all else. Olly paid big bucks - but zipped lips are part of the deal. And the man's a bloody octopus, tentacles everywhere.

But if I get caught again - posh horse as evidence and a blue-lipped giant left behind in a stable, can I face a third stint in the slammer? And,

Jesus wept, Fug's nasty toolkit's still on the back seat. Supposed to scalp the mane off the fucking horse and stash it, for later. Typical Olly - *Gonna send it to Lady Muck forra Christmas present.*

Lifting his head from the steering wheel, Manny saw the night slowly edge towards dawn. A strange mixture of emotions came over him. He liked Andalusian horses, had ridden a few, liked their sleek beauty and, yes, those long grey manes, flying in the breeze. But he wasn't going anywhere near *this* one – crazier than the Fucking Unfriendly Giant, and with a double-strength kick. What if he just unhitched the trailer and left it here? Someone was sure to find the nag. And it's not as if Lady Wake's feathers would go unruffled, not with her posh horse gone and a stone-dead *Fug* replacing her. Manny almost laughed at the thought of big-booted coppers clomping all over Wake Hall *again*. Plenty enough for him.

But for Olly Rutter? Huh. Never enough for bloody Olly. Beyond the windscreen, the high dark hedge loomed like a prison wall. Manny made up his mind. He wouldn't - couldn't - do a third stint inside. *For-gerrit!*

With rare resolve, and still in his latex gloves, he unhitched the stolen trailer, removed the false plates, and gathered up each suspect item from the 4x4, back seat and front. Into a sack it all went, and into the furnace soon. Not long after, the crusher would make the 4x4 disappear - and leave Manny in the clear.

He laughed, grimly. In the clear? From *Olly Rutter?* Need to put plenty of distance between the hairy ape's tentacles and Manny's wiry frame. Overseas this time? Maybe Spain? Horse country, Spain. Safer. And a useful connection there.

Before starting the engine, he dreamed up a tale to feed *Alison-Bloody-Handbag*, the cut-out between Manny, and the other shmucks…

…I grabbed the horse, but not before the horse clobbered Fug. That nutcase fucked up everything and got himself topped into the bargain - and there's only so much *one* man can do…

Would that satisfy Olly? Not in a million years. Manny added a touch of gloss.

…Crazy friggin' horse had a kick at me too, but I did the red paint, got the horse in the trailer and snuck away, despite a bruise the size of my arse and a dodgy leg. Have to lie low, can't risk A&E, in case the cops come looking. Don't worry, the car's in the crusher and all the evidence up in smoke...

As Manny started the engine, he heard the posh horse hammering her metal hooves against the unhitched trailer's sides. Plenty of oomph, that mare - like her bloody owner. And it could've been me, he thought, shuddering at Fug's dead eyes and the blue sheen on his lips. Maya's hooves still battered at the locked tailgate as Manny drove away. Someone'll find her, he told himself. And any reward's better than a kick in the chest...

By the time Manny Mcrory trundled from farm tracks to the reassurance of a tarmacked road, his breathing was back to normal. One small wiry man, alone, he'd achieved more than should be expected - and cleaned up all the mess.

As he turned onto the A303 and freedom, his whistles of relief were premature. It was still pitch-black when he cleared the back seat, and he failed to notice Fug's butcher's knife, vinegar-sharp, slide from the car as if it had a life of its own and nestle in the long grass. And in Fug's back pocket sat two flimsy sheets of paper. White scraps, vague numbers scrawled on them...but spelling serious trouble for Olly Rutter, should the police ever work out what they meant.

Thirty-nine

I ought to bill Her Ladyship for shoe leather, Batten thought, as he slogged towards the Hall, past what felt like an entire planet of stables. The ground frost was melting now, the track slippery underfoot. *This whole bloody place is slippery underfoot*, he muttered, totting up what little he knew. A body, male, dead, and not from natural causes. And Pavel Ducek still nowhere to be seen…

To his surprise, not Avril but Oksana Brok opened the double doors to him, and when he saw her pallor his fears for Pavel rocketed. The anteroom felt gloomy even in the white light of morning. Stepping into the cavernous hall, he was dwarfed by a full-height Christmas tree decked with glass baubles, fairy lights and shiny gold horses, incongruous beneath the sombre grey faces in the family portraits on the walls. He half-expected them to scream down at him: *Use the tradesman's entrance, you peasant!*

'Any updates?' he asked, keeping his words vague, not daring to ask about Pavel. 'I got next to nothing from the police.'

'Two of us, then. I can't remember a more confusing day since…' She closed her eyes briefly, as if to shake away the memory of her brother's disappearance, and Pavel's life-shaking flight to Spain. 'Best if you talk to…' She waggled her fingers at the trompe l'oeil door that was really a door.

Another one at Wake Hall saying *next to nothing*, thought Batten, raising his eyebrows in appeal.

'I'm in the dark,' she replied, her shoulders rising and falling. 'Today *began* as normal, but now, it's all confusion. And Pavel…I can't raise him…'

Batten choked off the possible reason why Pavel couldn't be raised. 'Surely Avril told you *something*?'

'*Something*? That Maya is gone? That a dead body was found in her stable? Does that count as *something*?' She took an apologetic breath. 'Even Allie Chant is saying nothing. Allie's never ill but went home with a migraine. Lady Wake staggered in, barely able to speak. She and Avril disappeared next door, two ghosts.' Oksana threw both hands at the sky. Frustrated, Batten strode towards the portal of the Hall of Secrets.

'Oh, no, I'm supposed – you're supposed to ask before you…'

Too late. Batten was through the trompe l'oeil door and striding down the carpeted walkway to Avril's office. He knocked, waited two seconds, and went in. The room was empty, and to his surprise, Avril's black padded coat was not hanging neatly on the back of her chair but discarded on the floor like a small black corpse.

The sight of it almost stopped him heading to Lady Wake's private domain, but he steeled himself, the sprung carpet almost bouncing him down the long corridor. Knocking and waiting, having seen Avril do the same, he opened the *portal* and stood in the doorway.

Lady Wake, alone, eyes closed, was slumped at her walnut desk, its pristine surface marred by a single white tissue, crumpled and stained. It had done little to stem the ruined make-up streaming down her cheeks. Her back was turned away from the infinite fields of horses where all but one of her equine children grazed - and from the nearest field in particular, empty now, its sweet grass forlorn. Whether she sensed his presence or heard his intake of breath, she opened her eyes and slowly turned toward him. Not diamond hard now, her eyes, but two sad orbs in a face more grey than white.

Batten wished he'd stayed outside.

With the slightest shake of her head Lady Wake silently conveyed *Not now*. Her haughty expectation of deference was gone, and he could almost read in her eyes a plea not for privacy, but solace. He hovered, unsure how to comfort an aristocratic employer – or if he was allowed to. With a nod of genuine sympathy, he withdrew, closing the door almost soundlessly behind him.

Beneath the jarring lights of the Christmas tree, neither Oksana nor Avril were anywhere to be seen, the place a cavernous courtroom, a whole jury of dead eyes staring down from the faded portraits on the walls. *What do I do now?* Only late morning but his presence clearly unwanted, here and at the stables.

He compiled a list of other people who might talk to him. Allie Chant came top but had fled the field, Susie Foreman too. Would Ben Roche, the HS&S officer be responsive, despite neither Health, Safety nor Security earning any brownie points today? The relevant tapes from Ben's CCTV system would by now be in an evidence bag, but maybe Ben had viewed them, and might cough up what he saw? Batten shuffled through the ante-room and softly closed the tall double doors behind him, feeling like a footman on unpaid overtime.

As soon as he stepped into the maintenance workshop, it was clear the police had pulled no punches with Ben, slumped against the workbench, young face scarlet with anger. '*Huh,*' he moaned, 'they know more about me now than I know myself. Implied it was *my* fault, this stables business. And that twitchy Sergeant - *Why weren't the new security cameras installed? You ordered them, didn't you? Why the delay?*'

Batten was asking himself the same questions. 'It's routine, Ben. The police have to check.' Sliding into the chair next to Ben's, he kept his voice as sympathetic as hypocrisy would allow. 'They're just eliminating you from their enquiries,' he said, while not eliminating Ben from his. 'A delay, is that right?'

Young but not stupid, Ben Roche spotted Batten's angle and narrowed his eyebrows – and his voice. 'I have the invoice, if you'd like to see? The *police* wanted to. I ordered infra-red cameras two weeks ago, hard disk recorder, colour monitors, the lot, and *Nightwatch Security* agreed to fit them before the weekend. But the brackets didn't arrive in time – so they said. *Tomorrow,* they said.'

Well, well, thought Batten, what a coincidence. 'But the old cameras? Too dark for them?'

'Too dark for detail,' said Ben. 'Prehistoric, black-and-white VHS, can you believe it? And anyway, your twitchy Sergeant took the tapes. He gave me a receipt. You can watch *that* if you like?'

Ben's sarkier than me, thought Batten. Guessing Hick's response if he asked for a shuftie at the tapes in question, he regrouped and tried a different tack with Ben. Nodding at the mugs and coffee jar by the workbench, he said, 'You look like a man who needs a coffee-break.'

'I must be a mirror,' said Ben, but with a faint smile he filled the kettle and switched it on. As Batten spooned coffee into mugs, Ben did some regrouping of his own. 'Sorry for being a grump,' he said. 'That Sergeant made me feel like a plonker. And I'm still naïve enough to think you're innocent till proven guilty.'

Batten nodded. *Nightwatch Security* will be thinking the same right now, he guessed, glancing at his watch. *The golden hours* – what the police called the first day of a suspicious death, when the body is cold but memories warm. Those hours were ticking away, fading into the air like steam from Ben's kettle.

Batten handed over a mug - *When Life Happens, Coffee Helps* stamped on its side – and Ben Roche regrouped some more. With a wry smile reminiscent of Doc Danvers, he said, 'Of course, they didn't ask about the back-up tapes. Sergeant What's-his-name can imply I'm useless at security, but I'm not. There's no sound, but you can watch them, if you like?'

With a chuckle of surprise, Batten clinked his cup against Ben's – and they sat at the console to view the tapes together…

As a horse trailer silently reversed towards Maya's stable, Batten imagined Hick's irritation at the fuzzy images – though the unreadable number plates were sure to be false. Two shadowy figures emerged from a 4x4, wearing what looked like ski-masks. From their profiles as they lowered the trailer's ramp, Batten assumed two males, up to no good.

Quick and wiry, the smaller of the two pointed what looked like a thin stick at the twin security lights. Soundlessly, in turn, the lights went out and the images grew fuzzier still.

The second man, little more than a shadowy giant, loped into the stable. Half-obscured, the camera picked up the neck and head of a long-maned horse, jerking and baulking, then disappearing up the ramp into the trailer. The wiry man seemed to react to something before dashing into the stall. When he emerged, the giant didn't.

Movements quicker now, even frantic, the small man locked the trailer's tailgate then reached into the 4x4 for what looked like another stick, a gun maybe, thicker and shorter. Batten froze the frame, and Ben tweaked the image as best he could. One of the vets suggested red paint was splattered on the horses with a paint ball gun - could this be what Batten was seeing?

Whatever, when the short man scurried back into the stable, thirty seconds of dead tape followed before he emerged again, dashing for the 4x4, stowing the gun - if that's what it was - and clambering into the driver's seat. Almost immediately, he drove away, without headlights.

And without the slow giant.

'Could you play it again?' asked Batten, almost certain where he'd seen that gait and those wiry movements before, five years ago, perhaps. And the wiry man's identity - Batten was almost certain of that too.

'I can do better. I can make you a copy – on condition you leave me less in the dark than these tapes.'

'Agreed,' said Batten, 'if you throw in a copy of that plumber's van coming and going, the day Oksana Brok's keys went AWOL, and someone burgled her cottage?'

'Ah,' said Ben, cottoning on. 'There's a connection?'

Batten paused for thought. Both crimes had the stamp of Olly Rutter and Luka Judd. 'There *might* be a connection. Need to compare the tapes, so…?'

'OK, a copy of each - with the same proviso?'

They sealed their agreement with a clink of coffee mugs. Ben Roche's rotten morning was beginning to improve, Batten's too, when he slid the copies into his new leather messenger bag, a gift from Sonia. With a cheerier thank-you, he set off for the car park.

Halfway there, he slapped himself on the forehead.

Hazel Timms had borrowed his car.

Forty

On the far fringe of Parminster, in darkness, at precisely 7pm, 'Prof' Andy Connor sneaked from the rear porch of his newly-thatched longhouse – a fully renovated dwelling Batten could only envy. Old woolly hat concealing his thinning hair and half his face, Connor stowed his overcoat in the back of Batten's Ford and sneaked his dark-clad body into the passenger seat. Once hunkered down, he muttered, 'Drive, Zig,'

'Drive where, Prof?' GCHQ? You're dressed like a spy.'

'*The Black Horse*, fast as is legal.'

'*The Black Horse?* Haven't we had enough of horses? And it's a dive. No-one goes *there*. Not even criminals.'

'Exactly. On the day a suspicious death pops up, I can't afford to be seen with the likes of you. All shall be explained…'

'Last pimped before the Boer War,' said Connor, staring at *The Black Horse's* peeling paintwork. Over the windows and doors, strips of tired Christmas tinsel made the place more funereal than festive. In a gloomy corner of the back bar Connor slid two pints onto a scarred tabletop held together with dirt, his language playful but his face deadly serious. 'There's trouble at t'mill, Zig. Isn't that what you Yorkshire folk say?'

'Never said that in my life, Andy. Cut to the chase?'

'I'd rather not *be* at the chase, Zig. And if anyone asks, I never was, right? But kindly apply your grey matter to the problem of Chris Ball and our esteemed bloody Wallingford.'

Batten inwardly groaned. Area Superintendent Wallingford was the Scrooge of the Somerset Force, quick to claim credit for other people's work and even quicker with a balance sheet. 'Don't tell me, Chris has had a run-in with him?'

'Not a bit of it. Chris's trouble is he doesn't do run-ins, though he'll have to learn. It's far worse. I'm not supposed to know, but since I'm a magnet for *data*…' Connor sampled his pint, pulled a face, and shuffled his chair closer. 'Ever wondered why Wallingford was lightning-quick to sign off your departure, invalidity pension and all?'

'*Efficiency*, Prof. His favourite word.'

'Huh. And why he was lightning-quick to nudge Chris Ball into your vacant seat, on a *'temporary acting'* basis?'

'Andy, my beer's flat enough already. Just spout, will you?'

'He's a devious bastard, Zig. To save more pennies he's trying to close down Parminster for good. His dream's a central Area Force covering the whole county – based many a mile from our neck of the woods, mind. A yokel bloody Flying Squad, with him in charge! So, he rapidly gets rid of you, and sneakily bungs inexperience in your place.'

'Chris Ball's had plenty experience, Prof. More than twenty years.'

'And none of it as an Inspector. I watched him at Wake Hall. He'll get there, given time, but right now the poor sod's struggling.'

With a wary sip of his beer, Batten realised he'd noticed too. He caught up. 'Chris is Wallingford's excuse? A new Inspector, new Sergeant, a bit green, so they make mistakes? Then the bastard claims they're a waste of money, and closes Parminster down - for *efficiency*?'

'That's about the size of it. Quick to sign off Hazel Timms' request for part-time, wasn't he? And when Nina Magnus lined up her maternity leave, well, the sourpuss sod must've come dangerously close to smiling.'

'But he's got to bring someone in, to cover for Nina. There *are* rules, Andy.'

'Dream on, Zig. This is Wallingford, not Mother Theresa. He's promoting PC Lee to *temporary acting* Detective Constable.' Connor warily sipped his pint. 'Did you slip cyanide in this beer when my back was turned?'

Batten smiled not at Connor but at the remembered face of PC Jon Lee, or 'Choirboy' as he was known. Pushing thirty now, but still a poster boy for the joke about policemen getting younger. 'Jon Lee's helped CID before, Prof. He's youthful, but no dolt.'

'Nor is he Superman. Nor experienced. Wallingford wouldn't have the nerve with you in the chair, Zig. But Chris…' Andy Connor shivered over his beer. 'Left my coat on your back seat. That'll teach me to assume the invention of heating had reached *The Black Horse*.'

'Sod the heating, Prof. What do expect me to do about Wallingford? You already reminded me I've been pensioned off, thank you very much.'

'Convergence Theory, Zig-'

'*Prof…*' said Batten, in his warning voice.

'Tuh, forgot you're a lesser mortal. Look, Chris and Hickie converge on Wake Hall, right? And you converge too because you're working for her divine Ladyship - who, despite a distaste for size-twelve police boots on her manicured lawns, will turn bright purple when she learns the nearest public-servant-detective will soon be a million miles away on the other side of Somerset? Luckily for us, she happens to know the Chief Constable - more convergence, hint-hint. On top of that, isn't the unsolved past still hovering at Wake Hall, waiting to converge?'

'The Tractor Thief murder?'

'The very same. And unless my jungle drums are off-key, a Wake Hall corpse might stir that particular pot? Oksana Thing might not want it stirred, in case her dodgy brother floats to the surface, but the pot's full of *summat*. Wake Hall's ripe for a great big spoon, seems to me. That's plenty convergence, which has the handy habit of converging into commonality.'

'Prof, just speak English, will you?'

'I did, you peasant. *Commonality*. In crowds, Zig, individuals converge - and find *common goals*...Get your tongue in Her Ladyship's ear, metaphorically speaking, so she gets hers in the Chief Constable's. But for God's sake share what you have with Chris Ball. He knows stuff you don't and, knowing you, there's a vice-versa. Put your stubborn heads together, the pair of you. A worthwhile common goal would be getting Parminster CID to show its mettle. And screwing Wallingford's plans would tickle the rest of us - *efficiently!*'

A worthwhile common goal, thought Batten, taking refuge in his flat beer, sour enough to keep an army alert, never mind an ambivalent ex-detective. What exactly was Batten supposed to do? Turn up at HQ, pretending to report a missing cat?

'Well?'

'Problem is, Prof, Chris was keen to point out I'm an outsider now. Not sure how to *converge*.'

'Then find a way, and quick, before Wallingford pins us all to a balance-sheet, like euthanised bloody butterflies.' Connor sipped beer, grimaced, and peered round the gloomy bar-room. 'In old British movies, there's always an aspidistra in a big pot, where the hero - that's me - dumps his undrinkable beer.' He pushed the half-full glass along the chipped table. 'My professional knowledge of toxins prevents me from swallowing this. And since my work is done, drive me home, Jeeves!'

Despite Connor's mock levity, the return trip was sombre. Batten pondered ways and means with his brow furrowed. The Prof did the same, beneath a ridiculous woolly hat. When they reached the house, Andy opened his mobile and told Batten to open his. 'Switch on your camera, Zig, if you'd be so kind?'

Connor took Batten's phone and photographed two images on the screen of *his* phone. 'I left the phone on my desk, Your Honour, taken short, you know how it is, and while I'm in the lav, someone copied what was on my screen!' His smile disappeared. 'Couldn't risk sending these funny numbers direct,' he said. 'Found in the dead man's back pocket. See what you make of them. Chris Ball's stumped at the mo, and so are we all.'

With that, he retrieved his winter coat, poked his head through the driver's window and lowered his voice. 'And I think something fell out of my coat, Zig,' he said. 'Might've landed on your back seat, thought I heard a thud. Might be a file full of *data*. Might help you *converge*.'

Batten stared, open-mouthed, at the 'Prof', but before he could speak, Connor said, 'For your eyes only, right? And it didn't come from me.'

'Prof, you're a-'

Connor's hand forestalled him, his serious voice whispering, 'Zig, this is *once-only*, for Chris. And I mean it.' Without waiting for an answer, the Prof crept into the shadow of his rear porch and disappeared.

When Batten viewed the snapshots on his phone, two random puzzles of numbers stared back at him. No wiser, he revved away, the 'misplaced' file teasing and tingling from the back seat, almost drilling a hole in his damaged skull.

Forty-one

The evening still young, and Sonia out on a rare night with the 'girls', Batten drove not to *Hillview* but to the old VHS player in his Ashtree cottage – to view the CCTV tapes in privacy and read the goodies in Connor's 'gift'.

To keep the pipes in the empty cottage from freezing, he'd left the central heating on low, and his study was warm enough, despite the pre-Christmas cold snap. Familiar prints on the wall, hand-built bookshelves, the old Turkish rug, all reminded him it was a well-loved place, whose future he must soon decide. Connor's file was a tingle of temptation, but first the VHS player and Ben Thorne's video tapes...

A muscled figure blurred across the screen, too slow and heavy to be Pavel Ducek, but identity still unknown. Even blurred, his wiry companion was all-too familiar, his gait, small body and jerky movements so distinctive Batten could almost hear his sharp Scouse voice. '*That* is Manny bloody McRory,' Batten told the walls. 'Sidekick of our Mr Rutter. And I thought the little shit was still inside!'

He played the other tape, in case the rogue van-driver of *Elliot's Plumbing Services* turned out to be McRory too. Though taken in daylight, the images were fuzzy, and what little of the driver was visible seemed too robust for McRory. The hands on the steering wheel looked a size up at least, the body-mass bulkier - though still the carefully selected 'average height, average build' that confused witnesses. 'Not McRory,' Batten mumbled to himself, 'but maybe the 'detective' with the fake warrant card who questioned Oksana? And one out of two is progress.'

Fingers tingling, he turned to Connor's file, almost afraid to open it. When he did, he was back at Parminster HQ, his old cubby-hole desk scattered with early witness statements, transcripts, photos, diagrams – though the ones in his hand were all photostats, with Andy's characteristic italic scrawl in the margins. Despite the ethical dilemma, Connor had taken a double risk for the greater good: sharing evidential documents, then annotating each one in handwriting so identifiable he might as well have signed his name. Batten twigged the reason. If the misdemeanour ever came to light, Connor's innocent staff would remain beyond suspicion. 'You're a caped crusader, Prof,' Batten told the empty room.

Switching on the desk lamp and fumbling for his specs, he began to read. The first document covered the usual – the scene, wider environment, personnel involved, initial timeline, and the rest. The second held more concrete information, something Batten lacked. He reached for the bottle of Aberlour on the shelf above his head and poured himself a much-needed single malt, before grabbing notebook and pen to make jottings of his own. *Two old habits*, he reminded himself, summarising the facts while sipping.

Connor's notes confirmed why Lady Wake's face had turned ash-grey. Maya, her favourite horse, was gone, enticed into a trailer driven, it now seemed, by no less than Manny McRory. A second man was involved – a giant, found dead in Maya's stable, possibly from cardiac arrest brought on by a kick from Maya's hooves. Batten found no death amusing but maybe there was such a thing as natural justice. He shook his head. *Strange, strange day.*

A photograph of Maya's 'decorated' stable echoed the recent past. *Red paint,* he scribbled, adding 'Olly Rutter's signature.' More photos cemented the presence of Rutter's old minion, Manny McRory, but if Inspector Ball had identified him, none of Connor's scribbles yet said so. *Find Manny, screw Olly,* Batten wrote - then bit the end of his pen. Luka Judd's name appeared nowhere. Was he once more the third man, the behind-the-scenes cut-out between troops on the ground and the four-star General? Batten scribbled, *Find Luka, screw Olly twice-over.*

As he sipped whisky and read on, the Wake Hall ducks quacked – fast and loud, shouting *Avril Dean* at him. Her unexplained drifts into the past; her frantic reaction to the Estate's endangered horses; the curious Morse Code blinks she shared with Lady Wake. Reasons lay there on the desk in front of him, next to his golden glass of Aberlour, but so unpalatable his pen pinged onto the desk when he read the details. 'Hell's teeth,' he murmured, the page hot as he dropped it next to the pen.

Despite his erratic memory, he recalled Avril's visit to his garden office. Then, with a different pen poised in his hand, he'd asked for her surname. 'Oh, it's Kerrig – I mean Dean,' she'd said. 'D.E.A.N. Avril Dean. Kerrigan was my married name.'

Awaiting fingerprint checks, the CID document gave the dead victim's *probable* identity. But three Wake Hall women, Avril amongst them, had separately agreed who the body was: Avril Dean's ex-husband, *Phil Kerrigan*.

'Thank God it's not Pavel,' Batten whispered, dispelling his knee-jerk response with whisky. Connor's private jottings, in neat italic letters in the margin, were the information cherry on the cake – with an underscored warning: <u>Use with care.</u>

Pre-divorce, Kerrigan worked various jobs at Wake Hall. Handy, eh, your wife chumming up to the owner? Food prep first – seems he was ex-Army Catering Corps, a trained butcher. Then horse supplies, very suggestive. And for a time, would you believe, Security?

Batten's new employers - Lady Wake and Avril Dean - could have told him all this on day one. *More confidentiality,* he mumbled. *More bloody secrets.* Finishing his whisky, he found a notelet clipped to the final document, written in Connor's well-worn style: jocular, to soften the toxic downsides of his profession.

Update from the Doc, Zig. Looks like the horse did it.

But where does that leave us? Batten wondered. Even if the police found Maya still in one piece, they don't arrest horses. Nor do horses sign witness statements.

Avril Dean must have, but her statement wasn't in Connor's pack. To get the full story he needed to ask her in person – another ambivalent trip to Wake Hall. But not tonight. He tucked tapes and documents into his messenger bag, swallowed the last of his whisky and rinsed the glass in the kitchen sink. After a final nostalgic glance at his much-loved cottage, he double locked the door and drove off.

All the way back to *Hillview,* he wished horses could talk.

Forty-two

Police alerts on social media sometimes came up trumps – sometimes not. Asking the public to report sightings of a missing horse did result in leads a-plenty, but also gave a soapbox to the crazies. On his first morning as *temporary acting* Detective Constable, Jon Lee was assigned a desk and a phone at Parminster HQ and told to follow up each possibility. He soon wished he was back in uniform. Most reports turned out to be stray nags who'd sidestepped a faulty electric fence in search of sweeter grass. Two came from lonely pensioners in need of human contact. Lee wanted to throttle the anonymous joker who dragged him on a wasted journey to a country lane, where a fly-tipped mound was topped by a broken clotheshorse.

Back at Parminster, an irate Lee followed up a call from a Dick Drumm, another joker with a made-up name, he assumed. The contorted yokel voice on the crackly phone only added to his suspicions.

'Could you repeat that, please, sir?'

'Yow deaf? Oy sez oy gotta 'orse-box!'

'Ah, you have a horse box.' *You and half of Somerset.* 'And why is that relevant, sir?'

'It's revelant 'cos oy 'ad no 'orse box yesserday.'

'Er…?'

'In moy field. Over to Brenner Wood. Council sez the 'edges round moy field, they be too tall. Oy don' even *use* the field, but oy goes to look. Good citizen, oy am.'

'Yes, sir. And?'

'An' they's a 'orse-box in moy field! Since oy don' own no 'orse-box, oy expeck it's *revelant!*'

Deciding he'd best see for himself, Lee gleaned directions. He was about to put down the phone when Dick Drumm added, 'An' there wor noises comin' from et. *Noises!* Waal, as oy left they wor…'

*

Emboldened by insider knowledge and a good night's sleep, Batten arrived at Wake Hall unannounced, strode up the steps and yanked the bell pull, chilling his fingers on the cold metal. The young eager-faced girl who'd brought him coffee on a silver tray - it felt like months ago - let him into the ante room and said she would 'go and check with Avril.' He almost asked her to bring coffee first, but his brass neck wouldn't stretch that far.

From previous experience he expected the bum's rush, but to his surprise Avril Dean appeared within minutes, her underbite taut, dumpy body stiff. Batten's resolve wilted when he took in the all too readable lines of pain on her face. She surprised him a second time by wordlessly walking him through the trompe l'oeil door to her office and waving him to a chair. Last time he was here, the window view was a dull mixed bag of parked cars and vans. Today, the pulled-down blinds obscured even the car park, and a single desk lamp cast funereal shadows across the walls. Avril's hands twitched in awkward silence between her desk and her lap, and back again. *Training to be a mime-artist*, Batten thought, but after an unsmiling pause Avril squeezed a few words past lips tightened by the turmoil of yesterday.

'I hoped you would give me a little more time,' she said, waving away his attempt at apology. 'But there never will be a good time. So?'

'It's still what the police call *the golden hours*,' he said. 'When memories are fresh.'

'Fresh? Oh, they're fresh, believe me. And painful. I wish-'

With a gentle knock on the door, the eager-faced girl ferried in a silver tray, placed it on Avril's desk and left without a word. When Avril poured, the welcome scent of coffee teased Batten's nostrils. Sonia said he drank far too much of it, but right now he needed to. 'You were about to say?'

She shook her head and sipped her coffee, black, like his. 'Nothing,' she said. 'Because nothing is how I feel. How *we* feel.' Her eyes flicked towards *ma'am's* private office, down the corridor. 'After yesterday, the pair of us are numb.'

But for different reasons? As he wondered how to ask, Avril continued.

'Whoever is behind the theft of Maya – and it's clear who tops the list – knew precisely how to drive a lance through Lady Wake's heart. And through mine, by proxy.' She paused to revive herself with coffee and

Batten took the opportunity to down a draught of his – rich, hot, and required.

'But you had other reasons, more personal reasons, to feel, well, numb?'

Avril eyed him over the rim of her cup, before clicking it into the saucer. The sound became a switch, turning Avril's silence into words. 'I suppose you're paid to be incisive,' she said. 'And since you're good at your job, can I assume you already know the facts?'

With 'Prof' Connor's sketchy notes in mind, Batten said, 'It would make more sense if you just told your story. Along the way, it'll fill any gaps.' *And you need to get it off your chest. If you don't, it could crush you.*

As if she read his mind, Avril nodded at a private memory, then made the pain of it public. 'Being small, I liked big men. And a man in uniform, well. He was fresh out of the army. When I was much younger, of course. Twenty, me. Far too young. But you don't know that till you're older, do you?' Her eyes drifted to the window, as if seeing the past in the drawn-down blind. She wrapped her fingers round her cup, perhaps for warmth. 'I'm sorry. I'm talking about the…body, in Maya's stable. You've found out who it is – who it was?'

Knowing when to keep silent, Batten gave a neutral nod.

'Phil. Phil Kerrigan. Heaven knows, we all make wrong turnings in life, and Phil was mine. The biggest. Because, yes, he was *big*. He preferred small women, so… What became clear was he found small women easier to control. Well, not me, in the end.'

When she paused, face knotted with pained experience, Batten topped up her coffee, and his, and waited. After a second or two, she took a breath and recovered herself.

'We use all sorts of coy phrases, don't we, instead of just saying 'mental health'? Phil's was a mess when he left the Army. But I can't blame them because Phil was Phil, and I suspect he'd always been close to the edge. Lady Wake, bless her soul, let him work on the Estate, one job after another because we had to keep 'moving him on'.' Avril paused to shake her head, perhaps at the irony of one of Kerrigan's jobs being in Security. 'The other staff were careful with their language, but the upshot was always the same. Phil was *behaving strangely* in the kitchen or *acting funny* in the Feed Store. One of the maintenance men said, *he's flown away to bird-land.* As if I didn't know. I lived in Phil's bird-land, a caged bird myself, every blessed day.'

'Did bird-land turn violent?' Batten recalled the giant looming figure from the CCTV tape.

'Not in the way you might mean - not at first. But he lost all sense of how strong he was. His big fists would grab me, and I bruise easily so my arms were technicolour tattoos. I stopped wearing short sleeves, even in summer. If you want the brutal truth, I lost my parents when I was just eighteen, and married Phil because I was lonely. But we just ended up being lonely together.'

Cripping a tissue from the box on her desk, Avril blew her nose. No tears, Batten noted. She stared at the pale carpet, as if healing truths might float up from the weave and weft. 'We had an argument once, well, more than once. But that day, he wouldn't let me go to work. I didn't live in then, you see. He just decided, on a whim, no debate. Grabbed me and held on till I screamed with pain. When he pushed me aside, I didn't go to work, I went to A&E. The doctor said I'd broken two ribs. When he saw my bruises, he asked if I'd been crushed by a giant python. That was Phil. *Gone funny in the head*, I heard a stable girl say. But he *went funny* in the street, too. In the shops, at the doctors. Even with Her Ladyship's support, I couldn't cope. For goodness' sake, I could barely cope with my son.'

'Your *son*?'

Avril's commune with the carpet snapped to a halt and she stared instead at Batten, almost surprised he was in the room. 'Oh. Yes. I thought I'd said.'

No, you bloody didn't! Another secret! 'Not come across him, your son, around here.'

'No. No. You won't…' Another tissue, to dab her brow this time. 'I told you, I was young, far too young. We called him George but, alas, he was no saint. George was his father's son, a giant like Phil, and like Phil he fought me - from the day he was born. Even when Phil became…oppressive, George took his side.'

Suspicious mind struggling to keep up with the emerging family saga, Batten said, 'How old was he, is he? George?' Avril's face surprised him - by turning even sadder than before.

'He'll be thirty, on Twelfth Night. 3.44pm, January 5th,' she said, voice no more than a whisper. 'I can't send a birthday card, because when he reached the so-called age of 'maturity', he left my life – and was brutally clear he meant *forever*. Phil was sectioned, you see, in the end. Best for Phil *and* me, they said and frankly I agreed. Not best for poor George, though. When Phil went through the doors of that mental hospital, I felt I'd betrayed both of them, felt it deeper than I can say – but I didn't need to, because George said it for me. Called me a *traitor* and didn't stop there. He hated me, he said, hated me, for letting them take his father away. I saw the piercing flames of hate in his eyes. *Hate.* What earthly *use* is it - to anyone?'

Batten wished he knew. Avril waved her tissue, a white flag, casting dark shadows across the desk.

'We divorced. Well, I divorced. Phil didn't know what day of the week it was. By the time they let him out, George had disappeared.' Anticipating Batten's question, she shook her head. 'I don't know where he went, or where he is now. I had no time to look, what with a living to earn and Phil to deal with *again*. I got a restraining order for my own safety. It worked – when Phil took his medication. But when he didn't… They took him in again, new treatment, which seemed to settle him. Without telling me, but to my great relief, my ex-husband wandered away, overseas.'

Spain? Batten wondered.

As if sensing his thoughts, Avril said, 'Which country, I couldn't tell you. Nor if he was reunited with our son. *His* son. I moved into the Hall, nice rooms, nice people, and yes I grew, and was trusted. Not something I ever experienced with Phil, or with George.'

Assuming she was done, Batten opened his mouth to speak, but she raised her hand to stop him. 'You see, I saw him, Phil, driving an old car on the A358, a week or two ago. *Can't be!* I told myself. Almost screamed the words out loud. But it was him. I was shocked, unsettled. *He'll never dare come back here*, I thought. I should have known better.'

And you should have told me, Batten thought. *Bloody secrets.*

'It was traumatic, seeing Phil again, even if through a car window. And when he turned up at the stables, in the dark - wearing a ski-mask, the policeman said - for God knows what mischief, and then…'

All gabbling spent, tears streamed down Avril's cheeks, her breath in gasps, her face a crumpled paper bag. Batten rose from his chair and in the half-light gently put his arm round her shoulders. I'm becoming a professional comforter now, he thought, as Avril sobbed the pain of memory into his chest. He cursed himself as casual sexism kicked in – *in the Force, we had WPCs for this…*

At a polite knock on the door, Avril straightened up, dabbed her eyes, and became Avril-who-gets-things-done. 'Yes?' she said.

The eager-looking girl shuffled into the doorway. Taking in Avril's face, and Batten's, she paused, unsure. 'Yes Jean,' said Avril. 'What is it?'

Jean glided across the carpet and whispered in Avril's ear. Batten heard every word. *An Inspector Ball is outside. He needs to see Lady Wake. It's very urgent.*

Batten didn't think Avril's face could turn any whiter.

But it did.

Forty-three

In Lady Wake's private office, Batten squatted awkwardly on the edge of a Queen Anne chair, *Her Ladyship* grey-faced in the other, and Avril Dean planted bolt upright on the sofa. The log fire blazing in the grate might just as well have been a block of ice. Inspector Ball had been asked to wait - *in the ante-room*, Batten guessed, *on that faded velvet chair.* He assumed *Jean* wouldn't be serving Ball coffee on a silver tray.

After ten careful minutes, part condolence, part dentistry, Batten was satisfied all *confidentialities* had been shared. 'I do wish you to be fully involved,' Lady Wake said. 'And I shall insist on this when…?'

'Inspector Ball, ma'am,' said Avril.

'When Inspector Ball is shown in.' She raised barely an eyebrow at Avril, who stood.

'I beg your pardon, ma'am, but…in *here?*'

A dazed Lady Wake stared at her private lair as if for the first time. 'Ah. No. Of course not. Thank you. Your office, perhaps?' Since her question was a polite command, the three of them trooped down the carpeted corridor. On the way, Avril pointed to a pair of hard chairs in an alcove and said, 'could you, please?'

Huh, furniture mover, now, Batten thought, doing the honours. *Two hard chairs, for me and Chris Ball,* he guessed. When Ball was shown into Avril's office, he was right.

Inspector Ball had changed his suit but looked just as awkward in the new one - grey, to match the mood. One glance at Batten and the grey suit seemed to darken. But Ball had already crossed paths with Her Ladyship and was careful not to directly question Batten's presence. 'You may prefer to discuss this in private, ma'am?' he said.

Two diamond-hard eyes sliced into him. 'No. I may not. My team here have my full confidence.' Her fingers took in Avril and Batten with the slightest of waves. 'Continue.'

But how do Ball and I continue? Batten asked himself - *continue being friends?*

Stone-faced, Ball did as he was told, though if there was an easy way to bring the worst news to Lady Wake, he failed to find it, his tragic message stumbling to a painful close. '...And it seems your vet, a Mr Markham, is up there now. At what is technically a crime scene. So, he...er, I...we need to know what your wishes are...?'

Lady Wake's wishes would need a time-machine, to return the tragic present to a happier past. For the briefest moment a raw, pained sadness filled her eyes, threatening to engulf her. Then her face silently closed, like an exquisite door on a Chippendale cabinet, as breeding kicked in – the *sang-froid* control of emotion when servants are in the room.

Glancing over at a crumpled Chris Ball, Batten transferred his empathy. At many a call of duty, his own tight lips had supressed his true feelings, and did again, now. He wanted to say, *Chris, wait till the job makes you tell a mother, as best you can, her beloved child is dead.* But Ball had done precisely that. And the 'child' was Maya.

Cutting into the two women's silent Morse Code, Batten raised his eyebrow in a question. After a breath-held pause, Lady Wake stood up, at first shakily, with visible effort, then ramrod-straight. 'Perhaps, Zig, on my behalf you might confer with Geoff Markham, whose advice I trust? And jointly make the... necessary arrangements? I'm afraid I must be elsewhere.'

Before Batten and Ball could fully stand, she was gone, and Avril too, leaving the two men half-squatting like a pair of awkward toads on two hard chairs, each waiting for the other to speak or move, as the room became one giant elephant.

'I don't know the way,' Batten said at last.

Ball managed just three words: 'Fifteen-minute drive.' Batten's long legs struggled to keep up with his old Sergeant's speedy escape through the trompe l-oeil door, past the huge Christmas tree a-glitter with sad, ironic horses, out through the ante-room, and down the long cold track to the all-too-*Official* car park.

A few miles beyond the walls and fences of the vast Wake Hall Estate, Ball skidded to a halt in a muddy lane beside a fierce-looking overgrown hedge. Hawthorn, Batten guessed. Ball would know, but Batten wasn't about to ask. He'd tried small talk in the car, getting only shrugs and silence for his pains.

Geoff Markham, the chief vet, his plastic apron thankfully unbloodied, shook Batten's hand and nodded at Ball. 'Your Forensics people just left,' he said.

'Yes, sir, I'm aware. In CID we're trained in the use of telephones.'

Bulky frame rebuffed by Ball's wrong-note sarcasm, the vet switched his focus to Batten. 'I'm glad *she* hasn't come. If I was her, I wouldn't either. All the same, she'd want me to show you.' Chin clenched, Markham led the two men through an open gate into the high-hedged field, rampant with untamed weeds and scrubby grass. Pointing to a daisy-yellow plant, he said, 'Senecio Jacobaea. You'll know it as Ragwort. Poisonous to horses. Gives them liver damage. Alas, that's not what killed her.'

Following the unmissable imprint of tyre-tracks, as DC Lee had done earlier, they tramped across to a grey metal horse-trailer, forlorn at the field's edge. A large, covered truck with an ominous winch attached was parked twenty yards away, two burly men inside, the driver tapping his meaty fingers on the steering wheel. 'Undignified,' said Markham, pointing at the truck, 'but there's no easy way to remove the dead weight of a dead horse. They'll be respectful. Not least because I'll stay here to keep an eye. And I'll make sure the ashes are sent back? I suppose she'll want to…?'

'Yes,' said Batten. 'Best send them to Avril?'

'No problem. I'll show *you* though. You'd like to say a quiet farewell, on Her Ladyship's behalf?'

Ball was here to view the crime-scene. A countryman all his life, viewing a dead carcass in close-up was nothing new. But for the ex-urban Batten this was a first, and he winced as Markham ushered him up the same ramp Maya had trotted - and a dying Phil Kerrigan had staggered down. Within, beautiful Maya lay on her side, her once-flowing mane crestfallen on the trailer floor, legs splayed, dead eyes open, emptily staring upwards at the cold blue sky. When Batten saw how ruined, how colossal she was, even prone on the matted straw, he understood the nearby truck and its winch, and understood why his employer could not bear to cast even one of her diamond eyes on the sad sight.

Wishing he was elsewhere, he asked Markham, 'If Ragwort didn't kill her, what did? When the time's right, Lady Wake will want to know.'

Markham's jaw clenched tighter still. 'Well, I hope you'll soften the truth. Because strictly speaking, *I* killed her, or we did.' He jabbed a thumb at co-vet Paula standing by the trailer, scribbling details into the blank spaces of an official form. 'Technically alive when the police called us, but with a leg broken – and badly. Kicking against the ramp, I suppose, poor beast. And a broken leg is a nightmare to fix. Blood struggles to reach the hoof, you see, and keeping a horse still while the bones heal, well, nigh-on impossible. She was seriously dehydrated, too, poor Maya. We had no choice but to euthanise her. The worst part of our job, but at least her soul's over the rainbow now.'

Batten wanted to ask Markham if horses had souls, but he was still talking.

'Hard to believe, but it could've been even worse.' Markham turned to the silent Inspector Ball. 'Your young colleague, he showed me that butcher's knife he'd found. Massive bloody thing.' He held his hands more than a foot apart, to demonstrate.

Ball nodded. DC Jon Lee might be inexperienced, but there was nothing wrong with his eyesight. He'd spotted the razor-sharp knife in the long grass and bagged it for Forensics. But had no business showing it to Geoff Markham. Ball would need to have a word – one more task on the burgeoning list. 'The knife is safely in evidence now, sir,' he said.

'Evidence!' spat Markham. 'Evidence of what they'd planned to do to her. Whatever scuppered them, thank God it did. But if I get my hands on the murderous bastards, you'll be arresting *me!*'

It wasn't Ball's place to tell Geoff Markham Maya had already despatched one of her captors, or that the police were searching hard for the other. He had enough on his plate. Batten saw him sneak a glance at his watch.

'Anything else to tell us?' asked Batten, hurrying things along.

Markham shook his head. 'Days like this, I wish I worked on the checkout in Tesco. I'm supposed to keep creatures *alive.*'

'I expect we have that in common, sir,' murmured Ball. 'I'll be on my way.'

Having come in Ball's car, Batten said an embarrassed thanks to Markham and followed the Inspector down the straw-scattered ramp, pausing one final time to stroke, with tenderness, the dead crest of Maya's grey magnificent mane, on behalf of her grieving owner.

And on his own account, too, his sad farewell to lost beauty. Then Ball started the engine and reluctantly drove back towards Wake Hall, in a silence too thick for even a butcher's knife to cut through.

Forty-four

In the car, swallowing a breath and his pride, Batten homed in on 'Prof' Connor's plea for *common ground* with Ball. He was about to bite the bullet when the car slowed, coming to a halt at the brow of a low hill, pale green pastureland rolling away to the far distance like a huge, mottled blanket. To Batten's surprise, Ball climbed from the car, planted his folded arms on a metal gate, and stared in silence at the early winter fields.

When Batten joined him, Ball kept his solemn eyes on the distance. 'This used to be our farm,' he said, the words a whisper. 'Mum and Dad's, mine. It was everything we owned.'

Batten realised he was staring at Ball's lost inheritance - the Ball family's bankrupt smallholding, purchased at a knock-down price by old Lord Wake and tacked on the edge of the vast Estate, making it vaster still. From the gloom on Chris Ball's face, Batten guessed he still blamed the Wakes for his parents' early deaths - and was ill-disposed to mucking out the stables of the current owner. *Who is currently paying my wages.*

'Not been this close to our lost fields since…I don't know when. I've dreaded coming here,' mumbled Ball. 'Having to walk into *that* place…' He waved an angry hand at rising ground on the horizon, topped by the white limestone speck of Wake Hall. 'Having to ring the doorbell, tug my forelock and…'

'And be professional?'

'*Professional*! It's a *curse*.'

It's the job, Batten almost said. His own job too, from a different angle now. 'We're both doing what we must, Chris. That's the territory.'

Ball wasn't listening. Respects paid, he climbed back into his old Volvo and was sweeping off before Batten had even clipped his seat-belt in place. They drove in a dark silence till Batten chanced his arm, wondering when Ball had last swallowed anything more than cold tea and stale cake. 'Chris, I don't suppose you've time for lunch?'

An eyeball flashed at the passenger seat. '*Time?* I have to make an appointment to scratch my arse!'

'It's just that we're not far from *The Horse and Groom*. They do a mean bacon sandwich…'

Bacon, an instant trigger to Eddie Hick, took longer to cut through Ball's gloom. After a few hundred yards, he muttered, 'Pubs are for cider' - his private law.

'They serve soft drinks, too?'

Another few hundred yards and the car slowed. 'It'll have to be quick,' Ball said, pulling up in the car park and clambering out. Batten followed him inside, remembering the last time he was in *The Horse and Groom*, Pavel Ducek's hand gripping his forearm like a pincer. He could still feel Pavel's iron fingers and hear his veiled threat. Today in the near-empty pub he hoped things would go better with *Inspector* Ball.

To neither man's relief, the surrounding walls brayed with equine paintings, one long-maned horse after another. At least their bacon sandwiches arrived promptly, with chips in a dainty wire basket and a token garnish of mixed leaves. 'Classy pub,' said Batten, 'they've even dressed the salad.'

To avoid replying, Ball filled his mouth with bacon, chewing thoughtfully for what seemed forever. Then he wiped his lips on a paper napkin, glared at Batten and said, '*Well?*'

Emboldened by chips, Batten reverted to his default position – direct. '*Luka Judd*,' he said.

No flicker of recognition passed across Ball's face. He shrugged his bulky shoulders. 'What, a pop star, is he? A rapper? Wouldn't have thought he'd be gracing your CD collection.'

'He's not. Olly Rutter, then.'

'Rutter? That hairy ape *does* sound like a rapper. What about him? He's still in Bristol Prison.'

'And still his nasty self. These *shenanigans* at Wake Hall? Could be Rutter's doing, with help from this Luka Judd.'

Putting down his fork, a half-eaten chip skewered on the prongs, Ball gave Batten a long stare. 'Leaving aside you not informing the *police*, until now - you know this *because?*'

Between mouthfuls, Batten told almost everything, 'leaving aside' any clues to the source. Ball's brow knotted at the mention of *Pavel Ducek* and *Oksana Vossialevydipsic*, whose names had recently graced his overflowing desk.

'I couldn't give a damn if she's changed her name to *Brok*. Her brother

Dave is still a *Vossialevydipsic*, far as I'm concerned. So why am I not hearing his name, too?' asked Ball. 'If someone burgles Oksana Brok's house, and nothing gets nicked, I'd be leaning towards Dipstick Dave being the object of attention. Wouldn't *you*?'

Batten held up his bacon-greasy fingers in surrender. 'Chris, until now, I've been juggling jigsaw pieces.'

Ball's lunch disappeared, but not his disquiet. '*Until now*, we didn't have two more dead bodies on our hands – one of them *human*! I ought to bloody arrest you!'

To ease the tension, Batten said, 'Waste of time, Chris. Lady Wake would spring me in no time.'

His dealings with Lady Wake still painful, Ball mumbled, 'Yes, she probably would. She knows the Chief Constable. And was bloody quick to remind me.' Crushing his serviette into a knot and dumping it on his empty plate, Ball stared at his two-pounds-of-sausage fingers. 'I'm not sure where all this leaves us.'

Clocking the 'us', Batten pitched in. 'Leaves us needing to track down Manny McRory - I'm 99 percent certain it was him behind the ski-mask. McRory could lead us back to Rutter? Rutter might give us Luka Judd – then from Judd to Dave *Vossialevydipsic*. Dave *is* still wanted for murder.'

'Thought I'd forgotten, did you? Tom Bowditch - bloody awful sight. A pair of bolt cutters sticking out of the poor sod's skull. I got to the body before you did, Zig. *Remember*?'

Relieved by the sudden use of *Zig*, Batten took a breath. 'Chris, if that big bundle of crime was to get solved, think of the justice – and the kudos for Parminster CID…?' With Wallingford's devious plans in mind, Batten let *kudos* hang in the air.

After five brow-wrinkled seconds, Ball pulled his phone from his suit pocket and opened his *Photos* app. 'See what you make of these,' he said, showing Batten two images, the first a pair of strung-out numbers, the second a jumble of numbers in some kind of pattern. Feeling hypocritical, Batten pretended he'd never seen them before. But his head-shake was truthful - because he still had no idea what they meant.

'I'm on my way to see the boss at *Nightwatch Security*,' said Ball. 'Hickie's already grilled the security guards who were supposed to be patrolling. Dragged them from their night-shift beds to the station and enjoyed it more than they did. But the bleary-eyed buggers seem pukka, so let's hope their boss can cast some light. Maybe about these numbers - they've got to mean *something*.' He stood up and reached in his back pocket for his wallet.

'I already paid, Chris, on my way back from the loo.'

'Next time, ask me first,' said Ball. He gave Batten a penetrating stare. 'And next time, where *shenanigans* are concerned, *tell* me first. Is that clear?'

'Crystal,' said Batten, using Ball's police nickname.

The faintest hint of a smile crept across the new Inspector's face. Then he turned away and strode to the car park.

Forty-five

Day is night and night is day, Walter Moon mumbled to himself. Since inheriting his dead father's security company, he'd spent too many days sleeping and too many nights working - enjoying neither. According to his birth certificate he was forty-two, but his mirror said fifty – and a thin, pale fifty to boot. His body clock was a poor fit for a night security firm, but as the old man used to say, 'Nobody wants our services in daylight - and when your surname's *Moon...*'

It was daylight now, and the police *did* want Moon's services – insisted on it. From behind his office desk, he watched an unfamiliar old Volvo crunch across the gravelled forecourt and come to a halt below his office window. *Inspector Ball*, said the scribbled note in Moon's hand. A grey-suited, ginger-haired man, squat and enviously robust, climbed out of the car, and moments later strode into *Nightwatch Security*'s reception area.

Ball hovered by the desk, expecting to see a receptionist, but found an empty desert. *Not exactly secure*, he mumbled to himself, glancing at the half-hearted gold tinsel draped over the windows and a wonky plastic Christmas tree that had seen better days. A connecting door opened and Walter Moon, who'd also seen better days, drew Ball into a small office, planners on the wall and a robust-looking safe standing in the corner like a large steel dunce. Wedging his spoon-shaped backside into the chair opposite Moon, Ball refused coffee, and explained his presence.

Moon was relieved Ball turned down the coffee - because he'd be making it himself. If Alison were here, she would have ferried in a plate of biscuits too, giving Moon something to fiddle with, to stop his nervous hands twitching on the arms of his chair. But this was the second day his Secretary/Receptionist had failed to turn up. 'Fibroids,' she'd said on the phone, which Walter knew was *woman stuff,* so he didn't probe, despite the hassle. When he worked nights, like last night, Alison always covered mornings - volunteered in fact - practically running the place so he could rest. This morning, though, she was nowhere, and he was half-asleep.

'Er, how can I help?' he said to the grey-suited Inspector, while failing to suppress a yawn.

Five minutes later, he was wide-awake and wide-eyed, staring at two photostats. Strings of all-too-familiar numbers stared back at him, and the cold sweat of realisation began to drip from his brow.

Walter Moon mumbled, 'How did...?' - and wished he was home in bed.

*

While Ball's pointed questions were draining the blood from Walter Moon, a chalk-faced Lady Wake stepped out of the Hall's double-doors, gripped the arm of dear, loyal Avril Dean, and steeled herself to visit what *Nightwatch Security* had failed to secure. Insistent as ever, Lady Wake had demanded access. And, as ever, Avril arranged it. The two women trudged in silence down the post-and-rail lined track towards the stable yards, not certain why. As mourners? Pilgrims? Exorcists?

Pulling winter coats tighter, they were relieved the Forensics tent had gone, but strips of blue and white police tape, still flickering in the wind, barred the entrance to Stall 20 in Stable Block D. They stared - breathless, silent - at the view beyond the tape, secretly glad they could not cross. Lady Wake withdrew her arm, took an unsteady step closer, a lone mourner now, and stared into the pit of sadness. At first she felt nothing, saw nothing, till the tears clouding her eyes trickled down her cheeks and she took in the stable's rubber matting and swept-aside straw, and to her distress, the jagged scars of blood-red paint on the floor and walls. And the emptiness.

She recalled Olly Rutter's dark stare of disdain when he'd rebuffed her desire for a child, her need for an heir to the vast Estate. With a shiver of ambivalence, she imagined her ancestors' reaction had the Wakes' future stemmed from the loins of a bed-warming stud-cum-criminal. The portraits on the high walls would have clicked their tongues in one giant collective *Tut!*

But the red-silked ex-gangster had done more than rebuff her longing for an heir. He had spirited away her beloved proxy child. For a moment, she was in riding gear, the reins loose in her fingers, dancing her thoroughbred mare across the show ring, horse and rider moving as one. 'My beautiful Maya,' she whispered, but the words were lost on the wind, and she staggered back from the empty stable to the support of Avril's arm.

'How he must *hate* me,' she said, more tears seeping from her eyes.

'He hates everything,' was Avril's response. 'Except himself. And what *use* is hate, to anyone?' Staring at the grave-like stall, she was thinking of *her* ex, too, Phil Kerrigan, and the malign part he had played in Maya's destruction. And of her lost son George, his departing eyes aflame with enmity. *Are creatures of hate drawn together?* she wondered.

'But I shall not hate,' Lady Wake was saying. 'Nor sink to his level. The law can deal with Mr Rutter. Though perhaps we might offer the powers-that-be a little…help and encouragement?'

'Um, what did you have in mind?' asked Avril. And in response to Her Ladyship's rediscovered business voice, she tacked on a 'ma'am.'

Turning back towards the Hall, Lady Wake said, 'I shall pay a discreet visit to the Chief Constable. *Noblesse Oblige* has many interpretations, mm? You, dear Avril, shall invite Mr Batten to a *strategy* meeting. Here.' She waved a glove at the Hall. 'In a day or two. Once things have…settled down.'

'What kind of strategy meeting, ma'am?'

'Oh, straightforward enough. I shall ask him to pursue anything and anyone that may lengthen Mr Rutter's sojourn behind bars. If along the way, dear Oksana's dilemma were to be eased, then so much the better. Should *Zig* demure, please tell him, from now on he has *carte blanche*.'

'And the cost, ma'am?'

Her Ladyship stared up at the burden of Wake Hall, a white limestone ship adrift in a vast green sea of pastureland.

'The cost?' she said. 'Immaterial.'

*

After leaving *Nightwatch Security* and a squashed Walter Moon, Ball pulled into the nearest layby, fired up his laptop and began to reshape the current state of play. Adding Moon's information and Batten's story to what he already knew, he listed fresh lines of enquiry for Hick and the team to get cracking on - pronto, starting yesterday…

…At his Parminster desk, littered with food wrappers and empty cups, Eddie Hick was soon gazing at new tasks and names on his laptop screen. He juggled them into a logical sequence and cracked on – after wiping bacon grease from his fingers.

Alison Brown.

Hick didn't recognise the name. Ball's summary said she was likely to be *Alice Brown* too, and that she didn't exist. In his early Detective Constable days, Eddie Hick would have groaned and said, *supposed to track down the invisible, am I?* A proud Sergeant now, he swiftly gutted Alison Brown's job application - for her Receptionist role at *Nightwatch Security*, all the while imagining the shock on Walter Moon's face. Her mugshot - dark-haired, attractive, thirty-something - smiled out from the top of page one, but not from any police database. He sent a copy to Oksana Brok, with an urgent request to confirm this was the *Alice Brown* who recently enrolled on a *Booker Prize Novels* course at Wake Hall – and burgled Oksana's house into the bargain.

The answer pinged onto his laptop within minutes. 'Yes and no,' it said.

Helpful, not, mumbled Hick, then read the rest. 'Same age, same face, but Alice Brown was blonde. And wore thick glasses, which didn't suit her. But she seemed nice enough.'

Delving deeper, Hick discovered Alice/Alison was not alone in being fake. Her references and employment history were fake too. Moon's own checks would have been diligent enough – had *Alison Brown* not been a seasoned fraudster. Her previous employers turned out to be shell or parent companies, real but deceptive.

Bolstered by bacon, Hick did what Moon didn't: he drilled through the crust, rooted around in the pie for inadvertent truths and pulled out a plum. Slogging through firms within firms in *Companies House*, one employer in particular rang out – *L.J. Property*. Hidden well enough to fool Walter Moon, it caught Hick's focused attention, and when he burrowed into a list of company directors, another name on Ball's list popped up: *Luka Judd – L.J.* Drilling deeper still, Hick pulled out the name of a second director: *Angie Bowen.*

'Two Browns and a Bowen? All with the initials *A.B.? Huh!*' said Hick, who had learned - from Batten - to distrust coincidence. And the relationship between *Angie Bowen* and *Luka Judd* – was it boardroom, or bedroom? Either way, Hick had firm leads to follow.

I'm gonna getcha!' he told the names on his laptop screen.

Engrossed in his task, Sergeant Eddie Hick belatedly noticed the sun had disappeared. With daylight fading into darkness, he grabbed his coat and nipped out for a second bacon sandwich, to fuel him up for more Batten-style digging.

Forty-six

With zero enthusiasm, Arnie Goole stared at his breakfast, then at the polished pine doors of the kitchen cupboards. Pointless rummaging beyond the doors because his wife had stripped every cupboard of suspect comestibles - 'to help you diet.' No blueberry muffins remained, not a grain of sugar for his decaffeinated coffee. A small brown bowl of unsweetened muesli and a thin slice of wholemeal toast stared back at him, *yum*. In months of trying, he'd lost eight miserable pounds – and all sense of pleasure. But as skimmed milk dribbled through his muesli, the memory of yesterday's events restored his spirits – though not the spirits of Prison Officer Kev Campbell, now detained on the wrong side of a cupboard-like cell, awaiting charges.

'What's that white thing in in your pocket, Kev?' Arnie had enjoyed asking.

Half-way through stirring a third spoon of sugar into his tea, a wary Campbell had said, 'White thing? It's a *hankie*. I use it to blow my nose.'

Arnie chewed unsweetened oats with a satisfied smile of memory. '*Paper* hankie, is it?'

Face turning whiter than the hankie in his other pocket, Campbell glanced left and right, beyond the cluttered staffroom table, towards the entry and exit doors. He turned whiter still when Arnie's two bulky colleagues stepped across to block the way. '*What?* Er, yeh. Paper hankie. You know, hygienic.'

'Little bird tells us there's writing on it, Kev, your *paper hankie*. Take a look, shall we?' Before Campbell could move, Arnie's un-slimmed frame had him against the wall. Unpocketing a square of white paper, he held it by a corner, in thumb and finger, and shook it open. Half an hour ago he'd watched its arrival and concealment, via the hidden surveillance camera he'd forgotten to tell Campbell about. Ex-CID, Arnie scanned the typewritten page for watermarks or printer codes then read the typed contents. '*Target successfully removed*. Now, what target's that, Kev, eh?'

A monkey, not an organ grinder, Campbell dropped his head to avoid the room of eyes, and muttered the truth, 'Dunno.'

'*Major impact achieved, but operatives injured. Task incomplete.* And I don't suppose you know which operatives, or what injured them?'

Another shrug. 'Found it tucked under my wipers, this morning, before work. In plastic, like a parking ticket.'

'Didn't bin it, though, eh, Kev? You brought it here, and we both know whose cell it's headed for, so I'll save you the tr-'

Before Arnie could finish, Campbell hissed, 'OK, *OK!*...But I want a deal.'

Goole's face clouded over. 'Your only deal's a day in court, you worm.'

'Maybe. Maybe not. I've other stuff, see, from before, stashed away. The other notes say a lot more than this one. If I get a deal, you get to look...'

Spreading low-fat margarine on his toast, Arnie Goole smiled once more at the deal currently being developed. After breakfast, he would ring Zig Batten with the gist, as promised, and spread a big beaming grin all over his face.

Olly Rutter wouldn't smile, though. Arnie would bet a whole pack of blueberry muffins on that.

*

At *Hillview*, breakfast over, Batten squatted at the desk in his garden office and glared at the phone. He'd never liked phones. They brought directions to a crime scene, or a summons to a reprimand - or news of a family death. Once in a while, they'd carried a female voice saying, *Goodbye, Zig.*

Torn between respecting Wake Hall's need to mourn and his own need to *bloody get on with it,* he deflected the problem to his fingertips. Tap-tap at first. Then tap-tap-tap, an impatient metronome. Then a louder drumming of febrile flesh on the desk's oak top – which must have made the phone ring, because it did. And to his amazement, Avril Dean was phoning *him.*

'...Yes,' she said. 'In the light of recent events, Lady Wake wishes you to widen your activities. In fact, *carte blanche* was the very phrase she used...Tomorrow, here? 10am?'

A gob-smacked Batten, his previous assaults on fortress Wake Hall achieved mostly by crowbar, would have preferred an imminent meeting to calm his fingers - and in case Her Ladyship changed her mind. But he readily agreed, replacing the phone all a-puzzle.

Impatient for tomorrow, he chanced his arm, grabbed the phone and rang Chris Ball's mobile. A robotic voice said, *the person you have called is not available, please leave a message.* Batten cursed. *What message could he leave?* Waiting was his only option.

Tapping fingers applied themselves to the puny paperwork of his new career, filing it in the near-empty cabinet which closed with a hollow *thunk*. He tried getting in the mood for Christmas, without success. Frustrated, he stood at the picture window to stare at the vast view of Ham Hill across the valley, the ancient hill fort showing off its morning coat of white frost beneath a sky of the clearest blue. *Wish my thoughts were as clear*, he mumbled to himself, eyes fixed on the distance.

Somewhere between zeal and *Zigland*, he heard a noise from the desk, and realised it was the phone.

'Eyup, Zig,' said Arnie Goole, his smug chuckle from fifty miles away sounding as if he was in the room.

And as Batten listened to Arnie's gleeful tale, his tapping fingers relaxed, slowed, and came to rest. Leaning back in the leather chair, he plonked his feet on the office desk without bothering to take off his shoes. The throaty sound of relief chuckled back down the phone to Arnie.

Forty-seven

Pacing up and down his cell took no time at all, so Olly Rutter did it again. A week without news was too bloody *long* in this rabbit-hutch, after sleep-free nights on a hard bed that doubled as an instrument of torture. Where was bloody Campbell? *The snivelling git better not be on holiday!* Olly glanced at his watch - a thick aluminium monstrosity so widget-swamped it was no mean feat to spot the time. His solid gold Rolex was stashed away in a very private safe-deposit box, along with a foot-high wad of bonds and readies, and no-one was getting their thieving hands on *that*.

Rutter's playbook rarely changed. *Leverage.* Get some leverage. And when you do, stick a knife in the shmuck's gut, and twist. Prison Officer Campbell's 'secret' extra-marital affair - with a fellow prison officer - was leverage a-plenty. And Campbell's shame at being Rutter's personal *conduit* was softened by the careful greasing of his palm – a task carried out by arms-length minions.

But snivelling git Campbell's palm would go ungreased if he didn't get in here soon with a new burner phone or the latest gen. Olly ached to hear how *The Witch's* bone-china face fell apart at the sight of her headless nag. And soon, on Christmas Eve, when his minions sent the poncy nag's severed mane to Wake Hall, gift-wrapped in blood-red tinsel, well…

His sadistic chuckle was interrupted by the jangle of key in lock. *About time,* he hissed, but when the cell door swung open, it wasn't PO Campbell standing there, but squitty little Arnie Goole. *If it didn't mean serving more time in this shithole,* Olly thought, *I'd poleaxe the podgy twat - with my little finger.* 'Being released early, am I?' he quipped, undisguised sneer on his face. 'About time my pricey lawyer earned his crust.'

'Have to disappoint you, Rutter,' retorted Goole. 'All the same, your pricey lawyer may come in handy. Prison Officer Campbell would've mentioned it, were he not currently detained at His Majesty's Pleasure. From Prison Officer to Prisoner, as if by magic, eh? And he's doubly desolate. Did you know, his wife buggered off? A little bird told her he was playing away, naughty Campbell. The poor sod's alone *and* arrested now. And just as well he's in a cage, because he's singing like a canary. Mostly about *you*.'

A purple-faced Rutter made a move towards the door, despite himself. As he did, Arnie Goole stepped to one side and a thick-armed giant replaced him, blocking both doorway and light. 'This is Prison Officer North. He's Campbell's replacement. North here, he's a lay preacher in his free time, aren't you?'

North gave a silent, unsmiling nod, which earned him a Rutter sneer. 'Oh, and when he's not preaching, he's teaching. Taekwondo, that is. Forgot to mention, he's a black belt…'

Digging into his chasm-deep stock of bravado, Rutter shrugged himself onto the mattress, folded one arm behind his head, and lit a cigar with the other, blowing the forbidden smoke pointedly at Goole and North. 'Thank you *greatly* for the information,' he said, glancing again at his monstrous watch. 'I usually manage a spot of bible study at this time of day, so do toddle off.'

Arnie Goole wafted Olly's sarcasm - and the smoke from his cigar - back towards the bed he sprawled on. 'Very gracious, Mr Rutter,' he said, stepping across the cell, swiping the illicit cigar from Rutter's lips and crushing it with his heel. 'North and me, we *are* about to toddle off, as it happens. With *you*. To the interview room, for an awkward little chat with CID. Your pricey lawyer's already there, so get your fat arse off that bed! *NOW!*'

*

HMP Bristol's interview room was not built for comfort, but Ball and Hick glided onto the hard seats with controlled panache. Rutter and his lawyer already squatted on theirs, wishing to be somewhere else. Inspector Ball introduced himself and his Sergeant for the tape, determined to apply what he'd learnt when Batten was the Inspector and he the Sergeant, even down to language and tone.

'Huh, been good little boys and got yourself promoted, the pair of you?' asked Rutter. After that, the mock-cordiality tumbled downhill. His lawyer, Hugo Tupp, smiled indulgently at the sarcasms, but swiftly shut them down when they crept anywhere close to evidence.

It mattered little. Ball drip-fed the damning facts, his confidence boosted by previous nods of approval from the Crown Prosecution Service. 'Did I mention Prison Officer Campbell has admitted supplying you with burner phones? And disposing of them afterwards?'

From the look on Rutter's face the news went down like a slug sandwich. 'Campbell? Talking out of his arse,' he snapped. 'Talking *horseshit*.'

'And did you know,' Ball added, 'the standard tariff for a prisoner in possession of an illegal phone is two more years inside – isn't that right, Sergeant?'

Hick's confirming nod collided with Tupp's acid glare. 'In possession of a phone?' said Tupp. '*Were* any found in Mr Rutter's possession, Inspector?'

'No, sir, but it seems instead of dumping them, Campbell kept each one...all plastered with your client's fingerprints.' Ball punctured the damning silence. 'Maybe you needed to phone a certain Phil Kerrigan, to renew your mutual past at Wake Hall?' Rutter's mitts flipped the suggestion at the piss-yellow walls. Tupp's response was to mumble, 'Happenstance...circumstantial.'

'Then let's turn to what isn't circumstantial,' said Ball. 'Were you aware PO Campbell kept more than your burner phones? He covered his miserable back by copying everything he brought into your cell, and everything you sent the other way - did you know that?'

Tupp's grim-faced stare coincided with a tightening of Rutter's jaw. Guaranteed silence from his minions was Chapter One in Rutter's playbook – till now. A different silence filled the interview room when Ball dropped a photostat on the table. Two innocent lines of seemingly random numbers stared up.

'I think you'll recognise these?' said Ball. '*We* do, now. They happen to be the encrypted frequencies for *Nightwatch Security*'s radios. More specifically, for the radios in the two vans that patrol Wake Hall. Now, for what possible reason would they find their way into your cell?'

'*Were* they found in Mr Rutter's cell, Inspector? I think not.'

'Neither here nor there, sir.' Ball turned from Tupp to Rutter. 'Very handy, all the same, these codes. Meant your henchmen could listen in, check the whereabouts of the vans and avoid them – particularly on the night Lady Wake's favourite horse disappeared?'

'I repeat, merely circumstantial, Inspector,' said Tupp, since he was paid to at least say *something*.

'The courts will decide that, I expect, sir. And decide what to make of this, too.' A second photostat landed on the table, more numbers but in a grid-like pattern. 'These numbers correspond precisely to *Nightwatch Security*'s zonal map of Wake Hall, though I expect you already know that. A doddle for your henchmen to dodge security when they knew which zones the vans would be in, eh? And in what sequence?'

'Again, these documents were *not* found in Mr Rutter's cell,' repeated Tupp, his nostrils so close Ball noticed the little white hairs could do with a trim. 'And since you have admitted Prison Officer Campbell had copies in *his* possession...?'

'Well, yes, sir, I do take your point. But that fails to explain another 'circumstantial' fact. Namely, that copies of these documents were also found in the back pocket of a Mr Phil Kerrigan. In the stable of Lady Wake's stolen horse, Maya. A growing chain of evidence, perhaps?' Ball allowed this news to filter past Rutter's clenched fist defiance. 'Remiss of me, I know, but I forgot to say - the documents in question were discovered on Mr Kerrigan's *corpse*.'

From Rutter's covert glance at Tupp, Ball guessed neither man knew. With a smile he added, 'I expect, of late, there's been a degree of disturbance in your channels of information? Not helped by the disappearance of a lady who sometimes calls herself Alice Brown? A curious woman, she turned up for a posh book club at Wake Hall, apparently with blonde hair and thick pebble specs but, would you credit it, she stole a set of house keys instead, then burgled one of the cottages. Seems she was looking for a rucksack which we suspect contains the proceeds of crime – and a rather large amount, to boot. As far as we can tell, she was whisked away in a stolen plumber's van driven by a man who'd previously visited the same cottage pretending to be from CID, and also on the lookout for purloined cash.'

Though Rutter said nothing, Ball watched his eyebrows puzzle together and his eyeballs dart a furtive glance at Hugo Tupp, who silently returned the puzzlement.

'Life is strange, isn't it, sir? Do you know, when this Alice Brown got herself a job at *Nightwatch Security,* for some reason she suddenly had black hair and 20/20 vision, and her name was *Alison* Brown! Her boss told me she even had a posh handbag with the initials *AB*, in gold letters. Pure coincidence, I'm sure, but she phoned in sick, the same day your pal Kerrigan met his maker, and she's not been seen since. We have her mugshot. Alison or Alice, she won't get far.'

'Inspector, this is becoming tedious. If you have no further questions…'

Ball had plenty, though some were staying in his pocket for now. 'Oh, three or four, sir. I'll just ask Mr Rutter if he knew the lady in question as *Angie Bowen*, which is of course her real name?'

Four mirthless eyes glared back across the table.

'And ask if your client remembers his old pal Manny McRory – who's disappeared too, would you credit it? Not been seen since turning up wearing latex gloves and a ski-mask in a recent Oscar-winning movie. A gunslinger part, I expect, because he used an air-rifle to shoot out the security lights, then splattered red paint all over a stable with what looked like a paintball gun. Now, *red paint?* Why would he want to use *red paint*, do you think?'

Ignoring Rutter's iron glare, Ball added, 'Oh, forgot to say, the movie was filmed at Wake Hall, the same night Phil Kerrigan went over the rainbow.'

A stone-faced Tupp got to his feet. 'I've not *finished*,' said Ball, with no trace of a smile, and Tupp slithered back into his chair. 'How recently has Mr Rutter renewed his business relationship with a certain *Luka Judd*? We understand Mr Judd is a colleague of Angie Bowen, and it seems pillow-talk is the least that's passed between them. Do forgive my indelicacy, sir.'

'Inspector, since Mr Rutter has been incarcerated in this…*building* for some considerable time, he has plainly had no opportunity to renew a business relationship with…*Angie Bowen*…or *Luka Judd* – or with anyone else!'

'Well, sir, it goes back to my initial question: why, then, did your client need so many burner phones?' Before Tupp could respond, Ball stood up. 'But I think Mr Rutter's looking tired, so we'll resume this conversation in a day or so. Give the Crown Prosecution Service time to process the burgeoning evidence, eh? If memory serves, Sergeant, when they saw Mr Rutter's file, didn't the CPS use the term, *silver platter?*'

Hick, the silent partner, twitched out something between a nod and a smirk. Ball gave Rutter a stare, then addressed Tupp's nasal bristles. 'Not saying much, sir, your client?'

Rutter spoke for himself *and* Tupp. '*No comment,*' he hissed.

'Nevertheless, expect to see us again soon. In here, I mean. Because Mr Rutter will be enjoying the fruits of this…*building* for a goodly while longer now. Unless he's moved to a tougher prison, of course.'

Turning their backs on Tupp's overpaid splutterings and the curious mix of poison and puzzlement in Rutter's eyes, Ball and Hick loped back to the car.

'Were you *trying* to sound like Zig Batten in there, boss?' said Hick.

Ball rolled his shoulders. Maybe he was. 'Well, Eddie, it worked for Zig.'

'It worked for *you*, boss. Rutter's *face!* Pissed off, and with a vengeance.'

'I might keep doing it, then,' said Ball, trying to wipe a hard-earned grin of triumph from his face – then deciding it could stay.

Forty-eight

Though Batten would have preferred to be updated by Chris Ball, when Arnie Goole rang again he was happy to echo the fresh laughter. And never had the view of Ham Hill looked so serene.

'The downside, Zig, is having to put up with Rutter's ugly mug for a lot longer. The upside is my low-fat diet's become almost bearable.'

'And I seem to remember I owe you a toasted sandwich, Arnie?'

'Can't, Zig. Eat it yourself. The wife's bought digital scales – she keeps weighing me!'

No sooner had the phone gone down on Arnie's chuckles than it rang again. Afterthought-Arnie, Batten guessed, settling for a blueberry muffin. Answering, he was amazed to hear the haughty voice of Hugo Tupp, Olly Rutter's lawyer. In alert mode now, Batten flipped his feet off the desk and onto the floor.

'...No, you did *not* misunderstand. Mr Rutter has asked to see you...*Of course* at HMP Bristol...*No*, he has not specified the nature of the conversation...Yes, *of course* I have advised him against it...*No*, he does not wish to talk to the *police*...*No*, I shall not be present - because he has specifically requested otherwise...'

Direct as ever, Batten cut in. 'Look, just tell me what's going on, will you?'

An expensive sigh was the initial response. 'It would seem *Mr Rutter* is best-placed to answer your questions...But you are aware, I surmise, that nothing said will have any value in a courtroom?'

Knowing Rutter backwards, Batten was only too aware. 'When?' he said.

'Mr Rutter has requested tomorrow. After lunch. I take it you can make yourself available?'

Batten could.

'In which case, *goodbye*.' Tupp rang off, but for several seconds the dead phone hummed in Batten's hand.

Bewildered, he replaced it. *This warrants a large single malt*, he thought - to pass the time, because tomorrow couldn't come soon enough. Swirling the whisky in his glass, he tried getting his ducks, and Rutter's, into a logical row.

When the ducks swam sideways, he gave up and savoured the golden nectar instead.

*

The 50-mile drive to HMP Bristol would have been a nightmare of potholed roads and traffic jams, had Batten's mind not been focused on Olly Rutter and Luka Judd. And this time, the twenty-minute wait for Rutter to grace the interview room's piss-yellow walls was spent in speculation. Why did Rutter *ask* for this meeting and what's his agenda? Because he'll have one, for sure. As the minutes ticked by, Batten became aware of the room's particular smell. Sweat? Bleach? Fear? *Rutter's sweet cologne will neutralise all three*, he thought. And it did.

When he stalked in and swallowed up the metal chair opposite Batten, Rutter was thinking too. Dark rumblings lined his face, his suntan long gone. He glared across the pitted table, in silence.

'I'm no priest, Rutter, but I'll happily hear your confession.'

More silence, and a still darker glare, as Rutter firmed up in his head what he intended to say – and what to leave out. He had problems a-plenty now, but *every problem is an opportunity*. A mantra, as far as he was concerned. He flexed and unflexed his fingers, hands clenching slowly into one giant fist.

'Been learning classical mime, Rutter?'

A low rasp emerged from Olly's lips. 'Screw that. And screw your confession. I'm here to do you a favour.'

Batten almost laughed the suggestion back in Olly's face. 'A *favour*? Magically reborn as a God-fearing citizen, are you?'

'Shut up and listen. Or piss off. I don't care which.'

Oh, yes you do, said Batten's eyebrows. He folded his arms and waited.

'Luka Judd.' Two short words, then Rutter folded his arms too.

'Wish I'd brought a chessboard,' Batten said to the silence.

'Do you want him, or not?' *Because the bastard's screwed me, and nobody gets away with that!*

'CID want him. I'm *ex*-CID.'

'*Ex*, my arse. Your blood's a fucking diluted warrant card.'

Rutter had a point, but Batten shrugged it away. 'Luka Judd. What about him?'

What about him? thought Rutter. *I call in a favour, pay through the nose for extra 'resources', and what does he do? Instead of sticking to equine, he moonlights - on my payroll - with Wake Hall 'business' of his own!* 'Theft, burglary, impersonating a police officer,' that's what squat bastard Ball had said. *And the fuzz added 'conspiracy' and tacked the lot on **my** charge sheet!* Olly wasn't having that. 'Cop or ex-cop, I assume you want to feel his collar?'

Batten could almost believe the man opposite was made of fire, so red with revenge was his face. 'And *I* assume you want something in return?'

Rutter's face relaxed. No, for once, he didn't. Not really. Screwing Luka was plenty. *Revenge*, is plenty. 'I want nothing. Maybe I *am* a reborn God-fearing citizen.'

'And the Pope's a reborn Hindu.' Whatever Rutter offered, there'd be a catch. 'Either put up or shut up. I've driven fifty miles to listen to this twaddle.'

'Huh, heartbroken. But you'll need to do more than fifty to find Luka...He's back in *Spain*.'

That figures, thought Batten. He awarded Rutter another eyebrow.

'Luka Judd is a property developer, on the Costa del Sol. Second-home apartment blocks. D'you know how much the last one sold for? Six million euros. Tidy, eh?'

'Fascinating. I've come all this way for Luka's bank statement.'

'Well, *smartarse*, in a way you have. Because the greedy twat ploughed the profits, plus some chunky secured loans, into an even bigger complex - just as the property bubble burst.' Rutter allowed himself a sneery chuckle. 'I know, because he tried to get *me* to invest, as if I've forgotten the meaning of *due diligence*. He's desperate now. Owes the Spanish banks a pile, can't repay till he sells the latest block - and can't sell till it's built. And, poor old Luka, the banks won't lend him any more cash to build it!' Rutter's laughter was so caustic it could unblock a drain. 'Which means the bastard's *fucked!*'

'Well if he is, that's Luka done with. Thanks for the wasted journey.' Batten got to his feet.

'Sit down and *listen*, plonker. Luka Judd is *never* done. He'll wriggle his way past any law you throw at him. Because he loves money – especially if it belongs to someone else.'

Batten heard Pavel's voice whisper in his head… 'And money will be another reason, be sure of it'…Then Ronnie Lopen saying, 'The staff used to call him *Filthy Luka*'. 'Sounds like he's taken a leaf from *your* playbook, Rutter. Except *you* got caught.' Batten perched on the edge of his chair and flicked a finger at the sturdy red brick of Bristol Prison.

Taking in the confined walls, his 'home' for the foreseeable, the thought of Luka wriggling past the law burned a hole in Olly's head - *I'm locked up, and Luka's free? Fuck that.* He selected more crumbs to feed bastard Batten. 'Did you suss it was *his* crew did that spot of burglary at Wake Hall - grubbing after more dinero? The devious sod knew *I'd* get the blame. And we both know whose house got burgled, don't we? And *I* know Luka didn't find any readies, so…' With a hint of theatre, Rutter unclenched his giant hands, threw them at the air and flopped them onto the tabletop.

Not bothering to ask how Rutter knew, Batten followed the money. *Desperate Luka*, searching for Dipstick Dave's hidden cash, to complete a building worth millions? And if Dave is in Spain…and Luka is in Spain…? A sense of urgency made Batten scrape back his chair and climb to his feet. 'Bored,' he told Rutter. 'I expect this'll be another of your fantasies.'

Staying in his seat, Rutter allowed a strange smile to crease his face, despite his predicament. *No*, said the smile. *For once, I'm telling the truth.* 'Ever heard of Casares?'

Batten nodded. 'I know where it is.' *Casares, the hillside village where Dipstick Dave lives. Maybe.*

'Well, this unfinished apartment block of Luka's, it's on the slopes below Casares. Near a golf course. With one of those seductive views towards the sea. I told you, he tried to get me to *invest*.' Re-clenching his hands into one giant fist of vengeance, Rutter kept to himself his 'deal' with Luka: *you* sort Lady Wake's horses, then *I'll* consider investing. Now, Olly's only investment was these piss-yellow walls. 'If you want Luka Judd,' he told Batten, 'try looking in Casares. Help yourself.'

Beneath Batten's tapping feet, Bristol Prison's scratched vinyl could have been the tarmac at Bristol Airport. He began to wonder who he was working for: Lady Wake, or Olly Rutter? *Neither - I'm working for me.* And without another word, he turned for the exit.

Rutter shouted after him, 'And, *Ziggy,* when he gets sent down, tell Luka to watch his back in the prison shower!'

The big ape's drain-clearing snort faded away as Batten trudged down the corridor, hoping never again to hear that sound - or any sound at all - from the sewer that Rutter used as a throat.

While Batten headed for the open air and his car, Olly Rutter lumbered back to a tight cell feeling tighter today, and no cigar to compensate. But what a good turn he'd done, steering plonker Batten towards Casares, towards crazy Luka Judd.

And didn't his good turn deserve a bonus? He chuckled at the thought of bastard Batten cornering Luka, and Luka's brawn making mincemeat of Batten's dodgy skull. Then the real fuzz locking Judd in a cell even tinier than Olly's, for years and years and years... *Yes,* he reminded himself. *Every problem is an opportunity.*

Slumped on his hard mattress, wishing he had a cigar, Rutter still managed to smile at the ceiling. Two birds. One nasty stone.

Perfect revenge.

Forty-nine

Ensconced in a Queen Anne chair by the banked-up log fire in Lady Wake's private office, Batten sipped Darjeeling tea and munched an exquisite wafer-thin shortbread. Nor did he care when the occasional crumb tumbled past his lap and drifted onto the owner's trampoline carpet. He didn't expect *Her Ladyship* did the hoovering. In any case, his latest news, of Olly Rutter and of Luka Judd's Spanish predicament, still twinkled in the air like fairy lights on the giant Wake Hall Christmas tree.

'That's settled, then?' said Lady Wake, standing with her back to the window, diamond eyes flashing from Avril to Batten. 'How soon can you travel?'

Batten brushed shortbread crumbs from his trousers. How soon? To Spain, without a parachute, in a nervy metal tube at 30,000 feet? With *Hillview* only half-renovated? And a relationship still in its infancy? He hesitated – till the driven-dog urge to *unearth* got the better of him.

'Er, after Christmas? Is that reasonable?'

Lady Wake would have preferred him to leave yesterday, and her eyes said so. '*Soon* after Christmas?' she asked, her question a veiled command, as ever. 'In the past, I may have been guilty of prevarication, and of a certain…blindness. I do not intend to repeat my mistake.'

'OK. Soon after Christmas. But when you say I have *carte blanche*, how literal is that?'

Marianne Wake turned to gaze through the glass at Maya's empty field. When the time was right, she herself would return to Spain, to find a mare even half as beautiful as Maya. She would run long fingers through her flowing mane and coax her round the *manege*, barely needing to use the reins. And it would soften her heart.

In the meantime… 'Yes, Zig. Literal. *Carte blanche*. A blank cheque, if you wish. Unlimited power to act.'

'Unlimited power to act – within the law, I take it?'

Lady Wake gave Batten the full force of her diamond eyes. Her answer, like her questions, carried a whiff of ambiguity. 'Within the law?' Her stately face became an impenetrable mask. 'Oh,' she said. 'Naturally.'

*

Back at *Hillview*, an upbeat Batten awarded himself a break, pulled on his walking shoes and, in househusband mode, hiked the mile and a half into the centre of Parminster. In the covered market just off the High Street he bought fresh prawns, shallots and salsify, to make Sonia her favourite pasta dish. On the return leg, shopping bag swinging jauntily by his side, he smiled again at Arnie Goole's news, and its implications for Olly Rutter - more visits from CID being one of them. How Batten envied *Inspector* Ball, staring across the interview table at *Mr* Rutter, shooting poisoned-arrow questions at him. And maybe, before long, at *Mr* Judd.

'Turn the screw, Ballie,' he told the empty street. 'For both of us.'

Though cooking for himself felt a chore, making prawn pasta for two and chilling a bottle of Pinot Grigio was a genuine pleasure, his only impatience being Sonia's slow arrival at dinner.

A tired, withdrawn Sonia Welcome had struggled through the front door, and now stared blankly across the dining table, as if awaiting arrest.

'Difficult day, love?' he said, the lame question earning a sad sigh in response. He wondered if she'd even noticed the antique serving dish and china plates, her grandmother's, carefully unpacked this very afternoon.

'We're becoming too much alike, Zig,' she said, her golden smile gone, and for five gut-tumbling seconds he feared she was about to bring their relationship to an end. 'I've begun to carry work home now, in my head, just like you. I used to leave it behind by switching off the desk lamp and reaching for my car keys. Now on bad days, my work climbs into the passenger seat, and I drive it here, to our new home, to *Hillview*.'

Batten back-pedalled, clumsily. 'I guess, on bad days, Sonia, a lot of people do much the same?'

'*Much the same?* And do this *lot of people* autopsy a three-year-old child, battered to death by its own parents – mere days before Christmas? And in the process, do they coolly dictate a report listing every bruise and cut and broken bone? I found forty-three injuries, on a child shorter than this table leg!' She swiped a fist hard enough against it to bruise her hand. 'How much *hate* must two parents feel, to batter their own child forty-three violent times?'

In CID, he'd seen bucketloads of violence and hate, and still couldn't explain them. He kept silent.

'I'm supposed to be *professional, Zig. Dispassionate. Objective.* And somehow, I manage it. But words alone can't block the darkness. I take a scalpel to a tiny life snuffed out, and it's a childhood of fear and pain I see, instead of hope and growth.' She swallowed a defensive glug of wine, staring at the pasta clamped around her fork but eating none of it.

Like Sonia, Batten took pride in being *professional*. But had he ever been truly *dispassionate* and *objective* in his work? He doubted it. Staring at Sonia's plate, he silently cursed. He'd made tagliatelle, and the white swirls curling round her fork could have been a child's intestines, streaked with red stains bleeding from the beetroot salad. *Well done, Zig, for easing Sonia's mind.*

He chewed on pasta and salsify, almost biting his tongue when Sonia dropped her fork onto the antique china with a *ching!* so loud he thought the precious plate would smash.

'Whether the house is finished or not, Zig, *please*, book us a holiday. As soon as Christmas is done, fly us somewhere warm. Anywhere. A do-nothing break, to rest my weary mind. Will you?'

Relieved, he said, 'Of course I will, love. Of course.' He bit into a garlic prawn, tasting the hint of lemon and basil, the sweetness of shallot. But it lumped down his throat like a pound of slime, heavy with guilt, as he pushed aside the conversation he had planned to have but wouldn't - couldn't - tonight.

…Er, Sonia, I have Dipstick Dave's address in Casares, in Spain. This Luka Judd is holed up there too. And Lady Wake has given me 'carte blanche' so, soon as Christmas is done, I'm flying back to the Costa del Sol, to find the pair of them, and tie things up. And, yes, it could be dangerous…So, er, I can't take you with me, I'm afraid…

With more wine than food inside her, Sonia pleaded exhaustion and went to bed. Batten breathed a temporary sigh of relief. Tomorrow, when she was rested, they would talk - openly, honestly. She was central to his world, and he would move mountains to sustain that. *Hillview* would never become a *Hall of Secrets.* Wasn't one enough?

After clearing up, he switched on the CD player and let *The Walk to the Paradise Garden* soothe his senses. He loved the Delius orchestration first time he heard it, and when he discovered *The Paradise Garden* was in fact a pub, it sounded better still. Clicking *Repeat*, it soothed him so deeply he nodded off on the new sofa, waking stiff-necked from a nerve-jangling nightmare, his aeroplane spiralling towards the ground, it and him exploding into fragments so tiny they were untraceable.

He stretched his spine and arms, but body and mind remained taut with conflicting demands: *Love. Work. Home. A* conjuring trick, a juggling act - and he was no stage performer. Locking the doors and switching off CD and lights, he struggled up the stairs to Sonia, knowing what a lucky man he was.

Yet every tread felt one step closer to 30,000 feet.

PART FIVE

CASARES, SPAIN

Fifty

Though at the very top of *Calle del Barrio Alto*, their tiny, rented house had advantages. Its hilltop position gifted them a stunning view over the beautiful white village of Casares, a mazy spiral of steep lanes dipping and winding past iron balconies and little patios clothed in sun or shade. Batten had lost his way twice, in the short time they'd been there. At night, said his companion, Casares *had atmosphere,* with ornate black streetlamps on the high walls casting deep dark shadows down its narrow streets. For Batten, the shadows were simply more places for *someone* to hide.

In daytime, the vista below the village fell away past steep rocky outcrops and sporadic trees skirting one apartment block after another, past the rolling greens of a golf course, and down to the blue coastline of the Costa del Sol. And January was warm, twenty degrees warmer than Bristol airport - the last of England for as long as their assignment took. Batten allowed himself a non-work moment to enjoy the morning sun on his face and the scent of saffron from the *restaurante* in the street below.

A second advantage was access. This highest part of Casares was pedestrian only, and steep. Batten had watched groceries and building supplies being carted up on little motorised platforms or improvised sledges and, once, on a donkey. And *Barrio Alta* ended in a cul-de-sac. He guessed why Dave had chosen this narrow street for his bolthole. Any 'visitor' must tackle the slope, on foot, on the only available route. And be clearly visible.

A third advantage was deliberate. Their rental's front porch sat diagonally across the street from number *338*, the Spanish home of Dipstick Dave Vossialevydipsic, its dark panelled door tinged by morning sun. *Good job we have sunshine,* Batten mused. Because, so far, they didn't have Dave. And if Luka Judd was also in search mode, there was no sign of Luka.

From his canvas chair in the canopied porch, a frustrated Batten gazed through a broad gap in the buildings opposite towards the cliff's edge, where a group of trainee climbers in yellow safety helmets waited their turn. An instructor was clipping a harness to the next in line and coaxing him over the parapet, pointing to handholds and crevices below, cooing words of encouragement in soft Spanish.

Batten was reminded of old Ronnie Lopen and his climbing club, though this instructor was forty years younger than Ronnie. Pointing to the youthful climbers, surrounded by coiled ropes and a jumble of assorted gear, he said, 'Miss it?'

From his chair in the shadows, Pavel Ducek shook his head. 'These boys are gumbies. I was experienced. This is climbing for beginners, on a safety rope. And see the metal chain, bolted to the cliff? There are two or three more like it, along the cliffside. They run from top to bottom, with stanchions every ten feet or so. The teacher, he clips each beginner onto the chain, so if they fall they fall only a little way. It gives them confidence.'

'And it's safer,' mumbled Batten, still acclimatizing to a take-off and landing, and to their house at the cliff's peak.

'Safer. But less exciting.'

'You stopped, didn't you?'

Pavel looked at his hands. 'I did.'

'Because of Luka? Would he really have pushed you off a cliff?'

The reddish rock seemed to stir Pavel's memory. 'Dave thought so. And Dave is black and white, straight.'

'Straight? For a crook, you mean?' Batten had stopped mincing his words with Pavel. He never asked him to come.

'A crook, perhaps. Who saved my life.' Pavel stood up to stretch. 'So, yes. I stopped. Some of these boys will stop,' he said, pointing to the group. 'But one day some will be instructors.'

'The wheat and the chaff,' mumbled Batten, hoping Dave would turn up and make today a wheat day. He was doing the lion's share of watching, his face unknown to both Dave and Luka Judd, while Pavel waited, a presence in the shadows, the same careful expression on his face as when he pressed the buzzer of Batten's garden office, days ago, though it felt like months…

… 'I thought you were Avril,' said Batten. 'She's driving me to Bristol Airport.'

'Do I look like Avril? *I'm* driving you. Ready?'

Batten was foot-tapping-ready, with photos of Dave and Luka Judd and Angie Bowen in his cabin bag. After a mile or two, his foot ceased to tap, and he dozed in the passenger seat while Pavel regressed to his old silent self. Only when the taciturn farrier drove not into the Drop-Off Zone but the Long Stay car park, did the penny drop.

'You're coming too? To *Spain*?'

'I've been before.'

'You said you'd had enough of it.'

Pavel found a parking space, opened the boot to retrieve his rucksack – a new one, larger – and locked the car. Facing Batten, he said, 'Oksana wanted to come, because of Dave. Insisted, till Lady Wake said, 'No, no. Pavel will go in your place.''

Though neither man knew it, Marianne Wake had reflected on the dangers of Batten's trip, without admitting a growing fondness for her Zig. 'What if I sent Ben Thorpe?' she asked Avril. 'After all, he has a Security brief.'

'Is Ben not a little…young, ma'am?' *With muscles like matchsticks.*

'Oh. Yes, I suppose so. Who, then?'

Avril Dean had already decided. 'Pavel has experience of Spain - the Costa del Sol in particular?' *And has the muscles of a farrier.*

It was decided. Pavel would share the load. And should danger arise, be a tacit bodyguard…

'As usual, *Her Ladyship* never ask Pavel.'

'And she never asked me. No surprise.'

'Yes. But, still, I am going. For Oksana, for Dave.'

'I'd set my mind on doing this alone,' said Batten. 'I'm not-'

'How is your Spanish?' said Pavel, with no hint of a smile. 'How will you persuade Dave to come back when you have never met him? What will you do if Dave and Luka turn up together? Ask them to hold hands, come quietly?'

Stumped, Batten picked up his cabin bag in silence. A private agent now, he could sidestep police procedure. But were his plans for Spain much more than a finger in the wind, a wait-and-see? Secretly, he was glad to have a sort-of sidekick, and he'd grown to like Pavel. All the same, as they headed for Departures, he said,' Just reassure me you don't have a sharpened bloody hoof-knife in your pocket. Eh?'

Pavel Ducek smiled, dipped his hand into his coat and pulled out a boarding pass…

…Another yellow-helmeted gumby in a safety harness disappeared over the side of the cliff. A sacrificial lamb, as far as Batten was concerned. He stared at the red rock – *bermejo*, according to Jorge, their nosy neighbour, a retired geologist all-too-keen to practise his English. Jorge's German Shepherd dog, *Ortega*, reminded Batten of Ronnie Lopen's *Cyril*. Two friendly dogs, like their owners, but Jorge was either too damn friendly or just plain nosey. Batten didn't know. What he *did* know was far too much about volcanic peridotites and ultramafic rocks. He needed no help from geologist Jorge to feel tiny beneath the grey limestone mountain that towered above even the tall pinnacle of Casares. He blew out his breath. *It's all bloody heights round here!*

Heights - and surveillance. He bought a wildlife camera, discreetly fixed it in the upstairs window of their rental and angled it to cover *338 Calle del Barrio Alto*. They took turns to scan the overnight footage. So far, it comprised cats, dogs, and a pair of acrobatic tipsy lovers. As a young Detective, Batten hated surveillance duty. In his head, he heard the voice of Ged Morley, his old pal from Leeds CID. 'You know what surveillance is, Zig? It's fishing, in a massive lake, in the dark - and you're not even sure there *are* any fish!'

The last few days felt much like that. In the streets below, he and Pavel consulted neighbours and toured the bars and *restaurantes* of Casares, subtly enquiring about Dave's whereabouts. At *Bar Nonina*, in a mixture of local dialect and broken English, a man called Luis said Dave was a *buen amigo*, a good bloke, who'd mended his motor bike, for free. When? *Oh, maybe a year ago?* Seen him since? *No, no, wish I had – especially if Dave is with his galanazo!* Luis made curvy female shapes with his rough hands as Batten threw a puzzled face at Pavel.

'I think a galanazo is…a hottie?' He and Luis babbled in Spanish, till Luis gave a leery grin and pretended to fan himself.

'Does he know this *hottie*'s name? Her whereabouts?'

More Spanish, more shrugs, more dead ends. Pavel translated Luis' final comment: *'If you see Dave, tell him my bike, it broke again!'* Hoarse laughter swamped the bar, covering Batten in a miasma of rancid garlic, in lieu of information.

Fifty-one

The two watchers shared the daily surveillance of Luka's apartment block on the slopes below, through strong binoculars, with a copy of *Birds of Spain* on hand as cover. The first time, Batten was shocked by the sight of a huge eagle, floating eerily above him on the thermals. But Luka Judd had either flown away - or was yet to nest.

'My turn to watch the birds,' said Batten, shouldering his binoculars. 'Your turn to watch for Dave.'

On Pavel's shrug, Batten strolled along the stony path beyond The Church of the Incarnation, shuddering his way past another climbing chain and another group of young climbers in hard-hats and harnesses. When he spotted nosy-neighbour Jorge taking *Ortega* for his daily walk, he ducked behind a wall till Jorge disappeared down the steep hill. Trudging with gritted teeth to the highest viewpoint, he tightly gripped the nearest lamppost and scanned the vista of rocks, trees, sky and sea. His true focus was *L.J. Property's* expansive apartment block on the slope below, still little more than holes in the ground. He scanned for a good ten minutes, the powerful lenses peering into every foundation trench, every excavated pit. Like yesterday, no cars or diggers were parked there, the high gates still padlocked, not a workman nor a Luka in sight. And no obvious hideaway where Luka might hole up.

A group of winter tourists strolled past, wondering why this tall, moustached man was squinting through binoculars while clinging to a lamppost as if his life depended on it. Embarrassed, he loped back to *Barrio Alta* and saw Pavel's head semaphoring at Dave's house across the street. Batten followed the frantic nods. A thirty-something woman had climbed the hilly street, stopped outside Dave's, and begun to fumble in her pocket – for keys? Short white leggings, tight pink top, a small shoulder bag strapped across her enviable curves. Was this Dave's *galanazo*, his hottie? She was certainly a looker - who spotted Batten looking.

'G'day. Ya English?' she said.

'Er, yes.' *And you're Australian.* 'Can I help?'

'If you're the Rental Agent, sure.' She consulted her phone. 'Mr Everett?' She pronounced it *Iveritt*.

In the absence of a clipboard, opportunist Batten flashed a Rental Agent smile. 'Er, that's me, yes. Am I early?'

'Don' care – at least you turned *up*. Not like that pushy Spinnish guy from your place – tell him if he rings me again, I'll sue. Chloe, Chloe Clark, by the way.' They shook hands, her grip like Pavel's. 'Ya get my litters?'

'*Litters*? Oh, letters, er, which ones?'

'*Which ones*? How minny do I need to write before you lot lissen? Fir crying out loud, this is Dave's place, not mine. Your Spinnish pal seems to think I can read Dave's *mind*, when I haven't *seen* him. I *used* to drop in, time to time, but now I'm dropping out, back to Oz, OK? As far as the *rint* goes, Dave paid ages in advance. If his shilling's run out, it's not *my* problem. So stop asking *me* to pay!'

'Er, well...'

'Look, here's the spare keys. I've a plane to catch. An' if you see Dave - 'cos I *haven't* - you can tell him Chloe said ta for the good times, and *adios*! Roight?'

Windfall keys jangling in his hand, Batten milked the situation. 'Er, I do see, about the rent, but you must know the Agency rules?'

It was Chloe Clark's turn to look puzzled.

'I can't accept the return of keys without inspecting the property. In the presence of a keyholder, that is. And since I'm here, and you're here...'

'An' since Dave's gone walkabout without paying the rint, ya mean?'

Batten gave her his hangdog, I'm-only-doing-my-job look. It worked.

'Aw, no need to git yer knickers in a knot, mate. Tin minnits – but then I'm *off*. Roight?'

Batten fitted the key into the ancient door of thick panelled wood, studded with lines of iron nails like black suspicious eyes, glaring at him. For a moment, the frowning double doors of Wake Hall flashed into his head. He expected a struggle, but the key turned with barely a click, the solid door soundlessly easing open.

'And that's another thing,' said Chloe. 'When the key snapped, Dave didn't whinge to *you*, did he? Some locksmith pal of his made him another. And I don't recall Dave sending you the bill!'

Following Chloe into the musty-smelling house, Batten weighed the key in his hand and improvised. 'He's done an excellent job, this locksmith pal. Be handy to have a good locksmith on our books?'

'I'll bit - but I nivver met him. Told you, I don't *live* here. He was Dave's boss – Lorcan? Lorcan Something?' She fished in her bag and handed Batten a business card. 'That's Dave's firm, well, this Lorcan's firm, but no-one's answering, because soon as you lot mentioned *rint*, I rang, tin times! If *you* get through, tell whoever answers to pay Dave's rint!'

Dave Voss, said the card. *Maintenance and Repair, L.J. Property, Estepona*. So, Dave and Luka Judd stayed connected in Spain…Batten thanked Chloe for the card and pretended to give the premises the once-over. Five smallish rooms, separated by more thick panelled doors in the old Spanish style he hated, with heavy black bolts and nails protruding from the dark wood. A small rear patio was penned in by a robust stone wall, five-foot high, its old whitewash now edging towards grey. Peering over it, Batten recoiled at the sheer drop on the other side. *Clifftops*, he mumbled with a shiver. *Always bloody clifftops*.

Chloe Clark gave an unsubtle cough. 'Y'inspected yit?'

'Er, yes.' Covertly, he'd watched her, checking her movements, hoping she'd give away a hiding place. But if she came to collect *something*, her behaviour said otherwise. 'Yes, all seems in order.' Nothing much *to* order, he thought. The bedsheets smelled stale but were uncreased, the pots and pans still stacked neatly in their cupboards, the wardrobe almost empty.

'Why am I not surprised? He's buggered off, hasn't he? Without so much as a 'nice knowing ya, Chlo.' Blokes, eh?'

'I'm sorry,' said Batten. 'I mean, if he…'

'Aw, chill, mate. Just fuck-buddies, me and Dave. You know, *when in the vicinity*. A beer, two grunts and a dick, that's Dave.' When she rolled her eyes at Batten's prissy response, he guessed he'd measured up as *Mr Iveritt*, even without the clipboard.

'We done?'

Batten paused. Did Spanish agencies normally require the rent *ages* in advance? Or was Dave deliberately holding onto his private bolthole – despite seeming to have 'buggered off' months ago? *And where does this leave Pavel and me?* Chloe twitched by the door, carrying only what she'd arrived in. 'Er, I don't suppose Dave left any documents or, er, *property* with you? Anything? Anything at all?'

Chloe pulled a sour face. 'Dave? *Nothing* at all! He wasn't exactly Mr Gift. Now - are we *done?*'

Better go, thought Batten, in case the real *Mr Iveritt* turns up. Dave's business card was handy. And with house keys, he and Pavel could take the place apart when the coast was clear. 'Er, yes, thank you. Done.'

'And you'll stop hassling me over Dave's *rint?*'

'I'll see to it,' he said, as Chloe Clark swished through the door on a lips-only smile. Dipstick Dave, who he'd pursued but never met, now felt somehow like a real person, with a place of abode, a business card and a relationship of sorts. He watched Chloe's pink and white curves disappear down the slope, strangely glad that, *when in the vicinity,* Dave Voss had at least enjoyed the well-toned comforts of her flesh.

Even while wanted for murder.

Fifty-two

Next morning, braving the hilly roads and the hire-car's unfamiliar left-hand drive, Batten trundled down to Estepona and parked two streets from the address on Dave's business card. *L.J. Property* occupied a decent-sized shopfront on the edge of the commercial area but when Batten strolled past, a *Closed* sign dangled from the door and the windows were smeared with dust and grime. At the street corner, from the dense shadow of an orange tree, he rang the firm's number, hoping to spot movement inside. Nothing. He wandered up and down, pretending to window-shop, then tried again. The same.

Drawing closer, he peered in. A pile of mail lay banked up beneath the letterbox. When a tap on the door brought no answer, he tapped harder and would have tapped harder still had a finger not tapped *him* – on the shoulder.

'*Señor?*'

Surprised, Batten took a now-automatic step back to safeguard his weakened skull. A dark, stocky man confronted him, wearing a grey nondescript suit, its jacket buttoned up despite the heat of the day. He'd never seen him before. 'Yes?'

'Ah, I thinked you are maybe English. My English is good. You have a moment?'

For what? 'A moment?'

From his pocket, the stocky man drew his ID and held it up.

Stalling, Batten fumbled for his glasses and said, 'It's in Spanish.' He'd already recognised the *Policia Nacional* logo and clocked the photograph. Glasses on, he deciphered the rank. *Inspector Jefe* - Chief Inspector. Remembering the fake detective who'd grilled Oksana in search of Dave's belongings, he felt a jolt of fear, and though the ID looked pukka, he took another step back after scanning it again. 'Look, just tell me who you are?'

'Of course, of course. My name is Rafael Delgado. Of the National Police.' He pointed to his name on the ID. 'My men, they call me Raffa.'

'Do they? Really?'

With a patient smile, the *Chief Inspector* crooked a casual finger at a side street off the main road. A uniformed *policia* emerged from an unmarked car and looked quizzically at the *Jefe*, who forestalled him with a raised palm. 'This *policeman*, he does, *really*.' Pointing to the tinted windows of a black saloon parked at the opposite kerb, he said, 'So, perhaps we will talk in my car?'

Not bloody likely! 'Perhaps we'll talk in there?' said Batten. *He* pointed to the neutral venue of a coffee-shop, a few doors away.

'Of course, if you wish. I will even pay...'

The coffee was so rich and aromatic, Batten drank a second cup. *Raffa* settled for one, which allowed him to do the talking - in the form of questions. At a corner table in the half-empty cafe, the two men kept their voices low as they fenced and fended. When Batten tried a few questions of his own, Delgado answered vaguely, with the same patient smile. He reminded Batten of Makis Grigoris, his good friend from the Greek International Police Co-operation Division. Different cops, different nationalities, same assumptions, same instincts.

'Mr Batten.' He pronounced it *Batt-ten*. 'My man - the one you see, in uniform - he is watching the shopfront of *L.J. Property* when you come there. He is a good policeman. He notice, shall we say, your *unusual* interest in who is inside? And knowing his job, he call me...Good coffee, yes?' he said.

Batten agreed, warily watching Delgado copy down his mobile phone number and check the notes he'd made.

'You are ex-CID, you say? An Inspector, once? But now a *private citizen*, and searching for a client's missing brother?'

Not liking the way 'private citizen' lingered on Delgado's tongue, Batten mumbled, 'Correct.' The snippets, though more or less true, were snippets only.

'And this brother, this Dave Voss, who once work for *L.J. Property*, he has somehow disappear, you say?' When Batten nodded back, Delgado raised an eyebrow, fell silent, then stared for ten slow seconds at the details on Dave's business card. 'This is no simple matter, Mr Batt-ten, but one thing is clear. *You* and the *Policia Nacional* are looking in the same place, for the same man. This *L.J*. This *Luka Judd*.'

'Seems we are,' said a cagey Batten.

'You have given certain *reasons* for your interest,' said Delgado, his tone suggesting he didn't much believe them. 'Of course, I cannot say my reasons…But much *fraud* perhaps. At the very least.'

'Does that mean there's *more*?'

Raffa's strong fingers fiddled with his cup for a moment. 'This information is official - and *you* are not, Señor.'

Huh, thought Batten, *more bloody secrets!* At least *Raffa* didn't tell him to get out of town.

'But for your own safety, I will say this: the man we seek is…resourceful. For example, we think an illegal firearm - along with many more suspicions. And I do not wish you to be hurt in attempting to…discover them.'

Keeping silent, Batten finished his second espresso. He, Pavel and the entire Wake Hall Estate had seen how *resourceful* Luka could be.

Toying with his cup, Delgado waved vaguely at the sky beyond the window. 'Spain is very beautiful country, yes?'

'Indeed.'

'So, please enjoy her beauty before - *soon* - you return to England? Which is also beautiful. I have been, of course.' He pushed his cup away. 'But do not rap on Mr Judd's office door. We will do that, and much besides. And we will find him. We, the *police*.' Delgado stood up, the 'meeting' over. 'Here, take my card. Perhaps for when you remember more than you have said, no? I have been polite, you agree?'

'Impeccably so, thank you.'

'But, if there is a next time - about Mr Judd, I mean - I may be *less* polite? You understand?' Pierced by the Chief Inspector's eyes, suddenly sharper, Batten understood alright. When he didn't say he would comply, Delgado's eyes narrowed further still. But with a tiny bow, the stout detective shook Batten's hand and said, 'Vaya con Dios, *Señor*.'

Watching the confident grey suit glide into the sunlit street, Batten felt nervous tremors darting through his veins. Those two strong coffees, he told himself – till he realised why Delgado's jacket was still buttoned up, despite the burgeoning heat of the day.

Fifty-three

When the light faded, they switched on the surveillance camera and nipped down to *Bar Nonina*. Nosy-neighbour Jorge, with *Ortega*, his German Shepherd curled up at his feet, was already there, boring the barman rigid with geology. Ignoring his sharp glance, Batten and Pavel carried their beers to a pavement table, well out of Jorge's reach, despite the coolness of the evening.

Pavel's face again tightened at the mention of *Policia Nacional*. It bled white when Batten admitted he'd given a false address. 'I told that Spanish cop I'd driven over from Malaga, from the hotel I stayed in when I was looking for you.'

'But that was months ago!' said Pavel, keeping his voice down despite the generic rock music thudding from the speakers inside.

'I *know*, but I had to think on my feet. It was the only address in Spain I could remember - apart from ours, and I wasn't giving him that.' Batten didn't tell Pavel the police had a dozen better ways to trace their whereabouts. 'We'll have to hurry things along.'

Pavel was unconvinced. 'Hurry? How? By *magic*?'

Draining his *Cruzcampo* beer, Batten said, 'What if we poke around Luka's unfinished apartment block - pretend we want to buy a flat, off-plan?' He hadn't even convinced himself, but they must do *something*.

'What if we *don't*?' said Pavel, clomping his empty glass onto the table.

'OK, then a deep search of Dave's place, tomorrow, when the streets are quiet?'

Pavel seemed happier with this suggestion. 'They still have siesta time in Casares. Mid-afternoon, that's when the streets are quiet.' He nodded at Batten's glass, nervous fingers tapping on his own. 'Another?'

It was Spain that made me drink – isn't that what Pavel had said? With both their best interests at heart, Batten declined. 'No. Early night for me.'

'To be ready for tomorrow?'

He got to his feet. 'Yes. Tomorrow. More surveillance. Then at siesta time, we search.'

*

By early afternoon, the wind had dropped but the sun hadn't, as he and Pavel nonchalantly turned the key in the silent lock of Dave's door, closing it noiselessly behind them. It was cooler inside, blue and white marble tiles on the floor, the windows locked and shuttered. When Batten switched on a pair of lamps, their thin beams fell on heavy doors and dark brown furniture, bringing more gloom than light to the place.

'Look,' said Batten, pointing to cracks in the floor tiles. 'Maybe Dave buried something underneath?'

Dropping to his hands and knees, Pavel inspected the cracks. 'Old,' he said. 'Old dirt in the cracks.'

'Dave might have *filled* them with old dirt, to fool us – or somebody.'

Pavel drew a large Swiss Army knife from his pocket and tried to prise up a cracked tile. Catching Batten's look of surprise, he said, 'Don't worry, it's legal. I bought it in Estepona.' After a minute, he shook his head. 'These are just cracks. The tiles are solid. Nothing here.'

Cursing, Batten scoured the upstairs, while Pavel went through every nook and cranny in the kitchen and *salon*. The little house had no loft, just an apex roof, beamed, with no place to hide even a matchbox. For over an hour, they tapped and pulled, pushed and poked but if Dave hid his cash in this Casares bolthole, he'd made it invisible. 'The patio?' said Batten.

The backyard yielded a broken flowerpot and a rusty spade. Shards of red rust fell from it when Batten picked it up. 'No-one's dug anything with this thing in a long time,' he said. Nor was there anything to dig, the concrete floor undisturbed, green with ancient mould and spotted white with lichen. 'There's a sort of locker, set into the side wall. Can you prise it open?'

Once more, out came the Swiss Army knife and the locker door clicked free. Old paint cans, a rotting rag, two decrepit brushes, and a frantic spider. Pavel tapped and prodded the sides and back. Solid.

'We could've missed something inside,' said Batten. 'We'll search again. Might be our last chance.'

'I'll see if Dave hid anything over the back wall,' said climber Pavel, heaving himself onto the stone for a better look.

'Rather you than me,' said Batten, shying away from the dizzying drop and heading back into the gloom. He realised, too late, that what flashed across his peripheral vision was not sunlight but the glint of a silver pistol

– which clipped him heavily on the shoulder, narrowly missing his skull but stunning him to the ground. A tall figure emerged from the back door's shadow as Pavel heard the commotion and dashed in – and for the second time in a few short months looked down the barrel of a shiny gun.

'This one is new, Pavel. But silver bullets, remember? Now, please reach down, very slowly, empty this man's pockets and slide the contents along the floor to me. Then *your* pockets. Miss anything, and I will put a silver bullet in you.'

A hazy Batten felt his pockets being stripped of his phone, wallet, his own and Dave's keys, and heard the jangle as they rolled across the floor. Then what Pavel had described as Luka's bank manager voice said, '*You*. Face down, please. Make an X on the floor, arms far apart, fingers spread.' From instinct and training, Batten did as he was told - for now.

Pavel's face was white with fear, hatred, indecision, his eyes on the silver gun.

'Ah, Pavel,' said Luka, 'you are thinking, *this room is small, what if I move quickly, wrench the gun from Mr Judd's hand, and be a hero?*' From the look on Pavel's face, he was thinking exactly that. 'I strongly advise against it.' He drew out the words with ice in his voice. 'And welcome back to Spain, Pavel - though did I give you permission to leave? Please, remain standing. I have a job for you.'

Batten slowly edged his head sideways to see his adversary. Now clean-shaven and suntanned, Luka's face was much less like his bearded photograph. No need to ask how this trained locksmith got in without making a sound, *but how did he know we were here?* Sensing Batten's movement, Luka glanced across, his bald head covered by a bright green baseball cap.

'Yes, I retrieved this cap from a pathetic little flat in Malaga. It was all Pavel left behind when he scurried away - like a little *mickey mouse!* But now, to work.' Luka Judd slid a backpack from his shoulders to the floor and, taking neither gun nor eyes off Pavel and Batten, one-handedly removed a spanner. His gun waved Pavel to the heavy panelled door between the salon and the kitchen. 'I will slide this spanner across the floor to you, Pavel. One false move and I will put a bullet in your knee, and in your friend's. I am an extremely good shot, by the way, and will risk the noise, within these shuttered walls.'

Batten watched the spanner and empty backpack slide across the tiles and come to rest against Pavel's trainers.

'You see those black bolts surrounding the large panel in the centre?' Pavel nodded, transfixed by the gun. 'Dave saw them too, but so did I. Handyman Dave - in secret, so he thought - had removed and replaced that panel. A hopeless actor, Dave. When, to his great surprise, I 'dropped in' one day, he stood a little too protectively in front of that very door. And the scratches on the black metal were so obvious a child could spot them. Dave is like the door, mm? Thick, heavy, slow, a *thing* of the old Spain. When *I* build, I build *modern*.'

Batten's addled mind told him he hated the heavy doors too. He shook away the ridiculous thought as Luka perched himself on a chair, the silver gun still staring like an eye. When Luka said, 'But that useful door has been my bank these last few months. Safe, secure, and of course tax-free,' Batten wanted to tell this bastard to zip the sarcasm.

'So, Pavel. Take the spanner - very slowly - and remove the bolts in turn. You will slide each bolt across the floor to me. Should you consider throwing them, I will revise my decision to shoot you in the knee and instead put a bullet in your groin. Might that spoil Oksana's honeymoon? *No.* You would bleed to death, you see, slowly, and in extreme pain.'

Incentivised, Pavel set to it as Luka watched, chatting in his sinister voice as if his two prisoners were partners in crime. As the first bolt rumbled noisily across the tiles towards him, he pointed his voice at Batten. 'You, sir,' he said, 'must be the man who visited a certain overmuscled gangster of my acquaintance, in Bristol prison? Not *quite* as slow as Dave, our foul-mouthed Mr Rutter. But slow, all the same. And he does not speak well of *you*. Ah, good,' he added as a second bolt rolled across the floor, followed by a third and fourth.

Batten counted six bolts in all, and tried not to think what would happen when the sixth was removed. From his prone position he had nil chance of beating a bullet by clambering to his feet to tackle Luka – who grinned as a fifth bolt rumbled against his foot.

Attempting to distract, Batten said, 'This panel's where Dave hid his money?'

A smug laugh. 'Ah, you have caught up. Dave's money, yes, but my money now. I 'drop in' here sometimes, to double-check. Dave is… elsewhere. With no need of it.'

The spanner twitched in Pavel's hand. He flinched and said, 'What of Tom? Tom Bowditch. His money's here too?'

'*My* money, Pavel, not Tom's. Why let it go to waste? And it was poor Dave who took it first.'

'By killing Tom?'

Luka laughed his dismissive, demon laugh, and Batten understood Pavel's deep hatred of the man. 'Ah, young Tom. He and Dave were wrestling on the ground when I drove up. In fact, Tom was winning. You could almost say Dave owed me his life.' Again, the laugh of a jackal. 'Even I was surprised by the *vulgar* noise a bolt-cutter makes when piercing a skull. Like cracking a boiled egg – or perhaps it's because my arms are so strong. And Tom was leaving, you see, with all that money. But without my permission.'

Adrenalin pumped another off-key thought into Batten's capricious mind. *Dave's not a killer!* But if Pavel thought the same, his grim face failed to show it when the final bolt rolled across the floor.

'The panel next, if you please. Lift it out - slowly - place it on the tiles and slide it over.' When Pavel did, Batten saw a deep and wide cavity in the door, stuffed with what looked like blue plastic freezer bags. As Pavel did as he was told and thrust them into the backpack, Batten realised that's exactly what they were. But instead of frozen meat, the bags bulged with fat wads of banknotes. Dozens of them.

To split Luka's focus, Batten took the lead. 'So, now you're rich?'

Steel eyes on Pavel, Luka spoke to them both. '*Almost* rich. Not all Dave' money is here, and since the wretch was too mean to spend any, he must have hidden the rest. But failed to say where, even after *persuasion*.'

Pavel winced, shoving the remaining blue bags into the backpack with fire in his face. Batten tried to keep Luka talking. 'You thought the rest was in Oksana's cottage, didn't you? But your clever burglars drew a blank.'

'Oh, the money will turn up, I'm sure. Though too late. Being *almost* rich is not rich enough, and banks can be so…greedy. Greedy, and uncooperative. To grub back their loans on my current venture, they have foreclosed. No matter, I will be long gone, with *my* money, and Tom's, and *some* of Dave's.' Luka grinned like a smug gargoyle at Dave's name. 'Poor repentant Dave... Do you know, he intended giving money to Tom's mother? It seems she's rather ill. *Aww*. Weak-minded *cretin!* And ungrateful. It was *me* found Dave a job, in Estepona - because of the money, yes, location unknown. But still he declined to invest. Like the banks - *uncooperative.*' Luka twitched the gun, a dismissive shrug. 'Black and white, Dave, and wanting to be only white. Sentimental fool, griping about his pathetic sister in England - *Don't!*' he hissed, as Pavel's arm jerked towards him.

The mention of Oksana squeezed the blood from Pavel's face. Despite the cold marble tiles, sweat was prickling Batten's limbs, his insides boiling with the anger of helplessness. *What now?* he asked himself. *Is my first case to be my last?*

Testing the weight of the backpack, Luka flashed a satisfied smile. 'Now, Pavel, you will also make an X on the floor, head down, by the far wall, and away from your friend. And the pair of you, arms and fingers spread wide, please, and facing the kitchen... *Good.*' He hoisted the spoils to his shoulder, the gun firm in his grip.

Luka's overshirt lifted as the backpack slid onto his arms, and Batten's penny dropped when from the corner of his eye he spotted the metal glint of a carabiner, dangling from a harness around Luka's waist. *The climbing chain! That's how this bastard gets in and out!* The same chain Batten had watched the instructor and his trainees use, only days ago.

But Luka was no trainee. He stared at his two spreadeagled prisoners and in his best bank-manager voice said, 'If only we had more time, we could play human noughts and crosses. But now I think it best if you close your eyes.'

Please let the bullet miss my skull! hissed Batten's maverick mind. Unable to catch Pavel's eye, he was overcome by the sheer black loneliness of death, there, helpless on the marble floor, waiting for the trigger to click and the gun to shoot. *No!* he urged himself. *Do* ***not*** *go meekly! Luka has a heavy pack now. Be quick, stay low, he might miss. Give Pavel time to act...*

About to spring, Batten froze when he heard a click – but no detonation, no acrid gunpowder sting, no echoes screaming off the walls or a pounding pulse of blood in the ears.

And no pain.

Twisting his neck, he heard a second faint click as the front door was locked almost silently, from outside. Turning, he saw their discarded wallets, but no phones, knife, keys - only a large wooden panel and six black bolts, lying forlorn on the tiles. And beyond them, Luka's empty chair.

Pavel saw it too and sprang at the door. Batten, slower, stiffer, joined him and together they yanked, hammered and kicked but like every godforsaken door in the house, the wood was dense and solid, the metalwork thick, strong and unyielding - the shuttered windows the same. And Luka had their phones. '*The back wall!*' shouted Pavel, adrenalin pelting him through the open rear door.

'What?' said Batten. '*It's a sheer drop!*'

'Not if you're a climber!'

'I'm not a bloody climber!' shouted Batten, as Pavel jumped onto the wall and clambered over. 'There's a narrow track,' said Pavel's now invisible voice. 'Come *on!*'

Stomach trembling, Batten peered over and down. Between the wall and nothing, Pavel stood on a strip of rock less than two feet wide, his frantic hand beckoning. Angry mind fixed on Oksana and Dave, his eyes burned with the heat of revenge. 'It's only thirty feet to the gap in the buildings. You won't fall. Come *on!*'

Barely conscious of his body, Batten somehow straddled the wall and slithered down the other side, sweat mantling his skin - from shock and from the sudden heat of mid-afternoon. One fleeting glance at the precipice below and he might have spiralled to the bottom if not for Pavel, his painful pincer grip welcome this time. '*Don't* tell me not to look down,' hissed Batten as he edged against the wall, inch by inch, fingers, eyes and toes to the stone, two hundred feet above the sheer drop.

Seconds, minutes, hours? Batten had no idea but when Pavel's grip on his arm relaxed, he realised they had reached the gap between the buildings. His breath a staccato rasp, Batten bent down, hands on his knees, to clear his head, and mumbled, 'the climbing chain'. Pavel's eyes aflame with anger, he once more grabbed Batten's arm, frantically dragged him back towards the cliff's edge where the climbing chain was bolted to the rock, and peered down it. Still siesta time, the peak of

Casares was deserted and silent, except for Pavel's voice echoing against the rock - *'He's not here!'*

Batten's first thought was *Good!* But Pavel was sprinting away, his judgement in shreds, crunching across the stony clifftop, past the Church of the Incarnation to the second climbing chain – then stopping so suddenly Batten almost careened into the back of him. Half of Luka was visible above the parapet, one hand on the chain, the other reaching into his waistband –

'Gun!' shouted Batten. Their reflex dive for the cover of rocks was followed only by silence. When they dared sneak a glance at the parapet, Luka had disappeared. 'He's fallen!' shouted Batten, in hope.

'No! He's climbing down!' said Pavel, dodging forward, rock to rock. 'He'll have a car, at the bottom. And we have no car keys!'

A flat stone, lodged in the path, peered up at Batten and he tried to claw it free. 'Help me! I'll throw this at the bastard!'

Once more, Pavel's grip was on his arm. 'You'll never shift it. Throw this.' He handed Batten one of the black iron bolts he'd unscrewed from Dave's door panel, pulling another from his pocket. 'Best I could do. He took my knife!'

They edged forward, not seeing Luka below but hearing him – or hearing his boots scrabble against the rock and his carabiner rattle down the chain till it hit the first stanchion. In a mindless crouch, Pavel was about to duck his head over the parapet when Batten jerked him back. 'He's got a bloody gun, Pavel. You trying to get your head blown off?'

In the shock of the moment, Pavel seemed not to care. *'He doesn't have three hands!* At every stanchion he must unclip, while holding on.' Pavel edged to the right, motioning Batten to the left. 'And how can he deal with two of us? Get ready to throw!'

Batten weighed the bolt in his sweaty hand, mind lurching between reality and farce -

- find a phone!
- call for help!
- get off this bloody cliff!
- stop Luka!

How? asked his rational mind. By making him *fall?*

Pavel was peering over the parapet, frantic anger clouding his judgement. '*Pavel,*' Batten began to hiss – but Pavel was on his feet and yelling, '*NOW!*'

A shock of heat and noise stunned Batten – the *clunk* of Pavel's bolt, bouncing off the cliff and tumbling pointlessly into space – the deafening *bark-bam* from Luka's pistol as he pulled the trigger – a stifled *nnngh* when the bullet seared the flesh of Pavel's arm – a loud *chung!* as it smacked against the same black lamppost Batten had clung to mere days ago.

Half-deaf, shocked but driven, and before his mind could tell him to rush to Pavel's aid, Batten did what he'd failed to stop Pavel doing. In pure reaction, he zoomed above the parapet and threw the iron bolt as hard as he could at the figure below. An *oof!* as it hit Luka's shoulder. A dull *clang!* as the gun jerked from Luka's hand and hit the rock. The *rrring!* of metal on metal as the loose pistol bounced onto the chain, skittered down it, and tumbled from the cliff to nowhere.

The gunshot had dragged a swarm of locals from their siesta to the clifftop and in a chaos of sweaty bodies they gasped at the blood on Pavel's arm. *A gunman!* they cried. *A gunman, in our Casares!* Seeing the prone but gun-less Batten, they helped him to his feet, firing not bullets but questions, one after the other, the Spanish rapid, incomprehensible. He pointed down, shouting one of the few Spanish words he knew – *alla, alla, there, there!*

Twenty pairs of eyes followed his finger to the parapet and peered over at the sweating figure of Luka, sixty feet below, frantically clipping and unclipping his carabiner, boots scrabbling past one remorseless stanchion after another. *Pistolero!* someone yelled. Other voices took up the cry, in Spanish and broken English, louder and louder, screaming at the fugitive – *Pistolero! Gunman! Para, para! Stop! Stop!*

Dazed still by the piercing *bam!* of the pistol and the sight of Pavel's bloodied arm, Batten felt the gathering anger in the crowd, his addled mind dragging up Andy Connor's mock-pompous guff about Convergence Theory - *in crowds, Zig, individuals converge - and find common goals...*

And this crowd did. Before Batten could intervene, a red-faced man picked up a stone and flung it. Others followed his lead, ignoring Batten's *Stop!* till an angry volley of stones showered the fugitive below, and then another. Some stones bounced off the red rock, some sailed into space, but others found their mark, forcing Luka's arm to jerk up to protect his head - as his other sweating hand was unclipping the carabiner from the chain.

Luka had no time to scream. In a sudden, gut-jolting silence the shocked crowd watched his fingers slide along the metal, his feet and hands scrabbling wildly at unyielding rock before his muscled body plummeted from the cliffside towards the jagged ground below. As his body looped and turned in the air, the contents of his backpack littered both him and the red *bermejo* onto which he crashed. Numb, the crowd converged again – this time in one long, collective gasp. Swallowing bile, Batten peered over the parapet to gaze down at the fallen man, dotted now with a blue confetti of plastic bags, each one stuffed with other people's money.

Fifty-four

Still half-dazed, Batten did a double-take when the man in the green baseball cap marched sternly towards him. *Luka, rescued by eagles, and brought back to life?* No. The green cap topped the uniform of the *Guardia Civil*, Spain's Gendarmerie. The nearest *Guardia Civil* post being less than a mile away was fortunate for Pavel, whose wound was quickly stemmed, but less so for Batten. Corporal Ruiz insisted on being addressed as *Cabo Primera* Ruiz, and if he possessed a smile, he kept it in a locked drawer. Big on procedure, he spoke just enough English to make life awkward, and worked tirelessly at doing just that.

Pavel, Batten and what seemed a random selection of Casares witnesses were ferried to the nearby police post and questioned in a loud confusion of Spanish and English. Two bilingual citizens served first as witnesses, briefly as suspects, then were pressganged as translators. Batten understood little of the babble that passed for an interview: *pistol, blood, fugitive, money – extranjeros!*

Getting nowhere, Ruiz regrouped, leading Batten and Sofia, the more capable of the two 'translators', to his sterile office at the rear of the building. Gradually, Batten explained why he couldn't produce his passport.

Because your house keys were stolen?
Yes, by Luka Judd.
Judd? The man who fired the pistol?
That's right.
And he is the body we have found?
Yes, he fell from the cliff.
You threw stones at him!
No! I certainly did not!

Ruiz stared down at Batten's wallet, which lay confiscated on the spotless desk. To deflect his confusion, he flicked through the contents as if they might bite him. When the self-importance drained from his face and he sat bolt upright, Batten assumed they had. Till he spotted Chief Inspector Delgado's business card in the Corporal's shaking fingers.

You know the Inspector Jefe?

We've met.
In England?
No. In Estepona.
But a long time ago?
No. Yesterday.
Ah…I will ask you-
Look, why don't you call Delgado, and ask *him*?

*

Chief Inspector Raffa Delgado swiftly commandeered the sterile office of *Cabo Primera* Ruiz, and Batten once again sat on the other side of his desk. Delgado's reaction to the death of Luka Judd was mixed, to say the least.

'Much mess,' he told Batten in a flat, unsmiling voice. 'Much…liaison. Stolen money, many document. And this…clown.' He flipped a hand at the closed door, in the vague direction of Ruiz. 'A good Corporal, but a bad General. You know, he want to arrest most of Casares?'

Batten said nothing. Ruiz wanted to arrest him, too. And Pavel. Right now, he wasn't altogether sure if Delgado would. When the *Jefe* removed his jacket, the sight of the holster on his waistband brought back the sound of gunfire, the harness round Luka Judd's waist, and the gut-shuddering plummet onto sharp red rock.

'We have closed a…difficult case,' said Delgado. 'With your *help*?' Batten didn't much like the question mark. 'But a quiet Pueblo Blanco? Gunfire, and theft, and death? *Catastrofico!* It will put off the tourists.'

'Or bring more?' said Batten, in hope.

Delgado blew out a sigh. 'Yes. Like rats to dead meat.'

Closing his eyes, Batten saw only the dead meat of Luka Judd, tumbling from the cliff in a shower of stones.

And the fatal stone, who is responsible? asked Batten's legal mind.

Luka is responsible, his moral conscience replied…

When he opened his eyes, Delgado was removing keys and phones from evidence bags and placing them on the desk. 'These were found at the base of the cliff,' he said. 'Of course the phones are broke, but you have your Sim cards. And with the house keys, you can retrieve your documents, yes?'

'Er, yes, thank you.'

Not in the thanks business, Degado's cool voice added, 'And with the car keys, you can drive to the *airport. Soon?*'

He's like Lady Wake, thought Batten, every question a command. He watched Delgado pick up a smashed phone.

'You made few calls, these last two days,' he said, shrugging away Batten's flash of anger. 'Of course we have listened. Perhaps you would do the same? And *Señor Navarro*, this afternoon, he made some calls about *you*. To a phone that is not…registered.'

Batten had no idea who *Señor Navarro* was.

'Jorge Navarro? Your neighbour?'

'Ah, Jorge.' *The nosy geologist next door.*

'Paid to watch, he admits. Paid by Luka Judd. To watch for strangers, near the house of this Dave Voss. Of course, Navarro is arrested. A minor accomplice.' Delgado shrugged away the inconvenience of *Jorge* then, to Batten's surprise, curled his lips into a satisfied smile. 'You know, he has a dog-'

'Ortega. A German Shepherd. Friendly dog.'

'Yes. I have told Corporal Ruiz he will care for this friendly dog, personally, while its owner is…detained. It may *improve* him.' Delgado's chuckle lasted a bare five seconds before his eyes narrowed again. 'Dave Voss is who you search for?'

'Well, yes.'

The *Jefe* pursed his lips in thought, stared at Batten, and pointed a stubby finger. 'I say only this, in private, and only to you, agreed?' Batten nodded. 'For a little while, one of my men work for Luka Judd, on buildings now sold. Undercover, you call it in England?' Batten nodded again, wondering where this was going. 'He tell me Señor Judd sometime do building work himself, alone – after the others leave? Dig, mix concrete for the…' Delgado pressed his hands towards the floor, unsure of the word.

'Concrete pad? Foundations?'

'Ah, yes. Foundations. And my people, we have much suspicion about Señor Judd…' He stared pointedly at Batten, allowing the thought to hang in the air, needing to say no more.

Half an hour ago, Delgado made Ruiz bring coffee. Now, Batten tasted it again, the churning, bitter sting of realisation. Dave Vossialevydipsic. Dipstick Dave. Oksana's only brother, Danuta's only son. A thief, yes, but no killer. And Luka's put him in a concrete grave.

Seeing the pain on Batten's face, Delgado said, 'Strong suspicion is not fact, but all the same... And I am afraid these buildings are sold - and occupied.'

'Don't you know which one? Can't it be dug up?'

As the *Jefe* splayed his hands in apology, a second realisation jolted into Batten. 'When did work stop on Luka's unfinished building, the one here, below Casares?'

Delgado told him. *A week or two after Luka made Pavel fly to Spain.*

More bitter coffee griped in Batten's gut as Luka's true intention for Pavel hit home. *If the building work hadn't stalled, Pavel's body would be in the foundations.*

'You are troubled, Mr Batt-ten?'

'Troubled?' *Tell Oksana her brother is dead, with no grave to visit? Tell Pavel he almost shared the same fate? And shatter their lives?* 'Troubled, yes.' *Why must truth be so costly?* 'Hard decisions to make. You know how it is.'

Chief Inspector Delgado was making hard decisions of his own. He assessed the recent events in England and Spain and recorded Chris Ball's details for future liaison. 'I regret, but your return, it is likely to be required? And Mr Ducek's? To give evidence?'

Batten shrugged. When it came to Luka Judd, he would tell the truth, all of it. The stress lines on his face had nothing to do with Luka, but life comes back to bite you, all the same.

The confidentialities, about Pavel and Dave - share them?
Or keep them secret?

PART SIX

SOMERSET, ENGLAND

Fifty-five

Throughout the flight home, knowledge of Pavel's close shave and Dave's sad 'burial' burned a hole in Batten's conscience. Despite being strapped in next to Pavel's solid frame, he kept quiet by pretending to read *Archaeology for Dummies*. The nervous jitters at take-off and landing required no pretence.

The pair of them emerged from Bristol Airport into a freezing January wind, Batten elated that Sonia was collecting him, Pavel insisting he was safe to drive, in spite of his bandaged arm. He shook Batten's hand in a familiar pincer grip and said, '*The Horse and Groom*? Six-o-clock, next Saturday?'

'One drink?'

Pavel grinned, carefully shouldering his rucksack. 'One drink, yes. And then dinner with Oksana, with me? We meet your Sonia?'

Batten smiled a *Yes*. 'Deal,' he said, and Pavel's back disappeared into the Long Stay Car Park.

The slow queue of cars at the Pick-Up Zone made Batten wish he'd packed a heavier coat. Though he missed the winter heat of Spain, a thousand miles away, the icy delay gave him time to reduce the perils of Casares to a Sonia-sanitised version. But when her old Vauxhall finally rolled up and he felt the warm softness of her lips, his conscience said, *No. Tell her everything. Trust and be trusted. Haven't you had enough of bloody secrets?*

He asked her to pull into the first convenient lay-by - and told the full story, warts and all, each remembered word a tremor in his veins. Expecting reproach, she surprised him with, 'Zig. Your hands are shaking.'

He looked down. They were, and he hadn't noticed. 'Truth is so *hard!* he said, and her arms coiled round him with such tenderness he wanted them to stay there forever.

'Not shaking now, my hands,' he said, as Sonia drove away. 'But my heart's going ten to the dozen.'

Looking across, concerned, she said, 'What is it? Stress? Shock?'

'No,' he said, eyes smiling. 'It's *you.*'

Stepping through the front door of *Hillview*, he did keep back one tiny truth - he wished they'd changed the name, because after two flights and the perils of a Spanish clifftop, he'd had enough of hills. But as he and Sonia gazed through the sweep of glass that used to be the back wall, and as they watched the sun brush golden light over magnificent Ham Hill, he decided: *Hillview* was staying.

The mail on the doormat was mostly bills, except for a posh envelope embossed with *Wake Hall Estate*. Inside was a second invitation to dinner, this one on a printed card edged in gold. At the top, Marianne Wake had written a few personal words in her italic script, perhaps while sitting at her exquisite walnut desk.

Zig, I wish to properly express my gratitude.

Batten flinched at the *gratitude* she might have in mind, till with relief he read the printed formality: 'Mr Zig Batten, and partner.'

*

Chris Ball's visit was swift, with no printed invitation – first thing next morning in fact. In the garden office, he refused coffee, lumped his spoon-shaped backside into the 'client' chair, and made it *crystal clear* he was here as *Inspector* Ball. Sharp words snapped back and forth across the desk, but after ten minutes of tension the heat cooled, and Ball got up to go.

'Chris. Have you got a moment?'

'I do. I've already scratched my arse this week.'

'Improved, at Parminster?'

'Steep learning curve. But I'm climbing.' He flopped back into his chair. 'Shoot.'

'Not the best choice of words, Chris, given recent events, but…' Batten shared his dilemma, hoping for wise counsel from his old Sergeant, who rubbed his chin with a two-pounds-of-sausage hand for five slow seconds.

'How much good, how much harm – isn't that the forever equation, Zig? Me, I wouldn't tell Pavel. It'd do him plenty of harm, and no bloody good at all. As for Oksana, what kind of closure would she get? *Your brother's encased in concrete, under some vague building in Spain, but there's no grave to put the flowers on?'*

'I have to tell her *something.*'

'Well, after you say Dave didn't kill anyone, tell her the Spanish police think he's disappeared. South America. Far East. A new identity. Then at least the poor woman can believe he'll come back someday.'

'You mean, leave her hanging?'

'Isn't hanging better'n *falling,* Zig?'

An image still haunted Batten, a body plunging from a Casares clifftop to the red rock below. He shook it away. 'Chris, this feels a bit like old times.'

Ball nodded, turned to go, then hovered by the door. 'Have *you* got a minute, Zig?'

'A coffee minute?' Batten jabbed a finger at Sonia's gift, the shiny espresso machine.

Face clouding over, Ball shook his head and slid back into his chair, voice a tired mumble. 'Might need something stronger than coffee...'

*

When Batten poured cider into Chris Ball's glass, at barely ten in the morning, the new Inspector said, 'Just as a lubricant. For the voice.'

'Long story?'

'I'll give you the short version. I've a dilemma, too. Good cider, by the way...It's to do with Wake Hall.' He flinched at the name. Batten guessed he always would. 'You're no stranger to police procedure, so after the recent shenanigans you'll know we drilled into every blessed bod at that godforsaken place, deep background, looking for motive...'

'*Shoot,* Chris,' said Batten, eyes glinting over his coffee cup.

Chris Ball smiled back - and retaliated. 'Remember when you first dropped Luka Judd's name into the conversation, and I'd never heard of him?'

'I do, Chris.'

'Well then, here's a name for *you. Nancy Hillam.*'

Batten raised his hands in surrender.

'She's the real mother of...*Avril Dean.* When the researchers dug down, a tricky morsel popped up. Avril Dean, they discovered, was adopted. Forcibly removed from her unmarried birth mother as a babe in arms. Then hustled over to the Deans to bring up as their own – can you believe it?'

'The narrow-minded bigots of England played God to thousands like that, Chris, right up to the 1970s, but it's hardly the point. Does Avril *know* she's adopted?'

'That's part of the dilemma. It's either yes, no - or not yet. But let me tell it my way.' Ball picked up his glass which disappeared into his giant hand. 'Nancy Hillam, while still alive, was a State Registered Nurse – not that names and pack drill matter. The problem's where and when, and the *where* is Wake Hall.' He sanitised the two words with a long glug of cider. 'This Nancy, *young, attractive,* it seems, she once worked at the Hall, nursing the previous Lady Wake – long slow decline, I'm told. And since even the Estate mares knew old *Lord* Wake's reputation with the ladies…And since old Lord Wake was *younger* then…'

His feet on the desk, as if in his cubbyhole office at Parminster, Batten caught up. 'Bit thin, Chris?'

'Thin, true. Till I factored in the *when*, and wished I hadn't. To be fair, it was Eddie Hick did the factoring. Do you know he's got a new nickname? He's not full of crap anymore, so we can't call him *Loft*. But since one whiff of a bacon sandwich gives him X-Ray vision, we call him *X-Ray Hickie* now.'

'You're turning into Andy Connor, Chris – disappearing down rabbit holes.'

'Ah, but you see, it was *X-Ray Hickie* sniffed out the documents – Nancy Hillam's employment records. And Avril Dean's. And of course, the *will.*'

'Whose sodding will? *Nancy's*? *Avril's*?'

'No, no. Old Lord Wake's. In Probate Records. Public property, once Probate's granted.'

'I know, Chris – the 1837 Wills Act. I once tried to read the bloody thing. What about it? Didn't he leave everything to Marianne Wake?'

'He did, more or less. Except for a string of small bequests. All to younger women – and none of them relatives, wink-wink. Lord Wake's nod to his bits of dalliance, sure as eggs is eggs.'

'At least he had the grace to remember them.'

'True, but *one* bequest was ten times bigger'n the others - Nancy Hillam's.'

'She nursed his sick wife, Chris.'

'She did – for barely three months. So how come the will mentions the *continuation* of monthly payments to Nancy Hillam? She upped and left the Hall pretty well overnight, with no record of official severance, so I'm thinking slush fund, under the table, then *keep quiet, Nancy, and I won't let you and the baby starve!* After she left, there's no record of her working anywhere else that year-'

'Chris-'

'- Which is the same year *Avril* comes into the world, get my drift?'

On a normal day, a mere sniff of a buried bone made Batten dig - but could he face more digging at Wake Hall? And what of his new loyalties? *This is private. It's other people's business…* At the risk of sounding like Olly Rutter's lawyer, he said, 'Merely circumstantial, Chris.'

'Wish it was. It's Hickie's fault – or yours, for being a bad influence. Kept ferreting, didn't he? And found another *when*, and then another. Seems Avril had just turned eighteen when the couple she thinks are her parents died in a car crash. Left her in pieces, no family, short on funds and even shorter on prospects. But two weeks after the funeral, by some *miracle*, her employment records say she was offered a maid's job. At Wake Hall!'

'Coincidence?' Batten didn't even persuade himself.

'Coincidence, my arse! It's Lord Wake, keeping tabs on his love-child. No need to confess to old Lady Wake – poor woman spent half her life on morphine. And since his 'proper' daughter was only six, I don' suppose he let on that she and the woman hoovering the playroom carpets were unofficial half-sisters! If the old devil wasn't pulling strings, then cider's penny a pint.'

Batten's damaged skull still flashed out staccato bursts of memory, and Ball's words fired him back to the portrait-hung Reception room at Wake Hall, after Oksana's cottage was burgled. A seething Avril, eyes aflame, had more or less accused him of skiving - something he would never do. To avoid glaring angrily at *her,* he'd glared instead at the giant mid-Century portrait of old Lord Wake on the wall above his head. Avril had hissed, *Kindly drag your attention from...portraiture, to the matter in hand!* But were the red flames in her eyes aimed at Batten, or at the looming figure of old Lord Wake? And if the latter, what was to be done?

Brow furrowed, Batten stared beyond the window at distant Ham Hill, hoping easy answers would flutter like tweeting birds from the Iron Age earthworks. But he heard only Professor Quinn's archaeology lecture, and saw only a PowerPoint image of 2000-year-old defleshed bones. *What right do we have to strip the living flesh from Avril Dean's? Or indeed from Marianne Wake's.* 'It's private, Chris. It's other people's business.'

'It's *my* business, Zig. *I'm* still CID. What if Avril Dean, Avril Kerrigan, found out she was half-sister to Lady Wake? And what if she knows all about her inheritance rights - to *Wake Hall?*'

Hoping his ex-Sergeant had a cloudy knowledge of the *Family Law Reform Act*, Batten stayed silent. His staccato mind spoke instead, reminding him of Marianne Wake and Avril Dean's curious relationship – their twitches of silent communication, their Morse Code connections, smooth, unspoken...Almost *sisterly.*

'You listening, Zig?'

'Sorry. Thinking.'

'Then think about this: with Avril Dean's inheritance rights in mind, is Phil Kerrigan's death a tad too convenient? They used to be married – so did he have a claim on the Estate? Would getting Kerrigan out the way avoid some nasty shocks and a stack of legal wrangling – and mean a bigger slice of pie for Avril?'

Draining the last dregs of his coffee, Batten wondered if even Avril Dean's unreadable face could conceal the machinations Ball was suggesting. The current evidence pointed elsewhere. Perhaps Avril's formal statement to the police lacked the deep emotional truth of her unburdening to *him* – a man no longer on the Force, not Ball's co-worker now, but Avril's. Sliding his empty cup onto the desk, he studied the fledgling Inspector. Theories were essential in CID – even creative flights of fancy. But with limits. Ball's own 'inheritance' had been swallowed up by old Lord Wake. Did the pain of it still gripe in Ball's gut? Was it niggling away at his judgement?

And if Ball's flight of fancy did have legs, what of *George* Kerrigan, the estranged prodigal son? When Avril Dean and the childless Marianne

Wake were no more, would George Kerrigan be heir to a vast Estate he might plunder - or erase? And how many livelihoods might he ruin along the way? Batten sucked in air, reluctant to flip that further complication onto the polished oak surface of his desk.

My home is Hillview. I don't own Wake Hall, thank God. And I'm not responsible for who does. 'It'll be a dog's breakfast, Chris, however you unpick it.'

Sunlight glinting through Ball's empty glass made him wish it was full. 'I'm over a barrel, Zig. Supposed to *inspect* crime, but if I unpick this one and there's a whiff of Lady Wake's perfume in the Kerrigan pie…? Bad enough with Wallingford on my back, but her and the Chief Constable too?'

'Didn't you call it the forever equation, Chris? How much good, how much harm?'

Climbing to his feet, Ball stretched his stubby body in a frustrated groan and stared through the window at the long high slope of Ham Hill, still tinged with January frost. 'So, I leave Avril Dean and her maybe-half-sister hanging?'

Batten slid his feet from the desk and stood beside his old friend, taking in the same long slope, the same January view. 'Hanging's better than *falling*. Isn't that what you told *me*?'

'*Buggeration!*' said Ball, with an even louder groan. Shaking his head, he thrust his empty glass at Batten. 'Zig, fill this up – and don't bloody remind me I'm on duty!'

Fifty-six

The monthly meeting of the *Parminster Cider Club* always began the same way. Four glasses were raised, and four voices mumbled the first three letters of *cider* - *C.I.D!*

Though an honorary member now, Batten still took his turn to arrange the venue - and pay for the group taxi - so he chose *The Five Bells*, not far from his empty cottage at Ashtree.

'What y'going to do with it, Zig,' asked Andy Connor. 'Sell or rent?'

'Dunno, Prof. I'll let you know when I'm less attached. Your shout next, by the way.'

When Connor went to the bar, Jess Foreman took up the theme. 'There's a pal of yours looking for a roof now, Zig. *Hazel Timms*. She's sold her parents' house, and the new owners are champin' at the bit to move in.' Foreman added a yokel smile. 'Just sayin', that's all.'

Batten smiled back, considering Foreman's nudge - till cider splashed the tabletop.

'Oops,' said Connor. 'Three Hail Marys, for spilling golden nectar.' He slid four fresh pints across the damp table. 'What you so quiet about, Chris Ball? You should be all a-whoop, from the kudos!'

Slow fingers tapping his glass, Ball said, 'Oh, you know. Loose ends. Stuff left *hanging*.' He and Batten shared a look.

'Zig's got some of that, haven't you, Zig? Passed your place t'other day and your new *venture* still has no sign on the wall. Doesn't a business need a *name*, Zig?'

'In hand, Prof.'

Foreman's rich Somerset burr broke in. 'I'd call it, *Baatten's Baad Boy Bureau.*'

'No, no, no,' said Connor, cider-laughter almost choking him. 'Call it, *Zig Will Dig!* Or maybe, *Trouble at t'Mill Solutions!*'

'Helpful,' chuckled Batten. 'Go on, Chris, let's have your sarkies, too.'

Ball was miles away, the Wake Hall dilemma furring his mind. 'Er... *confidential* something? Or...*private* such and such? One of those?'

'We'll see,' said Batten, raising fresh cider to his lips and filling his throat with the dry healing brew. He'd already chosen his new business name.

And it didn't include the word '*secret*'.

Acknowledgements

Many thanks to my patient beta readers, especially Pete and Yvonne, and to all the poor devils who listened to my ramblings while *A Secret Killing* gradually swelled inside the laptop.

Particular thanks to Chris and Carol for the fruitful trips to Malaga, Estepona and Casares, whose geography, yes, I have tweaked to fit the plot. Thank you to Mike and Wendy for their account of Remembrance Sunday on Ham Hill, to Ian for farrier information and to Yvonne for all things equestrian. Any errors are mine, not theirs.

Wake Hall is very loosely based on the many National Trust landscapes in Somerset, with a nod to Estates such as Ilchester, Dillington, and Melbury, though the personnel involved are entirely fictional. Also fictional is Parminster, an amalgam of Somerset market towns, notably Ilminster, Crewkerne and Chard.

The Prince of Wales at the top of Ham Hill is of course genuine, and well worth a visit. The other hostelries in the book are made-up, though loosely based on actual places. Indeed, discovering the real public houses behind the fictional ones might make for an interesting voyage of discovery. Alas, I am now busy on the next book, so must leave that voyage to you…

To the Reader

Reviews are an author's lifeblood. If you enjoyed *A Secret Killing*, please do tell others by leaving a review on Amazon.co.uk, Amazon.com, or on Goodreads.

Thank you for reading my latest Zig Batten crime novel. To learn more about the series, about special offers and e-books, please sign up for my newsletter at https://subscribepage.io/paultoolan

Inspector Zig Batten first appears in Book 1, *A Killing Tree*, where he struggles with his enforced move from urban Yorkshire to not-so-sleepy Somerset. Before he can blink, hikers discover a dead body slumped against a tree on a lonely hill... *www.amazon.co.uk/dp/B00V2B3ASK*

A January Killing sees Batten and his new love-interest at a traditional cider 'Wassail', in a pitch-black orchard on a winter night. Celebratory shotguns are fired into the trees, to deter 'evil spirits' and spark a fresh crop of apples. But not every shotgun fires blanks, and next day it's a dead body that has blossomed in the orchard... *www.amazon.co.uk/dp/B019KGW65G*

Crown of Thorns Hill overlooks the sleepy village of East Thorne. But on Good Friday morning, the village wakes to a malign vision at the hill's peak – a sight which catapults a flu-ridden Inspector Batten out of his holiday bed to a scene of desecration... *www.amazon.co.uk/dp/B07NPBMJLZ*

Who was the once-beautiful loner nicknamed 'Queen Mab'? And why would vicious hands rake a knife across her throat? For answers, Batten digs into Queen Mab's journals. But when he follows her trail from Somerset, Yorkshire and Cornwall to the shores and mountains of Greece, he digs up more than he bargained for... *www.amazon.co.uk/dp/B09N3ZGNGP*

We live life forwards, but understand it backwards. In these "beautifully poignant and funny stories", minds old and young journey through half-shaded landscapes of memory. Why not take the journey too, and see what they discover?
www.amazon.co.uk/dp/B075PGZPG

The novels can be read in sequence or standalone.

Printed in Great Britain
by Amazon